Grandmaster of Demonic Cultivation

MO DAO ZU SHI

Grandmaster of Demonic Cultivation

MO DAO ZU SHI

2

WRITTEN BY

Mo Xiang Tong Xiu

TRANSLATED BY

Suika & Pengie (EDITOR)

COVER ILLUSTRATION BY

Jin Fang

BONUS ILLUSTRATION BY

wenwen

INTERIOR ILLUSTRATIONS BY

Marina Privalova

Seven Seas Entertainment

GRANDMASTER OF DEMONIC CULTIVATION: MO DAO ZU SHI VOL. 2

Published originally under the title of《魔道祖师》
(Mo Dao Zu Shi)
Author ©墨香铜臭(Mo Xiang Tong Xiu)
English edition rights under license granted by 北京晋江原创网络科技有限公司
(Beijing Jinjiang Original Network Technology Co., Ltd.)

Seven Seas press and purchase enquiries can be sent to Marketing Manager Lianne Sentar at press@gomanga.com. Information regarding the distribution and purchase of digital editions is available from Digital Manager CK Russell at digital@gomanga.com.

Follow Seven Seas Entertainment online at sevenseasentertainment.com.

TRANSLATION: Suika
EDITOR: Pengie
SPECIAL THANKS: Moonsheen, Miki, Roquen
INTERIOR LAYOUT & DESIGN: Clay Gardner
COPY EDITOR: Jade Gardner
IN-HOUSE EDITOR: Tamasha
BRAND MANAGER: Lissa Pattillo
PREPRESS TECHNICIAN: Melanie Ujimori
PRINT MANAGER: Rhiannon Rasmussen-Silverstein
EDITOR-IN-CHIEF: Julie Davis
ASSOCIATE PUBLISHER: Adam Arnold
PUBLISHER: Jason DeAngelis

ISBN: 978-1-64827-920-1
Printed in Canada
First Printing: May 2022
10 9 8 7 6 5 4 3 2

GRANDMASTER OF DEMONIC CULTIVATION

CONTENTS

CHAPTER 8: The Stalk of Grass
(CONTAINS WEB SERIALIZATION CHAPTERS 33-42)

PART 1 9
PART 2 43
PART 3 72
PART 4 111
PART 5 147

CHAPTER 9: The Allure 185
(CONTAINS WEB SERIALIZATION CHAPTERS 43-46)

CHAPTER 10: The Beguiling Boy
(CONTAINS WEB SERIALIZATION CHAPTERS 47-50)

PART 1 237
PART 2 269
PART 3 335

APPENDIX: Character & Name Guide 355

Glossary 383

Contents based on the Pinsin Publishing print edition originally released 2016

8
The Stalk of Grass

— PART 1 —

THE SHUDONG REGION was inundated by countless river valleys and surrounded by tall mountains. With such rugged terrain breaking up the flow of winds, much of it was thus shrouded in year-round mists.

Wei Wuxian and Lan Wangji traveled in the direction that the ghost left arm had pointed, finally happening upon a tiny village. Mud houses with thatched roofs were encircled by a number of fences. A flock of many-colored hens and chicks pecked at grain as they wandered in and out of yards, and a big, bright-feathered rooster perched on one foot upon a roof. It shook its crest, twisting its neck as it surveyed the land with pride.

Fortunately, none of the households had dogs. The villagers probably didn't get to eat much meat themselves, let alone have extra bones to feed dogs.

The road split at the village entrance, branching off in three directions. Two of these roads were visibly worn and flattened with frequent use. The surface of the last path, however, was overgrown with weeds. A crooked, rectangular stone marker stood beside it, pointing in the same direction as the path.

The marker was aged and weather-worn, with a massive crack that stretched from top to bottom. Stalks of withered grass poked from the cracks. Two giant characters, presumably the name of the destination the road led to, were carved into the stone. The lower character was just barely legible as "City," but the upper character had many strokes and a complicated shape. The giant crack just happened to cut through it too, and many stone fragments had been chipped off. Wei Wuxian leaned over and peeled away the weeds, but even after studying the tablet for a long time, he couldn't figure out what that top character was.

Of course, the direction the left arm pointed in just had to be down that road.

"Why don't we go ask the villagers?" Wei Wuxian suggested.

Lan Wangji nodded. Needless to say, Wei Wuxian didn't expect him to do the asking. Face splitting into a wide smile, he walked toward a gaggle of farmer ladies who were sprinkling grain, feeding the chickens.

The women were a mix of young and old. When they saw a strange young man approaching, they all tensed, looking ready to drop their winnowing pans and escape back into their houses. Only after Wei Wuxian spoke to them, still smiling cheerfully, did they gradually calm down and begin to shyly answer his questions.

Wei Wuxian pointed at the stone marker and made an inquiry. All at once, the women's faces changed. It was with significant hesitation that they haltingly conversed with him on the topic, pointing and gesturing. During the conversation, they didn't dare glance at Lan Wangji, who still stood next to the stone marker. Wei Wuxian listened earnestly for a while, the corners of his lips raised the entire time. He seemed to change the subject toward the end, causing the farmer ladies to brighten, gradually relax, and bashfully return his smiles.

Lan Wangji stared at them from a distance. He waited for a while, but Wei Wuxian appeared to have no intention of returning. Lan

Wangji slowly hung his head and kicked at a small rock next to his foot. He flipped and fiddled with that innocent little rock, over and over, for quite a while. When he looked up again, Wei Wuxian had taken something from his robes and passed it to the chattiest of the farmer ladies.

Lan Wangji stood there dumbly until he could endure it no longer. Just as he was about to walk over, however, Wei Wuxian finally returned, strolling leisurely back over with his hands clasped behind him.

"Hanguang-jun, you should've gone over," he commented as he returned to Lan Wangji's side. "They keep rabbits in their yard!"

Lan Wangji did not react to this discovery. "What information did you obtain?" he said coolly, instead.

"This road leads to Yi City. The first word on the tablet is 'Yi,'" Wei Wuxian said.

"Yi for '*xiayi*,' chivalry?" Lan Wangji asked.

"Yes and no."

"Please elaborate."

"It's the same word but a different meaning," Wei Wuxian explained. "It's not the yi for chivalry but the yi for *yizhuang*—'charitable mortuary.'"

They started down the road, treading on tangled weeds and leaving the stone marker behind them as Wei Wuxian continued to share his findings.

"Those ladies said most people in Yi City are short-lived. It's been that way for ages. Whether naturally short or violently abbreviated, their lives end early, and so the city has a lot of mortuaries to store bodies in. On top of that, the local specialties are coffins, joss paper, and other kinds of funerary goods. Their craft is exquisite, whether it be coffins or paper funerary effigies. Thus did the city get its name."

There were barely-perceptible dips and ruts in the road, in addition to the broken rocks and windblown weeds. While Wei Wuxian talked and walked, Lan Wangji had been watching out for his every step.

"They said the people of their village rarely go to Yi City, and those from Yi City rarely leave it unless it's to deliver goods. They've barely seen anyone in recent years, and this road has been deserted for many more. It's going to be a difficult walk, indeed."

"And?" Lan Wangji prompted.

"And what?"

"What did you give them?"

"Oh, that? Those were cosmetics," Wei Wuxian replied.

In Qinghe, he had purchased a small box of rouge from the fake-cultivator quack doctor while grilling him for information. He'd been carrying it on him ever since.

"When you ask people for information, you've gotta give them something as thanks," Wei Wuxian explained. "I was going to give them money at first, but they were too nervous to accept it. I noticed they really liked the scent of that rouge, like they'd never used such a thing before, so I handed it over."

He paused briefly, then said, "Hanguang-jun, why are you looking at me like that? I know the rouge wasn't high quality, but I don't have flowers and accessories on me at all times to give to ladies like I did in the past. I really didn't have anything else to give them, and it was better than nothing."

Lan Wangji's brows furrowed, as if the statement had evoked an unhappy memory, and he slowly turned his head away.

As they pushed forward down the difficult road, the weeds gradually withdrew and shrank back to the sides, while the road itself grew increasingly wider. The fog, meanwhile, grew thicker and thicker.

A set of dilapidated city gates appeared at the end of the long road, and the ghost left arm clenched its hand into a fist.

The turret atop the city wall had missing tiles and peeling paint, and one of the corners was chipped. The overall impression was derelict and unsightly. The city walls themselves were choked with graffiti painted by unknown individuals. The red of the city gates had practically faded to white, and every single one of the doornails had rusted black. The gates were not firmly shut. It appeared someone had pushed them slightly ajar and slipped inside.

They had yet to set foot in the city itself, but the ominous atmosphere clearly warned that this was a hellish place. A place where evil swarmed.

Wei Wuxian had been examining the area along the way. Once they reached the city gates, he commented, "What terrible feng shui."

Lan Wangji nodded sagely. "A despairing landscape."

Yi City was surrounded by tall mountains and steep cliffs. The mountains tilted sharply toward the city in an oppressive, threatening manner, as if they might collapse at any moment. To be surrounded by such dark and massive mountains, hidden so shrunken and pitiful in this white fog—this place was as evil as could be. Simply standing here made one feel suffocated by anxiety, suffused with apprehension.

The saying "rich land fosters talent" had been in use since ancient times, and the opposite also held true. Some places had abominable feng shui simply due to their geography, as if the air was shrouded in lingering mildew. Those who resided in such places were commonly short-lived and doomed in all their endeavors. If they remained rooted there for generations, their ill fortune sank into the very marrow of their bones and festered there. Supernatural manifestations were also frequent in such places. Corpse reanimation, the rising of malicious ghosts, and other such things occurred far more often than usual.

Obviously, Yi City was such a place.

Places like these were usually remote, far from the reach of the prominent clans of the cultivation world. Of course, those clans never wanted to deal with them regardless. A Waterborne Abyss could be driven out, but the natural landscape was difficult to alter. If no one came knocking at their door crying for help, the clans kept their eyes closed and pretended to be unaware of any manifestations.

The best way for the city's residents to extricate themselves from their predicament was to move out, but if someone had been rooted there for generations, it was very difficult to find the resolve to leave the only home they knew. Even if more than half the people in their hometown were short-lived, perhaps they would be one of the lucky ones, they might think. Such thoughts made things seem bearable.

Wei Wuxian and Lan Wangji came to the city gates and exchanged a look.

Creeeak. The gate, misaligned due to the axles buckling under its hefty weight, slowly swung open.

The sight that greeted them was not a bustling street, nor lurching fierce corpses. There was nothing but white.

Thick fog permeated the air. It was several orders thicker than the fog outside the city walls, and they had to strain to make out a long, straight street ahead with houses on either side. Not a single person could be seen.

The two instinctively shuffled a couple of steps closer to each other before entering the city together.

Though it was daytime, it was still and quiet within the city. Not only were there no human voices to be heard, but even the clucking of chickens or barking of dogs was absent. Extremely strange.

Then again, since this was the destination indicated by the ghost left arm, it would be strange for the place to *not* be abnormal.

They walked along the long street for a while. The deeper they entered the city, the thicker the white fog grew, as if the air overflowed with evil energy. At first, they could still see about ten steps ahead. Then only five steps. Finally, they could hardly see their own outstretched fingers. The farther Wei Wuxian and Lan Wangji walked, the closer they pressed together, touching shoulders in order to be able to see each other's faces.

A thought surfaced in Wei Wuxian's mind: *If someone took advantage of this fog and snuck in between us, making us a group of three instead of two, we might not even notice.*

Just then, his foot kicked something. He looked down but couldn't make out what it was. Wei Wuxian grabbed Lan Wangji's hand so he wouldn't walk off on his own and bent down, squinting to get a closer look.

A human head, its eyes bulging with fury, assaulted his vision through the fog.

The head bore the appearance of a man: thick-browed and large-eyed, with unusually bright circles of blush on either side of his cheeks. Wei Wuxian had almost sent it flying when he kicked it, so he was aware of its weight—aware that it was too light to be a real head. He picked it up and squeezed it, and the man's cheeks caved in, smearing the blush in the process.

So, it was a human head made of paper.

The paper head was remarkably lifelike. While the makeup was exaggerated, its five features were quite exquisite. Yi City specialized in the production of funerary items, so the quality of their paper effigies was naturally excellent.

Funerary paper effigies included something known as a Substitute

Doll. Folk belief held that when a Substitute Doll was burned for the deceased, they could suffer in hell on their behalf, scaling the mountain of knives and plunging into the cauldron of boiling oil in their stead. There were also maids and beauties to serve the forebear in the netherworld, massaging their backs and legs. Of course, these were nothing but comforts the living craved for their own solace.

This paper head, then, should be from a Yin Muscleman. The Yin Muscleman, as its name implied, was a hired roughneck. It was said that once it went down below, it could protect the forebear from being bullied by malicious ghosts or wily judges, and would ensure that joss money burned for the forebear wouldn't get snatched up by beastly little ghouls. The head must've originally had a large, solid paper body to match, but someone had torn it off and tossed it onto the street.

Countless strands of lustrous, ebony-black hair flowed from the paper scalp. Wei Wuxian reached out and felt it, finding the hair firmly attached to the scalp, as if it had naturally grown there. *This craftsmanship really is excellent. Was real hair used and glued in place?*

Suddenly a scrawny little shadow darted right past him.

The appearance of this shadow was highly strange. It brushed right by him and ran past, disappearing into the thick fog in a flash. Bichen unsheathed on its own and attempted pursuit before it promptly returned and sheathed itself once more.

The thing that had scurried past him was much too fast—certainly too fast for a human!

"Keep your eyes open and be on alert," Lan Wangji cautioned.

Although it had simply brushed past, there was no telling what it might do next time.

Wei Wuxian stood up. "Did you catch that just now?"

"The sound of footsteps and a bamboo pole," Lan Wangji answered.

Indeed. In that short encounter, aside from the sound of frantic footsteps, they'd heard another strange sound. The *da-da-da* was crisp and clear, similar to a bamboo pole beating the ground in rapid taps. What had caused such a sound?

Just then, they heard more footsteps ahead in the dense fog.

This time the footsteps were very light, very slow, and also numerous and varied. It seemed to be a number of people cautiously approaching, attempting to remain undetected. Wei Wuxian flicked his hand, flipped out a yin-burning talisman, and casually sent it off in that direction. If anything ahead was boiling with resentment, the talisman would burn and the resulting firelight could at least brighten the area.

The newcomers ahead realized someone had thrown something at them and retaliated instantly. Multiple sword glares in a rainbow of colors, scathing and murderous, came hurtling at them. Bichen leisurely unsheathed itself and traced a half-circle before Wei Wuxian, beating all the sword glares back. The group of newcomers was battered into total confusion.

Having heard their angry noises, however, Lan Wangji immediately withdrew Bichen while Wei Wuxian wondered aloud:

"Jin Ling? Sizhui?"

He was not mistaken. Jin Ling's voice echoed from within the white fog. "You again?!"

"That's what I was gonna say!" Wei Wuxian said.

Lan Sizhui's voice was filled with delight, despite his best attempts at restraining himself. "Mo-gongzi, you're here too? Does that mean Hanguang-jun has also come?"

Jin Ling immediately shut up when he heard Lan Wangji might be there, as if the silencing spell had been cast upon him. Clearly, he was scared he'd be disciplined if caught in the act of any wrongdoing.

In contrast, Lan Jingyi also shouted, "He must've! That was Bichen just now, right?! That was Bichen?!"

"Yeah, he's here. He's right beside me as we speak," Wei Wuxian replied. "Come over here quick, all of you."

Learning the ones before them were friends rather than foes, the group of youths reacted as if they'd just been saved. Everyone hastily gathered together. Aside from Jin Ling and the Lan juniors, there were also seven or eight boys in the uniforms of other clans, the hesitation on their faces still unfaded. They were likely juniors from other highly-regarded cultivation clans.

"Why are you all here?" Wei Wuxian asked. "Attacking so fiercely right away—thank goodness I have Hanguang-jun here with me! What if you hurt ordinary folks?!"

Jin Ling rebutted, "There're no ordinary folks here. There's no one in this city at all!"

Lan Sizhui nodded. "Evil miasma pervades all, even under the light of day. Moreover, not a single store is open!"

"That's not important," Wei Wuxian said. "How did you all manage to gather here? Don't tell me you guys arranged to come out as a group for a Night Hunt?"

Jin Ling had an imperious temperament and a certain tendency to pick fights with anyone he considered intolerable—which was, in fact, everyone. Taking into account the previous friction between Jin Ling and the Lan juniors, how could they have willingly gone on a Night Hunt together?

Lan Sizhui, who was the kind to answer every question posed to him, explained accordingly. "That's a long story. We were originally..."

Right then, the unusually piercing sound of bamboo hitting the ground came from within the dense fog. *Ka-ka-ka, da-da-da.*

Startled, the juniors' faces changed color. "It's here again!"

The sound of bamboo hitting the ground would come suddenly and disappear equally suddenly. Sometimes far, sometimes near. It was impossible to determine its location, nor its source.

"Gather close and don't move. Don't draw your swords either," Wei Wuxian said.

The juniors frantically brandishing swords in this dense fog would probably end with them injuring themselves before the enemy suffered any blows. A moment later, the sound came to an abrupt stop.

After a long silence, one of the clan juniors whispered, "It's that thing again… How long is it going to keep following us?!"

"It's been following you guys?" Wei Wuxian asked.

"We stayed together since we entered the city, afraid of losing each other with how thick this fog is. And then we suddenly heard that noise. It wasn't this fast at first, and it only came every so often, with long intervals of peace. We even saw a small, indistinct figure in the fog ahead of us, but when we ran over, it had already disappeared. That sound has followed us ever since."

"How small?" Wei Wuxian asked.

Lan Sizhui gestured near his chest. "Very much so. Quite petite."

"How long have you guys been here?" Wei Wuxian asked.

"Almost half an incense time," Lan Sizhui replied.

"Half an incense time?" Wei Wuxian turned around. "Hanguang-jun, how long have *we* been here?"

Lan Wangji's voice came through the haze of the white fog. "Nearly one incense time."

"You see?" Wei Wuxian said. "We've been here longer, so how did you manage to get ahead of us? And only bump into us when you doubled back?"

Jin Ling finally cut in, despite himself. "But we didn't double back! We've been following this road forward."

If they were all going forward, then could this road have been tampered with? Turned into a recursive maze array?

"Have you tried mounting your swords to fly up and look down from above?" Wei Wuxian asked.

"Yes," Lan Sizhui answered. "It felt like I'd flown up a very long distance, but in reality, I didn't rise very high at all. Moreover, there were some blurry black shadows scurrying about in the air. I was afraid I wouldn't be able to handle them, so I came back down."

Silence blanketed the group. Shudong was a region rife with fog to begin with, so they'd paid the white fog of Yi City no mind in the beginning. However, it was beginning to look like this wasn't a naturally occurring fog but an evil miasma instead.

Lan Jingyi was alarmed. "This fog isn't poisonous, is it?!"

"Probably not," Wei Wuxian said. "We've been standing in it for a long time, and we're still alive."

"Had I known, I would've brought Fairy with me," Jin Ling said. "It's all the fault of that damned donkey of yours!"

When Wei Wuxian heard the dog's name, goosebumps shivered down his back.

Lan Jingyi shot back, "We didn't even blame your dog! It was the one who bit first and got walloped by Little Apple's hooves for it, so who's the one at fault? Either way, neither of them can move right now!"

"What?!" Wei Wuxian cut in. "My Little Apple got bitten by a dog?!"

Jin Ling scoffed. "How can you compare that donkey to my spirit dog? Fairy was a special gift to me from my little uncle![1] I'm telling

---

1 *Jin Ling refers to his paternal uncle Jin Guangyao as "xiao-shushu," which translates to "little (paternal) uncle." The use of "little" here indicates that Jin Guangyao is younger than Jin Ling's other paternal uncles. Jin Ling's maternal uncle, Jiang Cheng, is referred to as "jiujiu."*

you, if anything happens to it, even ten thousand donkeys won't be enough recompense!"

Wei Wuxian easily derailed this argument with some nonsense of his own. "Don't you go trying to intimidate people with Lianfang-zun's name. Furthermore, Little Apple is a steed that Hanguang-jun gifted *me*! Why would you guys bring Little Apple down the mountain to a Night Hunt? And allow it to be injured too?!"

"Liar!" the Lan juniors responded as one. They refused to believe that Hanguang-jun, with his taste and class, would pick such a steed as a gift. Even though Lan Wangji didn't refute the statement, they vehemently refused to believe it.

"Um...sorry, Mo-gongzi," Lan Sizhui explained. "Your Little A... donkey was making a racket every day at the Cloud Recesses. The seniors have been complaining for a long time. They told us we must drive it out the next time we descend the mountain for a Night Hunt, so we..."

Jin Ling also wasn't convinced the spotted donkey was a gift from Lan Wangji. "I loathe the sight of that donkey. And what's with that name, 'Little Apple'? So stupid!"

Lan Jingyi, thinking such harsh words would be unwise if the donkey really *was* a gift from Hanguang-jun, jumped to its defense. "What's wrong with the name 'Little Apple,' huh? It likes to eat apples, so it's called Little Apple. How sensible! It's leagues better than you naming your fat dog 'Fairy'!"

"How is Fairy fat?!" Jin Ling retorted furiously. "I dare you to find another spirit dog more agile..."

All of a sudden, everything went quiet.

After a few moments, Wei Wuxian asked, "Is anyone still here?"

There was a wave of *uhh* and *woo*, indicating they were all still around.

Lan Wangji replied coldly, "Clamor."

...So he'd actually silenced everyone at once. Wei Wuxian felt his own lips despite himself, feeling rather lucky.

At that moment, they heard footsteps ahead and to their left.

They sounded clumsy, pausing after every step. Soon after, the same noise could be heard in front, on the right, on the side, behind them—all around. Although the fog was too thick to see anything clearly, the stench of rot had already permeated the air.

Of course, Wei Wuxian didn't care about mere walking corpses. He blew a soft whistle with a rising end note, embedded with the intent to expel. When the walking corpses hidden in the fog heard that whistle, they faltered as expected.

Then the next second, they unexpectedly came hurtling over!

Never in his life could Wei Wuxian have imagined his expulsion command not just being ineffective but aggravating the walking corpses on top of that. He would never have mixed up the commands for "expulsion" and "aggravate"! But there was no time for him to think further. Seven or eight wobbling figures surfaced from the depths of the white fog. If they were visible through the thickness of Yi City's fog, then that meant they had already gotten very close!

Bichen's icy blue sword glare broke through the white fog. It slashed a sharp circle around the group, cutting the many walking corpses right at the waist, before swiftly returning to its scabbard. Wei Wuxian breathed a sigh of relief.

Under his breath, Lan Wangji murmured quietly: "Why?"

Wei Wuxian was pondering the same question. *Why did the whistle order fail to expel those walking corpses? With such a slow gait and rotten stench, they can't be high level. They should've been the type to flee in fright if I simply clapped. It's not like whistling runs on spiritual power. It's impossible for it to just suddenly lose its effectiveness. This has never...*

Abruptly a realization hit him, and a light sheen of sweat sprung up on his back.

No. It wasn't that this had never happened before. It *had*, and not just once. There was indeed a kind of fierce corpse or malicious spirit he couldn't command—the ones already under the control of the Yin Tiger Tally!

Lan Wangji undid the silence spell and Lan Sizhui could speak again. "Hanguang-jun, is the situation very dangerous? Should we leave the city immediately?"

"But with the fog so thick and the road impassable... And we can't fly out..."

One of the other clan juniors said, "I think there's more walking corpses coming this way!"

"Where? I didn't hear any footsteps!"

"I thought I heard strange breathing..." But the boy trailed off in embarrassment, realizing how silly he sounded the moment the words left his lips.

Another boy mocked, "I gotta hand it to you. Breathing. Those walking corpses are dead people, how can there be the sound of breathing?"

Just as he spoke, another burly figure lunged over. Bichen unsheathed once more, and the figure's head and body split with a strange popping noise. The clan juniors near it all screamed.

Worried they'd been injured, Wei Wuxian quickly called out. "What's wrong?"

"Something spurted from that walking corpse," Lan Jingyi said. "It looks like some sort of powder. It's bitter and sweet, and rank!"

He'd wanted to speak, but with extremely unlucky timing, had inhaled an abundance of powder when he opened his mouth. Disregarding all thoughts of proper conduct, he spat and sputtered a number of times.

The powder that had erupted from the walking corpse was no small matter. It was still wreaking havoc in the air around them, and if it found its way into their lungs, the effects would be much more dire than simply getting a mouthful of the stuff.

"Stand further away from that area, all of you!" Wei Wuxian ordered. "And you, come over here and let me take a look."

"Okay," Lan Jingyi answered. "But I don't see you. Where are you?"

Visibility was so low that it made moving around difficult. Remembering that Bichen's light cut through the white fog every time it was unsheathed, Wei Wuxian turned to address Lan Wangji.

"Hanguang-jun, draw your sword for a moment so he can come over."

Lan Wangji was standing right next to him. But he did not respond, nor did he move.

Suddenly, about seven steps away, there was a flash of translucent, icy blue sword light.

...Lan Wangji was over there?

Then who was the one standing beside him in silence this whole time?

Suddenly, Wei Wuxian's vision went black. A darkened face loomed in his vision. It was dark because it was covered by a thick, dense layer of black smoke!

This smoke-masked person grabbed at the evil-sealing qiankun pouch that hung from his waist. But the qiankun pouch abruptly swelled, breaking the strings tying it shut. Three malicious spirits, entangled as one and all boiling with resentment, burst from the bag and charged forth!

Wei Wuxian laughed. "Oh, you wanted to steal the evil-sealing qiankun pouch? Then you should get your eyes checked. What are you doing grabbing my spirit-trapping pouch?"

Ever since the encounter at the cemetery of the Chang Clan of Yueyang, when Wei Wuxian and Lan Wangji had taken the torso that the gravedigger had unearthed and forced them to retreat, they had been on the lookout. They figured they wouldn't give up so easily but would seek to wrest the torso from their possession at an opportune moment. Sure enough, when they entered Yi City, the gravedigger had taken advantage of the thick fog and the crowd to make a move. And they'd certainly succeeded...except Wei Wuxian had long since swapped the evil-sealing qiankun pouch carrying the ghost left arm with his spirit-trapping pouch.

Schwing. The other leapt backward and drew a sword. Spite-filled, resentful screeching immediately followed from the malicious spirits, thrown into confusion by that single slash.

An individual with high cultivation, just as I suspected, Wei Wuxian thought. He quickly called out, "Hanguang-jun, that grave-robbing guy is here!"

There was no need for the reminder. Lan Wangji's ears alone told him there was a problem. He remained silent, with Bichen's swift, relentless movement his only response.

The situation wasn't good. The gravedigger's sword was covered in black smoke to prevent its glare from shining through, and it was well hidden within the white fog to begin with—while Bichen could not block its own light at all. He was in the light, the enemy was in the dark, and their opponent's cultivation was not low—not to mention they were familiar with the sword techniques of the Lan Clan of Gusu. On top of that, while they were both fighting blind in the miasma, the gravedigger could strike without reservation while

Lan Wangji had to be careful not to injure his own party by mistake. Truly, he was at a grave disadvantage.

Wei Wuxian listened to the sounds of the clashing blades, and his heart lurched. He blurted out, "Lan Zhan? Are you injured?!"

From the distance came a muffled grunt, as if a vital point had been injured, but it was obviously not Lan Wangji's voice.

"Impossible," Lan Wangji replied.

Wei Wuxian laughed. "True!"

Their opponent seemed to sneer and then brandished the sword to fight again. Bichen's light and the sound of clashing swords moved farther and farther away. Wei Wuxian knew Lan Wangji had intentionally shifted the battleground to deal with the gravedigger, not wanting to hurt them by mistake. And so, the rest was up to him.

He spun around and questioned aloud, "How is everyone who breathed in the powder doing?"

"They're having trouble standing!" Lan Sizhui replied.

Wei Wuxian said, "Gather here at the center and give me a head count."

Thankfully, once the wave of walking corpses had been taken care of and the gravedigger led away, nothing else moved to harass them—not even the sound of the bamboo tapping upon the ground. The remaining clan juniors gathered together and counted their numbers. No one was missing. Wei Wuxian took Lan Jingyi and felt his forehead, which was a bit hot. It was the same for the other boys who had breathed in the powder the walking corpse spewed.

He peeled back one of Lan Jingyi's eyelids and said, "Stick out your tongue and let me see. *Aah...*"

Lan Jingyi obliged. *"Aah..."*

"Yup. Congratulations, you've got corpse poisoning," Wei Wuxian said.

"What's there to congratulate?!" Jin Ling barked.

"It's an experience, a tale to tell when you're old," Wei Wuxian said.

Normally one contracted corpse poisoning from being scratched or bitten by turned corpses, or from having a wound contaminated by a turned corpse's tainted blood. Very rarely did cultivators allow a walking corpse to get close enough to scratch or bite, and so no one made a habit of carrying the antidote on them.

Lan Sizhui was very worried. "Mo-gongzi, will anything happen to them?"

"Not immediately," Wei Wuxian replied. "But once it's in their bloodstream and makes it to the heart, then it's buh-bye."

"What...what will happen?" Lan Sizhui asked.

"Whatever the corpse is like is what you'll turn into," Wei Wuxian said. "Best case scenario, you'll just rot and stink. Worst case you'll turn into a long-haired *jiangshi*, doomed to hop about forevermore."

The poisoned juniors all drew in a sharp breath.

"You wanna be cured, yeah?" Wei Wuxian pressed.

They all nodded emphatically.

"If you want to be cured, listen up. From now on, heed well my every word. Every single one of you."

While a good number of the boys still didn't know who he was, they had seen how familiarly he treated Hanguang-jun, addressing him like a peer of the same generation, to the point of calling him by his birth name. They were also stuck in this eerie city choked with evil miasma, and furthermore, currently poisoned, feverish, and generally anxious and fearful. They instinctively wanted someone to depend on, and the way Wei Wuxian spoke carried an inexplicable confidence, as if there were nothing to be afraid of. This made it easy for him to lead them around by the nose.

They answered in unison: "Okay!"

Wei Wuxian received an inch and went on to take a mile. "You'll do everything I say without objections, understand?"

"Yes!"

Wei Wuxian clapped. "Everybody, on your feet. The unpoisoned will carry the poisoned. Best haul them on your backs, but if it takes two of you to lift them, remember to have their head and heart elevated over the rest of their body."

Lan Jingyi protested, "I can walk, you know. Why do I have to be carried?"

"Well, *gege*," Wei Wuxian began sarcastically. "If you gambol around, your blood will circulate faster and reach your heart faster too. So, you have to move less. Ideally not at all."

The boys immediately stood stiff as boards in a neat row and let their companions carry them. On his sect-mate's back, one of them grumbled, "I warned you. The corpse that spurted out that toxic powder really was breathing."

Lan Sizhui said, "Mo-gongzi, we're ready. Where are we going?"

As usual, Lan Sizhui was the most well behaved, obedient, and untroublesome of the lot. Wei Wuxian said, "There's no way we can leave the city for the time being. Go knock on doors."

"Knock on what doors?" Jin Ling asked.

Wei Wuxian turned that question over in his mind for a moment. "...Does anything else have doors, other than houses?"

"You want us to go into those houses?" Jin Ling demanded. "It's perilous enough outside! Who knows what's hiding inside those houses, spying on us?!"

The moment those words left his lips, everyone immediately felt like there really were many pairs of eyes hiding in the thick fog, within the houses, intently watching their every move and listening to their every word. It gave them the creeps.

Wei Wuxian said, "You're not wrong. It's hard to say if it's more dangerous out here or indoors. But since it's already this bad outside, no matter how terrible the inside is, it can't be much worse. Go on, then. There's no time to lose, we've got poison to cure."

Having already promised as such, the group had to do as he said. Following Wei Wuxian's instructions, everyone held on to the scabbard of the person in front of them to avoid losing each other in the fog and knocked on one door after the other. Jin Ling banged heavily for a long time but heard no response from within.

"There doesn't seem to be anyone inside. Let's go in."

Wei Wuxian's voice came drifting over. "Who told you to only go in if there's no one inside? Keep knocking. We want to enter an occupied house."

"You want an occupied one too?!" Jin Ling demanded.

"Yup. Knock properly. You were knocking too hard just now, it's very rude," Wei Wuxian scolded.

Jin Ling was so angry that he almost kicked down the wooden door, but in the end, he only...stomped his foot petulantly.

Every house on the long street had their doors shut tight, and no matter how much they knocked, they remained silent. The more Jin Ling knocked, the more irritated he became, though he did lighten his knocks significantly. Lan Sizhui, on the other hand, was good-humored the entire time. When they came to knock at the thirteenth shop, he repeated the same question he'd repeated many times before:

"Is anyone here?"

Suddenly the door moved slightly, cracking open a thin, black slit. It was very dark inside, and nothing was visible through the crack. Nor did the one who opened the door speak a word. The closest boys took an unconscious step back.

Lan Sizhui composed himself and asked, "May I ask if you are the shopkeeper?"

It was a while before a strange, old, and hoarse voice leaked from the crack. "Yes."

Wei Wuxian approached, patted Lan Sizhui's shoulder to have him move back, and then spoke up. "Shopkeeper, this is our first time in the area, and we got lost because of the thick fog. We're a little tired from walking for so long, might we be able to take a brief rest in your store?"

The strange voice replied, "This shop of mine is not a place for rest."

Wei Wuxian acted as if he found nothing amiss. He said, looking perfectly normal, "But there doesn't seem to be anyone occupying the other stores. Will you really not grant us this reprieve? We'll pay a handsome sum."

Jin Ling couldn't help but comment, "And where did you get the money to pay a handsome sum? Let's get this clear right now, I'm not lending you any money."

Wei Wuxian swung an exquisite little money pouch in front of his eyes. "Do you see what this is?"

Lan Jingyi was greatly alarmed. "The audacity! That belongs to Hanguang-jun!"

As they quarreled, the door opened a little further. Though the interior of the house still wasn't visible, they could now at least see that the one standing behind the door was an expressionless old lady with a head of grayish-white hair. Although her back was hunched and she looked aged at first glance, she actually didn't have too many wrinkles or age spots. Calling her an auntie would've been appropriate too.

She opened the door and then stepped aside. It would appear she had relented.

Jin Ling, greatly surprised, mumbled in a small voice, "She's really letting us in?"

Wei Wuxian whispered back, "Of course. I've got one foot stuck in the crack, so she can't close the door even if she wants to. If she didn't let us in, I would've just kicked it down."

"..." Jin Ling commented.

Yi City was already unnatural and eerie. Its residents were hardly ordinary either. This old lady was suspicious enough to have the juniors all grumbling in their heads, but although they loathed the thought of going inside a thousand times over—no, a million times—there was nowhere else to go. Desperate times called for desperate measures. They had no choice but to pick up their poisoned companions, who were standing stiff and afraid to move, and enter the shop one by one.

The old lady watched impassively, guarding the door. Once they were all inside, she immediately closed it. The interior was instantly plunged into total darkness once more.

Wei Wuxian asked, "Might Madame Shopkeeper turn on the light?"

"The light's on the table. Turn it on yourself," the old lady replied.

Lan Sizhui just so happened to be standing next to a table, so he groped around carefully until he came upon an oil lamp, smearing his hand with years of built-up dust in the process. He flipped out a fire talisman, but just as he brought it close to the wick of the lamp, he unwittingly glanced up. In that instant, chills shot from the soles of his feet to the top of his head. *Boom*. He was paralyzed with fear.

The main room of this shop was crammed full of people, packed densely elbow-to-elbow, all staring unblinkingly at them with bulging eyes!

He unconsciously slackened his grip. Before the oil lamp dropped to the ground, however, Wei Wuxian saved it. He leisurely swiped the burning fire talisman still in Lan Sizhui's hand and lit the wick before placing the lamp back on the table.

"Did granny make all these? Such excellent craftsmanship," Wei Wuxian complimented.

Only then did the group realize that the people packed into this house weren't real humans but a crowd of paper effigies.

The faces, heads, and bodies of the effigies were all sized like those of real people and exquisitely made. There were men and women, even children. The men were all Yin Musclemen, tall and well built, faces enraged. The women were all beauties with their hair coiffed in either the double-ring style or the top loose bun style. Their figures were noticeably slender and graceful despite being covered by their large paper robes, the patterns on which were finer than those of real brocade. Some were painted, heavy with vivid red and green, while some were left starkly, blank white. Every single one of the paper effigies had giant blush-circles applied to their cheeks to mimic the color on the faces of the living. However, none of their pupils had been dotted to finalize the work, leaving the sockets white. The richer the blush, the ghastlier they appeared.

There was another table inside the center room, and upon it were several candles of various heights. Wei Wuxian lit every single one, and the golden light brightened a good half of the house. Apart from the paper effigies, there were two large floral wreaths set on the left and right sides of the central room, and joss money of both bills and taels was piled in small heaps in the corners.

Jin Ling had drawn one third of his sword at first, but on seeing that this was nothing but a shop that sold funerary goods, he let out an imperceptible sigh of relief and sheathed it. Even when a cultivator passed away, the cultivation clans never carried out these messy and gloomy folk ceremonies. The boys had rarely seen anything like this, so after the initial fright had passed, their curiosity flared and they felt goosebumps all over. Truly, this was more exciting than hunting an average yao beast on a Night Hunt.

No matter how thick the fog was, it didn't enter the house. This was the first time since entering Yi City that they could easily see each other's faces, and it put them more at ease. Seeing them relax, Wei Wuxian turned to the old lady once more.

"May I borrow the kitchen?"

The old lady, who didn't seem to appreciate the firelight, was practically shooting death glares at the oil lamp. "The kitchen is in the back. Help yourself."

Then she ducked into another room like she was hiding from the God of Misfortune. She slammed the door extremely loudly, making everyone jump.

Jin Ling said, "There must be something odd going on with that old witch! You..."

"All right, that's enough," Wei Wuxian cut him off. "I need a hand, who's coming with me?"

Lan Sizhui quickly responded, "I'll come."

Lan Jingyi was still standing as straight as a broom. "Then what about me?"

"Keep standing. Don't move unless I tell you to," Wei Wuxian said.

Lan Sizhui followed Wei Wuxian to the kitchen in the back. The moment they entered, a putrid stench assaulted their faces. Lan Sizhui had never smelled anything so horrible in his entire life. His head swam for a moment, but he managed not to retreat. Jin Ling followed them in but then hopped immediately back out, fanning himself desperately for air.

"What the hell is this smell?! Why are you wasting time here instead of coming up with a cure?!"

"Hm? Oh, perfect timing," Wei Wuxian said. "How did you know I wanted to call you over? Come and help."

"I'm not here to help!" Jin Ling barked. "*Ugh!* Did someone forget to bury the body after they killed it?!"

"Young Mistress Jin, are you coming or not? If you're coming, get in here and help. If not, go sit outside and ask someone else to come over," Wei Wuxian said.

Jin Ling flew into a rage. "*Who's* Young Mistress Jin?! Watch what you say!!" He pinched his nose for a while, dillydallied for a while, and then finally humphed. "Well, I gotta see what the hell you're up to."

And thus, he lifted his hems and stormed furiously over the threshold. Unexpectedly, however, Wei Wuxian opened a box on the ground with a *bang*. That was where the awful smell was emanating from. A leg of pork and a chicken were sealed in that box, and the once-pink meat had turned completely green. It was pockmarked with little white larvae that coiled about.

Jin Ling was effectively forced back out again. Wei Wuxian picked up the box and passed it to him.

"Go toss this out. Anywhere's fine, as long as we don't smell it."

Jin Ling had a stomach filled with nausea and a head filled with misgivings, but he still obeyed and tossed the box out. He took out a handkerchief to violently wipe his hands, then tossed that handkerchief out as well. When he returned, Wei Wuxian and Lan Sizhui were unexpectedly washing the kitchen, having drawn two buckets of water.

"What are you two doing?" Jin Ling demanded.

"Washing the stovetop, as you can see," Lan Sizhui replied as he wiped diligently.

"Why wash that? It's not like we're cooking," Jin Ling said.

"Who said we aren't?" Wei Wuxian said. "Of course we're cooking. Come and help dust, get rid of those cobwebs up there."

He spoke with such conviction, so matter-of-factly, that when Jin Ling was randomly handed a broom, he confusedly began to do as he was told. The more he dusted, however, the more he felt something was wrong. But just as he was about to hurl the broom at Wei Wuxian's head, Wei Wuxian opened another box, and he dashed out in alarm. Thankfully there was no foul smell to assault their noses this time.

The three moved quickly, and soon the kitchen looked brand new. There were finally signs of life, and it no longer entirely resembled a decades-abandoned haunted house. There was chopped wood readily available in the corner, and they piled it into the hearth of the stove and kindled the flames with a fire talisman. They then placed a large newly washed pot on the stove to boil some water. Wei Wuxian poured glutinous rice from the second box, washed every grain, and then dropped the rice into the pot.

"You're making congee?" Jin Ling asked.

"Mhm," Wei Wuxian replied.

Jin Ling slapped the rag down. Wei Wuxian admonished him, "Look at you, losing your temper after doing only a bit of work. Look at Sizhui—he's worked the hardest, but has he said anything? What's so bad about congee?"

Jin Ling retorted, "What's so *good* about congee? Watery and tasteless! Wait, no... You think I'm angry about the taste of congee?!"

"Either way, it's not for you," Wei Wuxian said.

Jin Ling was even more incensed by that. "What did you say? I worked for so long and I don't get a bite?!"

Lan Sizhui spoke up, "Mo-gongzi, could it be that this congee can cure corpse poisoning?"

Wei Wuxian smiled. "Yes, but the cure isn't the congee, it's the glutinous rice. It's a folk remedy. Usually, you apply the glutinous rice to scratches or bite wounds. In the event you guys ever wind up in the same situation again, you can give it a try. It might hurt a lot, but it's definitely effective, and you'll see instant results. But they weren't scratched or bitten. They breathed in toxic powder, so we can only make glutinous rice congee for them to eat."

Understanding dawned on Lan Sizhui. "No wonder you were so adamant about going into a house, and specifically an occupied one. Only places where people live would have kitchens and therefore glutinous rice."

"Who knows how long this rice has been sitting around or whether it's still edible?" Jin Ling said. "Besides, it's been at least a year since anyone's used this kitchen—it's all dusty, and even the meat is rotten. Did that old lady not need to eat this year? There's no way she knows how to pull off inedia, so how did she manage to survive?"

Wei Wuxian calmly replied, "Either this house has always been empty and she isn't the owner of the store at all, or she doesn't need to eat."

Lan Sizhui said in a hushed voice, "Not needing to eat would make one a citizen of the dead. But that granny is obviously breathing."

Wei Wuxian randomly added whatever was in a series of bottles and jars to the pot, mixing them in with a spatula as he spoke. "Oh yeah, you guys weren't done telling your story. How did you all end up coming to Yi City together? There's no way you just so happened to run into us again by chance."

The two boys immediately turned solemn. Jin Ling replied, "Me, those Lans, and the ones from other clans—we were all chasing something. I came from Qinghe."

Lan Sizhui added, "We came from Langye."

"What something?" Wei Wuxian asked.

Lan Sizhui shook his head. "Not a clue. It's never shown itself, and none of us know exactly what it is, or who...or what organization."

Many days ago, after Jin Ling sent his uncle away on a wild goose chase and released Wei Wuxian, he'd been worried that Jiang Cheng really would break his legs. So he decided to slip away in secret, disappear for maybe half a month, and reappear after Jiang Cheng's temper had cooled. He handed off Zidian to one of Jiang Cheng's trusted subordinates and fled.

During his escape, he came to a small city at the border of Qinghe in the hopes of finding a good Night Hunt location. He stopped to rest at a large inn, and was memorizing incantations in his room that night when Fairy, who had been lying at his feet, suddenly started barking at the door. It was already late, and Jin Ling scolded the spirit dog to stop barking, but then he heard a knock.

Although Fairy had stopped barking, it was still agitated, scratching the ground furiously with its sharp claws as its throat rumbled with low growls. Jin Ling went on alert and sharply demanded to know who was at the door. Since there was no response, he ignored it. But an hour later, the sound of knocking came again.

Jin Ling hopped out of the window with Fairy in tow, then went around the building and rounded the stairs from the level above. He was ready to strike this person from behind, catch them off guard, and see exactly who was playing tricks in the middle of the night. Unexpectedly, he found only empty air. Even after spying on his door in secret for a while, he saw no one.

He kept his eyes open and had Fairy guard the door, ready to attack anyone lurking about at a moment's notice. They didn't sleep the entire night, but nothing else happened—except that he kept hearing a strange noise, a sound like dripping water.

Early the next morning, a scream came from outside the door. Jin Ling kicked the door open and rushed out, stepping right into a pool of blood. Something fell from above the door, only narrowly missing Jin Ling as he ducked back.

A black cat!

Someone had nailed a dead cat above his door without his knowledge. The strange sound he'd heard in the middle of the night was the dripping of the cat's blood.

"I switched between a number of inns, and the same thing kept happening," Jin Ling said. "So I decided to take the initiative and pursue the culprit. Whenever I heard about the body of a dead cat randomly appearing somewhere, I'd go there to check it out. I had to uncover who was playing these foul tricks."

Wei Wuxian turned to Lan Sizhui. "Are you guys the same?"

Lan Sizhui nodded. "Yes. Many days ago, we were Night Hunting in Langye. One night, during dinner, the head of a cat—with its pelt still intact—was suddenly ladled up from the soup... At first, we didn't know it was targeting us. But that same day, when we switched to a different inn to rest, another dead cat was discovered in the bedding. This went on for days. We followed it all the way to Yueyang, where we ran into Jin-gongzi. We discovered we were all investigating the same case, so we joined forces. It was only today that we found our way to this region. When we asked a huntsman in the village in front of a stone tablet, we were pointed to Yi City."

A huntsman? Wei Wuxian wondered.

The juniors should've passed by the village at the fork with the stone tablet later than he and Lan Wangji did. But they hadn't seen any huntsmen at the time—only a few shy farmer ladies feeding chickens and minding house, claiming their men had gone to deliver goods and wouldn't be back for a long time.

The more Wei Wuxian pondered, the more solemn he became.

Now that he'd heard their stories, it seemed the other party had committed no crimes other than killing cats and tossing their bodies around. Although it was surely horrifying to experience and behold, the boys had not been hurt. Instead, the incidents only roused their curiosity and desire to get to the bottom of things.

Furthermore, the juniors had met up in Yueyang, which also happened to be the place Wei Wuxian and Lan Wangji had just departed to come southward to Shudong. From the look of things, someone had intentionally led the oblivious kids to run into the two of them.

Guiding a bunch of naive juniors to a place full of unknown dangers to face the dismembered limb of a murderous fierce corpse—was this not exactly the same modus operandi as the case of the Mo Estate?

And that wasn't even the most complicated problem. Wei Wuxian was much warier of the fact that the Yin Tiger Tally could be here in Yi City at this very moment. Unwilling as he might be to accept the possibility, it was the most logical explanation. Since there existed someone who could restore the remaining half of the Yin Tiger Tally, there was no telling whose hands the restored Yin Tiger Tally had landed in, regardless of whether it was supposedly taken care of.

Lan Sizhui, who had been crouching and fanning the firewood, looked up and said, "Mo-qianbei, the glutinous rice congee seems to be done?"

Wei Wuxian snapped out of it and stopped mixing. He took the bowl Lan Sizhui had just washed and ladled out a bit to taste. "It's done. You can bring it out. Everyone who's poisoned gets a bowl. Feed it to them."

Lan Jingyi had only taken one bite after the congee was served, however, before he spat it out. "What is this?! *Poison?!*"

"What poison? This is the antidote! Glutinous rice congee," Wei Wuxian stated.

Lan Jingyi rebuked the very idea. "Setting aside why glutinous rice is the antidote, I've never eaten such spicy congee!"

The others who had taken bites all nodded in agreement with watery eyes. Wei Wuxian stroked his chin. He had grown up in Yunmeng, a place that was very fond of hot spices, and Wei Wuxian was as hardened as they came. Whenever he cooked, he invariably made the food so spicy that even Jiang Cheng couldn't stand it and would hurl the bowl away while loudly cursing its horrible taste. And yet, he remained forever unable to stop himself from adding spoon after spoon of spice. It would seem he had once again failed to control his hand.

Lan Sizhui tasted it out of curiosity and flushed from head to toe. He pursed his lips and managed not to sputter, but both his eyes were red. A thought crossed his mind: *This flavor...it's so terrible that it's giving me déjà vu...*

"Medicine is three parts poison. Spice helps you sweat, so you'll recover faster," Wei Wuxian said.

The boys *huhhh*-ed, expressing their disbelief, but still ate all the congee with scrunched-up faces. For a while after, everyone was bright red and drenched with sweat, suffering so greatly that they felt they might as well die.

Wei Wuxian couldn't help but ask, "Is this really necessary? Hanguang-jun is also a man of Gusu, but he can eat really spicy food, so why are you guys like this?"

Lan Sizhui had his hand covering his mouth as he spoke. "That's not right, qianbei. Hanguang-jun's tastes are very mild; he never eats spicy things..."

Wei Wuxian was slightly taken aback. "Really?"

He remembered once meeting Lan Wangji at Yiling in his previous life, after he'd defected from the Jiang Clan of Yunmeng. Although Wei Wuxian was still widely hated and condemned at the time, things hadn't yet reached the point where everyone was calling for his annihilation. So, thick-skinned as he was, he demanded Lan Wangji have a meal with him to catch up. All Lan Wangji had ordered at the time were spicy dishes rife with Sichuan peppercorns, so Wei Wuxian had always assumed they shared a similar palate.

Surprisingly, now that he thought back, he couldn't recall whether Lan Wangji had actually touched those dishes. But he'd even forgotten to pay for the meal despite saying it was his treat, leaving Lan Wangji to foot the bill in the end. Of course he wouldn't remember such minute details.

For some reason, he suddenly very, very much wanted to see Lan Wangji's face.

"...Qianbei, Mo-qianbei!"

"Hm?" Wei Wuxian snapped out of it.

Lan Sizhui said in a hushed voice, "The door to that old lady's room has...opened."

— PART 2 —

A GUST OF SINISTER WIND had blown in out of nowhere and pushed the door to the small room open a crack. It swung open and closed intermittently. It was pitch-black inside the room, and they could only vaguely see a hunched shadow sitting next to a table. Wei Wuxian gestured for them not to move and walked into the room himself.

The light of the oil lamp and the candles from the central room seeped inside. The old lady had her head bowed, as if she hadn't noticed anyone come in. There was a piece of cloth in her lap, tied taut to an embroidery frame. She appeared to be doing needlework. Her hands were stiffly pressed together as she tried to poke a thread through a needle.

Wei Wuxian seated himself next to the table. "Granny, why not turn on the lights when you thread your needle? Let me."

He took the needle and thread and fixed it in no time. Then he returned them to the old lady and walked out of the room like nothing was the matter, closing the door behind him.

"Leave her be," he said.

"Did you check if the old witch was alive or dead when you went in just now?" Jin Ling asked.

"Don't call her an old witch, it's rude," Wei Wuxian chided. "That old lady is a living corpse."

The boys exchanged looks of dismay. Lan Sizhui asked, "What's a living corpse?"

"A living corpse is when an individual has all the characteristics of a corpse, from head to toe, but the person themselves is still alive."

Jin Ling was greatly alarmed. "You're saying she's still alive?!"

"Did you guys see inside the room just now?" Wei Wuxian asked.

"Yes."

"What did you see? What was she doing?"

"Threading a needle."

"Did she succeed?"

"...No."

"That's right, she didn't. The muscles of the dead are stiff, so complicated actions such as threading a needle are impossible. Those aren't age spots on her face but rather livor mortis. And she doesn't need to eat. But she can still breathe, so, she's alive."

Lan Sizhui said, "But...but this granny's very old. Many old ladies have poor eyesight and can't thread needles by themselves."

"Which is why I did it for her," Wei Wuxian said. "But did you guys notice something else? In the time between opening the front door and now, she hasn't blinked a single time."

The youths themselves blinked.

"The living blink to prevent their eyes from drying out, but the dead don't need to do that," Wei Wuxian explained. "And when I threaded the needle, did anyone notice how she looked at me?"

Jin Ling answered, "She didn't move her eyes... It was her head that turned!"

"That's it exactly," Wei Wuxian said. "Usually when you look in a different direction, your eyes move at least a little. But the dead are not the same. Since they can't manage minute actions like moving their eyeballs, they can only move their whole head and neck."

Lan Jingyi was dazed. "Should we be taking notes?"

"A good habit to have," Wei Wuxian stated. "But where will you find time to flip through your notes during a Night Hunt? Use your brain, memorize it."

Jin Ling gritted his teeth. "Walking corpses are crazy enough. Why is there such a thing as a living corpse?!"

Wei Wuxian answered, "Living corpses are rarely formed naturally. They're usually deliberately made, like this one is."

"Deliberately?! *Why?!*"

"The dead have many shortcomings," Wei Wuxian lectured. "Stiff muscles, slow movement, and so on. But they have their advantages too—they don't fear pain, can't think, and are easy to control. Some people think those shortcomings can be improved upon, and that by doing so, they can construct the perfect puppet. That's where the concept of living corpses came from."

While the boys didn't blurt it out, their faces were already boldly written with an obvious sentiment: That person must be Wei! Wu! Xian!

Wei Wuxian didn't know whether to laugh or cry. *But I've never made such a thing!* he thought.

Although it did indeed sound like his style!

"Ahem. All right, it was Wei Wuxian who started the trend, but he successfully refined Wen Ning—that is, the Ghost General," he said. "To be honest, I always wondered who came up with that nickname. It's so stupid. Anyway. Others tried to mimic him but could only produce poor imitations at best. They ended up going down a deviant path and set their eyes on the living instead, coming up with living corpses like this." He concluded, "They're failed replicas."

At the mention of Wei Wuxian's name, Jin Ling's expression grew cold. He humphed. "Wei Ying was a deviant himself."

"Yeah, so those who make living corpses are *extra* deviant," Wei Wuxian agreed.

"Mo-qianbei, what should we do now?" Lan Sizhui asked.

"Some living corpses might not know they're already dead," Wei Wuxian said. "I see that old lady is one of those who hasn't quite figured it out, so it'll be fine if we refrain from bothering her for now."

Just then, there was suddenly a series of crisp taps—the sound of bamboo hitting the ground. It sounded like it was just outside a nearby window, which was sealed by black boards. The faces of the clan juniors in the central room turned pale. Having been consistently harassed by the sound since entering the city, they'd begun panicking upon hearing it.

Wei Wuxian motioned for them not to make a sound. They held their breath and watched as he stood next to the window, peering through an extremely thin crack between the planks of the door. At first, all he saw was white. He thought it was because the fog outside the house was too thick, leaving nothing visible...but then the white rapidly shrank away.

It was a pair of savagely white eyes, currently glaring fiercely through the crack in the door. All the white he'd seen wasn't the miasma, but this pair of eyes, which completely lacked pupils.

Jin Ling and the others' hearts were pounding, terrified he would suddenly be struck by disaster and fall, clutching his eyes. They heard Wei Wuxian let out an "*ah!*" and their hearts jumped into their throats, their hair standing on end.

"What is it?!"

Wei Wuxian whispered in the teeniest voice, "*Shh*, don't speak. I'm looking at it."

Jin Ling hushed his voice to be even teenier than Wei Wuxian's. "Then what did you see? What's out there?"

Wei Wuxian neither moved his eyes nor gave a direct answer. "Mm-hmm...yup...amazing. Wow."

His profile was filled with delight. The praise and awe he expressed seemed to come sincerely from the bottom of his heart, and the clan juniors' curiosity rapidly overtook their nervousness.

Lan Sizhui couldn't help but ask, "...Mo-qianbei, what's so amazing?"

"Aiyah! It's so interesting. Keep it down, don't scare it away, I'm not done looking," Wei Wuxian shushed him.

"Move! I wanna see!" Jin Ling said.

"Me too!"

"You really wanna see this?" Wei Wuxian asked.

"Yeah!"

Wei Wuxian slowly shuffled aside, acting incredibly reluctant. Jin Ling was the first to go over. Lining himself up with the thin crack in the wood, he peeked out.

Night had fallen by now. Nights here tended to be chilly, but surprisingly, the evil miasma circulating in Yi City had dispersed quite a bit. They could now see at least a few dozen meters of the street.

Jin Ling peered for a moment but didn't see anything "amazing" or "so interesting." A little disappointed, he thought, *Could I have scared it away when I spoke just now?*

Just as he had that thought, a scrawny, emaciated figure appeared in a flash. Jin Ling felt shivers scrabble up to his head and explode. He almost screamed out loud, but for some reason the burst of energy caught in his chest. He forced it down and stiffly maintained his bent pose, waiting for the numbing sensation to pass. Despite himself, he stole a glance at Wei Wuxian. The despicable man was leaning against the window boards with a corner of his lips curled up.

He wiggled his eyebrows at Jin Ling and smirked. "Isn't it very interesting?"

Jin Ling shot him a death glare, knowing full well he was messing with them on purpose, and replied through gritted teeth, "Yeah..."

Then his mind changed track and he straightened up, putting on an air of disinterest. "It's only so-so, barely interesting!"

He backed off to the side, waiting for the next fool. With the two of them taking turns at deception, the rest had their curiosity stoked as high as it could go. Lan Sizhui couldn't restrain himself. He went to stand in the same spot, but just as he placed his eyes to the crack, he let out a candid "*ah!*" and jumped back, his face full of helpless fear.

He spun around twice, disoriented, before he found Wei Wuxian and lamented his findings.

"Mo-qianbei! Outside! There's a...there's a..."

Wei Wuxian replied understandingly, "*That*, right? Don't tell. There'll be no surprise once you tell. Let everyone go see for themselves."

As if anyone else dared to go up after seeing the terrified state Lan Sizhui was in. What "surprise"? "Scare," you mean?! And thus, they all waved him off.

"No, it's fine, we're not looking!"

Jin Ling clicked his tongue. "Tricking people for fun at a time like this, what were you thinking?!"

"Weren't you in on it too?" Wei Wuxian said. "Don't imitate your uncle's tone. Sizhui, was that thing just now scary?"

Lan Sizhui nodded and replied honestly, "Yes."

"Scary is right," Wei Wuxian said. "This is a fantastic opportunity to further your training, you know! Why do ghosts scare people? Because when people are scared, their will falters and their primordial spirit becomes agitated. That's when it's easiest to drain their yang energy. So creatures like ghosts are most fearful of the brave—since the brave are fearless, they can't do anything to them or take advantage of them. Which is why, as clan juniors, your first priority is to strengthen your courage!"

Lan Jingyi was glad he couldn't move and therefore hadn't gone over to peep out of curiosity. Still, he grumbled, "Courage is innate. Some people are born chickens, what can you do?"

"Were you born knowing how to fly on a sword?" Wei Wuxian questioned. "Didn't you practice over and over until you got it? Same logic. Get scared again and again and you'll get used to it. Toilets stink, right? They're gross, right? But trust me, if you lived in toilets for a month, you could even eat in there without issue."

The boys were aghast at the thought and refuted him in chorus: "Nope! We don't believe you!"

"It's just an example," Wei Wuxian said. "All right, I admit I've never lived in toilets before, so I don't know if you'd actually be able to eat in there. That was an irresponsible remark. But with that thing out there, you guys have to try. Don't just look—you have to *examine* it. Scrutinize the details, and as quickly as you can, use those details to unearth any weaknesses it might be hiding. Remain steady in the face of danger and find an opportunity to strike back. Okay, I've lectured this long, do you all understand? People don't often have the chance to hear my lectures, you know. You have to cherish this opportunity. Don't back away now, come over and form a line. Take turns looking."

"...Do we have to?"

"Of course," Wei Wuxian said. "I am never one to joke around, nor do I play tricks on people. Let's start with Jingyi. Jin Ling and Sizhui have both had their turns already."

"Huh?" Lan Jingyi protested. "I can be excused, right? Those who were poisoned can't move, that's what you said."

Wei Wuxian directed, "Stick out your tongue. *Aah...*"

Lan Jingyi complied once more. *"Aah..."*

Wei Wuxian gave his blessing. "Congratulations, you're cured of the poison. Now bravely take your first step, come!"

Lan Jingyi balked. "Cured that fast?! You're lying, right?!"

His protests were ineffective, and so he had to force himself to boldly walk to the window. He looked, then looked away, looked, and looked away. Wei Wuxian knocked on the wooden plank.

"What are you scared of? I'm standing right here. It won't dare break through this board. It's not going to eat your eyeball."

Lan Jingyi jumped away. "I'm done!"

Then came the turn of the next person in line. Each person gasped sharply when they looked. Once everyone had taken their turn, Wei Wuxian said, "All done? Then why don't each of you share what you saw? Let's summarize."

Jin Ling rushed to answer first. "White eyes. Female. Very short, very skinny. Okay appearance. She's holding a bamboo pole."

Lan Sizhui thought for a moment, then said, "The girl's head reaches my chest. Her clothing is ragged and not too clean, kind of like the garb of wandering street urchins. The bamboo pole seems to be a cane used by the blind. It's possible those white eyes were not formed after death but rather that she was blind while alive."

Wei Wuxian commented, "Jin Ling saw a lot, but Sizhui saw details."

Jin Ling pursed his lips.

Another boy said, "The girl is about fifteen or sixteen years old. She has a heart-shaped face, very delicate and pretty, but there's a sense of vitality in those fine features. She uses a wooden hairpin to pin up her long hair. The end of the pin is carved with the head of a little fox. She's small, yet slender. Although unclean, she's not repellently filthy. If she was just given a chance to clean up, she'd definitely be cute—a real beauty."

When Wei Wuxian heard this, he instantly felt the boy's prospects were limitless. "Very good, very good," he praised energetically.

"A detailed observation with a unique focus. Our little friend will definitely be a romantic in the future."

The youth blushed, covered his face, and turned to face the wall, ignoring his companions' laughter.

Another youth said, "It seems the sound of bamboo hitting the ground was her walking. If she was already blind when alive, she'd still be unable to see after turning into a phantom in death. She has to depend on that cane."

Yet another youth countered, "But that's not right... You've all seen blind people before, right? Since their sight is hindered, they walk and move very slowly, scared to bump into something. But the phantom outside the door is quick and agile. I've never seen such an agile blind person."

Wei Wuxian smiled. "Mm, that's an excellent point. Very good. That's exactly how you should be analyzing the situation—don't overlook any points of suspicion. Now, let's invite her in and clear up those suspicions with answers."

Just as he said that, he immediately tore off one of the door planks. Not just the boys inside the house but also the phantom outside the window jumped in surprise at the abrupt action. She raised her bamboo pole, immediately on guard.

Wei Wuxian began by greeting the phantom. Then he asked, "Miss, you've been following them all this time. Do you have some business with them?"

That girl widened her eyes. If she were alive she would've been absolutely adorable, but with those blank white eyes exuding streams of blood, the motion just made her look doubly savage. Someone inhaled sharply behind Wei Wuxian.

Wei Wuxian asked, "What's there to be scared of? You'll see plenty of bleeding from the seven apertures in the future. Is two apertures already too much for you? That's why I'm telling you guys to practice more."

Prior to this, the girl had been fretfully pacing in circles before the window, hitting the ground with her bamboo pole, stomping, glaring, and flailing her arms. But now she suddenly changed course, gesturing like she wanted to tell them something.

Jin Ling wondered, "That's weird. Can't she talk?"

The phantom girl paused mid-action at this and opened her mouth to show them.

Blood poured from her empty mouth. It seemed her tongue had been yanked out at the root.

The clan juniors were covered with goosebumps, but at the same time, sympathy bloomed in their hearts. *No wonder she couldn't speak. Blind and mute—how unfortunate.*

"Is she using sign language? Can anyone understand?" Wei Wuxian asked.

No one did. The girl stomped her feet impatiently and used her bamboo pole to draw and scrape on the ground. But she obviously wasn't raised in a scholarly family and didn't know her letters. All she'd drawn was a mess of little people, making it impossible for anyone to decipher what she wanted to express.

Just then, from the far end of the street came the sound of frantic running and someone panting.

The phantom girl suddenly vanished. But she would probably come back on her own, so Wei Wuxian wasn't concerned. He swiftly stuck the door plank back in place and continued to spy on the outside. The other clan juniors also wanted to see what was happening, so they all squished by the door, a column of heads stacked from top to bottom, blocking the crack in the door with their eyes.

The evil miasma had thinned out earlier, but now it was circulating again. They saw an unkempt figure break through the white fog, rushing their way. This man was dressed all in black and appeared to be injured, stumbling as he ran. There was a sword at his waist, also wrapped in black cloth.

Lan Jingyi whispered, "Is it that smoke-masked man?"

Lan Sizhui whispered back, "It shouldn't be. The smoke-masked man's form is completely different from his."

There was a group of walking corpses following right behind the man, moving extremely fast. They caught up to him in an instant, and the man drew his sword to meet them, his sword glare bright and clear as he slashed through the miasma. Wei Wuxian cheered in his head: *Nice strike!*

But once the sword made its sweep, the familiar, odd spattering noise came again. Blackish-red powder spouted once more from the severed limbs of the walking corpses. Surrounded and with nowhere to dodge, the man could do nothing but stand on the spot and be blasted with a face full of powder.

Lan Sizhui was stricken by the sight. He whispered, "Mo-qianbei, that man, we..."

Just then, another group of walking corpses shambled close, outflanking the man as his figure shrank into the crowd. Another sweep of his sword, and more corpse toxin erupted into the air. He gasped in yet more of it, seeming to grow unsteady on his feet.

"We have to save him," Wei Wuxian said.

"How are you gonna do that?" Jin Ling questioned. "You can't go over there right now, the air is lousy with corpse toxin. You'll be poisoned if you get close."

After contemplating for a moment, Wei Wuxian moved away from the window and walked to the heart of the central room. The boys' eyes also unconsciously followed him as he went. They saw a group of paper effigies of various appearances standing quietly between the two giant floral wreaths. Wei Wuxian passed by them slowly and stopped in front of a pair of paper ladies.

The appearance of every paper effigy was different, but this pair seemed to have been intended to be twin sisters. Their makeup, attire, and facial features were all cast from the same mold. With crescent eyes and smiles on their faces, one could almost hear their giggling laughter. Hair coiffed in the double-ring style, they were adorned with golden bracelets, red pearl earrings, and embroidered slippers, fully suited to be the maids of a great and wealthy household.

"Let's go with these two," Wei Wuxian said.

He lightly swept his hand over one of the youths' unsheathed swords. Using the blood from the cut on his thumb, he spun around to dot the two pairs of eyes with four eyeballs.

He then took a step back and gave a light smile. "Coy eyes and seductive wiles, red lips part to chase a smile. Ask not of good or evil done, with these final dots, let the warrior come."

A gust of sinister wind blew from out of nowhere, abruptly engulfing the entire store. The boys unconsciously gripped their swords.

Suddenly, the pair of paper effigy twin sisters jolted.

In the next heartbeat, there came the sound of giggling laughter, drifting from those bright-red, painted lips.

The Final Eyes Summoning!

It was as though the pair of paper effigies had seen or heard something extremely funny. They giggled like tremulous flowering boughs. Those eyes, dotted with the blood of the living, rattled in their sockets as they twirled about, painting a picture that was both extremely charming and extremely horrifying. Wei Wuxian stood in front of them and inclined his head shallowly, giving them a courteous nod.

The pair of paper effigies reciprocated with a deep bow, showing him greater courtesy.

Wei Wuxian pointed to the door. "Go bring the living in. Obliterate everything else."

Shrill laughter shrieked from the mouths of the paper effigies. A blast of sinister wind rushed past and flung open the two doors of the entrance!

The two paper effigies leapt out, shoulder to shoulder, and dove right into the mob of walking corpses. It was hard to believe that fake humans, so clearly made of paper, could possess such fierce and destructive power. Stepping with their fine, embroidered shoes and fluttering their airy sleeves, they slashed off a walking corpse's arm with one sweep and sliced a head in half with another. It was as if the paper sleeves had transformed into sharp blades. That charming laughter echoed incessantly down the long street, rousing the mind yet raising the hair.

It wasn't long before over a dozen walking corpses had been sliced to mangled pieces by the pair of effigies. It was a complete victory for the paper maids. Obeying the command they were given, they picked up the weakened escapee and carried him inside before jumping out the door. The door closed automatically behind them, and they quieted down as they stood one on either side, watching the entrance like guardian lions.

The clan juniors inside the house were gaping.

In the past, they had learned stories of the deviant path from books and from their seniors. At the time, they couldn't understand: If it was so wicked, why were there so many people who wished to learn it? Why were there so many imitators of the Yiling Patriarch?

It was only now, after seeing it with their own eyes, that they understood. The deviant path had its own enticing and mysterious ways. And this Final Eyes Summoning was merely the tip of the iceberg.

Once most of the youths came around, there was surprisingly no revulsion on their faces. Instead, they were filled with unconcealable excitement. They felt as though they had gained immense insight and a wealth of topics to discuss with their fellow disciples when they returned. Only Jin Ling still looked upset.

Lan Sizhui went over to help Wei Wuxian assist the man, but Wei Wuxian said, "Stay back. And be careful not to touch the corpse toxin. You might get poisoned too if it catches on your skin."

By the time the paper effigies had carried the man inside, he was already drained of energy, only half-conscious. But now he was a little more alert. He coughed a few times but covered his mouth, seeming to be worried he'd infect the others if he expelled corpse toxin.

He asked quietly, "Who are you all?"

His voice sounded extremely exhausted. And he had posed the question not only because he didn't know anyone inside this house but also because he couldn't see.

A thick white ribbon was wrapped around the man's eyes. He, too, was probably blind.

And a very good-looking blind person, at that—with a straight, fine nose and thin lips of muted red, he could almost be called delicately handsome. He also appeared very young, between a youth and an adult, quite inspiring of sympathy. Wei Wuxian thought, *How come I keep running into blind people recently? Both alive and dead, both in the words of others and with my own two eyes.*

"Hey," Jin Ling said suddenly. "We don't know who this person is yet, or whether he's friend or foe, so why are we saving him so rashly? What if he's evil? Won't we have saved a snake, then?"

While he wasn't wrong, it was a little awkward to be so blunt in front of the man himself. The man wasn't angry, however, and he didn't seem concerned about getting thrown out. He smiled, revealing a pair of small, pointed canine teeth.

"The little young master is right. It's best if I leave."

Jin Ling, who had never expected that response, was taken aback for a moment. At a loss for words, he finally settled on humphing. Lan Sizhui quickly spoke up to smooth things over.

"But it's also possible that this gentleman isn't malicious. In any case, ignoring the dying would be against my family's precepts."

Jin Ling remained obstinate. "Fine. You guys are the good guys. Don't blame me if anyone croaks."

Lan Jingyi began angrily, "You..."

But before he could finish, his tongue tied itself.

This was because he saw the sword the man had placed on the table. Half the black cloth wrapping the sword had slipped off, revealing its body.

The sword was superbly forged, a paragon of craftsmanship. The scabbard was bronze, carved with fretwork of frost-like fractals. The body of the sword could be seen through that hollow pattern. Like silver stars twinkling in snowflake-shaped light, it had a sort of ice-pure and resplendent beauty.

Lan Jingyi's eyes bulged, looking like he was about to blurt something out. Wei Wuxian didn't know what he planned on screaming, but since the man had used a black cloth to cover his sword, he must not want anyone to see it. He also instinctively didn't want to alert the man, so he smothered Lan Jingyi's mouth with a hand while placing his index finger upon his own lips, gesturing to all the other shocked youths to not say anything.

Jin Ling mouthed two words, then reached out and wrote said two words on the dust-covered table:

Shuanghua.

...The sword Shuanghua?

Wei Wuxian mouthed his question soundlessly: "The sword Shuanghua that belonged to...Xiao Xingchen?"

Jin Ling and the others all nodded their conviction.

While the youths had never seen Xiao Xingchen in person, Shuanghua was a rare, famous sword. Not only was its spiritual power strong, but its physical appearance was also beautiful and unique. Once upon a time, it had been featured in countless editions of the *Illustrated Almanac of Spiritual Swords* and the *Atlas of Notable Blades*, making it unforgettable.

Wei Wuxian mulled over this information. If the sword was Shuanghua, and the man was blind...

One of the boys had arrived at the same conclusion and was reaching out to touch the bandage over the man's eyes, wanting to unravel it to see if his eyes were still there. But his hand had only just touched the bandage when the man seemed to be in extreme pain. He shifted back imperceptibly, apparently very scared of others touching his eyes.

The boy noticed his own impropriety and quickly withdrew his hand. "I'm sorry, I'm sorry... I didn't mean to."

The man raised his left hand, which was covered in a thin, black glove, and seemed to want to cover his eyes, even though he was afraid to touch them himself. Gentle contact already caused him unbearable pain. A thin sheen of sweat had broken out on his forehead.

He replied arduously, "It's fine..."

Still, his voice quivered.

Such a display was surely enough to deduce that this man was Xiao Xingchen, who had gone missing after the case of the Chang Clan of Yueyang.

Xiao Xingchen still hadn't realized his identity had been seen through. After enduring the wave of pain, he fumbled to reach for Shuanghua. Wei Wuxian's hand moved as fast as his eyes saw, pulling up the black cloth that had slipped off. Having felt Shuanghua, Xiao Xingchen nodded.

"Many thanks for rescuing me. I will take my leave."

"Don't go yet. You've got corpse poisoning," Wei Wuxian said.

"Is it serious?" Xiao Xingchen asked.

"Very," Wei Wuxian replied.

"Since it is serious, then why stay?" Xiao Xingchen said. "It is hopeless, regardless. Why not kill a few more walking corpses before I turn?"

Hearing he had no care for life or death, hot blood surged within the chests of the boys in the house. "Who said it's hopeless?" Lan Jingyi blurted in spite of himself. "Stay! He can cure you!"

Wei Wuxian said curiously, "Me? Sorry, are you talking about me?"

He really didn't have the heart to tell the truth. Xiao Xingchen had already breathed in too much of the corpse toxin; his face was tinted a faint blackish-red. He was poisoned too severely, and glutinous rice congee probably wouldn't work anymore.

"I already killed plenty of walking corpses in this city," Xiao Xingchen said. "They have been following me. More will shortly, and endlessly, follow. If I stay, you will all be overwhelmed by the mob sooner or later."

"Does my lord know why Yi City became this way?" Wei Wuxian asked.

Xiao Xingchen shook his head. "No. I am merely a wandering Daoi... I wandered here and entered the city for a Night Hunt after learning of the supernatural activity in the region. There are a great many living and walking corpses in this city. You have yet to experience the brunt of it. Some are agile and hard to defend against, while others expel corpse toxin from their bodies after being cut down. The poison infects instantly upon contact, but if those corpses are not cut down they tackle and bite, with the end result of poisoning you all the same. They are genuinely difficult to fight. Judging by your voices, there are many little young masters among you, am I correct? I urge everyone to leave this place as soon as possible."

Just as he spoke, they heard the sinister giggling of the paper effigy sisters outside the entrance. This time, the sound of their laughter was shriller than before.

Lan Jingyi leaned on the door to peek through the crack. Then he swiftly used his body to block the slit, his eyes wide and dumbfounded.

"So...so, so many!"

"Walking corpses?" Wei Wuxian asked. "How many is many?"

"I don't know!" Lan Jingyi exclaimed. "The entire street is full of them! Maybe a few hundred? And that number's growing! I don't think those two paper effigies can hold out for much longer!"

If the door-guarding effigies fell, all the corpses walking the street would swarm into the shop. Cut them down, and poisoning would be imminent—in fact, the more vigorous the slaughter, the faster the poison would circulate. Don't cut them down, and inevitably be torn apart or bitten to death.

Sword in hand, Xiao Xingchen clearly planned on pushing through the door to go out, probably hoping to fend off as many waves of those cadavers as he could with what strength remained in him. But his face suddenly turned purplish-red, and he fell backward onto the ground.

"Just sit tight," Wei Wuxian said. "This'll be resolved in a jiffy."

Once more, he casually swept the index finger of his right hand over the blade of Lan Jingyi's sword. Blood dripped.

"Are you gonna use the Final Eyes Summoning again?" Lan Jingyi asked. "How much blood would it take you to dot the eyes of every single effigy? How about I lend you some of mine?"

Other boys immediately rolled up their sleeves. "Me too..."

Wei Wuxian was caught between laughter and tears. "No need. Do you have any blank talismans?"

These juniors were still young, not trained enough to be able to draw talismans on the spot for immediate use. All the talismans they had on them were pre-drawn.

Lan Sizhui shook his head. "No."

"A pre-drawn one is fine too," Wei Wuxian said.

Lan Sizhui retrieved a stack of yellow talismans from his qiankun pouch. Wei Wuxian took only one sheet, glanced at it, and then pressed the index and middle fingers of his right hand together as his hand powerfully glided over the cinnabar paint from top to bottom. The vibrant red blood and the scarlet cinnabar formed a brand-new set of symbols.

He flicked his wrist, and the red-marked yellow talisman ignited midair. Wei Wuxian reached out with his left hand and caught the ashes drifting from the burning paper. He clenched his fingers and looked slightly downward. As he opened his palm, he gently blew the black ashes toward the row of paper effigies.

He murmured, "Wildfires cannot destroy, for life shall rise again in the spring breeze."[2]

The talisman ash stormed and whirled.

A Yin Muscleman standing at the forefront picked up a machete that was next to his feet and slung it over his shoulder.

Beside him was a sumptuously dressed paper beauty with her hair styled in a high, loose bun. She slowly raised her right hand, nimbly flexing her long and slender fingers. She appeared to be a languid noblewoman, haughtily admiring her long nails, which were painted blood-red.

Next to the beauty's feet stood a golden boy and a jade maiden. The golden boy yanked mischievously on the jade maiden's braid, and the jade maiden stuck out her tongue at him in response. A long tongue, almost thirty centimeters in length, abruptly slipped out of her small mouth and poked a giant hole in the boy's chest, like a venomous snake, before it was swiftly withdrawn with one vicious movement. The golden boy opened his mouth wide, revealing two chilling rows of white teeth, and bit her on the arm. Just like that, the paper effigy children started fighting each other first!

Twenty to thirty paper effigies started wobbling one after the other like they were working their joints, whispering to each other as they shook, while the sound of rustling undulated everywhere. They were not alive—no, they were far superior to the living.

"Hold your breath" Wei Wuxian instructed.

Then he sidestepped to make way to the entrance. He bowed slightly and made a gesture of invitation.

The wooden doors swung violently open once more. The sweet smell of corpse toxin gushed in, and everyone immediately covered their mouths, raising their sleeves in defense. The Yin Musclemen let

---

2 *A verse from "Farewell on the Ancient Grassland" by Bai Juyi, Tang Dynasty.*

out a loud roar and lunged first, before the rest of the paper effigies filed out.

The wooden door closed anew behind the last paper effigy.

"No one breathed any of that in, right?" Wei Wuxian asked the room.

Everyone quickly replied *no*. Wei Wuxian helped Xiao Xingchen to his feet. He'd thought to find a place for the man to lie down, but shockingly no such space could be found, leaving him no choice but to sit on the frigid, dusty ground. Xiao Xingchen was still tightly gripping his sword, Shuanghua. It was only with a strenuous effort that he roused himself from his half-conscious state.

He coughed a few times, his voice feeble. "Sir, that was...the Final Eyes Summoning?"

"My knowledge is rough at best," Wei Wuxian replied.

Xiao Xingchen pondered for a moment, then smiled. "Mn...that was indeed the best way to obliterate those walking corpses."

He paused, then added, "However, cultivators who walk this path can easily find themselves facing mutiny from subordinate malicious ghosts and belligerent spirits. Not even the founding father of this path, the Yiling Patriarch Wei Wuxian, could escape that fate. This is just my personal suggestion, but if my lord is not his match, then do be more careful in the future. Best not to use that magic unless absolutely necessary. Try cultivating another path..."

Wei Wuxian sighed inwardly. "Thank you for your exhortation."

Most acclaimed cultivators made their stance on the matter very clear, drawing lines in the sand to advertise their profound hatred for a certain someone. However, the fact that this dear martial uncle of his would still advise him so diplomatically, reminding him to watch out for mutiny even while he was half-dead himself—it only spoke to how exceedingly gentle he was, how kind and softhearted.

Looking at the thick layer of bandages over Xiao Xingchen's eyes, and remembering what the man had gone through, Wei Wuxian couldn't help but sigh regretfully.

Young juniors with scant worldly experience were usually too fascinated by the demonic path to regard it with contempt. So other than Jin Ling—who'd looked very upset the entire time—the other juniors were all crammed around the crack in the door to watch the spectacle unfold.

"Help...that effigy woman's nails are so scary. One slash leaves five gashes."

"Why is that little girl's tongue so long and so hard? Is she a hanged ghost?"

"That guy's so strong! I can't believe he can pick up so many walking corpses at once. He's gonna slam them down! Look, look, look! He's done it! They're all smashed!"

After he'd been pulled aside by Xiao Xingchen for a round of gentle counsel, Wei Wuxian grabbed the last bowl of glutinous rice congee on the table. "Your poisoning is severe. I have something here that might be able to give you a slight reprieve...but it also might not, and it tastes quite awful. Do you want to give it a try? If you no longer wish to live, don't worry about it."

Xiao Xingchen took the bowl with two hands. "Of course I want to live. If I may live on, then allow me to persist."

However, when he lowered his head and partook, the corners of his lips started to twitch. It was only by firmly pursing his mouth that he managed to not bring it right back up. It was a good while before he very politely uttered, "Thank you."

Wei Wuxian turned his head. "D'you guys see that? You see that? Hear what he said? You're the ones being delicate and difficult. All those complaints while eating the congee *I* slaved over!"

"Did *you* slave over anything?" Jin Ling accused. "Besides dumping a bunch of strange things into a pot, what else did you accomplish?"

Xiao Xingchen said, "However, upon further consideration...if I must eat this every day, then I choose death."

Jin Ling burst into mocking laughter without a shred of mercy, and not even Lan Sizhui was able to contain himself, letting out a *pfft*. Wei Wuxian looked at them, speechless, and Lan Sizhui immediately schooled himself.

Right then, Lan Jingyi exclaimed happily, "All right! They're all dead! We've won!"

Xiao Xingchen quickly put down the bowl. "Do not open the door yet. Be careful, there might be more..."

"Don't put down the bowl," Wei Wuxian said. "Pick it up and finish the congee."

He approached the wooden door to look out through the crack. After the inhuman slaughter, the street was permeated with thin white fog and purplish-red powder. The corpse toxin was gradually dissipating, and the paper effigies patrolled leisurely up and down the street. Pieces of the walking corpses were strewn all over the ground, and when they came across bits that still twitched, the effigies would viciously stomp down until those chunks were rendered into nothing more than puddles of blood and flesh.

Beyond that, everything was still and quiet. No new walking corpses had rushed onto the scene yet.

Just as Wei Wuxian was about to relax, there was a very, very light movement just above his head.

The sound was almost impossible to catch. It was as though someone was darting past on the roof tiles with the speed of a bird, their steps unusually light and agile, nearly silent. Were it not for Wei

Wuxian's sharp senses, he wouldn't have caught the minute sound of impact between the tiles.

The movement couldn't deceive the blind either. Xiao Xingchen alerted, "Above!"

Wei Wuxian barked, "Spread out!"

Just as he spoke, the ceiling over the central room tore open. Broken tiles, accumulated dust, and scattered straw plunged down like rain. The boys had quickly dispersed, so thankfully no one was hurt. A black shadow jumped down through the gaping hole in the ceiling.

This man was dressed in a set of black Daoist robes. He was tall, and his posture was straight as a pine tree. A Daoist whisk was tucked behind his back, and he wielded a longsword in hand. He was coolly handsome in appearance, and with his head slightly tilted up just so, he emanated a haughty and aloof demeanor.

But his eyes had no pupils. They were pure, deathly white.

A fierce corpse!

Everyone present had only just managed to realize that fact when he lunged, brandishing his sword.

He was aiming for Jin Ling, the one closest to him. Jin Ling drew his sword to parry, but the force behind the strike was immense and the impact numbed his arm. If not for the extraordinary spiritual power of his own sword, Suihua, he would probably have been struck dead.

His attack unsuccessful, the black-clad fierce corpse swung again, moving as smoothly and brutally as a flowing current, as if his hatred was as profound as the sea. He aimed for Jin Ling's arm, and in that moment of danger, Xiao Xingchen drew his sword and helped Jin Ling block his attack. Doing so must have caused the poisoning to surge, for he collapsed at last, unmoving.

Lan Jingyi was horrified. "Is he dead or alive?! I've never seen such a..."

...A fierce corpse with such agility and such expertise with the sword! But he'd trailed off because he suddenly remembered that yes, he had.

Because, of course, the Ghost General was the same!

Wei Wuxian's eyes had been firmly glued to this Daoist, his mind churning rapidly. He pulled out the bamboo flute tucked at his waist and played a long, shrill note, so piercing that everyone else covered their ears. When the Daoist heard the sound of the flute, his body lurched. Although the hand gripping the sword shook tremendously, in the end, he still lunged!

He could not be controlled. That meant this fierce corpse had a master!

Wei Wuxian dodged the lightning-fast attack, leisurely playing another tune as he sidestepped. Soon the paper effigies patrolling outside leapt onto the roof and jumped in through the gaping hole. Noticing the movement, the fierce Daoist corpse swung his sword back in two quick slashes. Two paper effigies were cut into four pieces, top to bottom. He drew his whisk with his left hand, and it was as if thousands of those soft white threads had suddenly transformed into metal whips and poisonous thorns. A simple swing would burst skulls and sever limbs. An accidental brush would turn a bystander into a sieve, pouring blood like water.

Though his hands were full, Wei Wuxian called out, "Don't come over here, stay in your corner!"

Then he continued issuing commands, the music of the flute whimsical and flighty and marked by ferocious chords. Although the fierce Daoist was fighting with both hands, endless paper effigies jumped down from above, surrounding and attacking him. If he struck here, there'd be more there; kill the one in front, and more would come from the back. His strength alone was inadequate.

Suddenly a Yin Muscleman dropped from above and grappled him, stomping down on his shoulder and pushing him to the ground. Three more Yin Musclemen followed right after, leaping down through the hole to pile onto him one after the other.

Legends told of the extraordinary strength of Yin Musclemen, so their crafters usually added extra weight to the effigies when crafting them. When wild ghosts were summoned to possess these bodies, each and every one became heftier than the next. Having one slam into you was already much like having a mountain bear down on your head. With four at once, it was amazing the Daoist-robed fierce corpse didn't puke his innards out at the impact. He was pinned completely in place, unable to move a muscle.

Wei Wuxian walked over, observing a section of damaged clothing on his back. When he flattened the tear to examine further, a thin, narrow gash could be seen by the corpse's left shoulder blade.

"Flip him over," Wei Wuxian ordered.

The four Yin Musclemen flipped the Daoist over to face the ceiling, making it easier for him to examine the man. Wei Wuxian reached out with the fingers he'd cut earlier and smeared them over the lips of each of the four paper effigies as reward. The Yin Musclemen stuck out their red paper tongues and cherished the blood with slow licks, seemingly savoring the delicacy. Only then did Wei Wuxian look down to continue his inspection. The area near the Daoist's heart seemed to have sustained the same damage as his back—the same tear, the same narrow gash. It was as if he had died from being stabbed through the heart.

The fierce corpse had been struggling all the while, a continuous low growl emitting from his throat. Jet-black blood trickled from the corners of his mouth. Wei Wuxian squeezed his cheeks, forcing him to open his mouth, and looked inside. It seemed the man's tongue had also been pulled out at the root.

Blind, pulled-tongue. Blind, pulled-tongue.

Why were these two characteristics appearing so frequently?

Wei Wuxian examined the man for a while, coming to the conclusion that this fierce corpse resembled Wen Ning when he was controlled by those long, black nails. Having formed this theory, he reached out, groping near the corpse's temples—and actually managed to find two small metal nubs!

These black nails were made to control high-level fierce corpses, causing them to lose their mind and their ability to think. Wei Wuxian didn't know this corpse's identity or character, so he couldn't recklessly pull the nails out. *He must be properly interrogated,* Wei Wuxian thought. But since his tongue was already gone, this fierce corpse wouldn't be able to speak even if he had his senses returned to him.

He asked the juniors, "Who among you have studied Inquiry?"

Lan Sizhui raised his hand. "Me. I have."

"Did you bring your guqin?" Wei Wuxian asked.

"Yes," Lan Sizhui answered. He immediately retrieved a guqin—simple, but lustrous in color—from his qiankun pouch.

Wei Wuxian noticed the guqin seemed brand new. "How's your guqin language? Have you used it in a practical setting like this? Will the invited spirits lie?"

Lan Jingyi cut in. "Hanguang-jun said Sizhui's guqin language is acceptable."

If Lan Wangji had said "acceptable," then it must be acceptable. He wouldn't have exaggerated, nor played it down. Wei Wuxian relaxed.

Lan Sizhui said, "Hanguang-jun told me to practice quality, not quantity. The invited spirits can choose not to respond, but they definitely cannot lie. So whatever they answer will be the truth."

"Let's start, then," Wei Wuxian said.

The guqin was placed on the ground above the Daoist's head. Lan Sizhui sat down, the hems of his robes spreading neatly out around him. He tried two notes and then nodded.

"First question: ask who he is," Wei Wuxian said.

Lan Sizhui thought for a moment, then mouthed the incantation to himself before daring to pluck out the first verse.

A good moment later the strings vibrated, and two notes blasted forth like bedrock splitting. Lan Sizhui widened his eyes.

Lan Jingyi urged, "What did he say?"

"Song Lan!" Lan Sizhui said.

...The best friend and fellow cultivator of Xiao Xingchen, Song Lan?!

Everyone turned to look at the unconscious Xiao Xingchen on the ground.

Lan Sizhui murmured, "I wonder if he knows this is Song Lan..."

Jin Ling also hushed his voice. "Probably not. He's blind and Song Lan is mute, not to mention he's become a mindless fierce corpse...so, best if he doesn't."

Wei Wuxian said, "Second question: ask who killed him."

Lan Sizhui played a verse seriously. This time, the silence lasted three times longer than before.

Just when they thought Song Lan's soul wasn't willing to answer this question, the strings trembled and three notes resounded with profound pain.

"Impossible!" Lan Sizhui blurted.

"What did he say?" Wei Wuxian asked.

Lan Sizhui was incredulous. "He said...Xiao Xingchen."

The one who killed Song Lan was Xiao Xingchen?!

They had only asked two questions. Who could've imagined each answer would be more shocking than the last?

Jin Ling was dubious. "You played wrong, right?!"

Lan Sizhui replied, "'Who art thou' and 'who killed thee' are the easiest and most frequently asked questions during a session of Inquiry. They're the first and second verses everyone who studies Inquiry learns. I've practiced them at least a thousand times, and I checked repeatedly before playing them. I most certainly did not make a mistake."

"Well, either your Inquiry was played wrong, or you've misinterpreted the guqin language," Jin Ling determined, adamant.

Lan Sizhui shook his head. "If the notes were not wrong, misinterpretation is even more impossible. 'Xiao Xingchen' is an uncommon phrase or name, rarely heard from invited spirits. If he had answered with a different name and I misinterpreted it, there's no way it would just so happen to be *this* name."

Lan Jingyi mumbled, "...Song Lan went to find the missing Xiao Xingchen, but Xiao Xingchen killed him. Why would he kill his best friend? He doesn't seem the type to do that."

"Don't worry about all that for now," Wei Wuxian said. "Sizhui, ask the third question: who is controlling him."

Lan Sizhui's face was serious, and he didn't dare breathe too hard as he played the third verse. Many eyes were glued to the strings, waiting for Song Lan's answer.

Then they heard Lan Sizhui interpret the response, one word at a time: "The. One. Behind. You."

Everyone's heads shot up. Xiao Xingchen, who had been lying on the ground unconscious, was now sitting up with one hand propping up his cheek as he smiled at them. He raised his black-gloved left hand and snapped his fingers.

— PART 3 —

THAT CRISP SOUND went right to the ears of Song Lan, who was on the ground. It was as if the sound had exploded in his skull. He suddenly seized the four Yin Musclemen who held him down and sent them flying! He leapt to his feet, brandishing his longsword and whisk once more, and sliced and diced the four Yin Musclemen, shredding them into multi-colored paper scraps. His longsword was pointed at Wei Wuxian, while his whisk was aimed threateningly at the clan juniors.

The tables had suddenly turned, here in this small shop.

Jin Ling put his hand on his sword. Wei Wuxian saw from the corner of his eye and quickly said, "Don't move, don't add to the problem. When it comes to swordplay, everyone here combined would still not be a match for this...Song Lan."

This body of his was weak in spiritual power, and his sword wasn't around. Besides, there was also Xiao Xingchen next to them to contend with; his motives unclear and whether he was friend or foe wholly unknown.

Xiao Xingchen said, "The adults are talking. Why don't you kids go out?"

He made a hand gesture at Song Lan, who obeyed silently, moving to herd the clan juniors out.

Wei Wuxian said to the boys, "Go on. You guys can't help here anyway. The corpse toxin outside should have settled by now, so don't go running around and stirring it up again. Slow your breathing."

When Jin Ling heard "you guys can't help here anyway," he was both indignant and frustrated, refusing to give up without a fight. But at the same time, he knew he was powerless, so he petulantly stormed out first. Lan Sizhui was hesitant to leave, looking as if he had something to say.

Wei Wuxian said, “Sizhui, you’re the most sensible here. Take the lead and guide them. Can you do that?”

Lan Sizhui nodded, and Wei Wuxian added, “Don’t be scared.”

“I’m not scared,” Lan Sizhui said.

“Really?”

“Really.” With that, Lan Sizhui laughed, surprisingly. “Qianbei, you and Hanguang-jun are so alike.”

Wei Wuxian was amazed. “Alike? How?”

They were clearly two drastically different people. Lan Sizhui did not answer but only smiled and exited, taking the rest of the boys with him.

I don’t know either, Lan Sizhui quietly thought to himself, *but they feel very similar. It feels like there’s no need to be scared of anything if either one of them is around.*

Xiao Xingchen fished a little red pill out of nowhere and swallowed it. “Such a moving display.”

Once he ate the pill, the purplish-red color of his face faded rapidly. Wei Wuxian asked, “Corpse toxin antidote?”

“Yes,” Xiao Xingchen replied. “Much more effective than that terrifying congee of yours, right? And it’s sweet too.”

“Really quite the performance, sir,” Wei Wuxian complimented. “From the brave charge against the corpses that exhausted you so terribly, to blocking the blow meant for Jin Ling and losing consciousness—was that all an act for us?”

Xiao Xingchen wagged a finger. “It wasn’t an act for ‘you,’ plural. It was for *your* eyes only. Very pleased to meet you, Yiling Patriarch. You are even more formidable than they say.”

Wei Wuxian didn’t react to this, his face remaining neutral.

Xiao Xingchen continued, "Let me guess. You still haven't told anyone who you really are, correct? That's why I didn't even expose you. I told them to go out so we can talk privately behind closed doors. What do you think? Aren't I considerate?"

"You're the one commanding all the walking corpses in Yi City?" Wei Wuxian questioned.

"Of course," Xiao Xingchen replied. "The moment you entered and blew that whistle I sensed something strange about you, which was why I decided to come out personally to test you. As I suspected—a low-level spell like the Final Eyes Summoning could only have such power if it was cast by the founder."

They were both cultivators of the demonic path, so neither could deceive the eyes of a peer. Wei Wuxian asked, "So what exactly did you want from me, holding a bunch of kids hostage?"

Xiao Xingchen chuckled. "I just want to ask qianbei for a favor. A small favor."

What a mess of hierarchy, for his mother's younger martial brother to defer to Wei Wuxian as his senior. Wei Wuxian was just laughing at this to himself when he saw Xiao Xingchen take out a spirit-trapping pouch and place it on the table.

"Please."

Wei Wuxian set his hand on the spirit-trapping pouch, feeling it like he was checking for a pulse. A moment later, he asked, "Whose soul is this? It's so shattered that not even glue could piece it back together. It's only got a single breath left in it."

"If this soul were easily glued back together, why would I ask you for help?" Xiao Xingchen said.

Wei Wuxian withdrew his hand. "You want me to restore this? Excuse my bluntness, but the scant bit of soul in here is just not enough. Besides, this person must've been immensely tormented while they were alive, subject to excruciating pain. They likely killed themselves and don't want to return to this world. If a soul has no desire to remain, it's most likely unsalvageable. If I'm not wrong, this remaining fragment of soul was forcibly pieced together, and once it leaves the spirit-trapping pouch it could dissipate at any time. I'm sure you're well aware of this."

"I'm not, and I don't care," Xiao Xingchen said. "You have to help whether you like it or not. Don't forget, qianbei—those kids you brought here are all watching pitifully outside the door, waiting for you to lead them out of danger, hmm?"

His tone was quite peculiar. It sounded almost affectionate, a little sweet even, but it carried an unwarranted maliciousness. It was almost as if he could happily call someone "brother" and "qianbei" one second, then turn hostile and kill them the next.

Wei Wuxian chuckled too. "You are also more formidable than they say, sir. Xue Yang, you're a perfectly fine thug, so why masquerade as a cultivator?"

There was a pause. Then "Xiao Xingchen" raised his hands and removed the bandage over his eyes.

As layers of bandages fell, they revealed a pair of shining eyes as bright as stars.

A pair of perfectly intact eyes.

It was a young and pleasing face. He could be called handsome, but when he smiled it revealed a pair of canine teeth, making him simply adorable instead. That air of childlike innocence masked the mayhem and ruthlessness concealed behind his eyes.

Xue Yang tossed the bandage aside. "Oops, you found out."

Wei Wuxian listed his observations. "Pretending to be in such frightful pain that no one with a conscience would be so impolite as to remove your bandage to inspect. Purposely showing a bit of

Shuanghua. Purposely letting slip you're a wandering Daoist. Not only do you know how to employ the trick of self-inflicted injury to gain the enemy's trust, but you know how to manipulate other people's sympathy too. What a fantastic show. Such cool and refined detachment, an excellent display of stern righteousness. If it weren't for the fact that there was too much you shouldn't have known and too much you shouldn't have been able to do, I really would've believed you were Xiao Xingchen."

Moreover, during Inquiry, Song Lan's answers to the last two questions had been "Xiao Xingchen" and "the one behind you." If "the one behind you" was also Xiao Xingchen, there was no reason for Song Lan to change his wording...unless "Xiao Xingchen" and "the one behind you" were never the same person in the first place. Song Lan wanted to warn them that this man was very dangerous, but he was afraid they wouldn't know who Xue Yang was if he said that name, so he had no other choice.

Xue Yang grinned happily. "It's his fault for having such a good rep. Mine's terrible. Of course I gotta pretend to be him if I want to gain others' trust."

"What expert acting," Wei Wuxian said.

"You flatter me," Xue Yang replied. "I have a famous friend, you see. *He's* the expert actor—I'm nowhere near his level. All right, enough chatter. Wei-qianbei, you *have* to help me with this."

"You made the long black nails controlling Song Lan and Wen Ning, right?" Wei Wuxian said. "If you can restore half of the Yin Tiger Tally, why ask me for help in repairing a mere soul?"

"It's not the same," Xue Yang said. "You're the founder. If you didn't forge the first half of the Yin Tiger Tally, there's no way I could've made the second half. Of course you're better than me. Which means you must be able to do everything I can't."

Wei Wuxian really couldn't understand why people he didn't know always possessed such baffling confidence in his abilities. He stroked his chin, not sure whether he should reciprocate this flattery among peers.

"You're too modest."

"It's not modesty, it's the truth," Xue Yang said. "I never exaggerate. If I say I'm going to kill someone's entire family, I mean it. I won't even spare the dog."

"The Chang Clan of Yueyang, for example?" Wei Wuxian said.

Before Xue Yang could respond, the doors suddenly burst open and a black shadow darted in.

Wei Wuxian and Xue Yang both backed away from the square table at the same time, Xue Yang snatching up the spirit-trapping pouch as he went. Song Lan lightly vaulted off the table with a hand, flipped in the air, and landed atop the table, letting it absorb the force of his landing. He then immediately looked to the doorway, black veins crawling up his cheeks.

Wen Ning, his body weighed down with chains, crashed heavily through the door. With him came a gust of white fog and black wind.

Wei Wuxian had sent out a summons for Wen Ning with the verses he'd played on his flute earlier. Now he instructed him, "Go fight outside. Don't smash him to bits. Keep the living safe, and don't let other walking corpses near."

Wen Ning raised his left hand, swinging a chain at Song Lan, who drew his whisk to parry. The two weapons clashed, tangling together. Wen Ning retreated, dragging the chain with him, and Song Lan didn't let go so he was dragged out as well. The clan juniors had already hidden away in another nearby shop, watching unblinkingly with outstretched necks. A whisk, facing iron chains, facing a longsword—*clink clank clink clank*, sparks were flying everywhere. The only thought in their minds was that the showdown between these two fierce corpses was truly, incomparably ferocious. Every move was brutal, every punch battered flesh. Only fierce corpses could brawl like this. If these were two live humans, there would surely have been severed limbs or bashed-out brains by now!

"Guess who's gonna win?" Xue Yang asked.

"Is there a need to guess? It'll be Wen Ning for sure," Wei Wuxian replied.

"It's too bad he refused to be obedient, despite my hammering so many skull-piercing nails into him. It really is inconvenient when things prove to be too loyal."

Wei Wuxian blandly noted, "Wen Ning is no thing."

Xue Yang burst out laughing. "You know, what you said has a double meaning!" When he reached the word "has," he suddenly drew his sword and lunged.

Wei Wuxian dodged. "Do you always ambush people like this halfway through talking?"

Xue Yang appeared surprised. "Of course? I'm a thug, you know this. It's not like I want to kill you either. I just want to immobilize you and drag you back with me, and then you can take the time you need to help me restore this soul."

"I already said there's nothing I can do," Wei Wuxian said.

"C'mon, don't be so quick to reject me," Xue Yang said. "If you're stumped, the two of us can put our heads together!"

He attacked again mid-sentence. Wei Wuxian dodged and evaded the attacks, stepping over ground covered with paper effigy shreds, and thought, *This little thug... His form really isn't too bad*. Seeing Xue Yang's sword swinging with increasing speed, aiming for progressively more artful and sinister targets, he couldn't help but say:

"Are you taking advantage of the fact that this body of mine is weak in spiritual power?"

"Yeah!" Xue Yang admitted happily.

Wei Wuxian had finally met someone even more shameless than him. He tittered right back. "When they say you should 'offend a good man rather than offend a thug,' they're talking about people like you. I'm not fighting you. Find someone else."

Xue Yang said with a gleeful grin, "Find who? That Hanguang-jun? I got over three hundred walking corpses to outflank him. He..."

Before he finished, a streak of white descended from the sky, and the icy cold, clear blue light of Bichen came striking at him.

Like an enveloping blanket of frost, Lan Wangji shielded Wei Wuxian. Xue Yang flung out Shuanghua to help him block Bichen's strike. The two famous swords clashed, then each flew back to the hands of their owners.

"Better to arrive in the nick of time than to arrive early, huh?" Wei Wuxian said.

"Mn."

As soon as Lan Wangji replied, he continued crossing swords with Xue Yang. While Xue Yang had been chasing Wei Wuxian all over the shop earlier, he was now being beaten back again and again by Lan Wangji. Seeing the situation turning against him, an idea came to Xue Yang, and his lips curled. He suddenly switched Shuanghua to his left hand and thrust the right inside his qiankun sleeve. Wei Wuxian tensed, thinking he might hurl some kind of powdered toxin at them or draw a secret weapon, but what he shook out instead was a longsword. Xue Yang attacked them again, seamlessly dual-wielding both blades.

The longsword he'd pulled from his sleeve had an eerie, gloomy glare. When swung, it emitted strands of black qi, making a stark contrast against the cool, bright silver of Shuanghua. Xue Yang lunged with both swords, the left and right flowing in perfect harmony, and his assault was immediately intensified.

"Jiangzai?" Lan Wangji thought aloud.

"Huh? Hanguang-jun knows this sword? What an honor," Xue Yang said, feigning shock.

Jiangzai, meaning "to call forth disaster," was Xue Yang's own sword. True to both its name and its master, it was an ominous sword that called forth death and destruction.

Wei Wuxian interrupted to comment, "Well, isn't that name just a perfect match for you?"

"Stand back," Lan Wangji said. "You are not needed here."

Wei Wuxian humbly took his advice and backed off. He backed all the way to the entrance and took a peek outside. Wen Ning was in the middle of stoically strangling Song Lan, lifting the man by his neck and slamming him into the wall, creating a giant man-shaped hole in the process. Song Lan, also expressionless, seized Wen Ning's wrist and flipped him over, crashing him into the ground. Loud, incessant bangs and booms accompanied the battle between the two stone-faced fierce corpses. Neither side could feel pain, nor were they afraid of injuries. Unless they were cut to pieces, they could keep fighting no matter how many limbs they broke.

"There doesn't seem to be a need for me here either," Wei Wuxian mumbled to himself.

Suddenly, he noticed Lan Jingyi waving wildly at him from inside the pitch-black shop across the street. *Ha! They must need me* there, *at least!*

He had just left when Bichen's glare grew by magnitudes. In a split second, Xue Yang's hand slipped and Shuanghua dropped from his grip. Lan Wangji took the chance and caught the sword. Seeing

Shuanghua had fallen into the hands of another, Jiangzai struck straight for the arm Lan Wangji had used to take it. The strike was unsuccessful, and a chilling fury flashed in Xue Yang's eyes.

He bit out darkly, "Give me the sword."

"You are unworthy of it," Lan Wangji stated.

Xue Yang sneered.

Wei Wuxian walked over to where the clan juniors were and was immediately surrounded by the group of boys. He asked aloud, "Everyone okay?"

"Yes!"

"We all listened and held our breath."

"Good," Wei Wuxian said. "If any of you don't listen, then I'll make more glutinous rice congee for the culprits to eat."

The few who'd already experienced the taste nearly retched. Just then, footsteps sounded all around them. Silhouettes began to come into view at the end of the long street.

Lan Wangji also heard the sound. With a wave of his sleeve, he flipped out his guqin, Wangji, and slammed it down flat on the table. He tossed Bichen into his left hand and continued to fight Xue Yang, the will of the sword undiminished. Even while keeping up the assault, he raised his right hand and swept his fingers over the strings.

The strings strummed, resounding far down to the ends of the street. What echoed back was the strange yet familiar noise of the walking corpses' heads exploding. Lan Wangji continued to parry Xue Yang with one hand while playing the guqin with the other. He swept a cool look around, unflustered and composed as he plucked at the strings, striking simultaneously with both left hand and right.

In spite of himself, Jin Ling blurted out, "Awesome!"

He'd seen Jiang Cheng and Jin Guangyao cut down yao beasts during Night Hunts and believed his two uncles were the strongest of all the distinguished cultivators in the world. He had always been more scared than reverent of Lan Wangji, afraid of his silencing spell and cold temper. But at this moment, he couldn't help but feel great admiration for the man's bearing.

Lan Jingyi was pleased. "Uh-huh. Of course Hanguang-jun is awesome; he just doesn't like to flaunt it everywhere. He's super low-profile, am I right?!"

The "am I right" was directed at Wei Wuxian, who was perplexed. "Why ask me? What's that got to do with me?"

Lan Jingyi grew upset. "You don't think Hanguang-jun is awesome?!"

Wei Wuxian stroked his chin. "Mm, yes, awesome, of course. Super amazing. The most formidable!"

As he spoke, he couldn't help but laugh as well.

This hair-raising night of peril was about to pass, day was about to break. However, that wasn't good news. The morning's light meant the evil miasma would thicken, and when that happened, moving around would become quite difficult again!

It wouldn't be so bad if it were only Wei Wuxian and Lan Wangji. But with this many live humans, escape would be difficult once they were surrounded by a large number of walking corpses—even if they sprouted wings. Just when Wei Wuxian's mind was spinning, trying to devise a plan, the crisp sound of a bamboo pole hitting the ground came again. *Ka-ka, da-da.*

The blind, tongueless phantom girl had come again!

Wei Wuxian made the decision right then and there. "Go!"

"Go where?" Lan Jingyi asked.

"Follow the sound of the bamboo pole," Wei Wuxian said.

Jin Ling was slightly shocked. "You want us to follow a phantom? Who knows where she'll take us?!"

"That's right. Follow her," Wei Wuxian repeated. "That sound has been following you ever since you entered the city, correct? You were heading into the city center but were being led back to the city gates when you ran into us. She was trying to drive you out. She was trying to save you!"

The strange, mysterious sound of the bamboo pole—sometimes distant, sometimes close—was her way of scaring the living who entered the city. But the intent to scare wasn't necessarily malicious. The paper Yin Muscleman head Wei Wuxian's foot had caught back then might also have been something she'd thrown there to warn and frighten them.

Wei Wuxian added, "And last night, she was clearly trying to tell us something urgent. She just couldn't express it. But the moment Xue Yang arrived, she vanished. She was most likely hiding from him. Either way, they're definitely not working together."

"Xue Yang?! Why is there a Xue Yang too? Wasn't it Xiao Xingchen and Song Lan?"

"Uh, I'll explain that later. Long story short, the one fighting with Hanguang-jun in there isn't Xiao Xingchen, it's Xue Yang impersonating him."

The bamboo pole was still beating the ground, making that *da-da* sound—as if waiting, as if urging. If they followed her, they might walk into a trap. If they didn't, they would be surrounded by walking corpses spewing corpse toxin, which was hardly any safer. The group of boys resolved to dash after the ground-beating sound with Wei Wuxian. Sure enough, as soon as they started moving the sound moved too. At times they could see a hazy, delicate little shadow in the thin fog ahead, and at times nothing was visible.

Lan Jingyi ran for a while, then asked, "Are we taking off just like that?"

Wei Wuxian turned his head back and yelled, "Hanguang-jun, I'm leaving this in your hands. We're going on ahead!"

The strings answered with a *beng*, sounding very much like someone uttered a "mn," and Wei Wuxian laughed out loud.

"That's it? Nothing else?" Lan Jingyi asked.

"What? What more do you want me to say?" Wei Wuxian said.

"Why didn't you say 'I'm worried about you, I'm staying!'? Then he'd say 'Leave!' Then you'd cry back 'No! I'm not leaving! If we have to leave, we leave together!' Isn't that the script?"

Wei Wuxian spluttered. "Who taught you that? Who said that sort of exchange has to take place? Never mind me—can you imagine your clan's Hanguang-jun saying anything of the sort?"

The Lan juniors all mumbled, "No..."

"Right? It's a waste of time," Wei Wuxian said. "Your clan's Hanguang-jun is such a dependable individual, I'm positive he can handle it just fine. I just gotta focus on doing what I gotta do and either wait for him to come find me or vice versa."

They had followed the sound of the bamboo pole for half an incense time, making many a turn, when the sound came to an abrupt stop ahead. Wei Wuxian extended an arm to stop the boys behind him and ventured a few steps forward. A lone house stood amidst the thickening evil miasma.

Creeeak.

The door of the house was already pushed open, silently waiting for this group of strangers to enter. Wei Wuxian had a hunch there must be something inside. Nothing perilous or life-threatening, but something that could answer some questions, solve some mysteries.

"Since we're already here, let's go in," he determined.

He lifted his foot and crossed the threshold. As he adjusted to the darkness, he reminded the rest without looking back, "Watch out for the threshold, careful not to trip."

One of the boys indeed almost tripped over the very tall threshold and was confused. "Why is the threshold so tall? It's not like this is a temple."

"It's not a temple, but it is also a place that requires a very tall threshold," Wei Wuxian explained.

A few of the boys ignited five to six illumination talismans, and the flickering orange-yellow light brightened the house.

There was straw scattered across the floor. At the very front of the house was an altar. Underneath it lay several small stools of various sizes, and next to it on the right was a small, pitch-dark room. Besides that, there were seven to eight ebony-black wooden coffins placed around the room.

"This is that charitable mortuary? The place that temporarily housed the dead?" Jin Ling wondered.

"Yep," Wei Wuxian confirmed. "Bodies unclaimed by their family, bodies too unlucky to be kept in a home, and bodies waiting to be buried are usually stashed in charitable mortuaries. You could say it's a postal station for the dead." The small room on the right was likely the overnight room for the caretakers of the charitable mortuary.

Lan Sizhui asked, "Mo-qianbei, why are the thresholds of charitable mortuaries built so high?"

"To guard against corpses that have turned," Wei Wuxian replied.

Lan Jingyi asked, looking blank, "Do taller thresholds stop corpses from turning?"

"They don't," Wei Wuxian explained, "But sometimes they can stop turned corpses from getting out." He turned and stood in front of the threshold. "Let's say I died and my corpse had just been reanimated..."

The boys nodded, watching in baffled confusion.

Wei Wuxian continued, "...The reanimation only just took place, so aren't my limbs all stiff? Wouldn't there be many actions I can no longer perform?"

Jin Ling replied, "Well, duh? You wouldn't even be able to walk. You can't move your legs, so you can only hop..."

He trailed off, understanding dawning on him.

"That's right," Wei Wuxian confirmed. "It's precisely because I can only hop."

He pressed his legs together and attempted to hop outside. But because the threshold was too high, he was obstructed every single time, his feet knocking against that barrier. The clan juniors found the sight absolutely hilarious. At the thought of a turned corpse trying desperately to hop out but being thwarted by the threshold each time, they burst out laughing.

Wei Wuxian continued, "You see? Don't laugh, this is folk wisdom. As tacky as it is, and as crude as it looks, it's effective against low-level turned corpses. Even if the turned corpse trips on the threshold and falls out, its stiff limbs won't allow it to crawl back up in a timely manner. By the time it can get to its feet, either the sky will be brightening and the roosters crowing, or it'll be discovered by the caretakers here. It's impressive, actually, for common folks without cultivation backgrounds to have thought of this method."

Jin Ling had laughed too, but his laughter faded immediately. "Why did she bring us to this charitable mortuary? Do walking corpses not surround this place? Where did she run off to?"

"Maybe they really don't," Wei Wuxian said. "We've been standing here for how long now? Have any of you seen walking corpses shambling around?"

Just as he spoke, the apparition of the girl suddenly appeared on top of a coffin.

Since everyone had carefully examined the girl's appearance earlier under Wei Wuxian's lead, including her bleeding eyes and tongueless mouth, no one felt nervous or scared to see her again. Just as Wei Wuxian had said, one's courage grew in tandem with the number of times one was spooked, and thus one could face these situations calmly.

The girl did not possess a solid body, and her spirit form emitted a faint, haunting glow. She was dainty in frame, the shape of her face similarly petite. If she was cleaned up, she would be the charming, lovely girl next door. But seeing how she sat cross-legged, she had none of the required manners. The bamboo pole she used as her cane was leaning sloppily against the coffin, and she dropped her two skinny little legs down to impatiently swing them back and forth.

Still sitting atop the coffin, she slapped lightly on the lid. Then she jumped down, circling around the coffin, making gestures at them. Her gestures were easy to understand this time: it was the motion of "open."

"She wants us to help her open this coffin?" Jin Ling asked.

Lan Sizhui speculated, "Could it be her body lying inside, and she's hoping we'll give her a proper burial?"

This was the most logical deduction. Many souls were not at peace because their bodies hadn't received proper burials. Wei Wuxian shuffled to one side of the coffin while several boys stood on the other, wanting to help him lift the lid.

"No need to help, stand back," Wei Wuxian instructed. "Gotta be careful that it's not a cadaver that gives you a face full of corpse toxin or something."

He lifted the coffin lid open by himself and threw it back, letting it fall to the ground. When he peered in, he indeed saw a cadaver.

However, it wasn't the dead body of the girl, but of someone else.

It was the body of a young man, placed in a very peaceful posture. Under the folded hands there lay a whisk. Dressed in a snow-white Daoist robe, the contours of the bottom half of his face were fine and elegant. His complexion was pale, and his lips were light in color. The upper half of his face was wrapped in layers upon layers of bandages, the width of four fingers. Under the bandage where the eyes should've been, however, there was no visible curve—it was sunken in. There were no eyes there at all, only two empty holes.

When the girl heard them open the coffin lid, she shuffled over and reached her hand in to fumble about. When her hands felt the corpse's face, she stomped her feet and two streams of blood tears flowed from her blind eyes.

Everyone understood, without the need of any words or gestures. This lonesome corpse, placed in this lonesome charitable mortuary, was the real Xiao Xingchen.

The tears of a phantom could not fall. The girl let her tears roll silently for a moment before suddenly gritting her teeth and rising to her feet. She *aah-aah*-ed at them, looking pressed and furious, like she desperately wanted to tell her tale.

"Should I use Inquiry again?" Lan Sizhui asked.

"No," Wei Wuxian replied. "We might not be able to guess the questions she wants us to ask. Besides, I think her answers would be very complicated, very hard to interpret."

Although he didn't say "you probably wouldn't be able to handle it," Lan Sizhui nonetheless felt somewhat ashamed. He inwardly resolved: *Once I get back, I must practice Inquiry more diligently.*

I must reach Hanguang-jun's level and know everything by heart, be able to ask and answer at will, to interpret and understand immediately.

Lan Jingyi asked, "What do we do then?"

"Use Empathy, I guess," Wei Wuxian said.

Every major clan had their own expert way of obtaining intelligence and gathering information from resentful spirits. Empathy was what Wei Wuxian was an expert at. His method wasn't as advanced as those other clans—anyone could use it. He'd invite the resentful spirit to directly possess him, using his own body as a medium to plunge into the deceased soul's memories. He would hear what they heard, see what they saw, feel what they felt. If the soul of the deceased had particularly strong emotions, his own body would be affected by their sorrow, their rage, their elation, and so on. Hence the name Empathy.

Of the various spiritual approaches, Empathy could be said to be the most direct, the simplest and swiftest—and thus the most effective. Of course, it was also the most dangerous. Possession by a resentful spirit was generally feared and avoided at all costs. Empathy was playing with fire. A single mishap would cause one to reap what they had sowed. If the resentful spirit changed its mind and took advantage of the situation, having your body be taken over was the best case scenario.

Jin Ling protested, "That's too dangerous! Not a single one of those evil spells would..."

Wei Wuxian cut him off. "All right, we're out of time. Stand in position, all of you, quickly. We still gotta go back to find Hanguang-jun when we're done. Jin Ling, you are the Monitor."

The Monitor was an essential actor in the Empathy ritual. To keep from sinking too deeply into the emotions of the resentful spirit and being unable to extricate themselves, the Empathizer needed to agree on a signal with the Monitor—ideally a phrase or a voice the Empathizer was very familiar with. The Monitor would supervise the entirety of the session. As soon as they sensed the situation turning sour, they needed to act immediately to pull the Empathizer out.

Jin Ling pointed at himself. "Me? You want m… You want me to supervise you doing such a thing?"

"If Jin-gongzi won't, let me," Lan Sizhui said.

"Jin Ling, did you bring that silver bell?" Wei Wuxian asked.

The silver bell was a signature accessory of the Jiang Clan of Yunmeng. Jin Ling had been raised by two families, staying at the Golden Carp Tower of the Jin Clan of Lanling half the time and at the Lotus Pier of the Jiang Clan of Yunmeng the other half. Thus, he should have things from both families on him.

Sure enough, though he looked immensely doubtful, he took out a quaint little bell. The Jiang Clan's insignia, the nine-petaled lotus, was engraved on its body.

Wei Wuxian stared at the silver bell for a moment. Jin Ling sensed something strange about that look and asked, "What?"

"Nothing," Wei Wuxian said and took the bell, passing it to Lan Sizhui. "The silver bell of the Jiang Clan of Yunmeng can steady the mind and bolster clarity. Let's use this as the secret signal."

Jin Ling snatched the bell back. "*I'll* do it!"

Lan Jingyi snorted. "Unwilling one second, willing the next, turning sunny or gloomy with caprice. A temper befitting a young mistress."

Wei Wuxian turned to the girl. "Come, enter."

That girl wiped her eyes and face, then hurtled herself into his body and forced her entire soul inside. Wei Wuxian slowly slid down along the coffin as he sank to the floor. The boys hustled together and dragged a bunch of straw over to cushion him while Jin Ling clutched the bell tightly, his thoughts indiscernible.

When the girl came crashing in, Wei Wuxian suddenly thought of a problem: *This little girl is blind. If I Empathize with her, won't I be blind too, unable to see a thing? The investigation won't be as effective.*

Whatever. Listening is pretty much the same.

The world spun about him in waves, until what was once a feather-light spirit seemed to land on solid ground. When the girl opened her eyes, Wei Wuxian's eyes opened with hers. Unexpectedly, his field of view wasn't pitch-black—the sight before him was a field of flourishing greenery.

He could actually see! Presumably, the girl wasn't yet blind at this point in her memories.

What Wei Wuxian saw in Empathy was the memories with the most intense emotions. The stories she most wanted to tell. All he needed to do was watch quietly, simply feel what she felt. In this moment, they shared the same senses. The girl's eyes were his eyes, her mouth was his mouth.

This girl sat by a small stream, using her reflection in the water to groom herself. Although her clothes were tattered, she still needed to keep up with the basics of tidiness. She tapped out a beat with the tips of her toes, humming a small tune as she did her hair, but no matter how she coiled it, she seemed to find it dissatisfactory. Wei Wuxian felt a thin wooden hairpin poking about here and there in her locks.

Suddenly she looked down at her own reflection in the water. Wei Wuxian's line of sight followed. Reflected in the stream was a young girl with a heart-shaped face curving to a pointed chin.

There were no pupils in the young girl's eyes. They were a blank field of nothing but white.

Wei Wuxian thought, *She clearly looks blind, but I can see right now...?*

Having done her hair, she dusted off her behind and leapt to her feet, picking up her bamboo pole as she went. She skipped as she traveled down the road and swung the bamboo pole as she walked, beating at the branches and leaves above her head, picking out the rocks at her feet, scaring the grasshoppers in the grass, not stopping for a single moment. Some distance ahead, people approached. The girl immediately stopped skipping and held the bamboo pole properly, hitting it against the ground as she walked at an exasperating pace, looking very careful and prudent. It was a group of village girls that had crossed her path. They all made way at the sight of her, whispering in each other's ears.

The girl nodded hastily. "Thank you, thank you."

One of the village girls seemed to be sympathetic at the sight of her. She peeled back the white cloth covering her basket to retrieve a hot, steaming bun to pass over.

"Xiao-mei, do watch your feet. Are you hungry? Here, take this."

The girl gasped and said gratefully, "How could I possibly? I, I..."

That village girl stuffed the bun in her hand. "Just take it!"

And so she took it. "A-Qing thanks jiejie!"

So, this girl's name was A-Qing.

Bidding the village girls farewell, A-Qing quickly gobbled down the steamed bun and began to bounce merrily again. Wei Wuxian, forced to skip along with her in her body, was getting quite dizzy.

This girl certainly knows how to cut loose. I get it now—she's pretending to be blind. She was probably born with those white eyes. While she appears to be blind, she can in fact see. She's using that, putting on an act to deceive others and win sympathy.

A lone, wandering, seemingly blind child. Since others thought she couldn't see, it was only natural they'd drop their guard around her—when in fact, she could see everything and react accordingly. All in all, it was a clever way to protect herself.

But A-Qing's spirit was truly blind. Meaning she had lost her sight at some point while alive. So how did she go from being fake blind to genuinely blind?

Could she have seen something she shouldn't have?

When there was no one around, A-Qing would skip. When there was, she'd cower and act like a blind person. Stopping and going in turn, she haltingly came to a marketplace.

The presence of a crowd meant she had to display her acting abilities to the fullest, of course. She was in her element, performatively tapping and knocking with her bamboo pole as she sluggishly moved through the stream of people. Suddenly she bumped headfirst into a middle-aged man dressed in vibrant, sumptuous clothes.

Appearing petrified, she stammered incessantly, "I'm sorry, I'm sorry! I can't see, I'm sorry!"

What did she mean she couldn't see? She was clearly targeting the man!

Having been bumped into, the man furiously whipped his head around, looking like he wanted to curse out loud. But when he saw it was a blind person—and a pretty young girl, at that—he knew he'd be criticized by those milling around him if he slapped her in the middle of the street.

So he only spat a nasty reply, "Watch where you're going!"

A-Qing apologized nonstop, but the man remained riled up even as he made to storm off. He reached out to give A-Qing's rear end a crass, hard pinch. It was as if he'd pinched Wei Wuxian's ass as well, since he felt what she did. The pinch made his skin crawl with acres of goosebumps, and he dearly wanted nothing but to knock that man to the ground.

A-Qing cowered into a ball, looking terrified. But when the man was gone, she tapped and prodded her way to a covert alleyway, where she immediately spat on the ground in contempt. *Bah!* She took a money pouch from her robes and poured out its contents. After she counted the money, she *bah!*-ed again.

"Stinkin' bastard. Dressed like he's all fancy, but barely a coin on him. Grab him by the neck and shake him and ya won't even get a clink for the trouble."

Wei Wuxian didn't know whether to laugh or cry. A-Qing was only in her teens—she probably wasn't even fifteen—but she sure was smooth when it came to spitting out insults, and smoother still when it came to picking pockets.

He thought, *If you'd picked my pocket, you definitely wouldn't curse like that. I was once rich, you know...*

He was still lost in wonder at his own impoverished state when A-Qing found her next target. She exited the alleyway, resuming her blind act. She walked for a stretch, then, employing the same trick, yelped as she bumped into a white-clad Daoist cultivator.

She cried again, "I'm sorry, I'm sorry! I can't see, I'm sorry!"

Wei Wuxian shook his head. *Not even going to change your lines, sweetie?!*

That cultivator swayed from the impact, then turned his head and helped steady her before considering himself. "I am fine. Can you also not see, miss?"

This man was very young, his Daoist robe simple and clean. Strapped to his back was a longsword wrapped in white cloth. The bottom half of his face was clean-cut and shapely, albeit somewhat emaciated. The upper half of his face was wrapped with a bandage the width of four fingers. From beneath the bandage there bloomed the faint color of blood.

A-Qing seemed to go blank for a moment before she could manage a reply. "Ah...yeah!"

"Then walk slower. Do not move so fast. It'll be no good if you bump into anyone else," Xiao Xingchen chided.

He didn't say a word about how he couldn't see either. Holding her hand, he led her to the side of the road.

"Walk on the side of the road. There are fewer people."

His speech and actions were both gentle and careful. A-Qing's hand reached out, then hesitated. In the end, she still speedily swiped the money pouch that hung on his waist.

"A-Qing thanks gege!"

"It's not gege, it's Daozhang," Xiao Xingchen replied.

A-Qing blinked. "It's Daozhang, but gege as well."

Xiao Xingchen chuckled. "Since you wish to call me gege, why don't you return gege's money pouch?"

Even if A-Qing's street hooligan fingers had been ten times faster, she still couldn't deceive the senses of a cultivator. Immediately knowing she was in trouble, she bolted with pole in hand but didn't even manage two steps before Xiao Xingchen seized her by the collar.

"Did I not say to not run so fast? What if you bump into someone again?"

A-Qing struggled and fought. Her mouth moved, upper teeth biting down on her bottom lip. Wei Wuxian thought, *Oh no, she's gonna yell "Harassment!"*

Just then, a middle-aged man whirled around the street corner in a rush. When he saw A-Qing, his eyes lit up. Swearing and grumbling, he stalked over. "I've caught you, you little tramp! Give me back my money!"

The cussing wasn't enough to exhaust his anger. He raised a hand to slap her, and A-Qing shut her eyes and hunched in fright.

Unexpectedly, the strike was stopped before it could land on her cheek.

"Please keep calm, sir," Xiao Xingchen said. "Is it not improper to treat a little girl like this?"

A-Qing cracked her eyes open and sneaked a peek. Though the middle-aged man had obviously put a great deal of force into the blow, his hand was, seemingly effortlessly, held in place by Xiao Xingchen. He couldn't move an inch.

The man was clearly nervous, but he remained stubborn. "Your blind ass butting in out of nowhere—what, are you tryin' to act the hero? For what?! Is this little tramp your lover? Do you know she's a thief?! She stole my money pouch! Since you're shielding her, you're a thief too!"

Xiao Xingchen was restraining the man with one hand, while his other held A-Qing by the scruff. He turned his head to her. "Return his money."

A-Qing quickly dug out the bit of money in her robes and handed it over. Xiao Xingchen released the middle-aged man, who counted the coins and then peered at Xiao Xingchen. The amount was correct, and it was clear the cultivator was no one to mess with, so he could only leave, shamefaced.

"You've got such nerve," Xiao Xingchen commented. "To think you'd dare go around stealing when you can't see."

A-Qing bounced furiously. "He felt me up! Pinched my butt! It hurt, y'know! So what if I took a bit of his money? Such a big pouch, with so little in there. How is *he* not embarrassed, being so mean, trying to hit people? Penniless bastard!"

You were the one who bumped into him and made a move with your sticky fingers. Now he's the one at fault? Such flawless logic, Wei Wuxian thought.

Xiao Xingchen shook his head. "If that were the case, it was even more reason for you not to provoke him. If no one else had been around today, this would not have ended with a single slap. Look out for yourself, miss."

He then turned and walked off in a different direction. *He didn't even ask for his own money pouch back, eh?* Wei Wuxian thought. *This shishu of mine sure was kind to the fairer sex.*

A-Qing clutched the small money pouch she had stolen and stood there dumbly for a while. Then she suddenly stuffed it in her robes and chased after Xiao Xingchen, still knocking around with her bamboo pole, until she ran headfirst into Xiao Xingchen's back so he had to steady her again.

"Is there something else?"

"Your money pouch is still with me!" A-Qing exclaimed.

"You can have it," Xiao Xingchen assured her. "There isn't much in there, but don't go stealing again before it has been spent."

"I heard that stinkin' penniless bastard cursing at you—so you're blind too?" A-Qing asked.

At the latter half of her sentence, Xiao Xingchen's face dimmed instantly and his smile almost vanished. The innocent, oblivious words of a child were the deadliest of all. Children were ignorant, and it was precisely their ignorance that most keenly wounded the heart.

Red bloomed and thickened beneath the bandage wrapped around Xiao Xingchen's eyes, nearly seeping through the cloth. He raised his hand and ghosted his fingers over it, arm shaking faintly as he covered it from view. The pain of plucking out his own eyes wasn't easily healed, and neither were the wounds left in its wake.

A-Qing, thinking he was just dizzy, declared happily, "Why don't I tag along with you from now on?!"

Xiao Xingchen gave an arduous smile. "Follow me for what? Are you going to become a Daoist priestess?"

"You're a big blind, I'm a little blind. If we travel together, we can watch out for each other. I've got no dad, no mom, and nowhere to stay. What does it matter who I go with or where I go with them?" She was very clever. Afraid Xiao Xingchen would reject her, and quite certain he was a good person, she added threateningly, "If you don't take me along—if you reject me—I spend money real quick. I'll spend every penny in no time, and then I'll have to steal and cheat again, and I'll get the beating of a lifetime and completely lose my wits! How awful would that be, huh?"

Xiao Xingchen chuckled. "You are such a clever little thing—you would be the one tricking people into losing their wits. No one could beat the wits out of you."

Having watched this scene, Wei Wuxian realized something interesting. With the real Xiao Xingchen present for comparison, he could tell that the impostor played by Xue Yang had truly been a remarkable imitation! Other than his appearance, every detail was vivid and accurate. If someone told him Xue Yang had been possessed by Xiao Xingchen at the time, he'd believe it.

A-Qing continued to pester and harass Xiao Xingchen, clinging to him the entire time, as she pretended to be both blind and pitiful. Xiao Xingchen told her many times that accompanying him was dangerous, but A-Qing refused to listen. Even when Xiao Xingchen paused at a village during their travels to exorcise an ox that was so old it had cultivated a mischievous spirit, it didn't scare her off. She insisted on calling him Daozhang and remained glued to him like a piece of sticky candy, never more than three meters away at all times.

As time went on, Xiao Xingchen tacitly permitted her to stick around, perhaps because he saw that A-Qing was smart, likable,

daring, and didn't get in his way, or perhaps because she was a little girl who was also blind like him, orphaned and alone.

At first, Wei Wuxian thought Xiao Xingchen had a destination in mind. But several segments of memories skipped past, and based on the local customs and dialects of the places they visited, his movements were scattered and unsystematic. It didn't seem he was headed anywhere in particular but more like he was going on Night Hunts at random. Whenever he heard of a place where evil had manifested, he'd go tackle the haunting.

Maybe what happened with the Chang Clan of Yueyang was too great a blow, Wei Wuxian thought. *Maybe he wanted nothing to do with cultivation clans ever again but couldn't bring himself to abandon his ideals, which was why he chose to wander from Night Hunt to Night Hunt. To help however he could, wherever problems arose.*

Presently, Xiao Xingchen and A-Qing were walking down a long, even road. The grass growing on the sides of the road was waist-high. Suddenly, A-Qing gasped.

Xiao Xingchen immediately asked, "What's wrong?"

"Oh, nothing. Just twisted my foot," A-Qing replied.

But Wei Wuxian could see perfectly well that she hadn't gasped because she'd twisted her foot. She was walking perfectly fine—if she wasn't acting the part of a blind girl to keep Xiao Xingchen from shooing her away, she could have flown into the sky in a single bound. A-Qing had exclaimed in shock because she'd glimpsed a black figure lying in the thick grass.

Although it was unclear whether the person was alive or dead, A-Qing probably considered them trouble either way. She obviously didn't want Xiao Xingchen to notice.

"C'mon, c'mon. Let's go to that whatchacallit city up ahead and take a break, I'm *exhausted*!" she urged.

"Did you not sprain your ankle? Do you want me to carry you?" Xiao Xingchen asked.

A-Qing was ecstatic at the prospect, excitedly tapping the ground with her bamboo pole. "Yes, yes, yes!"

Xiao Xingchen laughed, turning to present his back to her with one knee bent to the ground. A-Qing was just about to pounce aboard when he suddenly stopped her with a hand, keeping her down. He rose to his feet, his brows knitted.

"It smells of blood."

A-Qing's nose had also detected the faint smell of blood, but it was weak under the sway of the night breeze, only surfacing sporadically. She played dumb. "Oh really? How come I don't smell nothin'? Maybe some house nearby's butchering pigs or chickens?"

She had only just spoken when, as if the heavens were against her, the person in the grass coughed.

Though the sound was extremely feeble, it didn't escape Xiao Xingchen's ears. He immediately pinpointed its direction and stepped into the overgrowth, crouching next to the person. Seeing how the person had been discovered, A-Qing stomped her foot and pretended to fumble over.

"What's wrong?"

Xiao Xingchen was feeling the person's pulse. "There's a person lying here."

"No wonder it stank of blood so bad," A-Qing said. "Is he dead? Are we gonna dig a hole and bury him?"

A dead man was, of course, a little less troublesome than a live one. So A-Qing was anxiously hoping this man was just that.

But Xiao Xingchen replied with, "He is not yet dead. But he is gravely injured."

After deliberating for a moment, he gently lifted the person from the ground and put him on his back.

Seeing her rightful spot had been usurped by a stinking man drenched in blood, and that the promised piggyback ride into town had thus also fallen through, A-Qing pouted and jabbed a number of deep holes in the ground with her bamboo pole. But she knew Xiao Xingchen wouldn't be dissuaded from saving the man, so she couldn't exactly complain.

The two returned to the road and continued on their way. The more they walked, the more Wei Wuxian thought it looked familiar. Then suddenly, it came to him. *Isn't this the same road Lan Zhan and I took to Yi City?*

Sure enough, at the end of the road towered Yi City.

The city gates weren't quite as run-down at this point in time. The corner watchtower was in perfect shape, and there was no graffiti on the city walls. When they passed through the gates, the fog was thicker inside, but the difference was imperceptible compared to the suffocating miasma of the present. Candlelight shone from the doors and windows of the houses on either side, and there was the murmur of human voices. While still rather desolate, there were signs of life.

Bearing a heavily wounded, blood-soaked person on his back, Xiao Xingchen must have been well aware no inns would accept guests like them. He didn't bother asking around for overnight lodging but instead inquired directly with the approaching night watcher as to whether there were any unused charitable mortuaries around.

"There's one over there," the night watcher told him. "The old caretaker passed away last month, so there's no one managing it right now."

Seeing Xiao Xingchen was blind and would have trouble finding his way over, he voluntarily led him there.

It was the very same charitable mortuary that now housed Xiao Xingchen's corpse after his death.

After thanking the night watcher, Xiao Xingchen carried the injured man into the overnight chamber on the right. It was a mid-sized room with a cot, pots and pans, and other such cookware. He carefully laid him on the ground, then took a pill from his qiankun pouch and pushed it past the man's tightly clenched teeth.

A-Qing felt around for a bit, then exclaimed happily, "There's so many things in here! There's a pot!"

"Is there a stove?" Xiao Xingchen asked.

"Yes!"

"A-Qing, why don't you find a way to boil some water? Be careful not to burn yourself."

A-Qing pursed her lips and got to work. Xiao Xingchen felt the man's forehead, then took out another pill for him to swallow. Wei Wuxian really wanted a closer look at the person's face, but A-Qing, obviously uninterested and extremely irritated, refused to spare him a single glance.

Once the water boiled, Xiao Xingchen slowly washed the blood from the man's face. A-Qing stole a curious sideways glance and let out a soundless *huh*.

The reason for her *huh* was that, once the man's face was washed clean, he was actually fairly good-looking.

At the sight of his face, Wei Wuxian's heart sank.

Just as he suspected. It was Xue Yang.

Enemies are bound to meet on a narrow road, he thought. *Oh, Xiao Xingchen, you really...have the most rotten luck.*

Xue Yang looked like nothing more than a boy at this point in time, seven parts jauntily handsome and three parts childlike. Who could've imagined that a boy like this—with a smile broad enough to bare his canines when he grinned—could be an unhinged, clan-decimating maniac?

Estimating the timeline, this was around the time Jin Guangyao took the role of Cultivation Chief. Judging by Xue Yang's sorry state, he'd barely escaped death after being "taken care of" by Jin Guangyao. As the saying went—the good die young and scourges last for a thousand years. On the brink of death, Xue Yang had been saved by his good old foe, Xiao Xingchen.

Poor Xiao Xingchen, to have accidentally saved the very enemy who'd brought him to this sorry state, never thinking to even carefully feel the man's face. Though A-Qing could see, she was not part of the cultivation world. She did not know Xue Yang, nor the grudge between the two men that ran as deep as the sea. Honestly, she didn't even know Xiao Xingchen's name...

Wei Wuxian heaved another sigh. Xiao Xingchen's luck really couldn't be worse. It was like he'd decided to singlehandedly shoulder the weight of all the ill fortune in the world.

Just then, Xue Yang wrinkled his brows. Xiao Xingchen was checking him over and bandaging his wounds. Sensing the youth was about to wake, he said, "Do not move."

Xue Yang, being someone who'd done plenty of bad things himself, was naturally more vigilant than most. The moment he heard that voice, his eyes snapped open, and he immediately sat up, rolling to the corner of the room. He was tense and on guard, staring at Xiao Xingchen with murder in his eyes.

Those were the eyes of a cornered beast. They shone with obvious malice and ill intent, and that feeling passed into Wei Wuxian, making his skin crawl. He shouted mentally, *Say something! Xiao Xingchen must remember the sound of Xue Yang's voice!*

"You..." Xue Yang started.

The moment he spoke, Wei Wuxian knew it was over. Xiao Xingchen wasn't going to recognize Xue Yang, even if he started running his mouth. It seemed he'd hurt his throat, and coughing up blood had left his voice raspy enough that no one could possibly realize they were the same person.

Xiao Xingchen sat by the bed. "I told you not to move," he said. "You will reopen your wounds otherwise. Do not worry. I am the one who saved you. I will not hurt you."

Xue Yang, quick-witted, immediately figured out that Xiao Xingchen likely hadn't recognized him. Gears turned in his head. He coughed a few times and ventured a question. "Who are you?"

A-Qing interjected a question of her own. "You have eyes, can't you see? A wandering cultivator, duh. He worked so hard to carry you back, saved your life and fed you miraculous medicine, and yet you're so mean!"

Xue Yang turned his gaze on her immediately. His voice was chilly. "Another blindie?"

Oh no, Wei Wuxian groaned inwardly.

This little thug was sharp, cunning, and abnormally alert. Even A-Qing's white eyes wouldn't make him drop his guard so easily. Nothing suspicious got past him—he'd blow her cover in an instant if she wasn't careful.

Xue Yang had only spoken a few words. It would've been difficult to determine he was "mean" from those scant words alone...unless she'd seen his facial expressions.

Fortunately, A-Qing had been lying all her life. She immediately responded, "What, you look down on blind folks? Ain't it blind folks that saved you? You'd be rotting on the roadside otherwise and no one would care! Not even a word of thanks to daozhang when you wake up, how rude! And calling me a 'blindie' too, *humph!* ...So what if I'm blind...?"

She successfully changed the subject and shifted his focus, looking both indignant and aggrieved as she went off on a grumbling tangent. Xiao Xingchen hastily went to console her. Xue Yang, leaning against the wall in the corner, rolled his eyes. Xiao Xingchen then turned to him again.

"Do not lean against the wall. I have yet to finish bandaging the wound on your leg. Come here."

Xue Yang considered the idea with a cool expression. Xiao Xingchen added, "If you put off treating it for much longer, your leg might give out for good."

At those words, Xue Yang made his choice.

Wei Wuxian surmised his thought process went something like this: He was severely wounded, and having difficulty moving, making it unwise to refuse treatment. Since Xiao Xingchen was fool enough to offer himself up, why not accept that fool's help with open arms?

And so, he abruptly changed face. With gratitude suffusing his voice, he said, "Sorry for the trouble, daozhang."

Having witnessed Xue Yang's ability to change in an instant from smiling to heartless, Wei Wuxian couldn't help but break into a cold sweat on behalf of the two blind folk—one real, one fake. Especially for A-Qing, the faker. If Xue Yang ever found out she could see everything, he'd certainly kill her to protect his secret. Although Wei Wuxian knew A-Qing had most likely been killed by Xue Yang in the end, he still had to experience the journey, so he couldn't help but be on tenterhooks.

Suddenly, he noticed Xue Yang was subtly avoiding letting Xiao Xingchen touch his left hand. Upon closer examination, it turned out that hand had a pinky missing. The stump was an old injury, not new, and Xiao Xingchen must've known Xue Yang was nine-fingered. No wonder Xue Yang had worn a black glove on his left hand when he was impersonating him.

When it came to healing and helping other people, Xiao Xingchen gave it his all. His head was bowed low as he applied medicinal powder to Xue Yang's wounds, and when he finished, the wounds were bandaged beautifully. "All done. But you best not move around, lest that broken bone shift."

Xue Yang was now certain Xiao Xingchen hadn't recognized him. A dummy, indeed. Even while covered in blood and horribly disheveled, that lazy, pleased smile reappeared on his face. "Daozhang won't ask who I am? Or why I sustained such serious injuries?"

Anyone else would've carefully avoided the topic in order to conceal their true identity. But he just had to do the opposite by purposely bringing it up.

Xiao Xingchen lowered his head, tidying up the medicine box and bandages as he calmly replied, "Since you are not telling, why must I pry? I have done nothing but lend a helping hand to a stranger I met by chance. It was no difficult task for me. Once you are healed, we will go our separate ways. If I were in your place, there would be many things I would not wish others to inquire."

Wei Wuxian thought, *Even if Xiao Xingchen did ask, that little thug would've fabricated some elaborate, seamless story to throw him off the scent.* Having a messy past wasn't something a person could help. Xiao Xingchen was being respectful by not probing further. Who would've thought Xue Yang would just so happen to come along and abuse that respect?

Of this, Wei Wuxian was certain—Xue Yang wasn't just going to trick Xiao Xingchen into treating his injuries. He wouldn't obediently "go his separate way" once healed either.

Xue Yang rested in the caretaker's overnight room while Xiao Xingchen returned to the main hall of the charitable mortuary. He opened an empty coffin, gathered a few armfuls of straw from the ground, and laid a thick blanket of said straw at the bottom of the coffin. He then turned to A-Qing.

"The person in there is injured, so the bed is his. I'm sorry, but you will have to sleep here. With straw laid on top, it should not be cold."

A-Qing had been a street urchin since she was young. Having lived her whole life exposed to the elements, where in the world *hadn't* she slept? Wholly unconcerned, she replied, "What's there to be sorry about? Having a place to sleep is already a pretty sweet deal. It's not cold, so stop tryin' to give me your outer robe."

Xiao Xingchen patted her head, tucked away his whisk and strapped on his sword, and then went out the door. For safety's sake, he forbade her to follow him when he went on Night Hunts. A-Qing burrowed into the coffin and lay there for a while before she suddenly heard Xue Yang call to her from the room next door.

"Blindie, c'mere."

A-Qing poked her head out. "Whaddya want?"

"I'll give you some candy," Xue Yang tempted her.

A-Qing's mouth watered. It seemed she really wanted the candy. And yet, she refused. "No. I'm not comin' over!"

Xue Yang threatened her sweetly. "Are you sure? Are you saying that because you're scared? Do you really believe I can't go over there and get you if you don't come here?"

A-Qing shuddered at the odd tone of his voice. It was even more horrifying when she imagined that smiling, devilish face suddenly appearing over the side of the coffin. After a moment of hesitation, she picked up her bamboo pole, and tapped and beat the ground as she dragged her feet to the entrance to the overnight room. Before she could speak, something small suddenly came flying at her.

Wei Wuxian wanted to dodge, worried it was some secret weapon, but of course, he couldn't control this body. He immediately jolted, having realized: *It's a trap!*

— PART 4 —

XUE YANG WAS TESTING A-Qing. If she was really blind, she wouldn't be able to dodge that thing!

But A-Qing was a veteran faker, and shrewd to boot. When she saw the object come flying at her, she didn't bat an eye. She neither dodged nor evaded, but let it hit her chest before she jumped back.

"Hey! What did you throw at me?!" she exclaimed furiously.

His plot thwarted, Xue Yang replied, "Candy, duh. For you. I forgot you were blind and couldn't catch it. It fell by your feet."

A-Qing humphed and crouched down, feeling around quite believably until she found the candy. She'd never eaten anything like this before. She swallowed hard, gave it a quick wipe, then popped it in her mouth and happily crunched away. Xue Yang lay in bed on his side, propping his cheek up on one hand.

"It is yummy, blindie?"

"I have a name. And it's not 'blindie,'" A-Qing said.

"You won't tell me your name, so I've no choice but to call you that," Xue Yang retorted.

"Listen up, my name is A-Qing," A-Qing said. "Don't call me 'blindie' again!" Then she thought she might've sounded too harsh. Afraid she'd wind up setting him off, she immediately changed the subject. "Yer so weird. All covered in blood, so heavily wounded, but you still carry candy on you."

Xue Yang chuckled gleefully. "I've loved sweets ever since I was young, but I never got to have any. I could only watch other people eat them. So I thought to myself: One day, if I make it big, I'll always keep more candy on me than I could ever eat."

It just so happened A-Qing had finished the piece in her mouth. She licked her lips, not yet satiated. Apparently, the desire for candy overrode her dislike for this person. "Then do you have more?"

Xue Yang smiled. "Of course I do. C'mere and I'll give you another."

A-Qing stood up and tapped her bamboo pole as she went toward him. Halfway through her slow and careful trek, Xue Yang's smile remained unchanged even as an eerie look glinted in his eyes. Soundlessly, he drew a long, frightening sword from his sleeve.

Jiangzai.

He aimed the tip of the sword in A-Qing's direction. If she took a few more steps forward, she would be skewered through by Jiangzai. But if she hesitated even a moment, she'd expose the fact that she wasn't blind!

Wei Wuxian and A-Qing's senses were connected, so he felt the tension crawling over her. However, this young miss was proving to be impressively gutsy. She remained calm and collected, fumbling about like everything was normal as she moved forward. Sure enough, when the tip of the sword was only about a centimeter from her belly, Xue Yang withdrew his hand and tucked Jiangzai back into his sleeve. He exchanged it for two candies instead—one for A-Qing, the other for his own mouth.

"A-Qing, where did that daozhang of yours go in the middle of the night?" he asked.

A-Qing crunched on the candy as she replied. "I think he went hunting."

"Hunting? You mean a Night Hunt," Xue Yang scoffed.

A-Qing asked, "Is it? What's the difference? They both mean pretty much the same thing. Isn't it just helping other people fight ghosts and monsters? And for free too."

Wei Wuxian, however, thought to himself: *So astute.*

It wasn't that A-Qing didn't remember what it was. She remembered everything Xiao Xingchen ever said better than anyone else. She had purposely goofed the term "Night Hunt," and the fact that Xue Yang corrected her was equal to him admitting he was also a cultivator. Not only had Xue Yang failed to test her—he'd been tested *by* her instead. Though young, this girl possessed a sharp mind.

Disdain colored Xue Yang's face, but his tone was one of confusion. "Can he even go on Night Hunts if he's blind?"

"There you go again," A-Qing snapped back furiously. "So what if he's blind? Daozhang is super amazing, even though he's blind. That sword goes *whoosh, whoosh*—I got one word to describe it, and it's 'fast'!"

She was gesturing wildly when Xue Yang suddenly cut in. "It's not like you can see, so how do you know his sword attacks are so fast?"

A-Qing herself moved fast, and moved to counter even faster. She snapped back shrewishly, "If I say it's fast, then it's fast! Just because I can't see doesn't mean I can't hear! Really, what exactly are you tryin' to say here?! Are you mocking us blind people?!"

She sounded exactly like a naive young girl gushing about the one she admired. Her tone was more than convincing.

At this point, all three of his attempts to probe her having been fruitless, Xue Yang's face finally relaxed. He was probably now convinced that A-Qing truly was blind.

For A-Qing, however, alarm bells were sounding. The next day, Xiao Xingchen brought back some wood, straw, and tiling materials for roof renovations. The moment he entered, A-Qing quietly tugged him back outside to whisper complaints for a good while. She told him how suspicious Xue Yang seemed, how he clearly shared Xiao Xingchen's profession but kept hiding this and that. She told him how he couldn't be a good person. Unfortunately, she must have determined Xue Yang's missing pinky to be of no significance, and thus didn't mention the most critical point.

Xiao Xingchen appeased her concerns. "Since you have already taken his candy, stop trying to chase him off. He will leave on his own once he is healed. No one would want to stay with us in this charitable mortuary."

That was certainly true—there was only a single bed in the shabby place. Thankfully, there had been no storms, or the roof would have been an issue too. No sensible person would want to stay here.

A-Qing was gearing up to badmouth Xue Yang some more when his voice suddenly came from behind them.

"Are you guys talking about me?"

He'd actually gotten out of bed again. A-Qing didn't feel in the least bit guilty about being caught in the act. "Who's talking about you?" she snapped. "Don't flatter yourself!"

She picked up her bamboo pole and tapped about as she found her way inside. She immediately crept to the window and ducked down under it to continue eavesdropping.

Outside the charitable mortuary, Xiao Xingchen said, "Your injuries have not healed, but you refuse to listen to me and keep moving about. Are you sure you will be all right?"

"Injuries heal faster if you stay active," Xue Yang said. "Besides, it's not like both my legs are broken. I'm used to wounds like these. I grew up catching beatings."

Xiao Xingchen didn't seem to know how to respond to that. Should he console the youth or treat it like a joke? After a momentary pause, he said, "I see..."

Xue Yang continued chatting. "Daozhang, the stuff you brought back—you're thinking of repairing the roof?"

"Mmm. I will probably stay here for the time being," Xiao Xingchen said. "And with the sorry state the roof is in, it is no proper place for A-Qing or for your recovery."

"Need my help?" Xue Yang offered.

"No need to trouble you," Xiao Xingchen declined him courteously.

"You really know how to do this, daozhang?" Xue Yang asked.

Xiao Xingchen muttered a "much ashamed" with a smile and shook his head. "I have not attempted something like this before."

And so, the two began to fix the roof together. One worked while the other directed. Xue Yang was eloquent and quite the wisecracker, with a wit that carried the wild and crude tone of the streets. It was likely Xiao Xingchen rarely crossed paths with people like him. It was also clear he was easily entertained—it didn't take much to make him laugh.

Listening to their merry conversation, A-Qing soundlessly moved her lips. When carefully observed, she seemed to be hatefully hissing, *I'll beat you dead, you bad man.*

Wei Wuxian felt the same way A-Qing did.

Xue Yang was gravely injured and had almost died. It wasn't hard to surmise his old score with Xiao Xingchen had set that violence in motion. The hatred that existed between the two of them was irreconcilable. Xue Yang was probably desperate to see Xiao Xingchen die a violent death, bleeding from all seven apertures and resting in no peace whatsoever—and yet, he could still joke around with him like this. If Wei Wuxian really had been the one hiding under the window, he would've killed Xue Yang first and asked questions later to prevent the calling forth of future disasters.

Unfortunately, this wasn't his body. And even if she had the heart, A-Qing was powerless.

About a month later, Xue Yang had pretty much recovered under Xiao Xingchen's attentive care. Other than a slight limp, he had no major issues. However, he still hadn't brought up the subject of leaving and continued to squeeze into the charitable mortuary with the other two. Who knew what he was scheming?

One evening, after Xiao Xingchen had tucked A-Qing in and was about to leave on a Night Hunt, Xue Yang's voice suddenly came forth.

"Daozhang, how about taking me along tonight?"

Though his vocal cords must have healed by now, he purposely continued to mask his voice, changing his normal timbre to a different octave. Xiao Xingchen smiled.

"That won't do. I laugh whenever you speak, and if I laugh, my sword will not be steady."

"Then I won't talk," Xue Yang pleaded pitifully. "I'll just carry your sword and be a good helper. C'mon, don't brush me off like this, okay?"

He was used to playing cute, selling people on his charm. He spoke to older people as if he were their baby brother, and Xiao Xingchen, who seemed to have cared for his younger martial siblings during his time in Baoshan-sanren's sect, had very naturally accepted the boy as his junior. On learning that Xue Yang was also in the same profession as him, he happily agreed.

Xue Yang's definitely not helping Xiao Xingchen in Night Hunts out of the kindness of his heart, Wei Wuxian thought. *If A-Qing doesn't follow them, she's going to miss some important information.*

But as expected, A-Qing was a sharp girl and immediately knew that Xue Yang likely harbored ill intent. Once the two left, she hopped out of the coffin and followed. She kept her distance out of fear of being discovered, but the two walked quickly and it didn't take long for her to lose their trail.

Thankfully, Xiao Xingchen had mentioned while washing vegetables earlier that a small village nearby was being harassed by walking corpses, and had cautioned them both not to run around. A-Qing remembered that village and ran straight there, arriving not long after. She crawled through a small hole under the fence by the entrance, hid behind a house, and then stealthily poked her head out.

Wei Wuxian wasn't sure if A-Qing understood what she was seeing with that little peek, but his own heart froze.

Xue Yang stood smiling by the roadside with his arms crossed and head tilted. Xiao Xingchen was in front of him. The silver light of Shuanghua scintillated as Xiao Xingchen brandished his sword and stabbed a villager right through the heart.

That villager was a living human.

If A-Qing had been an ordinary young girl, she would've certainly screamed aloud right then and there. But she had faked being blind for many years. People often let down their guard in front of her, thinking she couldn't see, and as a result, she'd witnessed countless acts of ugliness and cruelty that had helped her forge a heart of steel. She forcibly kept herself from uttering a single sound.

Even so, Wei Wuxian sensed the wave of numbness coursing up her legs.

Standing at the center of a circle of slain villagers, Xiao Xingchen sheathed his sword. "Are there really no living humans left in the village?" he wondered aloud solemnly. "Everyone is a walking corpse?"

Xue Yang's lips were hooked upward in a smile, but the voice coming from those same lips sounded shocked and pained. "That's right. Thank goodness that sword of yours can automatically guide itself toward corpse qi—it'd be hard for the two of us to break through a siege like this, otherwise."

"Let's inspect the village one more time," Xiao Xingchen said. "If there really are no living humans left, we will have to burn these walking corpses as soon as possible."

They walked off side by side. After they'd gone some distance, feeling finally returned to A-Qing's legs. She slipped out from behind the house and approached the pile of corpses, keeping her head down and looking left and right. Wei Wuxian's sight flitted to and fro along with hers.

The villagers had all been killed by Xiao Xingchen with one clean stab to the heart. Wei Wuxian noticed a few familiar faces.

In prior segments of memories, when the three went out during the day, they had encountered a group of idlers siting at the intersection to the village and playing dice. When the men glanced over at them and saw a big blind person, a little blind person, and a little limping cripple, they all burst out laughing and pointing. A-Qing spat at them, angrily swinging her bamboo pole, while Xiao Xingchen pretended not to hear and walked past with a neutral face. Xue Yang had given them a smile. However, those eyes of his carried no mirth.

A-Qing flipped over a number of corpses in succession, peeling back their eyelids. They were all white-eyed, and some of their faces were already covered with livor mortis. She sighed in relief, but Wei Wuxian's heart was sinking lower and lower.

Although these individuals looked a lot like walking corpses, they were all real, live people. It was simply that they had been poisoned with corpse toxin.

Wei Wuxian noticed remnants of purplish-red powder near the mouths and noses of the bodies. Of course, the ones who'd been poisoned too deeply and lost their minds were beyond help. But there were some who weren't as deeply poisoned and could have been saved. These villagers hadn't been poisoned for too long. They exhibited the characteristics of a turned corpse, and emitted corpse qi, but they could think and speak. They were still alive, and if they were treated they could be saved, just as Lan Jingyi and the other boys had been. Killing them in error was no different from slaughtering the living.

They should've been able to talk, could've proven their identities, could've called for help. But the awful thing was that someone had cut out their tongues beforehand. Every single body had blood drooling from their mouth or dried by the corners of their lips.

Although Xiao Xingchen couldn't see, Shuanghua could point him in the direction of corpse qi. Since the villagers had no tongues and could only cry out strangely in a way that made them sound like walking corpses, he was certain that was what they were as he killed them.

Xue Yang was a complete maniac. Killing by proxy, repaying kindness with hatred—a vicious backstabber.

A-Qing didn't understand such intricacies, however. What meager knowledge she had was derived from things Xiao Xingchen mentioned offhand. "That bad man," she mumbled to herself, "could he really be helping daozhang?"

Don't believe Xue Yang so easily! Wei Wuxian thought. *Absolutely do not!*

Thankfully, A-Qing's instincts were sharp. While she couldn't find anything suspicious in what she'd witnessed, her guard against Xue Yang was already deeply ingrained. She instinctively disliked him. She couldn't relax around him. And so, whenever Xue Yang went with Xiao Xingchen on Night Hunts, she'd secretly follow. Even when they interacted under the same roof, she stayed constantly on her toes.

One evening while the wintry wind howled, the three of them squeezed together by the shabby hearth in the small room for warmth. Xiao Xingchen was repairing a torn basket, and A-Qing was curled by his side and wrapped snugly in the only blanket around.

Xue Yang, meanwhile, listened to A-Qing incessantly badger Xiao Xingchen to tell her a story, and looked quite bored with his cheek propped on his hand. "Stop your whining," he said, annoyed. "Keep that up and I'll tie your tongue."

A-Qing ignored him completely and continued to beg. "Daozhang, I want to hear a story!"

"No one ever told me stories when I was younger, so I do not know how to tell them," Xiao Xingchen replied.

But A-Qing continued pestering him, clearly ready to start rolling around on the ground. Xiao Xingchen relented.

"All right, let me tell you a tale from the mountain."

A-Qing said helpfully, "Once upon a time there was a mountain, and up on the mountain there was a temple?"

"No," Xiao Xingchen said. "Once upon a time there was a nameless immortal mountain, and on the nameless mountain there lived an immortal who had attained enlightenment. This immortal took in many disciples, but they were forbidden to descend the mountain."

Wei Wuxian understood immediately. *Baoshan-sanren.*

"Why were they forbidden to descend the mountain?" A-Qing asked.

"Because the immortal herself did not understand the world below the mountain. That was why she had hidden herself there. She said to her disciples: 'If you descend the mountain, do not bother to return. Do not bring the conflict of the outside world back with you.'"

"How could anyone endure that?" A-Qing wondered. "There must've been disciples who couldn't help sneaking down the mountain to play."

"Indeed," Xiao Xingchen said. "The first to descend from the mountain was an outstanding disciple. When he first descended, everyone admired and praised him for his strong abilities, and he became a distinguished cultivator on the orthodox path. But he later experienced something that greatly changed him and was suddenly transformed into an evil overlord who killed without batting an eye. In the end, he was cut down by the weapons of many."

This was the first of Baoshan-sanren's disciples to have "met a bad end," Yanling-daoren.

What, exactly, had Wei Wuxian's martial uncle encountered to make him change so drastically? It continued to be a mystery to this day, and it was unlikely anyone would ever learn the truth.

Xiao Xingchen finished repairing the basket and felt its surface to ensure it wouldn't prick one's hand. Satisfied, he put it down and continued his tale.

"The second was a female disciple, also outstanding."

Warmth enveloped Wei Wuxian's chest.

Cangse-sanren.

"Is she pretty?" A-Qing asked.

"I do not know," Xiao Xingchen replied. "She was said to be very beautiful."

A-Qing propped her face up with both hands. "Oh, I know, then. After she descended the mountain, there must've been a lotta people who liked her and wanted to marry her. She must've married a high-ranking official or the head of a major family! Hee hee."

Xiao Xingchen laughed. "You guessed wrong. She married a *servant* who attended the head of a major family, and the two ran off to faraway lands."

"I don't like that," A-Qing scoffed. "Why would an outstanding, beautiful fairy like her fall for a servant? This story is stupid. Some sour, broke-ass scholar probably made it up. And then? What happened after they traveled to faraway lands?"

"And then a mishap occurred during a Night Hunt, and they both lost their lives," Xiao Xingchen concluded.

"What kinda story is this?! *Bleh!* Marrying a servant, fine. But then they both died together?! I'm not listening to this anymore!"

Good thing Xiao Xingchen didn't tell her that those two also birthed a famously evil overlord whose demise everyone called for. Otherwise, she just might spit on me too, Wei Wuxian thought.

Xiao Xingchen was resigned. "This is why I said at the start that I am no good at telling stories."

"Then, daozhang, you at least remember your experiences from past Night Hunts, right?" A-Qing prompted. "I love hearing about those! Tell me, what kinda monsters have you fought in the past?"

Xue Yang's eyes were half-lidded this entire time; he only barely seemed to be listening. But at A-Qing's question, his eyes focused, his pupils contracted, and he looked askance at Xiao Xingchen.

"Well, there are too many of those," Xiao Xingchen replied.

"Really?" asked Xue Yang suddenly. "Then was daozhang still going on Night Hunts all alone in the past?"

The corners of his lips were curled in an obvious expression of malice, but his voice was full of innocent curiosity. Xiao Xingchen paused, then smiled softly.

"No."

A-Qing was interested now. "Who else was there?"

This time, Xiao Xingchen paused even longer. It was a good while before he replied.

"My most intimate friend."

There was a peculiar glint in Xue Yang's eyes. The smile hanging off his lips deepened. Picking at Xiao Xingchen's scars had given him considerable pleasure. A-Qing, however, was genuinely curious.

"What kind of person is your friend, daozhang? What's he like?"

Xiao Xingchen easily replied, "A sincere gentleman of high moral character."

Xue Yang rolled his eyes disdainfully at this. He seemed to have mouthed a few curse words, his lips forming their shape. Afterwards, he pretended to be puzzled. "Then, daozhang, where is your friend now? With the state you're in, how come he hasn't come looking for you?"

This guy is such a cruel little knife, Wei Wuxian thought.

Sure enough, Xiao Xingchen stopped talking. While A-Qing wasn't in the know, she still seemed to sense something amiss. She held her breath and sent a stealthy glare at Xue Yang, her teeth grinding like she desperately wanted to bite him. After staring into nothingness for a while, Xiao Xingchen broke the silence.

"I do not know where he is at the moment. But, I hope..."

He trailed off and patted A-Qing's head.

"All right, let us stop here for tonight. I really am no good at telling stories. It is much too difficult for me."

A-Qing replied obediently, "Oh, all right!"

Unexpectedly, Xue Yang suddenly spoke up. "How about I tell one?"

A-Qing hadn't accepted the disappointment of going without, so she immediately agreed. "Okay, yes, yes, you tell one."

Xue Yang began languidly.

"Once upon a time there was a child.

"This child loved eating sweet things, but because he had neither dad nor mom nor money, he couldn't have them often. One day, he was staring into nothingness as he always did, sitting on a porch. Across from this porch was a restaurant, and in that restaurant, a man sat at a table laid with a feast. When he saw the child, he waved to beckon him over."

While the opening of this story wasn't that great either, it was at least much better than Xiao Xingchen's cliché old tales. A-Qing's ears must have perked up like a rabbit's.

"The child was clueless and had no idea what to do with himself," Xue Yang continued. "So when he saw someone waving at him, he immediately ran over. The man pointed at a plate of desserts on the table and asked him: 'Do you want this?'

"He wanted it very much, of course, and nodded enthusiastically. The man gave the child a slip of paper and said: 'Then deliver this to a certain house, and I'll give it to you once you've done so.'

"The child was very happy. He only needed to run an errand, and he'd get a plate of desserts! A plate he earned himself, no less.

"He couldn't read, so he just took the slip of paper and headed to the appointed destination. When the door opened, a big, burly man emerged. This man glanced at the paper and then slapped the boy bloody. He gripped him by the hair and demanded: 'Who told you to deliver this?!'"

That child must have been Xue Yang himself.

Given Xue Yang's present shrewdness, Wei Wuxian was surprised to learn he'd been a naive and thoughtless child who did whatever he was told. Nothing good had been written on that paper, it seemed. There was probably some conflict between the restaurant man and the burly man, but the restaurant man didn't dare to insult the other directly, so he summoned a boy from the streets to deliver it instead. What an utterly foul stunt to pull.

Xue Yang continued, "Scared, the boy pointed in the direction of the restaurant. The burly man went there, dragging the boy by the hair all the while. But the man at the restaurant had long since fled, and the waiter had taken away the plate of leftover desserts. The burly man flew into a rage and flipped a number of tables before he stormed off, cursing.

"The child was anxious. He'd run the errand, gotten beaten, and been dragged back by his hair, feeling like his scalp was gonna peel off the entire way. If he didn't get to eat his desserts after all that, it wouldn't do at all. And so he asked the waiter, teary-eyed, 'Where's my dessert? Where's my promised dessert?'"

Xue Yang grinned widely. "The waiter was fuming at the state of the wrecked restaurant. He smacked the child out the door, slapped him silly. The boy crawled to his feet and walked around for a bit, and guess what happened? What a coincidence! He ran into the man who got him to deliver the message."

He stopped there. A-Qing, engrossed in the tale, urged, "And then? What happened?"

"What else? Ain't it just more smacks and kicks?" Xue Yang said.

"That was you, right?" A-Qing pressed. "A boy who loves sweets, that must be you! Why were you like that when you were younger?! If it were me, I would've *bleh, bleh, bleh*, spat in his food and drink, then beat 'im..." She gestured wildly and almost hit Xiao Xingchen.

Xiao Xingchen hurriedly chided, "All right, all right, the story is done, so time for bed."

A-Qing was still beating her chest in anger as he carried her to the coffin. "Gah! Both your stories are really killin' me! One's deathly boring and the other's deathly vexing! Oh my god, the man who sent the message is *so* annoying! I'm so annoyed!"

Xiao Xingchen tucked her in. After taking a couple of steps, he asked, "What happened afterward?"

"Take a guess?" Xue Yang said. "There is no afterward. Didn't you stop telling your story too?"

"No matter what happened next, you are doing reasonably well now. There is no need to dwell on the past."

"I'm not dwelling on the past," Xue Yang said. "It's just that blindie steals my candy every day and wound up eating it all. It made me recall the times when I couldn't have any."

A-Qing gave the coffin a hard kick and protested, "Daozhang, don't listen to his lies! I didn't take that many!"

Xiao Xingchen chuckled lightly. "Rest, both of you."

Xue Yang didn't follow him that night. Xiao Xingchen left to Night Hunt alone, and so A-Qing laid at ease in the coffin and didn't move. But she couldn't sleep.

Just as the sky was growing lighter, Xiao Xingchen soundlessly returned.

When he passed by the coffin, he reached in. A-Qing closed her eyes, pretending to be asleep, and only opened her eyes anew when Xiao Xingchen left the charitable mortuary once more. Lying next to her straw pillow was a tiny piece of candy.

She poked her head out and gazed toward the overnight room. Xue Yang was also awake, sitting by the table. She couldn't tell what was on his mind.

A piece of candy lay quietly by the edge of the table.

Following that night of stories by the hearth, Xiao Xingchen would hand both of them a piece of candy every day. A-Qing was elated, of course, while Xue Yang displayed neither gratitude for the gesture nor any intention of rejecting it. A-Qing was mad about that attitude of his for days.

Xiao Xingchen took care of their food and board in Yi City. Being blind, he couldn't pick out good vegetables and was too abashed to haggle prices. When he went out alone, it was fine if he found good-hearted vendors, but a number of times he ran into those who purposely took advantage of the fact that he couldn't see. The bundles would either be shorted by weight or the vegetables wouldn't be fresh. Xiao Xingchen didn't mind—or rather, he didn't really pay attention. But A-Qing was perfectly aware of the problem and mightily mad about it. She was furiously adamant in going grocery shopping with Xiao Xingchen to settle scores with those unconscientious vendors. Unfortunately, she had to hide the fact that she could see, so she didn't dare throw a fit and flip stalls like a shrew in front of Xiao Xingchen.

That was where Xue Yang came in handy. True to his unsavory character, his eyes were sharp and his tongue sharper. As long as he was present, the first thing he did was brazenly cut the price of any purchase in half. If the other party gave him an inch, he'd push further and take a mile. If they refused, his eyes would turn menacing. The vendors would think, *It's good enough that they'll pay at all, never mind fussing over how much is paid!* and then hurry them off; *go, go, get out of here.*

This must've been how Xue Yang used to lord over Kui Prefecture and Lanling. He likely never had to pay for anything he wanted.

Her grievances satisfied, A-Qing actually complimented Xue Yang a few times in delight. And with a piece of candy every day on top of that, for a time she and Xue Yang maintained a delicate peace. But she could never bring herself to entirely let down her guard around him, and that modest peace was often marred by numerous doubts and internal griping.

One day, A-Qing was doing the blind act again on the streets. She had played this game all her life and never once grown tired of it. Just as she was walking around tapping her bamboo pole, a voice suddenly came from behind her.

"Little miss, do not go so fast if you cannot see."

It was the voice of a young man, his tone somewhat cool. A-Qing turned her head and saw a black-clad Daoist cultivator standing several meters behind her. He had a longsword strapped on his back and a whisk in the crook of his arm. His sleeves were light and fluttering, and his posture was extremely upright, with a definite air of aloofness and pride.

It was, indeed, the face of Song Lan.

A-Qing tilted her head, but Song Lan had already approached. He laid his whisk on her shoulder and guided her to the side of the path.

"There are fewer people on the sides of the street."

As expected of a good friend of Xiao Xingchen's, Wei Wuxian thought. *What they call good friends are indeed those similar in temperament.*

A-Qing snorted and laughed. "A-Qing thanks daozhang!"

Song Lan withdrew his whisk and hooked it in the crook of his arm anew. He swept a look over her. "Do not run about so wildly," he chided. "Also, this place is heavy with yin energy. Do not loiter outside when the sun sets."

"Okay!" A-Qing replied.

Song Lan nodded and continued onward. A-Qing couldn't help but twist her head to watch him. After he'd walked on for a bit, he stopped a passerby.

"Please wait. Might I inquire whether anyone in this area has seen a blinded Daoist carrying a sword?"

A-Qing listened with rapt attention as the passerby replied, "I'm not too sure. Why don't you ask the people ahead, daozhang?"

"Many thanks," Song Lan said.

A-Qing went over, tapping her bamboo pole. "Daozhang, why are you looking for that other daozhang?"

Song Lan whipped around. "You have seen him before?"

"I might've, or I might not've," A-Qing replied.

"What can I do to make it a 'might've'?" Song Lan asked.

"Answer me a few questions and I might just might've," A-Qing said. "Are you that daozhang's friend?"

Song Lan was taken aback, and it took him a moment before he answered, "...Yes."

Why the hesitation? Wei Wuxian wondered.

A-Qing also felt his answer was a little forced. She grew suspicious. "Do you really know him? How tall is that daozhang? Is he pretty or ugly? What's his sword like?"

Song Lan immediately answered, "Similar to me in height, exceptional in appearance, and his sword is carved with frost fractals."

Seeing how his answers were all correct and he didn't appear to be a bad person, A-Qing said, "I know where he is. Why don't you come with me, daozhang?"

At this point, Song Lan had been traveling in search of his good friend for many years. After being disappointed countless times, now that there was finally news, he almost couldn't believe it. Maintaining his calm with considerable effort, he replied, "...Th... thanks for the trouble..."

A-Qing led him near the charitable mortuary, but Song Lan stopped and remained frozen in the far distance.

A-Qing asked, "What's wrong? Aren't you going in?"

For some reason, Song Lan's face was extremely pale. He stared at the entrance to the charitable mortuary, looking like he wanted nothing more than to charge in but was too afraid to do so. All the aloof coolness from before had melted away.

Could he be nervous now that he's so close?[3] Wei Wuxian wondered.

But when he finally seemed ready to enter—another figure did so ahead of him, swaggering languidly through the entrance of the charitable mortuary.

Seeing that figure, Song Lan's face went from pale to dark in a flash.

The sound of laughter came from inside the charitable mortuary, and A-Qing humphed.

"The pest is back."

"Who is he? Why is he here?" Song Lan questioned.

A-Qing whined and complained and explained. "A rotten guy. He won't tell us his name, so who knows who he is? Daozhang saved him, and now he pesters daozhang all day. So annoying!"

Shock and fury suffused Song Lan's face, a mixture of pale white and dark and dismal. A moment later he said, "Do not make a sound!"

The expression on his face scared A-Qing. She was quiet, as directed. The two soundlessly approached the charitable mortuary, and one stood by the window while one hid underneath. They heard Xiao Xingchen speak inside.

"Whose turn is it today?"

The moment he heard that voice, Song Lan's hands shook so hard that even A-Qing noticed.

"Why don't we stop taking turns from now on? Switch it up," Xue Yang suggested.

---

3 *Wei Wuxian is referencing an idiom: 近乡情怯 / "The closer you are to home after a long absence, the more nervous you become."*

"You always have something to say when your turn comes. Switch it up how?"

"Here, I've got two small sticks," Xue Yang said. "The one who picks the longer stick won't need to go, but the one who picks the shorter stick does. How's that?"

After a moment of silence, Xue Yang laughed out loud.

"You picked the shorter one. I've won. You go!"

Xiao Xingchen had no choice but to say helplessly, "All right, I will go."

He seemed to have stood up and started walking toward the door. *Very good,* Wei Wuxian thought. *Hurry out. Best if Song Lan can grab you and run the moment you step outside!*

Unexpectedly, he didn't get that far before Xue Yang spoke again, "Come back. I'll go."

"Why are you suddenly willing?" Xiao Xingchen asked.

Xue Yang rose to his feet. "Are you a dummy? I was lying to you just now. I drew the shorter stick, but I had another, longer one hidden. No matter which one you picked, I could always take out a longer one. I'm just messing with you since you can't see, that's all."

He poked fun at Xiao Xingchen for a bit before leisurely picking up the basket and heading out the door. A-Qing looked up to see that Song Lan's entire body was shaking. She was puzzled as to why he was so angry. Song Lan indicated for her to remain silent, and the two left soundlessly. Only after putting some distance between them and the mortuary did Song Lan begin questioning A-Qing.

"That person. When did Xing...the daozhang save him?"

His tone was grave. A-Qing understood now that this was no trivial matter, so her voice became solemn as well.

"A long time ago. It's been many years now."

"And that entire time, the daozhang hasn't known his identity?" Song Lan questioned.

"He hasn't," A-Qing confirmed.

"While staying at the daozhang's side, what has that person done?"

"Talk all slick, bully me, scare me. And... Oh, and he goes on Night Hunts with daozhang!"

Song Lan's brow immediately furrowed. He must not have expected Xue Yang to be so altruistic either. "Night Hunt? Hunting what? Do you know?"

A-Qing didn't dare give a careless answer. After thinking for a moment, she replied, "They used to hunt for walking corpses all the time. Now they hunt ghosts or haunted livestock, or something."

Song Lan questioned her thoroughly, also seeming to feel something was off without being able to pinpoint exactly what it was. "Do he and the daozhang get along well?"

Despite her reluctance to admit it, A-Qing gave him the truth. "I feel like daozhang isn't very happy on his own... So, to finally have someone from the same profession... And it kind of seems like he enjoys listening to that rotten guy's wisecracks..."

Dense clouds of gloom covered Song Lan's expression, storming with indignation and heartache. Amidst this confusion and disbelief, one thing alone was clear:

Xiao Xingchen must never find out about this!

"Do not tell that daozhang anything unnecessary," he said. Then he moved to follow in the direction Xue Yang had gone, his expression grave.

A-Qing called after him. "Daozhang, are you heading off to beat up that bad man?"

But Song Lan was already far away. Wei Wuxian thought, *He won't just settle for a beating—he's gonna butcher Xue Yang alive!*

Xue Yang had left with the grocery basket, and A-Qing knew the usual route he took to the market. She took a shortcut through a forest, running as fast as the wind while her heart pounded, and finally spotted him up ahead. He was yawning as he walked lazily along, dangling the basket from one hand—which was stuffed full of green vegetables, radishes, steamed buns, and other such goodies. It seemed he was on his way back from the grocery run.

A-Qing was an old hand at hiding and eavesdropping. She moved sneakily along with him, stooped low and hidden behind the forest brush. Suddenly, Song Lan's cold voice came from ahead.

"Xue Yang."

As if a bucket of cold water had been thrown in his face, or he'd been slapped awake from a dream, Xue Yang's expression was instantly ghastlier than ever before.

Song Lan stepped out from behind a tree. His longsword was already drawn and brandished, the tip pointing at the ground.

Xue Yang pretended to be shocked. "Oh my, if it isn't Song-daozhang? What a rare guest. Here to bum a meal?"

Song Lan raised his sword and lunged. Xue Yang shook Jiangzai out from his sleeves with a *sching* to block the attack. He backed up a few steps to safely set the basket down by a tree, then spat.

"Stinkin' cultivator. The one time I felt like heading out on a grocery run, and you had to fuckin' kill the mood!"

Song Lan was utterly mad with fury, each of his moves aiming to end Xue Yang's life. "What demonic tricks are you playing?!" he bellowed, the tenor deep and words harsh. "What are you planning, getting close to Xiao Xingchen?!"

"I was wondering why Song-daozhang held back from delivering a fatal blow. So it was to ask about that?" Xue Yang laughed.

"Speak!" Song Lan shouted angrily. "As if scum like you would be so kind as to help him with his Night Hunts!"

The qi from his next swing only narrowly missed Xue Yang's face, leaving a gash across his cheek. But he wasn't the least bit alarmed. "I'm shocked that Song-daozhang knows me so well!"

One of them practiced the Daoist orthodox way, while the other was a practitioner of rogue techniques honed through criminal acts. Song Lan was obviously more skilled at swordplay. With a thrust, he pierced right through Xue Yang's arm.

"Speak!"

He was desperate to know the truth of this unsettling situation, or he would surely have aimed his sword at Xue Yang's neck instead. Despite being stabbed, Xue Yang's expression remained unchanged.

"You really wanna know? It's just that, well, I worry you'll go crazy if I tell you. Some things are best left without gory details."

Song Lan snapped coldly, "Xue Yang, my patience for you is limited!"

Clang! Xue Yang knocked aside an attack that aimed for his eyes. "All right, you're the one who asked to hear this. Do you know what that good cultivator friend of yours, your good bosom friend, has done? He's killed many walking corpses. Exterminating evil without asking for anything in return. So moving. He's blind—dug out his eyes to give them to you—but the great thing about Shuanghua is that it can guide him toward corpse qi.

"Oh, let me tell you something even more amazing: I discovered that if you take someone poisoned by corpse toxin, then cut out their tongue to make them unable to speak, Shuanghua can't tell the difference between those who are just poisoned and the real walking dead..."

Song Lan's hands and sword began to tremble as he heard this mercilessly detailed explanation.

"You swine... You inhuman swine..."

"Song-daozhang, you know, sometimes I really pity you cultured gentlemen when it comes to cussing. It's always the same words, nothing new at all. Completely toothless. I haven't used those two flaccid words since I was seven."

Beside himself with anger, Song Lan attacked again, now finally aiming for his throat. "You took advantage of his blindness! Woe upon him, beset by your lies!"

His thrust was both fast and brutal. Xue Yang barely managed to dodge, though his shoulder was still impaled once more. His brows didn't even twitch, as if he was senseless to pain.

"Bringing up the blindness, eh? Song-daozhang, don't forget—for whom did he dig out those eyes of his, hmm?"

At this, Song Lan's expression and movements both froze.

Xue Yang continued on. "And what leg do you have to stand on, criticizing me? Gonna claim to be his friend? Do you really still have the *nerve* to call yourself Xiao Xingchen's friend?! Ha ha ha ha! Song-daozhang, need I remind you what you told him after I massacred Baixue Temple? He was worried about you. He wanted to come help you. But how did you greet him? What did you tell him?"

Song Lan was devastated. "I—! At the time..."

Xue Yang cut him off and shut him up. "At the time—you were in the throes of lamentation? In pain? Grieving? Or just lacking any other targets? To be fair, I did slaughter your temple because of him. You had every reason to take it out on him. But that was exactly what I wanted."

Every single word struck home. Both Xue Yang's hand and words closed in with each step. His sword attacks grew more and more languid, but also increasingly sinister and shrewd, and he was imperceptibly gaining the upper hand. And yet, Song Lan didn't seem to notice at all!

Xue Yang sighed dramatically. "Who was the one who said there was 'no need to ever meet again'? Wasn't that you, Song-daozhang? He listened to your demand and vanished from sight after digging out his eyes for you, so why have you come shuffling around here now? Aren't you just making it awkward for everyone involved? Do you agree, Xiao Xingchen-daozhang?"

Startled into hesitation, Song Lan's sword faltered! Xue Yang had thrown both his mind and movements into chaos, allowing him to be fooled by such a cheap trick.

Xue Yang could hardly let such a perfect opportunity pass. With an upward sweep of his hand, corpse toxin choked the air. The powder was so meticulously refined that even Song Lan had never seen anything like it before. When it spread, he gasped in several mouthfuls. Knowing instantly that he was in danger, he tried forcing himself to cough up the stuff—but Jiangzai was waiting. Light glinted coldly off the sword's tip as Xue Yang brutally burrowed it into Song Lan's open mouth!

In that instant, Wei Wuxian's sight went pitch-black. A-Qing had shut her eyes in fright. But he already understood—they were witnessing Song Lan's tongue being cut out.

The sounds were too horrible to comprehend.

The rims of A-Qing's eyes were hot, but she fiercely bit her tongue and didn't make a peep, opening her eyes with a shudder. Song Lan's sword barely propped him upright. He covered his mouth with his other hand as blood spilled ceaselessly from between his fingertips.

Having fallen for Xue Yang's trap and lost his tongue so suddenly, he was in such intense pain that he could barely walk. Yet he pulled his sword from the ground and staggered forward to lunge at Xue Yang, who dodged easily as a twisted smile contorted his face.

A moment later, Wei Wuxian learned why he was smiling like that, just as the silvery glint of Shuanghua ran Song Lan through.

Song Lan looked down at Shuanghua's blade, its tip piercing his heart, and then slowly looked up. He saw Xiao Xingchen, Shuanghua in hand and wearing a calm expression.

"Are you here?" asked Xiao Xingchen, completely unaware of what was happening here.

Song Lan moved his lips soundlessly.

Xue Yang smiled. "I'm here. Why are *you* here?"

Xiao Xingchen withdrew Shuanghua and sheathed it. "There was something off about Shuanghua, so I let it lead me here." He sounded amazed. "Walking corpses have not visited this area in a long time. And one lone straggler too. Did it come from somewhere else?"

Song Lan slowly dropped to his knees in front of Xiao Xingchen.

Xue Yang gave him a condescending glance. "I suppose. Its cries are awfully menacing."

If Song Lan passed his sword to Xiao Xingchen, he would know who he was. He'd recognize his dear friend's sword with a single touch. But that was no longer an option for Song Lan. How could he give his sword to Xiao Xingchen, and in doing so, tell him who he'd just killed with his own two hands?

Xue Yang was betting on this and didn't feel the slightest bit of fear. "C'mon, let's head back and make dinner. I'm hungry," he said idly.

"The shopping is done?" Xiao Xingchen asked.

"Shopping's all done," Xue Yang confirmed. "Too bad I had to run into that thing on the way back. How unlucky."

Xiao Xingchen left first. Xue Yang gave the wounds on his own shoulders and arm a pat, then picked up the basket again. As he passed in front of Song Lan, he smiled lightly and lowered his head to murmur.

"You're not invited."

A-Qing waited until Xue Yang had walked far, far away—probably even until he'd made it back to the charitable mortuary with Xiao Xingchen—before she stood up from the bushes.

She had crouched for too long; her legs were asleep. Hobbling as she leaned on her bamboo pole, she tremblingly approached Song Lan's stiff, kneeling corpse. It showed no sign of toppling over.

Song Lan had died with his eyes still open, a sign of everlasting regret, and A-Qing jolted in fright at the sight of that wide, empty stare. Then she saw the blood gushing from his mouth, spilling down his chin and drenching his clothes, soaking the ground. Enormous teardrops spilled from his eyes.

Terrified, A-Qing reached out and helped close Song Lan's eyes. She knelt before him and placed her hands together in a prayer.

"Daozhang, *please* don't blame me or the other daozhang. It'd be certain death for me if I came out, I had no choice but to hide. I couldn't save you. The other daozhang was deceived by that bad man. He didn't mean it, he didn't know the one he killed was you!"

She sobbed.

"I'm going back now. May your spirit in heaven *please* bless me with success in getting Xiao Xingchen-daozhang out! Bless the both of us so we can escape that devil's clutches and make that monster die a horrible death. We'll shred his corpse to a million pieces and send him to hell—never to be absolved!"

She kowtowed soundly three times, wiped her face hard, then stood up and gathered herself before heading back to Yi City.

The sky was already dark by the time she returned. Xue Yang was sitting by the table, peeling apples and cutting all the slices into rabbit shapes. He looked like he was in an exceptionally good mood. Anyone who saw him would think him simply a mischievous young lad. No one could ever imagine what he'd just done.

Xiao Xingchen came out carrying a plate of green vegetables. When he heard her, he called out a question.

"A-Qing, where did you go today, coming back so late?"

Xue Yang peered at her, and his eyes suddenly flashed. "What happened? Her eyes are all swollen."

Xiao Xingchen hurried over. "What is the matter? Did someone bully you?"

"Bully her? Who could manage to bully *her*?" Xue Yang scoffed.

Although he was smiling, his suspicion was obviously aroused. Suddenly, A-Qing threw down her bamboo pole and burst out into hysterical wailing.

She was all snot and tears, crying so hard she was short of breath. She flung herself into Xiao Xingchen's arms, her body racked with sobs. "Am I very ugly? Am I? Tell me, daozhang, am I really very ugly?"

Xiao Xingchen stroked her head. "Of course not, A-Qing is so beautiful. Who said you are ugly?"

Xue Yang scoffed disdainfully, "*So* ugly. More so when you cry."

"Do not say that," Xiao Xingchen admonished him.

A-Qing cried even harder now, and she stomped her feet. "It's not like you can see, daozhang! What's the use if *you* tell me I'm beautiful? You must be lying! He can see, and he said I'm ugly. So it seems like I'm really ugly! Ugly and blind!"

The two naturally assumed she was throwing a fit because she'd been called "ugly freak" or "white-eyed blindie" by some random child and was feeling aggrieved.

"They called you ugly, so you ran back here to cry?" Xue Yang commented with contempt. "What happened to that usual shrewishness of yours?"

"You're the shrew!!" A-Qing snapped. "Daozhang, do you still have money?"

Xiao Xingchen paused, then said somewhat sheepishly, "Mmm... I think so."

Xue Yang cut in, "I've got money, I'll lend you some."

"You've stayed with us all this time, but when it comes to a bit of money you'll still only *lend*?!" A-Qing said harshly. "You loser! Aren't you embarrassed?! Daozhang, I wanna go buy pretty clothes and pretty accessories, won't you come with me?"

She's trying to steer Xiao Xingchen out with her alone, Wei Wuxian observed. *But what if Xue Yang wants to follow? What to do then?*

"I can, but I cannot help you determine if something looks good on you," Xiao Xingchen said.

Xue Yang interrupted again, "I'll help her."

A-Qing jumped, almost hitting Xiao Xingchen's chin as she did so. "I don't care, I don't care! I want *you* to accompany me! I don't want him to come. He only knows to call me ugly! He calls me 'little blindie'!"

It was hardly the first time she'd thrown a hissy fit. They were used to this by now. Xue Yang made a face at her, and Xiao Xingchen said obligingly, "All right. How about we go tomorrow?"

"I want it tonight!" A-Qing whined.

"Where are you gonna go if you head out at this time of night? The market's closed," Xue Yang said.

A-Qing had no other options. "Fine! Then tomorrow! You promise!"

Her plan hadn't worked, and if she continued to make a fuss

about going out, then Xue Yang would definitely get suspicious again. Forced to relent, A-Qing sat down at the table to eat.

While she'd performed that act just now exactly as she always had—which was to say, incredibly convincingly—her belly was tense the entire time. She was still extremely nervous, and her hand was a little shaky as she held her bowl. Xue Yang was seated to her left. He eyed her askance, and A-Qing's legs tensed again. Too frightened to eat, she conveniently pretended to have lost her appetite from anger. She spat out every mouthful she took, pushing the bowl around hard, mumbling strings of curses under her breath.

"Damn tramp. Rotten bitch. It's not like *you're* that good-looking either. Tramp!"

The other two listened as she cussed out that non-existent "rotten bitch," and Xue Yang rolled his eyes hard while Xiao Xingchen chided her.

"Do not waste food."

And thus, Xue Yang's eyes moved from A-Qing to Xiao Xingchen's face.

It's no wonder the little thug was so accurate in his impersonation of Xiao Xingchen, Wei Wuxian thought. *After all, they sat facing each other every day. Plenty of opportunity to scrutinize him in detail.*

Xiao Xingchen was completely unaware of the eyes on him, however. At the end of the day, the only blind person in this house was him.

Once they'd finished their meal, Xiao Xingchen cleaned away the dishes and utensils and went inside. Growing agitated, A-Qing wanted to slip in after him, but Xue Yang suddenly called out to her.

"A-Qing."

A-Qing's heart jumped into her throat, and Wei Wuxian could feel how her blood ran cold.

"What are you calling me by my name for, all of a sudden?!" she snapped.

"Didn't you say you don't like me calling you 'little blindie'?" Xue Yang asked.

A-Qing humphed. "There's always something fishy about people being nice for no reason! Whaddya want?"

Xue Yang chuckled. "Nothing. I just wanna teach you what to do next time you're insulted."

"Oh yeah? What?" A-Qing said.

"If someone calls you ugly, just make them uglier," Xue Yang explained. "Slash her face a few dozen times with a knife and make her too ashamed to ever leave her house again. She calls you blindie, you sharpen one end of that bamboo pole of yours and put out both her eyes, make her a blindie too. See if she'll talk shit after that!"

A-Qing was disturbed but still managed to pretend she thought he was scaring her on purpose. "You're messing around with me again!"

"Take it as you will." Xue Yang humphed. Then, he pushed a plate of rabbit apple slices toward her. "Here."

Looking at the plate of adorable little bunny apple slices—jade-white, red-skinned, gold-fleshed—wave after wave of deep revulsion seized both A-Qing and Wei Wuxian's hearts.

The next day, A-Qing started whining bright and early for Xiao Xingchen to take her out to buy pretty clothes and cosmetics. Xue Yang was annoyed.

"If you guys head out, doesn't that mean I'm the one going for groceries again?"

"What's wrong with that?" A-Qing snapped at him. "Daozhang's done it so many times already! You're the one playing dirty tricks, cheating and bullying him!"

"Yes, okay, fine. I'll do the run. I'll go right now," Xue Yang relented.

Once he was out the door, Xiao Xingchen asked, "A-Qing, are you not prepared yet? Are you ready to head out?"

A-Qing made sure Xue Yang had gone far enough before she went back inside and closed the door. She posed a question in a trembling voice.

"Daozhang, do you know someone named Xue Yang?"

Xiao Xingchen's smile froze.

The words "Xue Yang" were a heavy blow to him. He never had much color in his complexion, but when he heard that name, what color there was drained away in an instant and his lips turned the color of chalk.

His voice came out in a near whisper, as if he wasn't sure he'd heard correctly. "...Xue Yang?" Then he suddenly snapped to his senses. "A-Qing, how did you come to know this name?"

"That Xue Yang is the one living here with us! He's that bad man!"

Xiao Xingchen was still dazed. "The one with us? ...The one with us..." He shook his head like he was dizzy. "How did you find this out?"

"I heard him kill someone!" A-Qing said.

"He killed? Who?" Xiao Xingchen asked.

"A woman!" A-Qing replied. "Her voice was young, and she probably carried a sword. And this Xue Yang also had a sword hidden on him, because I heard them start fighting and making an awful racket. That woman called him 'Xue Yang' and said he 'slaughtered a temple' and 'committed atrocious crimes.' She said 'everyone has the right to execute you.' My god, that guy is homicidal! Who knows what he's up to, hiding next to us all this time?!"

A-Qing hadn't slept but had instead stayed up fabricating an entire night's worth of lies. First, she must not let daozhang learn that he had mistaken living humans for walking corpses and killed them. Second, he must not learn that he had killed Song Lan with his own two hands. So, as unfair as it was to Song-daozhang, she could never confess the circumstances of his death. The best scenario would be if Xiao Xingchen would just hurry up and flee as soon as he learned Xue Yang's identity—flee as far as he could, as soon as possible!

But her revelation was hard to swallow, and it sounded horribly absurd at first. Xiao Xingchen could hardly believe it so easily. "But the voice was wrong. Besides..."

A-Qing was so anxious that she beat her bamboo pole against the ground incessantly as she spoke. "He faked his voice! Because he doesn't want you to find him out!" Suddenly, it struck her, and she humphed. "Oh, that's right! He has nine fingers! Daozhang, did you know that? Does Xue Yang only have nine fingers? You must've seen him before, right?!"

Xiao Xingchen lost his footing all of a sudden.

A-Qing quickly caught him and slowly helped him to the table, sitting him down. It was a good while before he found his voice.

"But A-Qing, how do you know he only has nine fingers? Have you touched his hand? If he really is Xue Yang, why would he allow you to touch his left hand and discover his defect?"

A-Qing clenched her teeth tightly. "...Daozhang! Let me just tell you the truth! I'm not blind, I can see! I didn't touch his hand, I saw it!"

— PART 5 —

EACH NEW CLAP of thunder was louder than the last. Xiao Xingchen was stunned by all the noise. "What did you say? You can see?!"

A-Qing was scared, but this couldn't remain a secret any longer. She apologized over and over again. "I'm so sorry, daozhang, I wasn't purposely trying to deceive you! I was scared that once you knew I wasn't blind, you wouldn't let me be with you any longer. I was afraid you'd chase me away! But please don't blame me right now. Let's run away together. He'll be back as soon as he's done getting groceries."

Abruptly, she shut her mouth.

The bandage wrapped around Xiao Xingchen's eyes was usually snow-white, but now twin blots of blood were growing on it. The blood spread and spread until it gradually soaked through the fabric and rolled from his empty sockets.

A-Qing screamed. "Daozhang, you're bleeding!!"

It was as if Xiao Xingchen had only just noticed. He let out a soft *ah* and touched his face, his hand coming away soaked in blood. A-Qing helped him wipe his face, her hands shuddering as she did, but the more she wiped, the more blood there was. Xiao Xingchen raised his hand.

"I'm fine... I'm fine..."

In the beginning, his wounded eyes would bleed when he overthought things or grew overly emotional, but the wounds hadn't opened up in a long time. Wei Wuxian had thought they'd healed by now, but here he was, having a relapse and bleeding once more.

"But...but if it really is Xue Yang, why would it be like this?" Xiao Xingchen mumbled. "Why did he not kill me at the very start?

Why did he stay by my side for so many years? How could this be Xue Yang?"

"Of course he wanted to kill you at the start!" A-Qing replied. "I saw those eyes of his, they were mean and scary! But he was wounded and couldn't move. He needed someone to take care of him! I didn't know who he was, but if I did—if I'd known he was some homicidal maniac—I would've stabbed him to death with my bamboo pole while he was lying there in that grass! Daozhang, let's run away, 'kay?!"

Wei Wuxian, however, sighed inwardly. *That's no longer possible. If you hadn't told him, he'd have continued to live together with Xue Yang. But you did tell him, and he'll never run off just like that. He feels compelled to question Xue Yang face-to-face. It's unavoidable.*

Sure enough, once Xiao Xingchen had calmed himself with an effort, he said, "A-Qing, you go on."

His voice was slightly raspy. A-Qing replied, a little scared, "Go? Daozhang, let's leave together!"

Xiao Xingchen shook his head. "I cannot leave. I have to find out what he is thinking. He must have a goal in mind, and it is most likely in pursuit of that goal that he has stayed by my side all these years. If I leave... If he is left alone here, he will slaughter the people of Yi City. That is who Xue Yang has always been."

This time, A-Qing's tears were no longer pretend. She tossed the bamboo pole aside and clung to Xiao Xingchen's leg. "Daozhang, how do I leave on my own?! I wanna go with you. If you're not leaving, I won't either! Let him just kill both of us. I would've died alone and wretched out there by myself anyway. If you don't want things to end like that for me, we have to run away together!"

Unfortunately, with the secret of her not being blind exposed, this trick of playing pitiful was no longer effective. Xiao Xingchen soothed her, "A-Qing, you can see, and you are smart. I believe you can live your life very well. You do not understand how terrifying this Xue Yang is. You cannot stay, and you must never go near him again."

Wei Wuxian heard A-Qing's internal screaming: *I know! I know how terrifying he is!*

But she simply couldn't tell him the entire truth!

Suddenly, there came the sound of spry footfalls. Xue Yang was back!

Xiao Xingchen snapped his head up. As keen and alert as if he were on a Night Hunt, he pulled A-Qing close to whisper to her. "When he comes in, I will handle him. You take that chance and run away. Be good!"

Frightened to tears, A-Qing nodded confusedly. Xue Yang kicked at the door a couple times.

"What're you guys doing? I'm back already, but you're still not gone? If you haven't left yet, undo the latch and let me inside. I'm exhausted."

His words and tone were exactly those of a good boy next door, a sprightly little martial brother! No one could ever have guessed that an inhuman monster stood outside the door. A crazed fiend, a demon wearing a handsome human skin, walking and talking like a man!

The door wasn't locked, but it was barred from the inside. If they didn't open the door soon, Xue Yang would surely become suspicious—and when he entered he would be on guard.

A-Qing wiped her face and yelled, "Exhausted, my ass! It's how far to go and get groceries, and you're already tired?! Your big sis got caught up changing into a couple of outfits, what's it to you?!"

Xue Yang's reply was full of scorn. "And how many sets of clothes do you own? They're all the same, no matter what you change into. Open up."

Even though A-Qing's legs shook uncontrollably, she still sounded vigorous and confident. "Bah! Well, I *won't* open it for you. Kick the door open yourself if you're so amazing!"

Xue Yang laughed aloud. "You're the one who said it. Daozhang, don't blame me if you've got to repair the door later."

True to his word, he kicked the wooden door open with a single punt. He crossed the tall threshold and entered, one hand holding the basket full of vegetables, the other a vibrantly red apple. He had just taken a crisp bite out of it when he looked down and saw Shuanghua's blade, burrowed into his belly.

The grocery basket fell to the ground. The green vegetables, the radish, the apples, the buns, all rolled across the floor.

Xiao Xingchen barked in a low voice, "A-Qing, run!"

A-Qing bolted, charging out the front door. She ran madly for a bit, then changed course and turned back, furtively circling back to the mortuary. She crawled to the hidden spot she was most familiar with, where she often went to eavesdrop. This time, she even poked her head out a bit to peer inside the house.

Xiao Xingchen asked coldly, "Did this amuse you?"

Xue Yang took a bite of the apple still in his hand and chewed unhurriedly before swallowing. "It did. Why wouldn't it?"

He had returned to using his normal voice.

"What exactly were you planning, staying by me all these years?" Xiao Xingchen questioned.

"Who knows," Xue Yang said. "Maybe I was just bored."

Xiao Xingchen withdrew Shuanghua, about to attack again.

"Xiao Xingchen-daozhang, that story I never finished..." Xue Yang continued, "...you probably don't want to hear the rest of it anymore, right?"

"No." But despite this harsh rejection, Xiao Xingchen still tilted his head slightly, his sword pausing.

"Well, I'm gonna tell you anyway," Xue Yang said. "If you still think I'm at fault once I'm done, you can do whatever you want."

He casually rubbed the wound on his belly, putting pressure on it to stop himself from bleeding out. "When the child saw the man who had cajoled him into delivering that message, he felt both aggrieved and happy. He flung himself at him, overflowing with tears, and told him: the message was delivered, but the dessert is gone, and I got beaten too. Can you give me another plate?

"But the man's face was bruised too—the burly man must have found and beaten him as well. When he saw this dirty little kid clinging to his leg, he was sorely irritated and kicked him away.

"He mounted an oxcart, telling the driver to go, now.

"The child crawled up off the ground and chased and chased the cart. He wanted so badly to eat that plate of sweet desserts. When he finally caught up, he waved in front of the cart, wanting them to stop. The man was annoyed by all the crying, so he snatched the whip from the driver's hand and lashed the boy's head, whipping him to the ground."

Xue Yang then emphasized each word: "And then, one by one, the cart's wheels rolled over each finger on that child's hand!"

Not caring whether or not Xiao Xingchen could see it, he raised his own left hand.

"Seven years old! The bones of his left hand were completely shattered, and one finger was crushed to mush on the spot! That man was Chang Ping's father.

"Xiao Xingchen-daozhang, how righteous and stern you were when you dragged me to Golden Carp Tower! You condemned me, demanding that I explain why I'd massacre an entire clan over a little grudge. Is it because that finger wasn't yours that none of you could understand the pain?! You don't know what it's like to hear screams of such excruciating agony from your own mouth! Why did I kill his entire family? Why don't you ask him why *he* played *me*, toyed with me for no good reason! The Xue Yang of today has Chang Ci'an to thank for his existence! The Chang Clan of Yueyang was simply reaping what they sowed!"

Xiao Xingchen was in utter disbelief. "When Chang Ci'an broke your finger—if you wanted revenge, why not also break one of his fingers? If you genuinely could not let go of this grudge, then break two of his fingers. Ten fingers! Even an entire arm would have been fine! Why did you have to kill his entire family? Did a single finger of yours need to be compensated by over fifty lives?"

Xue Yang actually considered this seriously. "Of course," he replied, as if it was an odd question. "The finger was mine, but those lives belonged to others. No number of lives would've been enough. It was only fifty or so people—how could that be enough to pay for my finger?"

Xiao Xingchen's face was growing increasingly pale. Furious at Xue Yang's matter-of-fact tone, he shouted, "Then what about bystanders?! Why did you massacre Baixue Temple? Why did you have to blind Song Zichen-daozhang?!"

Xue Yang argued back, "And why did you stop me? Why did you keep butting in my business? Why did you stand up and help those Chang nobodies? Were you helping Chang Ci'an? Or was it Chang Ping? Ha ha ha ha, remember how Chang Ping cried tears of gratitude at first? And how he *begged* you to stop helping him, later?

"Xiao Xingchen-daozhang, you were in the wrong from the very start. You shouldn't have gotten involved in other people's quarrels.

Who was right, who was wrong, was there more gratitude or more grievance—is that something an outsider can determine? Maybe you shouldn't have descended that mountain in the first place. Your master Baoshan-sanren was real smart, wasn't she? Why didn't you listen to her and stay on your mountain to cultivate your path? If you don't get how this world works, then don't enter it!"

Unable to endure this any longer, Xiao Xingchen gritted out a response with effort. "...Xue Yang, you really are...repulsive."

At those words, the murderous glint that had been absent from Xue Yang's eyes for so long flashed anew.

He chuckled darkly. "Xiao Xingchen, this is why I hate you. What I hate, hate, *hate* the most is self-righteous people like you. So morally superior, thinking you can just do a few good deeds and the world will suddenly transform into a better place. You utter fool! You naive, idiotic dumbass! You're repulsed by me? Fine, then. Do you think I'm afraid of repulsing people? But...do you even have the *right* to be repulsed by me?"

Xiao Xingchen was taken aback. "What do you mean?"

Both A-Qing and Wei Wuxian's hearts were ready to jump out of their chests.

Xue Yang said sweetly, "We haven't gone out to kill walking corpses recently, have we? But a couple years ago, didn't we kill whole groups of them pretty regularly?"

Xiao Xingchen's lips moved uneasily. "Why are you bringing that up now?"

"No reason," Xue Yang said. "It's just too bad you're blind. Since you plucked out those eyeballs of yours, you couldn't see those 'walking corpses' back then. Oh, how scared, how in pain they were when you stabbed them with your sword. There were even those who knelt and wept, kowtowing and begging for you to spare their families. If I hadn't cut out their tongues beforehand, they would've been wailing, crying 'Daozhang, have mercy.'"

Xiao Xingchen's whole body began to shake.

It was a good moment before he said, arduously, "You are lying to me. You want to deceive me."

"Yeah, I'm lying to you, I've always been lying to you," Xue Yang said. "Who woulda thought—you bought every single lie, but now that I'm telling the truth it's a no-sell?"

Xiao Xingchen took a staggering lunge at him, yelling, "Shut up! Shut up!"

Covering his belly with his right hand, Xue Yang snapped the fingers of his left as he backed away leisurely. The expression on his face could not be called human anymore. There was a mad glint in his eyes, and when he smiled and bared those tiny canine teeth, it made him look like a devil manifested in flesh.

"*Sure*, I'll shut up!" he shouted. "If you won't believe me, then trade a few moves with the one behind you and have *him* tell you whether or not I'm lying to you!"

A gust from a swung sword whipped close by Xiao Xingchen, who reflexively blocked with Shuanghua. But when the two swords clashed, he was stupefied.

Not just stupefied—he seemed to have hardened into a haggard statue.

Carefully, so very carefully, Xiao Xingchen ventured aloud, "...Is that you, Zichen?"

There was no answer.

Song Lan's corpse stood there behind him. He appeared to be staring at Xiao Xingchen, and yet his eyes had no pupils. The longsword in his hand was the one that had clashed with Shuanghua.

The two had studied swordplay side by side in the past. They had crossed blades many a time for such purposes and could recognize each other by the feel of the strike alone. Yet Xiao Xingchen still seemed unsure. Shuddering, he slowly turned around and reached out to feel the blade of Song Lan's sword.

Song Lan didn't move. Xiao Xingchen moved his hands upward along the blade until finally, bit by bit, he traced out the two characters carved on the hilt: *Fuxue*.

His face was growing paler by the minute.

He felt the blade of Fuxue, so overwhelmed he didn't seem to realize when it cut his palm. He was shaking so hard even his words seemed to have scattered all over the ground.

"...Zichen... Song-daozhang... Song-daozhang... Is that you...?"

Song Lan watched him quietly, without a single word.

The bandage around Xiao Xingchen's eyes, soaked by the incessant stream of blood, was marked by two horrifying red, sunken holes. He wanted to reach out to touch the sword-wielding man himself but didn't dare to; he extended his hand, then withdrew it. Waves of excruciating pain roiled in A-Qing's chest, so intense that both she and Wei Wuxian had trouble breathing. Their tears flowed like a spring.

Xiao Xingchen stood there, confused and helpless. "...What is the matter... Say something..." He was utterly crushed. "Somebody, say something?!"

As he wished, Xue Yang spoke. "Do I need to bother telling you who the walking corpse you killed yesterday was?"

Clang!

Shuanghua dropped to the ground.

Xue Yang burst out in uproarious laughter.

Xiao Xingchen knelt woodenly before the standing Song Lan. He burst into wailing tears of agony and clutched his head.

Xue Yang was laughing so hard his eyes watered. "What's wrong?!" he bit out fiercely. "Has this reunion of two good friends moved you to tears?! Are you gonna give him a big hug?! Huh?!"

A-Qing covered her mouth firmly, not allowing a single sob to slip free. Inside the charitable mortuary, Xue Yang paced back and forth, spitting insults in a frightening tone filled with both crazed fury and wild joy.

"Save the world! What a joke, you can't even save yourself!"

A fresh wave of acute pain filled Wei Wuxian's mind. However, this pain didn't come from A-Qing's soul.

Xiao Xingchen knelt there on the ground, unkempt, prostrated at Song Lan's feet. He curled into a ball, seeming very, very small and fragile, as if he wished desperately to disappear from this world. The Daoist robe that was once flawlessly clean and white was now stained with blood and grime.

"You've accomplished nothing!" Xue Yang screamed at him. "Failed utterly! You only have yourself to blame! You reap what you sow!"

In that moment, Wei Wuxian saw himself in Xiao Xingchen.

The him who suffered a crushing defeat while drenched in blood. The him who accomplished nothing, was criticized by all, furiously rebuked by all, and left powerless to fix his desperate circumstances. The him who could do nothing but wail!

The white bandage was thoroughly dyed red. Xiao Xingchen's face was covered in blood. Without eyes, the only tears he could shed were crimson. He'd been deceived for years, taken a foe for a good friend, had his kindness crushed underfoot. When he thought he was exorcising evil, his hands were instead stained with the blood of innocents—and with those same two hands, he had killed his own dear friend!

He moaned in agony. "Please have mercy."

"Weren't you about to stab me dead with your sword? And now you're suddenly turning around and begging for mercy?" Xue Yang taunted.

He clearly knew that, with the protection of Song Lan's fierce corpse, it was impossible for Xiao Xingchen to take up the sword once more.

He had won again. A complete victory.

Suddenly, Xiao Xingchen snatched up Shuanghua, which had been lying on the ground. He turned the sword and placed the blade against his own neck. A clear and clean silver gleam slashed across Xue Yang's deep and dayless black eyes. Xiao Xingchen's grip loosened, and deep crimson blood rolled down Shuanghua's blade.

At the crisp clatter of the longsword hitting the ground, Xue Yang's laughter and movement came to an abrupt halt.

He was silent for a moment. Then he approached Xiao Xingchen's unmoving dead body. He looked down. The twisted curve of his lips slowly drooped, and blood crawled into his eyes. Maybe Wei Wuxian was mistaken, but the rims of his eyes seemed to have reddened.

He then furiously gritted his teeth. "*You're* the one who forced my hand!!"

Then he sneered and muttered to himself, "It's better that you're dead! More obedient when you're dead."

Xue Yang felt for Xiao Xingchen's breath and pinched at his wrist for a pulse. As if he thought Xiao Xingchen wasn't dead enough, the body not stiff enough, he stood up, went into the overnight chamber and came out carrying a basin of water. Using a clean cloth, he washed Xiao Xingchen's face clean of blood and even attentively wrapped a brand-new bandage around his eyes.

He drew an array on the ground, set up the necessary materials, then carried Xiao Xingchen's body in and arranged it properly. Only after doing all that did he remember to dress his own stomach wound.

Probably convinced the two of them would meet again shortly, his mood became jollier by the minute. He picked up all the vegetables and fruits that had been strewn across the ground and neatly placed them back into the basket. He cleaned the house in a sudden bout of diligence and even laid down a new layer of thick straw in the coffin where A-Qing usually slept. Once he'd finished, he took out the candy Xiao Xingchen had given him the night before from his sleeve.

Just when he was about to pop it into his mouth, however, he stopped himself and thought for a moment. Xue Yang put the candy away. He sat by the table, a hand propping up his cheek, and waited in sullen boredom for Xiao Xingchen to sit up.

But Xiao Xingchen never did.

The sky grew increasingly dark, as did Xue Yang's dimming expression. His fingers tapped impatiently on the table.

When dusk had fallen completely, he kicked the table, cursed, and swept back the hem of his robe as he stood up. He half-knelt by Xiao Xingchen's corpse to inspect the array and the symbols he had drawn. He checked them repeatedly, but there didn't appear to be anything wrong. His brows furrowed as he pondered, but in the end, he still wiped it all away and redrew it.

This time, Xue Yang sat directly on the ground and stared at Xiao Xingchen with great patience. Another period of waiting followed. A-Qing's feet had already fallen asleep three times and were painful and itchy, like millions of ants were nibbling on them. Her eyes were also swollen from crying, and her sight was a little blurry.

They waited for another two hours before Xue Yang finally realized things had gotten out of control.

He placed his hand over Xiao Xingchen's forehead, then closed his eyes to search. A moment after, his eyes snapped open. Wei Wuxian knew what he'd likely found was the few, feeble fragments that remained of a broken soul.

And a soul this broken could not be used to forge a fierce corpse.

It seemed Xue Yang had never foreseen such an accident. For the very first time, that forever-smiling face was blank.

Without thinking, he used his hands to cover the gash on Xiao Xingchen's neck. However, the blood had already run dry. Xiao Xingchen's face was as white as a sheet, and large blotches of darkened blood were dried around his nape. It was completely pointless to compress the wound now.

Xiao Xingchen was already dead. Thoroughly and utterly.

Even his soul was shattered.

The disparity between the Xue Yang of the present and the Xue Yang in his story, who bawled when he didn't get to eat dessert, made it very hard to connect the two. But in that moment, Wei Wuxian finally saw the shadow of that confused child.

In the blink of an eye, Xue Yang's eyes were bloodshot, and he abruptly rose to his feet, his hands clenched tightly into fists. He thrashed about inside the charitable mortuary, breaking and throwing things, creating a huge racket as he wrecked the house he had just tidied up earlier himself.

His expression and the sounds he made were more maniacal than all of his previous abominable behavior combined.

After smashing up the house, he calmed down once more and crouched back in the same spot.

He called out in a whisper, "Xiao Xingchen. If you don't get up, I'm gonna make your good friend Song Lan go kill people.

"I'll kill every single person in Yi City and make them all into living corpses. You've lived here for so long. Is it really okay for you to not care?

"I'll strangle that little blindie A-Qing to death. I'll leave her body outside and have wild dogs tear her corpse to shreds."

A-Qing shuddered violently without a sound.

No one answered.

Xue Yang suddenly shouted, enraged, *"Xiao Xingchen!"*

He grabbed the collar of Xiao Xingchen's Daoist robe and shook, glaring at the dead man's face.

Suddenly, he pulled at his arms and hauled him up.

Carrying the corpse on his back, Xue Yang walked out the door, mumbling under his breath like an insane man. "A spirit-trapping pouch, a spirit-trapping pouch, that's right, a spirit-trapping pouch, I need a spirit-trapping pouch, a spirit-trapping pouch, a spirit-trapping pouch..."

He'd been gone quite a while before A-Qing dared to move.

She couldn't stand upright and wound up rolling to the ground, where she squirmed for a while before crawling back to her feet. She took a few arduous steps, shaking out her bones and muscles, then walked faster and faster, faster and faster, until she finally broke into a run.

She ran for a long time, leaving Yi City far, far behind her, before she dared release the wail stifled in her chest.

"Daozhang! Daozhang!" she sobbed. "Daozhang...!"

The scene changed. Suddenly, they were in a different place.

By now, A-Qing seemed to have been on the run for a while. She walked in a strange city, pretending to be blind with her bamboo pole in her hand, and she asked whoever she encountered:

"Excuse me, are there any major clans in this area?"

"Excuse me, are there any really strong masters in this area? Cultivation masters, I mean."

She's searching for someone who can avenge Xiao Xingchen, Wei Wuxian observed.

Unfortunately, no one took her inquiries seriously. Most simply walked off after a few placating words. However, A-Qing wasn't discouraged. She tirelessly asked one person after the other and continued to be waved off and chased away. Seeing her search was bearing no fruit here, she left and walked down a small path.

She'd been walking and asking around for the entire day, leaving her exhausted beyond measure. Dragging her heavy feet, she came to a small stream. She cupped her hands and drank a few swallows of stream water, moistening her throat, which was so raw it burned.

The reflection of the wooden hairpin in her hair caught her attention, and she reached up and removed it.

The wooden pin was originally crudely made, like an uneven chopstick full of bumps and holes. Xiao Xingchen had helped her smooth it out and even carved a little fox at the end of it. The little fox had a very pointy face with a pair of large eyes, and it was smiling. When A-Qing first received the hairpin, she felt it and exclaimed in delight:

"Ah! It looks like me!"

Staring at this pin, A-Qing pursed her lips, wanting to cry. Her stomach grumbled, and she fished a small white money pouch from her robes—the same one she'd swiped from Xiao Xingchen, so long ago now. She dug a tiny piece of candy from the money pouch and carefully licked it. When the tip of her tongue sensed sweetness, she tucked the candy back into the pouch.

That was the last candy Xiao Xingchen had left her.

A-Qing had her head down as she put away the money pouch.

With a passing glance, she suddenly noticed another shadow beside her reflection in the water.

In that reflection, Xue Yang was looking at her, smiling.

A-Qing let out a shriek of fright and scrambled along the ground as she dodged away.

Somehow, Xue Yang was already standing behind her. With Shuanghua in his hand, he opened his arms to gesture for a hug and said happily, "A-Qing, what are you running for? We haven't seen each other for ages, don't you miss me?"

A-Qing screamed, *"Help!"*

However, this wild, mountainous little path was very remote. There was no one around to save her.

Xue Yang arched his brows. "I was on my way back from finishing up some business in Yueyang when, amazingly, I ran into you in the city while you were asking this and that. What unstoppable destiny, don'tcha think? Speaking of which, what an excellent faker you are. I can't believe I was deceived for so long. Amazing."

A-Qing knew she couldn't escape. This was certain death. After the initial surge of terror, a feeling of calm washed over her. Having determined she was going to die anyway, she might as well curse him to her heart's content. All her shrewish energy surged forth again, and she hopped up and spat.

"You animal! *Traitor!* Bitch worse than a dog!! Yer ma and pa must've screwed in a pig's pen to have conceived a mutt like you!! *Shit-eating rotten dick!!*"

Having roamed the streets for so many years, she'd heard plenty of obscene abuse. Now, she spewed nothing but profanity at Xue Yang, who listened with a wide grin.

"You're so good at this. How come I never heard you be so feral in front of Xiao Xingchen? Got any more?"

"Screw you, you shameless bastard!" A-Qing cussed further. "You dare mention daozhang?! That's daozhang's sword! You think you're worthy of it?! You're dirtying his things!"

Xue Yang raised Shuanghua in his left hand. "Oh? You mean this? It's mine now. How pure did you think your daozhang was? Well, it's mine from now on, in any case..."

"Yours, my ass!" A-Qing snapped. "Dream on, why don't you?! Where do you get the right to say whether daozhang was pure or not?! You're nothing but snot! Daozhang must've had eight lifetimes of bad luck to have the misfortune to be tainted by you! The only dirty one is you! You! Repulsive snot!"

Xue Yang's face finally dimmed.

A-Qing had been on edge for so long, always on the run. Now that this dreaded moment had finally arrived, her heart was strangely light.

Xue Yang sneered darkly. "Since you enjoy pretending to be blind so much, why don't I help you make it a reality?"

He swept his hand up and a strange powder assaulted A-Qing's face, blasting into her eyes. Her vision was nothing but blood red all of a sudden, before everything turned black. Stabbing pain overwhelmed her eyeballs, and A-Qing gave a blood-curdling scream.

Xue Yang's voice came again. "Such a long tongue in that big mouth of yours. I don't think you'll be needing it either."

A sharp and bone-bitingly cold object burrowed into A-Qing's mouth. Just as Wei Wuxian felt the pain at the end of his tongue, he was forcefully pulled back.

The crisp jingle of the silver bell was only inches away. Wei Wuxian was still submerged in A-Qing's emotions, unable to snap out of it for the longest time. His surroundings seemed to spin around him.

Lan Jingyi waved in front of him. "No reaction? He didn't go stupid, did he?!"

Jin Ling retorted, "I told you all Empathy was super dangerous!"

"Wasn't it *you* who didn't ring the bell in time? What was going on in your head?!" Lan Jingyi countered.

Jin Ling's face froze. "I..."

Thankfully, Wei Wuxian finally got a hold of himself. He stood, supporting himself on the coffin as he did. A-Qing had already broken away from his body and was also leaning over the side of the coffin. The boys scurried around him like a litter of piglets, squishing together and talking all at once.

"He's up, he's up!"

"Thank goodness, he didn't go stupid."

"Wasn't he already stupid?"

"Don't talk nonsense!"

The chirping by his ears was incessant. Wei Wuxian waved them off. "Quiet, I'm so dizzy."

They quickly quieted. Wei Wuxian looked down and reached into the coffin, peeling aside the clean and tidy collar of Xiao Xingchen's Daoist robe. Just as he expected, at his throat was a thin yet fatal wound.

Wei Wuxian sighed. He turned to A-Qing. "You've worked hard."

The reason A-Qing was a blind ghost but didn't move slowly or carefully like someone who had been blind in life was because she'd only been truly blinded right before her death. Before that, she'd always been agile and energetic, a young girl who moved like the wind.

In the years since, she had hidden alone in Yi City, which was choked with evil miasma, skulking about and setting herself against Xue Yang. She scared away the living who entered the city, giving them warnings and herding them out. How great her courage and dedication must be!

A-Qing was leaning over the side of the coffin. She put her hands together in a praying motion, as if begging for something. Then taking her bamboo pole for a sword, she swung it in a "kill, kill, kill" motion, just like she used to do when playing around.

"Don't worry," Wei Wuxian assured her. He turned to the clan juniors. "You guys stay here. The walking corpses in the city won't enter this charitable mortuary. I'll be right back."

Lan Jingyi couldn't help but ask, "What exactly did you see during Empathy?"

"The story's too long; I'll give a full report in the future," Wei Wuxian said.

"You can't shorten it? Don't keep us in suspense!" Jin Ling yelled.

"I could." And Wei Wuxian did exactly that with his next words: "Xue Yang must die."

Amidst the confounding evil miasma that filled the air, the *ka-ka* of A-Qing's bamboo pole led the way. One man and one ghost moved swiftly, speedily arriving at where the fight still raged.

Lan Wangji and Xue Yang's battle had already moved outside. Bichen and Jiangzai's sword glares clashed with each other—he'd clearly arrived at the battle's critical moment. Bichen, calm and collected, had steadily gained the upper hand. Jiangzai, wild as a mad dog, was barely keeping up. However, the dreadful white fog kept Lan Wangji from seeing clearly, while Xue Yang had lived in Yi City for many years. Like A-Qing, he knew the roads like the back of his hand. This was the cause of their stalemate.

Every so often, the guqin's angry cries cut through the clouds to expel the hordes of walking corpses that relentlessly circled them. Wei Wuxian had only just pulled out his flute when two streaks of black crashed heavily in front of him like iron pagodas.

Wen Ning had Song Lan pinned to the ground. The two fierce corpses were strangling each other, their knuckles cracking.

"Hold him down!" Wei Wuxian commanded.

He stooped and swiftly found the ends of the skull-piercing nails in Song Lan's head. He relaxed. *These nails are much thinner than the ones in Wen Ning, and the material's different too. It shouldn't be hard for Song Lan to return to himself.*

He immediately pinched the pointed ends and pulled slowly. Feeling the strange objects in his brain twist, Song Lan's eyes snapped open, and he hissed and snarled low. Wen Ning had to increase the strength of his grip to prevent him from struggling free. When the skull-piercing nails were pulled out, Song Lan instantly slumped to the ground, like a puppet whose strings were cut, and stopped moving.

Just then, there was a rage-maddened roar from the scene of combat.

"*Give it back!*"

Lan Wangji's sword had slashed across Xue Yang's chest. Bichen's tip didn't only spill blood, it also plucked free the spirit-trapping pouch hidden in his robes.

Wei Wuxian, unable to clearly see what was happening, yelled in response, "Xue Yang! What do you want him to give back? Shuanghua? It's not like Shuanghua is your sword, so where do you get off saying 'give it back?' Are you that shameless?"

Xue Yang burst out laughing. "Well, Wei-qianbei, aren't you insensitive!"

"Go ahead and laugh. You can laugh yourself to death, and you still won't be able to piece Xiao Xingchen's soul back together. He finds you repulsive, and yet you still had to try and drag him back to play with you."

Xue Yang went from laughing uproariously one second to yelling hatefully the next. "Who wants to play games with him?!"

"Then why did you kneel so pitifully before me, begging me to restore his soul?"

Xue Yang was very astute. He had to be able to see that Wei Wuxian was trying to disrupt him on purpose, first by angering him to distraction and then by making him yell, so Lan Wangji could determine his position and attack. And yet, he couldn't help himself from answering again and again.

"Why? Humph! Like you don't know?!" he spat furiously. "I'm gonna turn him into a fierce corpse, an evil spirit for me to command! He wants to be some kind of moral, virtuous cultivator, doesn't he? I'll make him kill nonstop without a day of peace!"

"Huh?" Wei Wuxian commented. "You hate him that much? Then why did you go and kill Chang Ping?"

Xue Yang laughed derisively. "Why did I kill Chang Ping? Do you even need to ask, Yiling Patriarch?! Didn't I tell you? If I said I was going to kill the entire Chang Clan of Yueyang, then I wouldn't even spare the dog!"

Every time he ran his mouth, he announced his own location. The sound of a blade piercing flesh echoed through the air again and again. Xue Yang must have been near-impervious to pain. Wei Wuxian had already witnessed this during his session of Empathy: the youth could be stabbed through the belly and still joke around like nothing had happened.

"That certainly is a nice excuse, but the timing doesn't line up," Wei Wuxian continued to needle him. "Someone like you—who would take a thousand eyes in exchange for a single lost eye, who works with such viciousness and efficiency—why put it off for so many years if you genuinely meant to kill the whole family?

You know full well for whose sake you really went to kill Chang Ping for."

"Why don't you tell me, then?" Xue Yang spat. "What do I know full well, huh? *What do I know?!*"

The last part was screamed aloud.

"If you just wanted to kill him, why did you use lingchi?" Wei Wuxian pressed him. "It's a form of torture meant to punish sinners. If you were avenging yourself, why did you use Shuanghua rather than Jiangzai? Why did you have to pluck out Chang Ping's eyes, just like Xiao Xingchen?"

Xue Yang screamed his response for all he was worth. "*Bullshit!* That's all *bullshit*! What, should I have let him die an easy death when I wanted revenge?!"

"Well, I agree that it was vengeance," Wei Wuxian assured him. "But who, exactly, were you avenging? What a joke. If you really wanted vengeance, the one to suffer the thousand cuts of lingchi should've been your own damn self!"

Two sharp whizzing sounds snapped through the air, shooting toward him. Wei Wuxian didn't move an inch, but Wen Ning darted in front of him and intercepted the two gleaming, vicious black skull-piercing nails. Xue Yang let out the hooting laugh of a mad owl and then stopped abruptly. He fell silent, no longer responding, and continued to fight Lan Wangji in the dense fog.

This little thug's life force is too strong. It's like he can't feel pain at all, no matter where you hurt him, Wei Wuxian thought. *If he'd just keep yapping, Lan Zhan could stab him some more. I refuse to believe he could still jump around with his limbs cut off. Too bad he's not taking the bait anymore!*

Just then, a series of clear, crisp taps—*ka-ka*—came from within the fog.

It quickly clicked in his head. Wei Wuxian ordered, "Lan Zhan! Stab where that bamboo pole is tapping!"

Lan Wangji immediately attacked. Xue Yang grunted. A moment later, the bamboo pole sounded again from a different place, dozens of meters away!

Lan Wangji continued to strike wherever the sound directed him. Xue Yang threatened in a dark tone, "Little blindie, trailing so close behind me. Aren't you scared I'll crush you between my fingers?"

A-Qing had been constantly on the move in Yi City ever since she was murdered by Xue Yang, hiding so he wouldn't find her. For some reason, Xue Yang seemed to ignore her wandering ghost, perhaps thinking her too insignificant to be of concern. But A-Qing was now following him like a shadow within the thick fog, beating her bamboo pole against the ground to expose his position and guide Lan Wangji's attacks!

Xue Yang was extremely fast, able to disappear from one place and reappear almost instantly in another. However, A-Qing was quick as well—even quicker as a ghost than she'd been when alive. She stalked him like a curse, hot on his heels, wildly beating the ground nonstop with the bamboo pole in her hand. The sound of that *ka-ka, da-da* was suddenly far, suddenly close, suddenly left, suddenly right, suddenly in front, suddenly behind. Xue Yang couldn't shake her off. And as soon as the sound rang out, the glare of Bichen was sure to follow!

Xue Yang had been like a fish in water in this fog at first, able to hide and lay ambush. But now, he had to split his focus to deal with A-Qing as well. He cursed under his breath and whipped a talisman behind him—but in that split second of distraction, guided now by the sound of A-Qing's horrible scream, Bichen pierced through his chest!

A-Qing's ghost had been shattered by Xue Yang's talisman. She could no longer expose his location with the tapping of her bamboo pole, but Bichen had finally delivered a fatal blow. Xue Yang was no longer able to move as stealthily as before, no longer so difficult to catch!

From within the fog there came thick, bloodied coughing noises. Wei Wuxian threw out an empty spirit-trapping pouch to salvage A-Qing's damaged soul. Dragging his feet with great effort, Xue Yang took a few steps before he suddenly lunged forward, screaming with hands extended.

"Give it to me!"

Bichen's blue light flashed. Lan Wangji had cleanly chopped off one of Xue Yang's arms.

Blood gushed forth. Ahead of Wei Wuxian, a large area of the hazy white mist was suddenly dyed crimson. The stench of blood was overwhelming, a humid, rusty smell that dominated the senses, but Wei Wuxian had no time to care. He was busy concentrating on locating and squirreling away the pieces of A-Qing's shattered soul.

Although Xue Yang still did not moan in pain, there came the sound of knees heavily hitting the ground. Having finally lost too much blood, he collapsed, unable to walk a step further.

Lan Wangji readied Bichen once more, its next attack poised to send Xue Yang's head rolling. Unexpectedly, a burst of blue flames erupted suddenly from within the white miasma.

The spell fire of a transportation talisman!

Wei Wuxian knew disaster was imminent. He charged over, having no time to worry about the perils within the fog. In his rush, he nearly slipped; where the stench of blood was thickest, there were rivers of it all over the ground, all spewed from Xue Yang's severed arm.

But Xue Yang himself had vanished.

Lan Wangji walked over, and Wei Wuxian asked, "The gravedigger?"

Xue Yang had suffered a fatal blow from Bichen *and* lost an arm. Judging by the amount of blood, he was undoubtedly dead. He couldn't possibly have had enough energy or spiritual power left to use a transportation talisman. Lan Wangji inclined his head.

"I struck three times at the gravedigger. His capture was imminent. A sudden assault from a large crowd of walking corpses aided him in his escape."

Wei Wuxian's brows furrowed as he thought aloud. "So he was already hurt but didn't hesitate to spend an immense amount of spiritual power just to take Xue Yang's corpse with him. Which means he probably knew Xue Yang and his history. Taking the body...he was hoping he had the Yin Tiger Tally on him."

Rumor had it that the Yin Tiger Tally was lost after Xue Yang was "taken care of" by Jin Guangyao. But, judging by the looks of things, the tiger tally was likely on his person. Yi City had become a hive filled with millions of living corpses, walking corpses, and even fierce corpses. Corpse toxin and skull-piercing nails would hardly help control so many of them. Only the presence of the Yin Tiger Tally explained how Xue Yang could command such absolute obedience from the corpses, ordering them to advance and attack in wave after wave.

Someone as paranoid and cunning as Xue Yang would never let the Yin Tiger Tally out of his sight. He would only ever keep it on him, where being able to feel it every waking moment would give him a sense of security. By taking his corpse, the gravedigger had as good as taken the Yin Tiger Tally itself.

This was no trivial matter. Wei Wuxian said gravely, "With things as they are, we can only hope there's a limit to what the restored Yin Tiger Tally can do."

Right then, Lan Wangji lightly tossed something at him.

Wei Wuxian caught it easily. "What is it?"

"The right arm," Lan Wangji replied.

What he had tossed over was a brand-new evil-sealing qiankun pouch. Only then did Wei Wuxian remember their original objective for coming to Yi City. He brightened.

"Our good buddy's right arm?"

"Mn," Lan Wangji replied.

That Lan Wangji had actually had time to successfully find the right ghost arm while surmounting innumerable hurdles—the gravedigger, the walking corpses, the evil miasma—really, Wei Wuxian had to hand it to the guy.

"As expected of Hanguang-jun!" he praised vigorously. "We're ahead in the game again. It's too bad it's not the head. I really wanna get a look at our good buddy's face, y'know. But we'll get there soon enough… Where's Song Lan?"

Once Xue Yang's body disappeared, the white fog swirled faster and began to thin out. Visibility was improving, which was precisely how Wei Wuxian had suddenly realized Song Lan had disappeared. Only Wen Ning now crouched in the spot where he had lain, gazing in Wei Wuxian's direction as if in a stupor.

Lan Wangji placed his hand on the hilt of Bichen, which had only just been sheathed. Wei Wuxian assured him, "It's fine, no need to be alarmed. Song Lan was the fierce corpse from before. He should have no intent to attack anymore, or Wen Ning would've given warning. It's likely his mind returned to him, and he left on his own."

Wei Wuxian blew a soft whistle. Wen Ning stood up at the sound and retreated, head bowed, his figure disappearing into the white mist. As the sound of dragging chains gradually faded, Lan Wangji made no comment aside from a calm, "Let us go."

Just as they were about to go, Wei Wuxian suddenly said, "Hold on."

In the pool of blood, he spotted a lonesome object.

It was Xue Yang's severed left arm. The hand was missing a pinky, and the four remaining fingers were tightly balled into a fist.

They were clenched hard; Wei Wuxian, crouching down, had to pull with all his strength before each finger peeled back. In the now-opened hand, he found a tiny piece of candy sitting in the palm.

The candy was slightly blackened, certainly no longer edible. It was a little crushed from the force of that grip.

Wei Wuxian and Lan Wangji returned to the charitable mortuary together. The doors were wide open. Sure enough, Song Lan stood beside the coffin where Xiao Xingchen lay. His head hung low as he gazed into it.

The clan juniors, their swords brandished, were all squished together and bunched to one side, staring in alarm at this fierce corpse who had attacked them earlier. At the sight of Wei Wuxian and Lan Wangji's return, they looked as if their lives had been spared—but still didn't dare to yell, terrified they might rouse Song Lan from his stupor or provoke his ire.

Wei Wuxian crossed the threshold and gave Lan Wangji an introduction. "Song Lan, Song Zichen-daozhang."

Still standing vigil beside the coffin, Song Lan looked up and turned his gaze their way. Lan Wangji lifted his robe lightly to elegantly step over the high threshold and inclined his head in greeting.

Song Lan's mind had returned, and his pupils had rolled back into place. The eyes that gazed at them were clear and black.

And those eyes, once Xiao Xingchen's own, were full of indescribable sorrow.

There was no need for further questioning. Wei Wuxian had his answers. Song Lan had seen everything during the period he was under Xue Yang's control as a fierce corpse, and he remembered it all. To ask more questions, to even say anything else, would do nothing but add to his helplessness and pain.

After a moment of silence, Wei Wuxian took out two small, identical spirit-trapping pouches and passed them over. "Xiao Xingchen-daozhang and Miss A-Qing, respectively."

Although A-Qing was terrified of Xue Yang, she still trailed after the murderer who had killed her with his own two hands. She was the one who kept him from hiding and guided Bichen's blade to make sure he finally reaped what he'd sowed. The assault of Xue Yang's vicious talisman had almost dissipated her soul. Wei Wuxian had put the utmost effort into salvaging what pieces he could, but it was fragmented and scattered now, much like Xiao Xingchen's.

The two feeble souls were curled up in the twin spirit-trapping pouches, so fragile it almost seemed like the slightest bump would make them disperse inside their bags. Song Lan's hands shook slightly as he received them. He cradled them in his palms, not even daring to dangle them by the drawstrings for fear the swaying would damage them.

"Song-daozhang, what do you plan to do with Xiao Xingchen-daozhang's body?" Wei Wuxian asked.

One hand carefully holding the two spirit-trapping pouches, Song Lan pulled out Fuxue with his other and wrote on the ground: *Cremate the body, nurture the soul.*

Given how fragmented Xiao Xingchen's soul was, it would definitely never return to its body. Cremation wasn't a bad idea. With the body turned to ash, and only the pure soul left behind, perhaps one day—with patience and care—it could return to the world.

Wei Wuxian nodded. "What are your plans for the future?"

Song Lan wrote: *Carry Shuanghua, walk the worldly path. Exorcise evil together with Xingchen.*

He paused briefly, then wrote: *Once he wakes, tell him—it was not your fault.*

The words he was unable to say to Xiao Xingchen while he was alive.

The evil miasma of Yi City gradually dispersed. They could already see the long streets and intersections. Lan Wangji and Wei Wuxian led the group of clan juniors out of the barren ghost town.

Song Lan bade them farewell at the city gates. He was still dressed in the same ink-black Daoist robe. Alone, he carried two swords—Shuanghua and Fuxue—and two souls—Xiao Xingchen and A-Qing. And thus, he walked a different path.

It was not the path they'd taken to get to Yi City.

Lan Sizhui lost himself for a moment gazing at that retreating form, then said, "*Xiao Xingchen, bright moon, cool breeze, ever-distant; Song Zichen, dauntlessly scorns the snow and frost...* I wonder if reunion will ever come for them?"

As Wei Wuxian trekked down this road, so overgrown with weeds, he noticed a field. *This was where Xiao Xingchen and A-Qing saved Xue Yang back then,* he thought.

Lan Jingyi spoke up. "*Now* can you tell us what exactly you saw during Empathy? How did that guy turn out to be Xue Yang? Why was he impersonating Xiao Xingchen?"

"And, and—was that really the Ghost General? Where did the Ghost General go? Why isn't he around anymore? Is he still in Yi City? Why did he suddenly appear in the first place?"

Pretending not to have heard the second set of questions, Wei Wuxian replied, "Well, this is a complicated story..."

Once he was done telling the tale as they walked down the path, there were nothing but gloomy clouds of melancholy all around him. No one remembered the Ghost General anymore.

Lan Jingyi was the first to start crying. "How could something like that happen in this world?!"

Jin Ling flew into a rage. "That Xue Yang—scum! Scumbag! That death was too kind for the likes of him! If Fairy were here, I'd send it forth to bite him to death!"

Wei Wuxian was horrified—if Fairy were here, he would likely have died of fright himself before it could get around to chomping Xue Yang to death.

The boy who had complimented A-Qing's beauty while they spied through the door beat his chest with grief and regret. "Oh, Miss A-Qing, Miss A-Qing!"

Lan Jingyi cried the loudest, utterly losing control of himself, but there was no one to remind him of the rules regarding clamor since Lan Sizhui's eyes had gone red as well. Thankfully, Lan Wangji didn't silence him.

"Let's go burn some joss money for Xiao Xingchen-daozhang and Miss A-Qing, huh?" Lan Jingyi suggested, all snot and tears. "Isn't there a village at the intersection ahead? Let's go buy some stuff and pay respects to them."

The group all agreed. "Okay, okay, okay!"

They'd reached that village by the stone tablet as they spoke. Lan Jingyi and Lan Sizhui impatiently ran over and bought a mess of incense sticks, candles, and red and yellow paper money. They walked to the side of the road and used earth and mud blocks to build something resembling a windproof stove. The boys crouched together on the ground around it and began burning paper money, mumbling as they did. Wei Wuxian hadn't made many wisecracks on the way, as he wasn't in the best of moods. But watching them now, he snapped out of it.

He turned to Lan Wangji. "Hanguang-jun, look at what the children have gotten up to, right on other people's doorsteps. Why didn't you stop them?"

Lan Wangji replied blandly, "Why didn't *you* stop them?"

"Fine. I'll help you manage them," Wei Wuxian said.

And so he went. "You've gotta be kidding me. Each and every one of you is a junior of a cultivation clan—did your daddies, mommies, shushus, or bobos never teach you that the dead can't receive paper money? What do the dead need money for? They won't get any of it. Besides, burning the paper money here, in front of other people's homes..."

Lan Jingyi waved dismissively. "Go away, go away, you're blocking the wind! The fire won't start with you in the way. Besides, it's not like you've died before—how would you know whether the dead can receive paper money, huh?"

The other boy, tears and soot smearing his face, also looked up and agreed. "Yeah. How would you know? What if they can?"

Wei Wuxian mumbled, "How would *I* know?"

Of course he knew! Because in the ten-something years he was dead, he hadn't received a single sheet of paper money!

Lan Jingyi added another knife to his heart: "Even if you didn't receive it, it's probably because no one burned you any."

How could that be? Wei Wuxian asked himself. *Could I have been* that *much of a failure that no one would burn me any paper money? Could it really be that I didn't get squat because no one burned anything for me?*

The more he thought about it, the more he thought it was impossible. He turned his head to Lan Wangji and whispered,

"Hanguang-jun, did you burn any paper money for me? At least *you* did, right?"

Lan Wangji cast a glance at him, then lowered his head and brushed off the bit of ash staining the end of his sleeve. He gazed quietly into the distance, not providing a single comment.

Wei Wuxian watched his serene profile and thought, *No way?*

He really didn't?!

Just then, a villager with a bow strapped to his back walked over, clearly upset. "Why the heck are you burnin' all that here?! This is in front of my house! It's unlucky!"

"See, got yelled at, didn't you?" Wei Wuxian tutted.

The boys, never having done anything like this, hadn't realized burning paper money in front of someone else's door was considered unlucky. They apologized profusely.

Lan Sizhui wiped his face. "Is this your house, sir?"

That villager replied, "Hah! What're you sayin', kid? My family's lived here for three generations. If it's not my house, is it yours?"

Jin Ling grew upset at his tone and made to stand up. "Watch your tone, mister!"

Wei Wuxian pushed him back down by the head.

Lan Sizhui added, "I see. I apologize, I didn't mean anything by my question. It's just, the last time we passed by this house, it was a different huntsman we encountered, hence my question."

The villager looked at him blankly. "Another huntsman? Who?" He held up three fingers and said, "My family only had one son per generation! I'm the only one, no brothers! My dad died a long time ago, I ain't got a wife and sired no children, so what other huntsman is there?"

"But it's true!" Lan Jingyi insisted, also standing up. "He was all bundled up tight, wore a big hat, and was sitting in your yard repairing his bow and arrows, like he was getting ready to go hunting. When we arrived, we even asked him for directions. He was the one who pointed us to Yi City."

That villager *tsk*-ed. "What bull! You sure you saw him sittin' in my yard? There ain't anyone like that in my house! That dingy little backwater, Yi City—even the ghosts there will kill you. Pointed the way for you? I think he wanted to end you! I think what you saw was a ghost!"

He spat a number of times to counter the bad luck, then turned away, shaking his head. The boys were left looking around at each other in dismay.

Lan Jingyi was still arguing, "But he really was sitting in this yard, I remember it clearly..."

Wei Wuxian gave Lan Wangji a brief account and then turned to them. "Do you understand now? You guys were lured to Yi City. That huntsman who pointed you there wasn't a local villager at all. It was someone in disguise, with ulterior motives."

"Was someone intentionally leading us here with the cat-killings? Was the fake huntsman the one who did it?" Jin Ling asked.

"Most likely," Wei Wuxian replied.

Lan Sizhui was puzzled. "Why would he go to all that trouble to lead us to Yi City?"

"We don't know yet, at least for the time being. But be very careful from now on," Wei Wuxian advised. "If you encounter these kinds of strange happenings, don't investigate on your own. Contact your families first, have them send help and work together. If it wasn't for the fact that Hanguang-jun was also in Yi City, your little lives might've been snuffed out."

Cold sweat rolled down the juniors' backs as they thought of how things could've ended if they fell at Yi City. Whether it was a death surrounded by walking corpses or being killed by that real-life devil Xue Yang, either scenario was terrifying.

Lan Wangji and Wei Wuxian kept going for a while, leading the group of clan juniors behind them. Just as the sky was darkening, they made it to the city where they had left the dog and donkey earlier. The lights were bright, and the air was abuzz with human voices. At this sight, everyone in the group felt the same thing: *This is where the living should be living.*

Wei Wuxian flung his arms open at the sight of the spotted donkey and exclaimed joyously, "Little Apple!"

Little Apple brayed furiously at him. Then Wei Wuxian heard the barking of a dog and immediately burrowed behind Lan Wangji. Fairy had come charging over as well, and the dog and donkey faced each other, baring their teeth.

"Tie them up properly," Lan Wangji said. "It is meal time."

Dragging along Wei Wuxian, who remained practically glued to his back, Lan Wangji ascended to the second floor as he followed the waiter. Jin Ling and company were going to follow, but Lan Wangji glanced back and gave them all an indiscernible sweeping look.

Lan Sizhui immediately said to the others, "Seniors and juniors must be separated. Let's stay on the first floor."

Lan Wangji gave a light nod, then continued up the stairs with a cool expression. Jin Ling stood hesitantly on the steps, not knowing whether to go up or down. Wei Wuxian turned back, giggling.

"Adults and children must be separated. There are some things you guys had best not see."

Jin Ling pursed his lips. "Who wants to see?!"

Lan Wangji ordered a table for the juniors on the first floor, while he and Wei Wuxian sat face-to-face in a private booth on the second floor.

"Hanguang-jun, listen to my one piece of advice," Wei Wuxian started. "Absolutely do not let your family shoulder the entirety of the cleanup for Yi City. A giant city like that will be a massive expense to sort out, and incredibly tricky at that. Shudong was never under the jurisdiction of the Lan Clan of Gusu. Take a count of the juniors downstairs. See which families they're from and count each of those families in. It's their duty to contribute."

"Worth considering," Lan Wangji agreed.

"*Really* consider it, yeah?" Wei Wuxian said. "Everyone loves to jump into a fight when there's glory to be had but fobs off the task when there are responsibilities to shoulder. If you guys hold your tongues and handle everything, you'll just wind up spoiling the other clans. And they might not fully appreciate your kindness or understand the trouble you've undertaken. If you do this too often, people will start assuming they can leave everything to you whenever something happens. That's how the world works."

After a brief pause, he added, "Still, this really is rotten luck. Yi City is so remote, and there happens to be no watchtower in the area either. If there were, Jin Ling and the boys wouldn't have barged in by mistake, and it wouldn't have taken so many years for Miss A-Qing and Xiao Xingchen-daozhang's souls to be freed."

There were as many cultivation clans as there were stars, big and small and scattered across the land. Most resided in prosperous cities that were accessible from all directions or in spiritual lands with lush, auspicious landscapes. No clans wished to set up in remote, impoverished areas. Even skilled rogue cultivators rarely ventured that far in their ascetic travels. Thus, when evil hauntings occurred, the locals of these remote lands often suffered untold misery with nowhere to go for help.

When the former family head of the Jin Clan of Lanling—that is,

Jin Guangshan—was still around, Jin Guangyao had posed the idea of the watchtowers. But Jin Guangshan showed no enthusiasm for the project, which would have been monstrously expensive. Furthermore, the Jin Clan of Lanling didn't have the power to rally enough people behind them at the time. The plan got no attention, and nothing wound up happening.

Once Jin Guangyao formally succeeded the seat of the family head and ascended to the position of Cultivation Chief, he began rallying and allocating both manpower and clan resources, determined to put into action the idea he'd conceived in the past. At first, the voices of dissent were the loudest. Many suspected the Jin Clan of Lanling would profit from this opportunity and were only interested in lining their own pockets. But Jin Guangyao, smile in place, persisted relentlessly for a full five years. In those five years, he formed alliances with countless people and clashed with just as many others. Using both hard and soft tactics, employing every trick up his sleeves, he finally persevered long enough to see his plan come to fruition, building over twelve hundred watchtowers.

These watchtowers were distributed in remote and impoverished lands, and every tower was allocated a number of sect disciples from various clans. Should there be any abnormal activity, these disciples would take immediate action. Should the problem be beyond their ability to resolve, they would swiftly report to and seek help from other clans or rogue cultivators. If the cultivators who assisted asked for compensation and the locals were unable to bear the financial burden, the Jin Clan of Lanling was able to raise enough money every year to support a payment pool.

All of this had happened after the Yiling Patriarch's time. It was only after traveling by a number of watchtowers that Wei Wuxian heard about their origins from Lan Wangji. Rumor had it that Golden Carp Tower was currently raising funds to initiate construction on a second batch of watchtowers, increasing their numbers to three thousand and covering an even greater area. Since the watchtowers were already visibly effective, the second set would no doubt be well received soon after they were established. That being said, the voices of doubt and mockery had never fully quieted. When the time came, it was sure to be another grand mess.

It didn't take long before the food was served, and with that the liquor. Wei Wuxian glanced over the table, seemingly nonchalant. Most of the dishes were red with spice. He paid attention to what Lan Wangji took, noticing most of the dishes he reached for were plain and bland. He only rarely went for the vibrantly red ones, though his face remained unchanged when he took a bite. An idea came to Wei Wuxian.

Lan Wangji noticed his staring and asked, "What is it?"

Wei Wuxian languidly poured himself a cup and replied, "I kind of want someone to drink with me."

9
The Allure

NOT REALLY EXPECTING Lan Wangji to join him, Wei Wuxian tossed back a drink. Lan Wangji looked at him. After a moment of silence, the man drew back his sleeve with care and unexpectedly reached out to pour himself a cup. He steadied himself for a moment, then raised the cup and slowly drank it down.

Wei Wuxian was amazed. "Hanguang-jun, you're being far too considerate. Are you really going to join me tonight?"

He hadn't paid close attention to the man's expression the last time they drank together. This time, he made sure to take it all in. Lan Wangji shut his eyes when he drank. He wrinkled his brows, finished the cup in one swallow, and pursed his lips imperceptibly before he opened his eyes once more. The flowing glance that he swept over Wei Wuxian seemed slightly dewy.

Wei Wuxian propped his cheek on his hand and started counting mentally. Sure enough, when he got to eight, Lan Wangji set the wine cup down, placed his forehead against his fingers, closed his eyes—and fell asleep that way.

Wei Wuxian had to hand it to the man. He really was one to sleep first and be drunk later!

An inexplicable eagerness surged to his head at this opportunity. He chugged the remaining liquor in one go, then stood up and paced back and forth in the private room with his hands clasped behind him. A moment later, he strolled up next to Lan Wangji and stooped down to whisper softly into his ear.

"Lan Zhan?"

No response.

Wei Wuxian tried again. "Wangji-xiong?"

Lan Wangji was supporting his forehead with his right hand, and his breathing was steady and even. His face and the hand supporting it were both fair and flawless as fine jade. The faint scent of sandalwood permeated the air around him. It had been a cold, somber aroma, but it was now mixed with the richness of liquor, suffusing the cool scent with hints of warmth, much like the sweetness of mind that overcame those who were slightly drunk. It was surprisingly intoxicating.

When Wei Wuxian moved close, that fragrance mingled with his breaths. He unconsciously lowered himself further and shifted closer. His thoughts were fuzzy. *That's weird... Why does it feel a bit warm in here?*

Captivated by this heady sandalwood blend, Wei Wuxian was drifting closer and closer, though he was wholly unaware of the motion. His voice dropped to a low murmur and acquired a flighty, teasing flavor.

"Lan-er...ge..."

"Gongzi..." an indistinct voice suddenly called to him.

Wei Wuxian's face had come within inches of Lan Wangji's own, and the "gege" on his tongue had nearly rolled over his lips. But that voice snapped him out of it, causing him to almost fall over as he jolted upward.

He immediately shielded Lan Wangji and turned to face the window from where the voice had come. There was a careful tap on that window, and the tiny voice once again floated through the wooden slats.

"Gongzi..."

Only then did Wei Wuxian notice his heart was beating a little faster than before. Mumbling a comment on the strangeness of it, he steadied himself and walked over to prop the window open.

A black-clad man hung upside-down outside the window with his feet hooked onto the eaves. He was about to knock again when Wei Wuxian thrust open the window and bonked his head in the process. The man let out a soft *ah* and caught the shutter, coming face-to-face with Wei Wuxian.

The chilly night breeze whirled in from the outside. Wen Ning had his eyes open, but they were no longer deadly white. Instead, he gazed at Wei Wuxian with a pair of quiet black eyes.

The two stared at each other like that for a good while, one standing and one hanging.

"Come down," Wei Wuxian finally said.

Wen Ning's feet slipped from the eaves and he fell, crashing heavily to the ground below. Wei Wuxian wiped the non-existent cold sweat from his forehead.

What an excellent choice for a place to eat! he thought with relief.

Thank goodness they'd picked this tavern. To add a tranquil atmosphere, the window of this private room faced a small patch of woods and not the streets. Wei Wuxian took a pole and propped the window fully open before leaning half of his body out to look down below. Wen Ning was dead weight, and his heavy fall had created a man-shaped pit. His eyes were still trained on Wei Wuxian even as he lay there.

Wei Wuxian called out to him in a hushed voice, "I told you to *come* down, not *go* down. Do you understand the word 'come'?"

Wen Ning stretched his neck to look up at him, then crawled out of the pit and patted off the mud smeared on his clothes. He replied hastily, "Oh. I'm coming."

He hugged one of the inn's posts, ready to climb up to the window once more. Wei Wuxian exclaimed, "Stop! Stay right there, I'll go over to you."

He returned to Lan Wangji's side and bent to whisper in his ear. "Lan Zhan, oh Lan Zhan, *please* stay asleep a while longer. I'll be right back. Be good, 'kay?"

Once he was done, he felt his hand itch. He couldn't help but flick Lan Wangji's eyelashes with the tip of his finger. Those long lashes trembled slightly at the teasing touch. Lan Wangji seemed a little unsettled, his brows wrinkling.

Wei Wuxian withdrew his claws and leapt out the window, hopping over eaves and branches and leaves before finally landing on the ground. He'd only just turned around when Wen Ning knelt in front of him.

"What are you doing?" Wei Wuxian asked.

Wen Ning did not speak a word and simply hung his head.

"Do you have to talk to me like this?" Wei Wuxian sighed.

Wen Ning murmured in a low voice, "Gongzi, I'm sorry."

"Fine."

And then Wei Wuxian knelt in front of Wen Ning as well. Startled, Wen Ning hastily kowtowed once to him, and Wei Wuxian instantly returned the kowtow. Wen Ning jumped to his feet in alarm, and only then did Wei Wuxian stand back up. He dusted himself off.

"Should've stood tall to talk like this from the start. Not so bad, is it?"

Wen Ning had his head bowed and was clearly afraid to speak.

"When did you regain your senses?"

"Only just now," Wen Ning replied.

"Do you remember anything from when those skull-piercing nails were in your brain?"

"Some things, yes...some things, no."

"What do you remember?" Wei Wuxian asked.

"I remember being chained up in a pitch-black place. There might've been someone who'd periodically check on me."

"Do you remember who it was?"

"No. I only remember someone nailing something into my head."

"It was probably Xue Yang. He used skull-piercing nails when he controlled Song Lan too. He used to be a guest cultivator of the Jin Clan of Lanling, but we don't know whether he did it on their orders or for his own schemes." Wei Wuxian thought for a moment, then added, "It was probably on their orders. Back then, they publicly announced that you'd been reduced to ashes. If the Jin Clan of Lanling wasn't involved, he couldn't have hidden you all on his own. And then? How did you end up finding your way to Mount Dafan?"

"Later...I don't know how much later...I suddenly heard clapping," Wen Ning said. "I heard gongzi say 'Awake yet?' so I...broke the chains and ran out..."

That was the command Wei Wuxian had given the three fierce corpses back at Mo Manor.

The Yiling Patriarch had issued countless such commands to the Ghost General once upon a time. So of course, he also heard and obeyed the very first command Wei Wuxian gave upon his return to the world. In that muddled and confused state, Wen Ning began searching for him with his own undead kind and Wei Wuxian's command pointing the way.

As for the Jin Clan of Lanling, they knew the fact that they'd been privately hiding the Ghost General could not be allowed to get out. If the news did break, it wouldn't just hurt their clan's reputation but also incite panic. So even though Wen Ning ran off, they didn't dare pursue him with fanfare or put out an order for his arrest. Their hands were tied.

Wen Ning, meandering across the land, had finally made it to Mount Dafan in time to heed Wei Wuxian's flute summons. And so the two were successfully reunited.

Wei Wuxian heaved a sigh. "That 'don't know how much later' is over a dozen years." He paused briefly, then said, "But it's pretty much the same for me. Do you want me to tell you some of the things that happened over these years?"

"I've heard a little," Wen Ning said.

"What have you heard?"

"I heard the Burial Mounds is gone. That everyone there...they're all gone."

Wei Wuxian had wanted to tell him some fun, inconsequential gossip—like how the Lan family precepts had gone from three thousand to four thousand, or other such things. He hadn't expected Wen Ning to bring up something so heavy from the get-go and could think of nothing to say.

But as somber as the topic was, Wen Ning's tone wasn't one of profound grief. Instead, he sounded like he'd known all along that it had to be so...and it certainly was the case. They'd already predicted this worst-case scenario many times over a dozen years ago.

After a moment of silence, Wei Wuxian asked, "What else have you heard?"

Wen Ning said softly, "Sect Leader Jiang—Jiang Cheng—brought forces to besiege the Burial Mounds. And killed you, sir."

"That one I gotta clarify," Wei Wuxian stated. "He didn't kill me. I died from spiritual rebound."

Wen Ning finally raised his head to look him in the eye. "But Sect Leader Jiang was clearly..."

"No one can walk along a single-plank bridge their entire lives and never fall," Wei Wuxian explained. "It can't be helped."

Wen Ning seemed to want to sigh, but he had no air to exhale.

"All right, that topic is closed," Wei Wuxian said. "Did you hear anything else?"

"Yes." Wen Ning gazed at him. "Wei-gongzi...how horribly you died."

"..."

Seeing the mournful look on his face, Wei Wuxian sighed. "Have you not heard a single piece of good news?"

Wen Ning knitted his brows. "No... I really haven't."

"..."

Wei Wuxian actually had no response.

Just then, there came the loud crash of something porcelain breaking from inside the main hall. Lan Sizhui's voice quickly followed the sound.

"Weren't we discussing Xue Yang? How did the argument end up here?"

"Yes, we were discussing Xue Yang, but was I wrong?" Jin Ling said furiously. "What did Xue Yang do? He's an inhuman piece of scum, but Wei Ying was even more nauseating! What do you mean, 'can't be lumped together'? Those demonic deviants are a plague on the world! They *deserve* to all be killed, they *deserve* to all die, to go extinct!"

Wen Ning moved, but Wei Wuxian waved, motioning for him to stop. Then they heard Lan Jingyi joining the fray, complaining loudly.

"Why are you so angry? Sizhui didn't say Wei Wuxian didn't deserve to die, he just said that those who practice the demonic path might not all be like Xue Yang. Did you need to chuck plates around? I didn't even get to try that..."

"Didn't he also say 'the founder of the path might not have intended it to be used for harm'?" Jin Ling sneered. "Who is this 'founder'? Why don't you tell me?! Who else could it be, if not Wei Ying? How perplexing. You Lans of Gusu are also a distinguished cultivation clan. Didn't plenty of your people die at Wei Ying's hand? Wasn't it a headache to kill those walking corpses and all those minions? Lan Yuan, why are you arguing such a bizarre stance? Just listen to you... Are you trying to exonerate Wei Ying?!"

Lan Yuan was Lan Sizhui's birth name. He defended himself, "I was not trying to exonerate him. I was only suggesting that we not jump to any conclusions until we know the full story. Recall that, prior to our arrival in Yi City, plenty of people claimed that Xiao Xingchen-daozhang killed Chang Ping of the Chang Clan of Yueyang as revenge. But what was actually the truth?"

"No one actually witnessed Xiao Xingchen-daozhang kill Chang Ping," Jin Ling argued. "They weren't 'claiming' anything, just speculating. But how many cultivators died at Wei Wuxian's hands, at Wen Ning's hands—not to mention the effects of the Yin Tiger Tally during the Qiongqi Path Ambush and the Nightless City Massacre?! *That's* the truth that countless people witnessed. *That's* the irrefutable, undeniable truth! And I will *never* forget the fact that he had Wen Ning kill my father and that it was he who caused my mother's death!"

If Wen Ning's face had had any color to begin with, it would've been completely drained at this point. He asked in a low voice, "...Miss Jiang's son?"

Wei Wuxian was still.

Jin Ling continued his furious screed. "My uncle grew up with him, my grandfather saw him as his own child, and my grandmother didn't treat him all that badly. But what about him? It was his fault that Lotus Pier was infested by the Wen rabble, reduced to nothing but their devilish nest. He broke up the Jiang Clan of Yunmeng and caused the death of my grandparents *and* my parents. Only my uncle is left! Wei Wuxian brought his death on himself through the crimes he committed—for all the hell he raised, his fate was to die without a corpse! The full story is right there. What's there to consider? What's there to exonerate?!"

He argued back aggressively, and Lan Sizhui did not respond. A good moment later, another boy spoke up.

"Why do we have to fight over this for no reason? Let's just not bring it up anymore, okay? We're eating right now and the food's getting cold."

Judging by the voice, the boy who'd spoken was the one Wei Wuxian teased as "romantic." Another boy agreed aloud.

"Zizhen is right, stop fighting. Sizhui was just careless with his words, that's all. How could he have put so much thought into a casual comment? Sit down, Jin-gongzi, let's eat."

"Yeah! We just escaped from Yi City—we've forged an unbreakable bond by escaping the jaws of death together! So why start an argument over something unintentionally said? C'mon."

Jin Ling humphed. Only then did Lan Sizhui speak, polite as always.

"Forgive me. I thoughtlessly misspoke. Please take a seat, Jin-gongzi. If the noise persists, Hanguang-jun might come downstairs, and that would be bad."

Mentioning Hanguang-jun really was miraculously effective. Jin Ling immediately stopped making so much as a single peep. He didn't even huff again.

The sound of the table and benches being moved followed, suggesting they had sat back down. Noise returned to the main hall, and the youths' voices were quickly drowned in the clatter of cups, plates, and chopsticks. Wei Wuxian and Wen Ning, however, still stood quietly there in the woods, their faces somber.

As the silence stretched on, Wen Ning soundlessly knelt again. It was a while before Wei Wuxian noticed his movement, and he waved listlessly.

"It's got nothing to do with you."

Wen Ning was just about to speak when his eyes suddenly moved to a spot behind Wei Wuxian, looking taken aback. Wei Wuxian started to turn when he saw a white-robed blur dart past him, raise a foot, and kick Wen Ning's shoulder.

Wen Ning was sent crashing backward, creating another man-shaped pit.

Lan Wangji was about to kick again when Wei Wuxian hurriedly pulled him to a stop. He begged repeatedly, "Hanguang-jun, Hanguang-jun! Peace!"

It would appear "sleep" time was over, and "drunk" time had arrived. And Lan Wangji had come seeking him.

This situation was oddly familiar. It truly was shocking how history repeated itself. Lan Wangji looked more normal than he had during the previous incident though. He wasn't wearing his boots on the wrong feet, and even when he was boorishly kicking Wen Ning with said boots, his face remained stern and righteous and flawless in its perfection.

Once Wei Wuxian stopped him, he adjusted his sleeves and nodded. He stood there looking wholly proud and, as per Wei Wuxian's request, rained down no further kicks.

Wei Wuxian seized this moment of peace to attend to Wen Ning. "You all right?"

"I'm fine," Wen Ning answered.

"If you're fine, then stand up! What are you still kneeling for?" Wei Wuxian admonished.

Wen Ning crawled to his feet, hesitated briefly, and then gave a greeting. "Lan-gongzi."

Lan Wangji screwed up his eyebrows, then covered his ears and turned his back to Wen Ning, facing Wei Wuxian instead. He used his own body to block Wei Wuxian's line of sight.

"..." Wen Ning was speechless.

"You best not stand there," Wei Wuxian explained. "Lan Zhan, uhm, doesn't like seeing you very much."

"...What's wrong with Lan-gongzi?" Wen Ning asked.

"Nothing. Just drunk," Wei Wuxian replied.

"Huh?!" Wen Ning went blank, as if this was too much to believe. A good moment later, he finally asked, "Then...what should we do?"

"What else?" Wei Wuxian shrugged. "I'll take him inside and toss him in bed."

"Okay," Lan Wangji said.

"Huh? Don't you have your ears covered? Why can you hear me perfectly all of a sudden, hmm?" Wei Wuxian prodded him.

Lan Wangji didn't respond this time, but he still covered his ears firmly, as if he hadn't been the one to interrupt just now. Caught between laughing and crying, Wei Wuxian turned to Wen Ning.

"Take care of yourself."

Wen Ning nodded but couldn't help but steal another glance at Lan Wangji. Just as he was about to retreat, Wei Wuxian called out again.

"Wen Ning. You... Why don't you find a place to hide first?"

Wen Ning looked taken aback.

"You've technically died twice now," Wei Wuxian continued. "Get some good rest."

Once Wen Ning left, Wei Wuxian peeled Lan Wangji's hands from his ears. "All right, he's gone. You can't hear him, and you won't see him either."

Only then did Lan Wangji drop his hands. His light-colored eyes stared blankly at Wei Wuxian, their gaze too clear, too forthright. The desire to prank Lan Wangji surged like a tempest within Wei Wuxian, like something inside him had been ignited. He smiled slyly.

"Lan Zhan, will you still answer whatever question I ask of you? Do whatever I ask of you?"

"Mn," Lan Wangji replied.

"Take off your forehead ribbon," Wei Wuxian commanded him.

Sure enough, Lan Wangji reached behind his head and slowly undid the knot to remove the white forehead ribbon embroidered with rolling clouds.

With the ribbon now in his clutches, Wei Wuxian examined it closely, flipping it over and over, this way and that. "Well, drat. There's nothing particularly special about this. And here I thought it was hiding some big scandalous secret. Why did you get so angry when I snatched it back then?"

Could it be that, back then, Lan Wangji simply disliked him and hated anything he did?

Suddenly, he felt something tighten around his wrists. Lan Wangji had used the forehead ribbon to bind his hands together and was now tying a knot at an unhurried pace.

"What are you doing?" Wei Wuxian asked.

He wanted to see exactly what Lan Wangji was up to, so he allowed him to continue. The man bound his hands tight. At first, he tied a slipknot. Then he gave it some thought, seemed to conclude that was unsuitable, and undid the bonds and changed tactics to a dead knot. He thought some more. Then, still concluding it wasn't enough, tied another knot atop that one.

The draping ends of the Lan Clan of Gusu's forehead ribbons were meant to drift beautifully in the wind, fluttering and free. This came with the requirement that they be quite long. Lan Wangji tied seven to eight dead knots in succession, piling them all into a string of ugly little bumps before he was able to stop, seemingly satisfied.

"Hey, do you not want this forehead ribbon anymore?" Wei Wuxian asked.

Lan Wangji's frown had relaxed. Taking the other end of the forehead ribbon, he lifted Wei Wuxian's hands and raised them to his eyes, like he was admiring his grand masterpiece. With his hands suspended, Wei Wuxian thought, *I look like a criminal... Wait, why am I playing along with him? Shouldn't* I *be the one playing* him*?*

Snapping out of it, Wei Wuxian demanded, "Untie me."

Repeating the same old trick of deliberate misunderstanding, Lan Wangji happily reached out for Wei Wuxian's collar and sash.

"Don't untie *that*!" Wei Wuxian exclaimed. "Untie the tie on my hands! This thing you trussed me up with, this forehead ribbon."

If Lan Wangji stripped him naked with his hands still bound—it was horrifying to even imagine!

Lan Wangji's brows furrowed again at his demand, and he was still for the longest time. Wei Wuxian raised his hands in front of him and coaxed, "Didn't you say you'd listen to me? Hmm? Untie this for gege. Good boy."

Lan Wangji gave him a look, then calmly turned away, as if he couldn't understand what he was saying. As if his words required painstaking and lengthy consideration.

"Oh, I get it!" Wei Wuxian complained loudly. "You jump at the chance to tie me up, but when I tell you to let me go, suddenly you don't understand, huh?"

The Lan family's forehead ribbons were made of the same material as their outfits. They looked light and airy but were in fact incomparably sturdy. Lan Wangji had bound his hands tight and put a series of dead knots on top of that. Wei Wuxian couldn't struggle free no matter how he twisted and contorted himself.

Well, I really shot myself in the foot, he thought. *Thankfully it's just a forehead ribbon and not something hellish like an immortal-binding rope, or he'd really have me tied up good.*

Lan Wangji was gazing into the distance as he tugged at the dangling ribbon in his hand. He really seemed to be having a splendid time, pulling at it and swinging his arm.

"Untie me, 'kay?" Wei Wuxian begged piteously. "Hanguang-jun, you're such a graceful and transcendent soul. How can you do something like this, huh? Why do you need to tie me up? How unsightly, right? What if other people see it? Hm?"

Having heard the last part, Lan Wangji led him out of the woods.

As he was tugged stumbling along the path, Wei Wuxian exclaimed, "Wait, wait, wait a sec. I meant it'd be no good if other people saw! I wasn't *telling* you to show it to other people. *Hey!* Are you still pretending you don't understand? You're doing this on purpose, aren't you? You only understand what you *want* to understand, isn't that it? Lan Zhan. *Lan Wangji!*"

As he spoke, Lan Wangji had already dragged him out of the woods and circled around to the street, entering the main hall of the tavern from the first floor.

The juniors were still eating, drinking, and having a swell time. Although there had been a minor disagreement earlier, young people were good at quickly forgetting such things, and they were currently in the merry throes of drinking games. A few of the braver Lan Clan juniors wanted to sneak drinks, so someone had been watching the stairs to the second floor to prevent their plot being discovered by Lan Wangji.

None of them could have imagined Lan Wangji would suddenly drag Wei Wuxian through the front doors, which were left unguarded. When they twisted their heads to see, every single one of them looked stunned.

Clink clank, Lan Jingyi threw himself onto the table to hide the wine cups. He toppled several plates and bowls in the process, rendering the concealment completely ineffective and making the objects all the more conspicuous instead.

Lan Sizhui stood up. "Han...Hanguang-jun, why are you entering through here again..."

Wei Wuxian laughed. "Ha ha, your Hanguang-jun was feeling a bit warm, so we went out for a breath of fresh air. We thought we'd ambush you guys on a whim. See? We caught you sneaking drinks."

He prayed inwardly, *Please let Lan Zhan drag me right upstairs. Please don't say or do anything unnecessary!* As long as he maintained that icy cold facade and said not a word, no one would know there was something wrong with him.

He was just thinking this when Lan Wangji dragged him right to the table where the juniors sat.

Lan Sizhui was greatly shocked. "Hanguang-jun, your forehead ribbon..."

He hadn't finished the sentence when his eyes fell on Wei Wuxian's wrists, with Hanguang-jun's forehead ribbon binding them. As though miffed that not enough people had noticed, Lan Wangji raised the ribbon high, lifting Wei Wuxian's arms to show everyone present.

A chicken wing fell from Lan Jingyi's mouth. It landed in his bowl, splashing sauce everywhere and staining his robes.

Only one thought filled Wei Wuxian's head: *Lan Wangji will have lost all face once he sobers up.*

Jin Ling asked, sounding unsure, "...What is he doing?"

"He's demonstrating a unique use for the Lan Clan's forehead ribbon," Wei Wuxian hurriedly explained.

"What unique use..." Lan Sizhui began to question before trailing off.

"When you encounter a very strange walking corpse and want to bring it back for closer examination, you can remove the forehead ribbon and apprehend it like so," Wei Wuxian stated.

"That's not right?" Lan Jingyi protested. "Our forehead ribbons are..."

Lan Sizhui quickly crammed the chicken wing back in Lan Jingyi's mouth and said hastily, "I see. I didn't realize there was such a marvelous use!"

Ignoring the odd looks in the onlookers' eyes, Lan Wangji dragged Wei Wuxian straight upstairs.

Lan Wangji entered the room, turned around, closed the door, and then locked the door. The last step was to push the table against the door, as if blocking some enemy from the outside. As Lan Wangji busied himself with these tasks, Wei Wuxian watched helplessly.

"Are you planning on butchering someone in here?"

There was a painted wooden screen installed inside the private room which divided the space in two. One side was set up with a table and seats to eat and converse at, while the other half had a long, curtain-draped divan to rest on. Lan Wangji dragged him to the latter side and shoved him onto the bed.

Wei Wuxian's head knocked lightly against the divan's wooden headboard. He yelped a token "ow," but his real thoughts were, *Is he gonna force me to sleep with him again? It's not hai time yet, is it?*

Hearing his pained cry, Lan Wangji swept aside the hem of his white robe and sat down most gracefully on the side of the divan. He reached out and stroked Wei Wuxian's head. Although his expression was stoic, his touch was gentle, as if asking: *"Did it hurt?"*

As he stroked, the corners of Wei Wuxian's lips twitched. "Owie, ow ow oww."

Slight worry began to color Lan Wangji's face at his continuous complaints, and his touch became even gentler. He even patted his shoulder as an act of consolation. Wei Wuxian raised his hands to show him.

"Let me go, won't you? Hanguang-jun, you've tied me up so tight that I'm gonna bleed, it hurts. Undo the forehead ribbon and let me go, okay? Okay?"

Lan Wangji covered his mouth in an instant.

"Mffmffmffffff? Mffmffmfffffffff?!"

When it comes to things you don't wanna do, you pretend you don't understand me. And when you can't pretend you don't understand, you simply won't let me talk?! So despicable! Wei Wuxian thought. *Well then, don't blame me for what comes next!*

Lan Wangji had one hand firmly covering his mouth, so Wei Wuxian parted his lips. The tip of his tongue swiftly and lightly flicked over Lan Wangji's palm. It was the lightest of touches, like a dragonfly skimming the surface of water, but Lan Wangji's hand recoiled as if his palm had been licked by a flame instead.

Wei Wuxian drew in a deep breath, briefly feeling like his grievances were satisfied. But then he saw Lan Wangji turn around and hug his knees. Lan Wangji sat on the divan with his back facing him, cradling the lightly licked hand near his heart, and went still.

"What's up?" Wei Wuxian asked. "What are you doing?"

Lan Wangji looked as though he'd lost all will to live after being violated by a pervert. Those who didn't know the situation at hand would assume Wei Wuxian had done something awful to him.

Seeing him look like he'd suffered a huge blow, Wei Wuxian commented, "Didn't like that? Well, that's too bad. It's your fault for being such a bully and not letting me speak. Why don't you c'mere and I'll give it a wipe for you?"

He reached out with his bound hands to touch Lan Wangji's shoulder, but the man dodged away. Seeing the way Lan Wangji hugged his knees and silently curled up at the corner of the bed, another wave of desire to bully him surged in Wei Wuxian's chest.

He knelt on the bed and scooted closer and closer to Lan Wangji. He chuckled in the most alluring tone he was capable of. "Scared?"

Lan Wangji jumped off the bed at once. He kept his distance, his back still turned to Wei Wuxian as if he was scared of him.

Now Wei Wuxian was really gonna cut loose. He languidly slipped off the divan and giggled.

"My, why are you hiding? Don't run away! You still have my hands bound! I'm not afraid, so what are *you* scared of? Come, come, come. Come here!"

He laughed as he closed in. Lan Wangji rushed to the other side of the painted screen and was met with the table he had pushed against the door himself to block the entrance. Wei Wuxian stepped around the screen to chase after him, circling to the other side. The two chased each other in circles around and around the screen seven to eight times. Wei Wuxian was just starting to enjoy himself when his mind finally caught up with him.

What am I doing? Playing tag? What the heck, did the doors shut on my brain? Lan Zhan's drunk, but why am I playing along with him too?

When Lan Wangji noticed his pursuer had stopped, he stopped as well. Hiding behind the screen, he silently peeked out a sliver of his snow-white face to spy on Wei Wuxian.

Wei Wuxian scrutinized him. The man appeared wholly serious and upright, as if it were an entirely different person behaving like a six-year-old and running around and around the screen with Wei Wuxian.

"You want to keep going?" Wei Wuxian asked.

Lan Wangji nodded expressionlessly.

Wei Wuxian was holding back so much laughter that he was going to hurt himself.

Ha ha ha ha, my god! When Lan Zhan gets drunk, he wants to play tag!! Ha ha ha ha!!

His suppressed laughter wracked him like an overwhelming tempest. It was only with great pain that he kept it in, his whole body shaking with the effort. *This Lan Clan of Gusu. No clamor allowed, no fooling around allowed, no walking fast allowed. Lan Zhan must've never gotten to cut loose like this when he was younger. Tsk-tsk-tsk, so sad. Either way, he won't remember anything when he sobers up, so it's fine if I play with him a little.*

He ran at Lan Wangji for a couple of steps, feigning a chase. Sure enough, Lan Wangji also resumed fleeing. Wei Wuxian decided to treat this like he was playing a game with a little one and did his best to humor Lan Wangji, chasing him around for a few more laps.

"Run, run, run, run faster, don't let me catch you! Every time I catch you, I'll lick you! You scared?"

He had intended this to be a threat, but Lan Wangji unexpectedly walked around the screen and deliberately collided with him. Wei

Wuxian was trying to *catch* him—why would he deliver himself to his doorstep?

He was speechless for a second, forgetting to even reach out. Seeing he wasn't moving, Lan Wangji took Wei Wuxian's bound hands and looped his arms around his own neck, like he was voluntarily sticking his head into an indestructible noose.

"You caught me."

Wei Wuxian was confused. "...Uh? Mmm, yes, I caught you."

Lan Wangji appeared to be waiting in anticipation for something. After a good while of waiting, it had not arrived, so he repeated the three words again—with more emphasis this time, as if impatiently urging him.

"You caught me."

"Yeah. I caught you," Wei Wuxian agreed.

He caught him. And then?

What did he say again? Every time he caught him, he'd what, again?

...No way.

"This time doesn't count," Wei Wuxian said. "You walked over on your own..."

He trailed off when he saw Lan Wangji's face drop. His expression frosted over, and he looked incredibly unhappy.

No way, Wei Wuxian thought. *Lan Zhan doesn't just like playing tag when he's drunk—he also likes being licked?*

He meant to remove his arms from around Lan Wangji's neck, but Lan Wangji refused to free them, pinning them firmly in place with his own. Wei Wuxian saw one of his hands was on his upper arm. After a moment of contemplation, he tilted his head, tentatively pressed his cheek close, and like the ghost of a kiss, let his lips brush the back of Lan Wangji's hand. The tip of his tongue lightly swept that cool jade skin.

It was a very, very light touch.

Lan Wangji shrank back fast as lightning. He removed Wei Wuxian's arms and then scurried off to face the wall with his back facing him again. He hugged the hand that had been licked to his own chest, his head bowed and lips unspeaking.

So is he afraid, or does he like it? Wei Wuxian pondered. *Or is it both?*

As he considered this question, Lan Wangji turned back around. His face calm once more, he requested, "Again."

"Again? Again, what?" Wei Wuxian asked.

Lan Wangji ducked behind the screen again and peeked half his face out to peep at him.

That meaning was more than obvious: *Let's play again. You chase, I run.*

Briefly speechless, Wei Wuxian followed along and did it "again." This time, he'd only chased him for two steps before Lan Wangji came colliding with him on his own again.

"You really *are* doing this on purpose," Wei Wuxian griped.

Lan Wangji looped Wei Wuxian's arms around his own neck again, like he understood none of what had just been said, and waited once more for Wei Wuxian to fulfill his promise.

I'm letting Lan Zhan have such a great time by himself, Wei Wuxian thought. *That won't do at all. Either way, he won't remember anything I do to him once he sobers up, so lemme raise the stakes.*

He continued to plot against Lan Wangji as the two moved to sit on the wooden divan.

"You like the licking, right?" Wei Wuxian asked. "Don't turn your head away. Tell me. Do you like it? If you do, we don't necessarily have to run around every time. I'll do it as much as you want."

He raised one of Lan Wangji's hands, then lowered his head

and dropped a kiss between those fair fingers, so long and so slender.

Lan Wangji began to shrink back again, but Wei Wuxian held his hand tight, not letting him withdraw. Then he pressed his lips against those defined knuckles, his breath feather-light. His lips traveled along Lan Wangji's fingers until they found the back of his hand, where he dropped another kiss.

Lan Wangji couldn't pull his hand back, no matter how hard he tried. He curled his fingers, clenching them into a fist.

Wei Wuxian pulled back a bit of his sleeve, revealing his snow-white wrist, and dropped a kiss on it too. He didn't move his head after this kiss, only raising his eyes.

"Is that enough?"

Lan Wangji's lips were tightly pursed, unspeaking. Only then did Wei Wuxian languidly straighten up.

"Did you burn me any paper money?" he asked.

No response. Wei Wuxian snorted a laugh, then pressed close. He dropped another kiss over his heart, against his robe.

"If you don't talk, then I won't give you any more. Tell me, how did you recognize me?"

Lan Wangji closed his eyes, his lips trembling. He looked as though he was about to confess.

However, it just so happened that Wei Wuxian had been staring at those pale, red, soft-looking lips. As though bewitched, he dropped a kiss upon them. His tongue followed after, licking along his lips as though unsatiated.

Their eyes widened at the same time.

A good moment later, Lan Wangji suddenly raised his hand. Wei Wuxian snapped to his senses, his body drenched in cold sweat. Thinking Lan Wangji was going to slap him silly right then and there, he quickly rolled off the divan. But when he looked back, he saw Lan Wangji slap his own forehead—forcefully knocking himself unconscious—before collapsing onto the wooden bed.

Here in this private room, Wei Wuxian sat on the floor while Lan Wangji was slumped on the divan. A gust of cold wind blew in through the open window, sending cold shivers down Wei Wuxian's back—but it helped clear his head somewhat. He rose to his feet, pushed the table back in place, and sat down next to it.

He stayed dazed for a while. Then he lowered his head and painstakingly bit at the forehead ribbon around his wrists until the mess of dead knots was loosened at last.

Once his hands were free again, he very naturally reached to pour himself a cup of liquor to deal with his shock. But when he delivered the cup to his lips, there was not a single drop to be had. He looked down to find nothing in the cup at all. He had chugged the entire contents of the jug much earlier but somehow hadn't noticed that nothing had come out when he poured now.

Wei Wuxian put the empty cup back on the table. *Why bother? That's enough booze for today.*

When he turned his head, he could see just enough around the screen to catch sight of Lan Wangji lying quietly on the divan. *I really had too much today, I crossed the line. Even if Lan Zhan's drunk and probably won't remember anything after he wakes up, I shouldn't have teased a perfectly good and proper man like him so outrageously... It was far too disrespectful.*

But when he remembered exactly how he had been "outrageous," Wei Wuxian couldn't help but raise his hand and softly touch his own lips.

He stroked the forehead ribbon in his hand until it was straightened out again, then walked to the side of the divan and placed it next to the pillow. He forced himself to not sneak even a single look at Lan Wangji's face as he crouched down and helped him remove his boots, arranging him in the standard Lan Clan sleeping position.

After completing his task, Wei Wuxian leaned against the divan and sat on the floor. His mind was running wild and in complete disarray, but one thing was absolutely clear.

He couldn't let Lan Zhan drink again. If he acted like that with everyone when drunk, then that wouldn't be good at all.

For some reason, Wei Wuxian felt indescribably guilty tonight. He didn't dare squeeze into the same bed as Lan Wangji as he usually did and spent the night on the ground instead, passing out against the divan some time after his head lolled against it. The morning arrived fuzzily. He felt someone gently pick him up and lay him down on the divan. Wei Wuxian blearily cracked his eyes open, and Lan Wangji's eternally cool face entered his vision.

He was immediately half-awake. "Lan Zhan."

Lan Zhan answered him with a "mn."

"Are you sober or drunk right now?" Wei Wuxian asked.

"Sober."

"Oh... Is it mao time?" Wei Wuxian wondered.

Lan Wangji woke punctually every day at mao time, which was how Wei Wuxian could determine the time without looking at the sky. Lan Wangji lifted Wei Wuxian's wrists, upon which were countless red welts. He retrieved a little light-green porcelain bottle and bowed his head as he applied a fine medicinal cream to the welts, which instantly cooled them. Wei Wuxian squinted his eyes.

"Owie... Hanguang-jun, you really are such a rude drunk."

"You suffer the consequences of your own actions," Lan Wangji said without looking up.

Wei Wuxian's heart lurched. "Lan Zhan, you really don't remember what you get up to when you're drunk, right?"

"No."

Probably true, Wei Wuxian thought. *Or he would've been so furiously embarrassed that he'd have butchered me by now.*

He was glad Lan Wangji didn't remember but also a little disappointed. It was like having secretly done something bad or eaten a forbidden treat on the sly. You'd hide in a corner snickering, secretly delighted that no one discovered you but disappointed you had no one with whom to share the unmentionable joy. Unconsciously, his eyes traveled to Lan Wangji's lips once more.

Although those lips never curved upward, they always looked very soft. And they were, indeed, very soft.

Wei Wuxian unconsciously bit his own lips as his mind began to wander off to the vast universe. *The Lan Clan of Gusu is so strict, and Lan Zhan is completely immune to romance, so he must've never kissed a girl before. What should I do? Should I tell him I took his first? If he found out, would he be so angry he'd cry? Heh, maybe when he was younger, but he probably won't now. Besides, he's like a wooden monk. Maybe he's never even thought about that sort of thing... Wait! Last time he got drunk, I asked if he liked anyone and he told me "yes." So maybe he's already kissed someone? But with Lan Zhan's chronic restraint, love must've ended at virtue. They probably never kissed, probably never even held hands. Maybe he never understood the type of "like" I was referring to in the first place...*

After Lan Wangji finished applying the cream, someone lightly knocked three times at the door. Lan Sizhui's voice followed.

"Hanguang-jun, are you both up? Shall we be departing?"

"Wait downstairs," Lan Wangji replied.

Once the group left the city, they would go their separate ways at the gates. The clan juniors had originally only known each other by sight, having at most dropped in during symposiums hosted by one clan or the other. But over these last few days, they'd investigated the cat-killer case and passed a terrifying day and night in a foggy ghost city. They'd burned paper money together, snuck drinks together, argued with each other and argued with other people together. They were well acquainted with each other by now, making them reluctant to say their farewell.

They dragged their feet at the city gates, promising to visit during a symposium hosted by one family or to travel to another family's domain for a Night Hunt. Lan Wangji didn't rush them. He stood underneath a tree, tall and silent, letting them chatter away. He was also keeping an eye on Fairy, so it didn't dare bark or run around and could only cower under the tree, gazing pitifully in Jin Ling's direction while rapidly wagging its tail.

Taking advantage of Lan Wangji watching the dog, Wei Wuxian put his arm around Jin Ling and strolled off.

Mo Xuanyu was one of Jin Guangshan's illegitimate sons. He was Jin Zixuan and Jin Guangyao's younger half brother, born of the same father but a different mother from either of them. In terms of bloodline, he was technically also Jin Ling's little uncle, which meant he could matter-of-factly exhort him using the tone of an elder.

"Don't quarrel with your uncle anymore when you go back," he said as he walked. "Listen to him, and be more careful from now on. Don't rush off on Night Hunts on your own."

While Jin Ling was from a distinguished sect, gossip spared no one. As an orphan, it couldn't be helped that he was eager to secure accomplishments, eager to prove himself.

"You're only in your teens," Wei Wuxian added. "None of the clan juniors your age have brought down any formidable evil creatures, so why be so impatient to snatch your first?"

Jin Ling mumbled, "My uncle and little uncle were teenagers when they first won acclaim."

Is that even comparable? Wei Wuxian thought. *Everyone was on edge back then, thanks to the tyranny of the Wen Clan of Qishan. If you didn't train with everything you had, if you weren't ready to kill at all times, who knew when your luck might run out? Everyone was drafted into battle during the Sunshot Campaign. No one cared if you were a teenager, or how old you were. But things are peaceful now. The clans are all stable. The atmosphere isn't as tense, and people have stopped killing themselves cultivating because there's no need for it anymore.*

"Even that damned dog Wei Ying was in his teens when he slaughtered the Xuanwu beast," Jin Ling added. "If he could manage that, why can't I?"

Wei Wuxian shuddered when he heard his own name with that word in front of it. He painstakingly shook off the goosebumps. "Did he kill that thing? Wasn't it Hanguang-jun?"

At the mention of Hanguang-jun, Jin Ling gave him an indiscernible look, like he wanted to say something but forced it back down. "You and Hanguang-jun... Never mind. It's between you and him, and anyway, I don't want to concern myself with you. Go be a cut-sleeve if you love it so much. It's an incurable disease."

Wei Wuxian laughed. "How is that a disease?"

Inwardly, he was in stitches, doubling over. *He still thinks I'm shamelessly throwing myself at Lan Zhan?!*

"I now know the meaning behind the forehead ribbon of the Lan Clan of Gusu," Jin Ling declared. "Since this is how it is, stay by

Hanguang-jun's side properly. If you're gonna be a cut-sleeve, you have to cut in a chaste and honest way! Stop courting other men, especially ones from our families! Otherwise, don't blame me for coming after you."

His "families" included the Jin Clan of Lanling as well as the Jiang Clan of Yunmeng. It would appear his tolerance for cut-sleeves had increased. As long as Wei Wuxian didn't pursue people from those households, he could look the other way.

"Such a brat!" Wei Wuxian tutted. "What do you mean 'courting other men'? Saying it like I'm so *that*. And forehead ribbon? There's a meaning behind the forehead ribbon?"

"Don't give me that!" Jin Ling exclaimed. "You got what you wanted, so don't get carried away. I don't wanna talk about this anymore. Are you Wei Ying?"

He tossed that out suddenly at the end, cutting straight to the point to catch him off guard.

Wei Wuxian replied easily, "Do you think I look like him?"

Jin Ling was quiet for a moment, then suddenly blew a short whistle. "Fairy!"

Having been called by its master, Fairy dashed over with its tongue hanging out and flapping in the wind. Wei Wuxian bolted off.

"Just talk to me properly, why release the hounds?!"

Jin Ling humphed. "Bye!"

Having said his farewells, he took off gallantly in the direction of Lanling with his head held high. It would seem he still didn't dare go see Jiang Cheng at Lotus Pier in Yunmeng. The other clan juniors went off in different directions in groups of twos and threes, heading home. Finally, only Wei Wuxian, Lan Wangji, and the Lan juniors remained.

The juniors continuously looked backward as they walked, unable to control themselves. Although Lan Jingyi said nothing, he looked a little forlorn and reluctant to part ways.

"Where are we going next?" he asked.

"Zewu-jun is currently attending a Night Hunt in the Tan Prefecture area," Lan Sizhui said. "Are we heading straight back to the Cloud Recesses, or should we join him there?"

"We will join him in Tan Prefecture," Lan Wangji stated.

"Good, good, maybe we can give him a hand or something," Wei Wuxian said. "We don't know where our good buddy's head has gotten to anyway."

The two of them walked ahead while the boys followed far behind. After they'd traveled a while, Lan Wangji said, "Jiang Cheng knows who you are."

Wei Wuxian was riding Little Apple, letting the spotted donkey walk at a leisurely pace. "Yeah, he knows. But so what? He has no proof."

Unlike possession, a spiritual sacrifice left no evidence that could be traced. Jiang Cheng was only basing his conclusion on Wei Wuxian's reaction at seeing a dog. But he'd never told anyone Wei Wuxian was afraid of dogs, and only people close to each other could dissect reactions and facial expressions thus. Such things hardly served as concrete evidence. Even if Jiang Cheng were to post public bulletins everywhere announcing that the Yiling Patriarch Wei Wuxian cowered at the sight of a dog, everyone would only take it as a sign that Sandu Shengshou had finally gone mad after his years of unsuccessfully pursuing the Yiling Patriarch.

"That's why I'm so curious," Wei Wuxian said. "How in the world did you recognize me?"

Lan Wangji replied dryly, "I am also curious as to why your memory is so dreadful."

It was only a few days before they arrived in Tan Prefecture.

Prior to their meeting with Lan Xichen, the group passed by a massive garden that was extraordinarily beautiful, if rather neglected. Unable to control their curiosity, the juniors entered to take a look. As long as it wasn't against the family precepts and rules, Lan Wangji never stopped them, and so they explored as they pleased.

Inside the garden were stone gazebos and banisters, stone tables and stone chairs, all provided for visitors' convenience during blossom and moon viewings. But the gazebo was chipped after enduring many years of exposure to the elements, and two of the stone chairs had toppled over. There were no flowers or other greenery visible anywhere in the garden, only withered branches and leaves. It had clearly been abandoned for many years.

The juniors strolled around in high spirits, making half a circuit before Lan Sizhui asked, "This is the garden that belongs to the Damsel of Annual Blossoms, right?"

"Damsel of Annual Blossoms? Who's that?" Lan Jingyi asked, looking blank. "This garden has an owner? How come it's so run-down? It looks like it hasn't been tended for a long time."

Flowering periods were short, and flowers that bloomed with certain seasons were thus called annuals. There was an abundance of varieties, each with their own varied colors. When they blossomed, gardens would be awash in their fragrance.

A memory flashed in Wei Wuxian's mind when he heard that name.

Lan Sizhui stroked the columns of the gazebo and thought for a moment. Then he said, "If I remember correctly, this must be that garden. It's famous, I've read about it in books. The chapter 'The Blooming Soul of the Annual Damsel' states: 'There is a flowerbed in Tan Prefecture, and in this bed, there is a damsel. Recite poetry beneath the moonlight—should the poem be excellent, one shall be gifted a single annual flower, its bloom unwithering for three years and with lingering fragrance. Should the poem be undesirable, or should there be errors in its recitation, the damsel will appear, hurl flowers at one's face, and vanish after.'"

"Recite a poem wrong and she'll pelt you in the face with flowers?!" Lan Jingyi exclaimed. "I hope those flowers don't have thorns, or I'd definitely get all scratched up if I gave it a shot. What kind of monster is that?"

"Not so much a monster but a spirit," Lan Sizhui corrected. "It is said that the first owner of the flowerbed was a poet, and he planted these flowers with his own hands, considering the blooms to be his friends. He recited poetry here every day, and the scholarly fragrance and affection lingering in the verses overflowed into the flowers and plants of this garden. Eventually, the wisp of a spirit took shape. This was the Damsel of Annual Blossoms. When outsiders visit, they will be gifted a single flower if they should make her happy by reciting poetry agreeably and reminding her of the one who nurtured her. If they should recite poorly or incorrectly, she will emerge from the flowering bushes and use those same flowers to pelt their faces. Those who are hit lose consciousness, and when they wake, they find themselves thrown out of the garden. A dozen years ago, the crowds visiting this garden were said to be endless."

"Elegant. Simply elegant," Wei Wuxian commented. "But there's no way the books in the Lan Library Pavilion would have anything like this in their records. Fess up, Sizhui. What did you read, and who let you read it?"

Lan Sizhui blushed and snuck a glance at Lan Wangji, afraid of being punished.

"Is the Damsel of Annual Blossoms very beautiful?" Lan Jingyi asked. "Is that why so many people wanted to come?"

Seeing Lan Wangji had no intention of scolding him, Lan Sizhui secretly breathed a sigh of relief before answering with a smile. "She must be very beautiful. She's a spirit of great elegance, after all, coalesced from wondrous things. But in reality, no one has ever seen the face of the Damsel of Annual Blossoms. Even if you can't compose a poem yourself, how hard is it to recite one or two? For that reason, most visitors received a gift of a flower from the Damsel. And even if there were occasionally some who got pelted due to incorrect recitation, they lost consciousness immediately and had no chance for an audience thereafter. However...there was one exception."

"Who was it?" another boy asked.

Wei Wuxian cleared his throat quietly.

"The Yiling Patriarch, Wei Wuxian," Lan Sizhui replied.

Wei Wuxian cleared his throat again. "Um, why him again? Can we not talk about something else?"

No one paid attention to him. Lan Jingyi waved him off anxiously. "Be quiet! Wei Wuxian, what? That big evil overlord? What did he do? Did he forcibly drag forth the Damsel of Annual Blossoms?"

"No, it's not like that," Lan Sizhui said. "He came from Yunmeng to Tan Prefecture, to this garden, expressly to try and see the face of the Damsel of Annual Blossoms. He recited poetry incorrectly each time, provoking the Damsel to hit him with flowers and toss him out. When he woke up, he crawled back in and continued to loudly and incorrectly recite poetry. He did this over twenty times. Finally, he got a good look at her face and then headed out to praise her looks to everyone. However, the Damsel of Annual Blossoms was so angered by him that she didn't emerge for a very long time. And whenever *he* entered thereafter, there would be a storm of crazed blossoms, flurries of flowers hitting people, the most extraordinary sight you can imagine..."

The boys all laughed.

"Wei Wuxian is such an annoying character!"

"Why is he so frivolous?!"

Wei Wuxian stroked his chin. "What do you mean? Who hasn't done a thing or two like that in their youth? And speaking of, why do people know something as insignificant as this? For a serious book to record such an anecdote—*it* must be the one that's frivolous."

Lan Wangji regarded him. While his face remained stoic, there was an odd twinkle in his eyes, like he was laughing at him.

Heh, Lan Zhan, you dare make fun of me? Wei Wuxian thought. *I know at least eight embarrassing stories from your younger days, if not ten. Sooner or later, I'll tell them all to these kiddos and destroy the noble, incorruptible saintly image they have of Hanguang-jun. Just you wait.*

"You kids are untranquil in the heart and unclean in the mind," Wei Wuxian declared aloud. "Reading such idle books every day instead of concentrating on your cultivation! When you get home, tell Hanguang-jun to punish you by having you transcribe the family precepts. Ten times!"

The color drained from the boys' faces. "Ten times while doing handstands?!"

Wei Wuxian was shocked, as well. He turned to Lan Wangji. "Your family sentences people to transcribe texts as punishment—*while* doing handstands to boot? Brutal."

"There will always be those who do not learn their lesson through transcription alone," Lan Wangji replied dryly. "Handstands simultaneously reinforce memory and serve as training."

Wei Wuxian was, of course, the person who did not learn his lessons. He pretended not to understand the implication, then turned around and strolled off, quite glad he didn't have to do handstands during transcription back in the day.

The youths were in high spirits after listening to the story and decided to camp out that night in the Annual Blossoms Garden. Camping out was a standard affair during Night Hunts, so the party knew to scout for kindling and quickly gathered a pile of withered branches and leaves to start a campfire. Lan Wangji went out on patrol to ensure the area was safe and set up an array while he was at it to prevent any surprise attacks in the middle of the night. Wei Wuxian stretched out by the fire. Seeing Lan Wangji had finally left, he decided this was his chance to clear up some confusion.

"Oh yeah, I've got a question. What exactly is the meaning behind your family's forehead ribbon?"

The boys' faces all changed drastically at the mention of this, and they started hemming and hawing. Wei Wuxian's heart stalled, then started racing.

Lan Sizhui asked carefully, "Qianbei, you don't know?"

"Would I have asked if I did?" Wei Wuxian asked right back. "Do I really look that frivolous?"

Lan Jingyi grumbled, "Yeah, you do... You went as far as tricking us into lining up to look at that thing..."

Wei Wuxian poked at the fire with a branch, making sparks dance. "Wasn't that because I was helping you guys to train properly, to push yourselves? It was clearly very useful. Remember my words and you will reap infinite benefits in the future."

Lan Sizhui seemed to be considering what to say next. He deliberated for a while before he began to explain. "It's like this. The forehead ribbon of the Lan Clan of Gusu symbolizes self-restraint—you know this, qianbei. Right?"

"Yes. And then?" Wei Wuxian said.

"And as per the words of the founding father of the Lan Clan of Gusu, Lan An: Only in the presence of your fated person, in the presence of the one your heart belongs to, can you allow yourself to be free of restraint," Lan Sizhui continued. "The teachings passed down through the generations have always stated that our family's forehead ribbon is, uhm...a very, very personal item. Very sensitive and precious. No one other than you is allowed to touch it. It cannot be easily removed, and it most definitely cannot be tied onto someone else. That's forbidden. Mm, except, except..."

There was no need to elaborate on that "except." The young, tender faces by the campfire were all flushed red, and not even Lan Sizhui could keep going.

Wei Wuxian felt at least half the blood in his body surge to his head.

That forehead ribbon, that forehead ribbon, that, that, that—

The meaning behind that forehead ribbon was pretty significant, huh?!

He suddenly felt he very much needed fresh air. He shot to his feet and scurried off, and only managed to steady himself by clinging to a wizened tree. ...*My god! What have I done?! What has HE done?!*

Back at Qishan, the Wen Clan had once hosted a Grand Symposium that spanned seven days. There was a different recreational event each day, and one was an archery competition.

The rules of the competition were as such: young juniors of each clan who had yet to reach crowning age would enter the grounds to battle for prey. There were over a thousand life-sized paper doll targets that fled swiftly about the arena. However, only one hundred of these had a fierce spirit sealed within. If one should shoot the wrong target, they must immediately withdraw. Only those who consistently shot the paper dolls containing the fierce spirits could remain. Those who shot the most by number and the most accurately would be calculated and ranked accordingly.

On these occasions, it was a given that Wei Wuxian would participate as one of the contestants from the Jiang Clan of Yunmeng. Prior to the competition, he had already spent an entire morning listening to debates. His head was swimming, and it was only when he strapped on the bow and quiver that he finally regained some energy. He yawned as he headed toward the hunting grounds.

On the way, he cast a casual glance beside him and noticed a handsome young man whose face was fair as powder and cold as ice. He was dressed in a red, round-collared and narrow-sleeved robe bound with a nine-ringed belt. It was the standard event attire for the juniors attending this Qishan Grand Symposium, and it looked particularly good on him: three parts refined, three parts gallant, but handsome in every way. An eye-catcher.

This youth had a quiver of arrows with snow-white fletching strapped on his back. His head was lowered as he tested the bow. His fingers were long, and when he plucked the bowstring, the sound thrummed like a strummed guqin—pleasant to the ear, bold and vigorous.

He also looked a bit familiar... After pondering this briefly, Wei Wuxian slapped his thigh and greeted him excitedly. "Well now! If it isn't Wangji-xiong!"

Over a year had passed since he was sent back to Yunmeng after studying at the Cloud Recesses. On returning, he'd told others of the things he'd seen at Gusu, and these stories included a massive number of digressions regarding how, although Lan Wangji's face was good-looking, he was so, so stiff, so, so dull, and so on and so forth. Still, it hadn't taken him long to leave those days well behind him and return to raising waves on the lakes and going wild in the mountains.

Before today, he had only ever seen Lan Wangji in the Lan Clan of Gusu's simple "funeral clothes," and never in anything so vibrant and eye-catching. Combined with Lan Wangji's beautiful face and the suddenness of the reunion, he was so dazzled that he hadn't immediately recognized the boy.

As for Lan Wangji—done testing his bow, he twisted his head away and left. Having been snubbed, Wei Wuxian turned to Jiang Cheng.

"He ignored me again. Heh."

Jiang Cheng shot him a cool look, also planning on ignoring him. There were over twenty entrances to the range, and every clan started at a different one. Lan Wangji approached the entrance for the Lan Clan of Gusu, but Wei Wuxian had sneaked over first. Lan Wangji shifted to the side, and Wei Wuxian matched his movements. Lan Wangji moved away, and he did too. In short, he blocked him, refusing to let him pass.

At last, Lan Wangji stood still and raised his head. He said, sternly, "Pardon."

"Gonna stop ignoring me now?" Wei Wuxian commented. "Were you pretending not to know me earlier, or were you pretending not to hear me?"

Not far away, the boys of the other clans were all looking in their direction, curious and amused. Jiang Cheng smacked his lips irritably and strapped on his quiver before heading off to the other entrance.

Lan Wangji raised his eyes and coldly repeated, "Pardon."

A smile hung off of Wei Wuxian's lips. He wiggled his brows before turning to the side to allow him to pass. The entrance was narrow, and Lan Wangji had to press close to him in order to squeeze through.

Once he entered the grounds, Wei Wuxian called after him.

"Lan Zhan, your forehead ribbon is crooked."

Juniors from prominent clans were very mindful of their bearing and poise, especially those from the Lan Clan of Gusu. Hearing him, Lan Wangji unthinkingly reached to right his ribbon—but it was clearly fastened correctly. He shot a peeved look at Wei Wuxian, but the latter had already turned and left for the Jiang Clan of Yunmeng's entrance, laughing all the way.

Once the competition formally began, the number of participants dwindled as they shot ordinary paper dolls in error. Wei Wuxian brought down one doll with every arrow fired. He was shooting slowly but never missed once, and it didn't take long before seventeen or eighteen of the arrows in his quiver were gone. Just when he was considering switching to his off hand, something fluttered into his face.

It was light, soft and tickled like silk thread or willow catkins. He looked back to see that Lan Wangji had unwittingly wandered near him. He was aiming at a paper doll, his back turned to Wei Wuxian.

Those fluttering ribbons were swept up by the wind, dancing gently as they brushed Wei Wuxian's skin.

His eyes squinted in a smile. "Wangji-xiong!"

Lan Wangji had his bow drawn as full as a full moon. After a momentary pause, he still answered. "What is it?"

"Your forehead ribbon is crooked," Wei Wuxian said.

This time, however, Lan Wangji did not believe him. The arrow flew. Without a backward glance, he left one word for Wei Wuxian. "Frivolous."

"It's true this time!" Wei Wuxian insisted. "It really is crooked. Look at it if you don't believe me. I'll fix it for you."

His hand moved as he spoke, catching the ends of the ribbon fluttering in front of him.

The awful thing was that he just couldn't keep his hands to himself. He'd gotten into the habit of tugging on the braids of the girls in Yunmeng, and whenever his hands found anything long and string-like, he couldn't help but want to yank it. And so, without thinking, he yanked this time as well. But because this forehead ribbon was already a little crooked and a little loose, this made it slip completely off Lan Wangji's forehead.

Lan Wangji's hand instantly shuddered on his bow.

It was a good while before he stiffly turned his head. His eyes very, very slowly turned to Wei Wuxian.

"Sorry about that, I didn't mean to," Wei Wuxian apologized sheepishly, still holding that silky forehead ribbon. "Here, you can retie it."

Lan Wangji looked extremely upset. A dark cloud enveloped his face, the back of the hand that held his bow was popping with veins, and his entire body was so tense with anger that he seemed about to start shaking. Seeing red crawling into his eyes, Wei Wuxian couldn't help but give the forehead ribbon a squeeze. *This thing I pulled off really is just a forehead ribbon and not a body part, right?*

Seeing him actually daring to squeeze it too, Lan Wangji brutally snatched the forehead ribbon back from him. Wei Wuxian let go as soon as he grabbed it.

The other juniors from the Lan family also stopped shooting and came to surround them. Lan Xichen had his arm around his little brother's shoulders, whispering something to the deeply silent Lan Wangji. The others looked serious, like they were about to face a formidable foe, talking and shaking their heads and sending indiscernible weird looks at Wei Wuxian.

He vaguely heard the words "accident," "no need to be angry," "pay it no mind," "a man," "family rules," and other such things, and grew increasingly confused.

Lan Wangji shot him a glare, then turned and left with a sweep of his sleeves, heading straight out of the grounds.

Jiang Cheng walked over. "What did you do now? Didn't I tell you not to tease him? Can't be happy without courting death at least once a day, can you?"

Wei Wuxian shrugged. "I told him his forehead ribbon was crooked. The first time was a lie, but the second time was true. He didn't believe me, was even angry at me. I didn't yank his forehead ribbon off on purpose, why do you think he's so mad? Mad enough to ditch the competition."

"Need me to spell it out?" Jiang Cheng mocked him. "It's because he finds you particularly abominable, of course!"

The quiver on his back was almost empty. At the sight of that, Wei Wuxian focused on the game once more.

He'd never once recalled that memory in all these years. It wasn't that he never suspected there was something special about the Lan forehead ribbon, but he'd tossed the whole mystery to the back of his mind after the competition. Now that he thought back on it, the looks the other Lan juniors present at the scene had given him...

To have his forehead ribbon forcibly plucked off by a little bastard like him... And Lan Zhan had actually managed to not shoot him dead on the spot. What terrifying self-restraint! As expected of Hanguang-jun!!

And now that he really thought about it, he'd touched Lan Wangji's forehead ribbon on more than one occasion since his return!

"What is he doing, pacing back and forth by himself like that?" Lan Jingyi wondered doubtfully. "Restless after having filled his belly?"

"The color of his face keeps changing too..." another boy added. "Did he eat something bad...?"

"But we didn't eat anything odd... Is it because of the meaning behind the forehead ribbon? There's no need to get so excited over that, right? He must really be infatuated with Hanguang-jun. Look how happy he is..."

Wei Wuxian circled a wilted flowering bush over fifty times before he managed to finally calm down. When he caught that last comment, he didn't know whether to laugh or cry.

Right then, behind him came the sound of withered leaves being crunched underfoot.

The footfalls were heavy, meaning it wasn't a child. Thinking it was Lan Wangji returning to camp, Wei Wuxian quickly smoothed out his expression, spun around, and was met with a black figure standing not far away in the shadow of a wizened tree.

The figure was very tall, stood very straight, and veritably thrummed with power.

However, it was missing a head.

As if a bucket of cold water had been thrown on his face, the upturned curve of Wei Wuxian's lips froze.

The giant figure stood beneath the wizened tree, facing in his direction. If there had been a head on top of its neck, it would have been quietly staring at Wei Wuxian.

Over by the campfire, the Lan juniors had also noticed the shadow. Every hair was standing on end, their eyes were wide, and they were ready to draw their swords. Wei Wuxian placed his finger to his lips and softly hushed them.

He shook his head and used his eyes to signal "do not." Seeing that, Lan Sizhui soundlessly pushed the sword Lan Jingyi had half-drawn back into its sheath.

The headless man reached out and placed his hand on the trunk of the tree beside him. He felt around, seeming to ponder something, or perhaps trying to confirm what he was touching.

He took a small step forward, and Wei Wuxian finally saw most of his body clearly.

The headless man wore slightly ragged funeral robes—the same robes they'd dug out of the Chang cemetery and used to dress the ghost torso. Furthermore, the ground by its feet was scattered with tattered fabric. Wei Wuxian could just make them out as the remaining shreds of the evil-sealing qiankun pouches.

We've been careless, Wei Wuxian thought. *Our good buddy pieced himself back together!*

He and Lan Wangji had been constantly in action from the moment they entered Yi City until now. It had been more than two days since they had last played "Rest." They'd done all they could to keep the body parts separate on their travels so far, and just barely managed to suppress them. But now the corpse's four limbs were all together, and the attraction between them was greatly heightened. Perhaps they sensed each other's resentment, causing their desire to reassemble to grow too powerful. When Lan Wangji went out on patrol, they seized the opportunity and impatiently rolled their respective evil-sealing pouches together, broke through their bindings, and joined together into a body.

Unfortunately, this corpse was still missing a particular part. The most important part.

The headless man placed his hands over his neck, feeling the neat scarlet wound there. He felt around for a bit but still couldn't find what should've been there. As if this truth had angered him, he suddenly struck out and slapped the tree next to him! The tree trunk cracked at the impact.

What a temper, Wei Wuxian thought.

Lan Jingyi brandished his sword in front of him, his voice trembling. "What...what is that monster?!"

"Just from that, I can tell you don't do your homework," Wei Wuxian admonished. "What's a yao? What's a monster? This is obviously a corpse, of the ghost category. How can it be classified as a monster?"

Lan Sizhui asked in a hushed voice, "Qianbei, you...are so loud. Aren't you afraid he'll notice you?"

"It's fine," Wei Wuxian assured. "I just realized that it actually doesn't matter how loud we are, because he doesn't have a head—and so, no eyes and no ears. In other words, he can't see, nor can he hear. If you don't believe me, try shouting at him."

Lan Jingyi was amazed. "Really? Lemme try."

Sure enough, he immediately shouted twice. Just as he did, however, the headless man spun around and walked toward the Lan juniors.

The boys were scared witless. Lan Jingyi wailed, "Didn't you say it's fine?!"

Wei Wuxian cupped his hands around his mouth and yelled at the top of his lungs, "*It really is fine, look! See how he's not coming here even though I'm so loud?* The problem isn't that you're loud, it's the firelight! It's hot! With lots of living humans! And all men too! It's bursting with yang energy over there! He can't see, he can't hear, but he can go toward places where he senses the bustle of life. Put out the fire now and spread out! Hurry!"

Lan Sizhui swept his hand, and a gust blew out the flames. The boys scattered throughout the abandoned garden in a rush.

Sure enough, once the campfire was out and the people dispersed, the headless man lost his sense of direction. He stood rooted in place for a while, but just as they sighed in relief, he suddenly started moving again, heading unerringly for one of the boys!

Lan Jingyi wailed again, "Didn't you say it'd be fine once the fire was put out and we scattered?!"

Wei Wuxian didn't have the time to answer him. "Don't move!" he barked at that other boy instead.

He picked up a rock by his foot, flicked his wrist, and hurled it toward the headless man. The rock hit him squarely in the back, and he immediately stopped in his tracks. He turned around, weighed his options, and seeming to think Wei Wuxian's side was more suspicious, walked toward him.

Wei Wuxian very, very slowly shifted two steps away just in time, brushing shoulders with the headless man, who stomped over with leaden footsteps. "I told you guys to spread out, *not* run around. Don't run too fast—this headless ghost's cultivation level is very high. If you move too fast and kick up wind with your movements, he'll notice that."

"He seems to be searching for something..." Lan Sizhui observed. "Is he searching for...his head?"

"Correct," Wei Wuxian replied. "He's searching for his head. There are so many heads here, but he doesn't know which one is his. So he plans to wrench the heads off of every single neck here and try them on to see if one fits. If it does, he'll use it for a while. If not, he'll toss it. So you guys have to walk very slowly, dodge very slowly, and not get caught."

The boys shuddered violently as they imagined their heads being wrenched off by this headless fierce corpse and worn so gruesomely on his neck. Their hands flew to their necks to shield them as they slowly and carefully began to "flee" about the garden. It was like they were playing a perilous game of tag with this headless ghost, where whoever was caught by "it" would have to hand over their heads. Whenever the headless man caught a whiff of a boy's trail, Wei Wuxian would hurl a rock to divert his attention and lure him his way.

Wei Wuxian moved at an easy pace, hands clasped behind his back, and observed the movements of this headless corpse as he walked. *There's something strange about our good buddy's posture, eh? He keeps swinging his arm with a loose fist. That action...*

He was still thinking when Lan Jingyi spoke up, having had enough. "How much longer are we gonna keep this up?! Are we just gonna keep walking around like this?!"

Wei Wuxian contemplated for a moment, then replied, "Of course not." He raised his voice and yelled, "Hanguang-jun! *Hanguang-juuun!!* Hanguang-jun, are you back yet?! Help!!"

At the sight of him, the others started yelling too. This fierce corpse had no head and couldn't hear, so they each screamed louder than the one before them, each more tragic than the other. In an instant, there came the murmuring moan of a xiao within the dark of the night, followed closely by the brisk strum of a guqin.

Having heard the two instruments, the group of juniors were practically ready to cry tears of joy. "Hanguang-jun! Zewu-jun!" they sobbed.

Two tall and slender figures appeared before the run-down garden entrance in a flash. Similarly tall, slim, and graceful, similarly colored like ice and snow—one held the xiao while the other carried the guqin, walking side by side. When the two saw the headless figure, they were both taken aback.

Lan Xichen's expression was especially obvious—he was practically stricken. His xiao Liebing had fallen silent, but Bichen was already unsheathed. The headless man sensed the hurtling approach and incredible power of that bone-bitingly cold sword glare and raised his arm, swinging it downward once more.

That action again! Wei Wuxian thought.

The headless man's form was remarkably swift and nimble too—he leapt, just missing Bichen's sharpness as it grazed past. He flipped his hand and, astonishingly, managed to seize Bichen's hilt just like that!

He raised Bichen high into the air, seeming to want to inspect this object now in his hand. Alas, he had no eyes. Seeing how the headless man had actually stopped Hanguang-jun's Bichen with his bare hands, the juniors all paled at once. Lan Wangji appeared unaffected, however. He took out his guqin, lowered his head, and plucked a string. The strummed note howled and spun toward the fierce corpse, as if it had transformed into a sharp but intangible arrow.

The headless man swung Bichen and struck the note to bits. Lan Wangji swept his hand down, and the seven strings of the guqin all vibrated at once, belting out a high and intense note.

At the same time, Wei Wuxian pulled out his bamboo flute. With an unusually sharp timbre, he harmonized with the guqin. In an instant, it was as if the sky were raining blades!

The headless fierce corpse brandished Bichen and returned in kind, but Lan Xichen had snapped out of it by then. He pressed Liebing to his lips once more, knitting his brows as he played. Perhaps it was only a figment of the imagination, but the moment the elegant and peaceful sound of the xiao sang through the night air, the corpse's movements seemed to falter. He stood rooted in place to listen for a moment, then turned, seeming to want to see who the musician was. But that was impossible, of course. He had no head, and no eyes with which to see.

First the guqin and flute assailed him in unison, and now he was being attacked by three tones at once. The headless fierce corpse finally swayed and collapsed, like his strength had left him. Technically speaking, he didn't collapse—rather, he fell apart. The arms, the legs, the torso, all lay brokenly on the ground piled with fallen leaves.

Lan Wangji flipped his hand to withdraw his guqin and summoned his sword back to its sheath, then approached the severed body parts with Wei Wuxian. He glanced down at them and then took out five brand-new evil-sealing qiankun pouches. The group of juniors came circling them, still shaken. They bowed to Zewu-jun first. Before they could start blabbering, however, Lan Wangji gave them a command.

"Go rest."

Lan Jingyi looked confused. "Huh? But Hanguang-jun, it's not hai time yet?"

Lan Sizhui tugged at him and answered respectfully, "Yes, sir." He asked no further questions and led the other juniors to start a new campfire in a different part of the garden and rest.

Only the three of them remained, standing next to the corpse pieces. Wei Wuxian nodded at Lan Xichen in respect, then crouched, ready to seal the corpse back into the pouches anew. He took up the left ghost arm and started stuffing it into the qiankun pouch but had only gotten half of it in when Lan Xichen interrupted him.

"Please wait."

Wei Wuxian had known there was something up when he saw Lan Xichen's expression earlier. Sure enough, the man's face was deathly pale.

"Please...wait," he repeated. "Allow me to look at the corpse."

Wei Wuxian stopped what he was doing. "Zewu-jun knows this man's identity?"

Lan Xichen didn't answer right away, as if unsure. But Lan Wangji gave Wei Wuxian a slow nod.

"All right. I know who it is now too," Wei Wuxian remarked. He lowered his voice. "It's Chifeng-zun, right?"

During their game of "tag" earlier, the headless corpse had continuously repeated the same actions: make a hollow fist, swing the arm, slash horizontally, cleave vertically. It looked very much like he was miming swinging some kind of weapon.

The first thing Wei Wuxian thought of was a sword. But he was a sword-wielder himself and had crossed blades with many distinguished swordsmen in the past without ever seeing a master use a sword like that. The sword was considered the "king of weapons," and those who practiced its art always strove for noble bearing or lithe grace in their forms. Even the vicious and sinister sword of an assassin could boast agility. Overall, the art of the sword had more lunging and flicking than slashing and cleaving.

The way the headless man moved while using a sword was too weighty. His moves possessed a sort of ruthless energy, a burning intent to slaughter. Besides, all that hacking and chopping was neither elegant nor noble.

But if what he was holding wasn't a sword and was rather a saber—a powerfully murderous and hefty saber—then everything made sense.

The temperament and martial form of sabers and swords were vastly different. The weapon this headless man had used while still alive was probably a saber. The art of the saber was fierce—it demanded power alone, with no pretensions of elegance. As the corpse searched for his head, he was also searching for his weapon. That was why he kept repeating the saber-swinging movement and even caught Bichen to use like his own saber.

The corpse had no unique markings such as birthmarks, and being cut into so many pieces made it impossible to easily determine its identity. Never mind that Nie Huaisang hadn't recognized the leg at the Saber Offering Hall—even Wei Wuxian wouldn't dare assume he could recognize his own leg if he chopped it off and tossed it somewhere. It was only when the four limbs and the torso were temporarily reunited by resentment and had managed to piece themselves together into a moving body that Lan Xichen and Lan Wangji could recognize him.

"Zewu-jun, Hanguang-jun told you about the things we saw during our travels, right?" Wei Wuxian asked. "The Mo Estate, the gravedigger, Yi City, and all that."

Lan Xichen inclined his head.

"Then Hanguang-jun must have told you that the smoke-masked man who fought to take the torso knew the sword techniques of the Lan Clan inside and out," Wei Wuxian continued. "There are two possibilities. One, he's from the Lan family and practiced the Lan Clan's techniques since he was young. Or two, he's not from the Lan family but is very familiar with their swordplay, meaning he either sparred frequently with members of the family or is unusually smart and can remember every move and approach."

Lan Xichen was silent. Wei Wuxian added, "Him fighting so hard to take the body means he doesn't want others to notice Chifeng-zun has been dismembered. Once Chifeng-zun's corpse was assembled, he'd be at a disadvantage. This is someone who knew the secret of the Saber Offerings Hall of the Nie Clan of Qinghe. Someone who might be very close to the Lan Clan of Gusu. And someone who is... significantly connected...to Chifeng-zun."

There was no need to say aloud who, exactly, such a person might be. Everyone knew.

Lan Xichen still looked somber, but after Wei Wuxian's summary, he immediately said, "He would never do this."

"Zewu-jun?" Wei Wuxian asked curiously.

"The two of you investigated the case of the dismembered corpse and encountered the gravedigger within this month. And he has spent practically every night of this month deep in conversation with me," Lan Xichen firmly explained. "A few days ago, we were still planning for the Grand Symposium to be hosted by the Jin Clan of Lanling next month. He's had no time to sneak away. The gravedigger cannot be him."

"What if he was using a transportation talisman?" Wei Wuxian asked.

Lan Xichen shook his head. While his tone was gentle, it was resolute. "A transportation talisman requires the study of transportation magic. It is exceptionally difficult to learn, and there were no lingering magical traces on him to indicate that he had done so. Furthermore, this magic consumes an enormous amount of spiritual power. But we attended a Night Hunt together not long ago, and he performed magnificently. I can confirm that he absolutely did not use a transportation talisman."

"He need not go himself," Lan Wangji pointed out.

Lan Xichen still shook his head slowly.

"Sect Leader Lan, you're well aware of who the most suspicious person is," Wei Wuxian said. "You just refuse to admit it."

The flickering campfire cast light and shadows over their faces, erratic and unpredictable. Complete silence reigned within the abandoned and decaying garden.

After a while, Lan Xichen broke the silence. "I know that, for various reasons, people hold many misconceptions regarding him and his actions. But...I believe only what I have seen with my own eyes all these years. I believe he is not such a person."

It wasn't hard to understand Lan Xichen's urge to defend this person. To be honest, Wei Wuxian didn't have a bad impression of their suspect, himself. Perhaps because of his origins, the man always treated everyone he met with great humility and amity. He offended no one and made anyone he interacted with feel at ease. Not to mention the friendship he'd shared with Zewu-jun for many years.

The Nie Clan of Qinghe had been under Nie Mingjue's control while he lived. The clan had been at the peak of its power and influence, posing the most direct threat to the Jin Clan of Lanling. Who would have benefited the most from Nie Mingjue's death?

To qi deviate and then die of that madness in public... It seemed to be nothing more than an unfortunate tragedy, with no one to blame. But was the truth really that simple?

10
The Beguiling Boy

— PART 1 —

THE GRAND SYMPOSIUM hosted at Golden Carp Tower was fast approaching.

Most prominent cultivation clans constructed their residences in open areas with lush, auspicious landscapes, but the Golden Carp Tower of the Jin Clan of Lanling was situated at the heart of the prosperous city of Lanling. The principal road for visitors was a sloping carriage path, about one kilometer long. This road, however, only opened to the public during banquets, symposiums, and other such major events.

According to the rules of the Jin Clan of Lanling, running and hurrying were not permitted on this avenue, which was lavishly decorated with murals and reliefs on both sides. Each work of art depicted the heroic tales of past family heads and other distinguished cultivators of the Jin family. Sect disciples of the Jin Clan of Lanling drove the carriages that ferried guests and would narrate these stories as they passed through.

The current family head, Jin Guangyao, was the subject of four of the most striking of these works of art. They were named "Espionage," "Assassination," "Oath," and "Merciful Power," and depicted, respectively, these four scenes: Jin Guangyao's tenure as a spy in Qishan, delivering intelligence on the Wen Clan to the forces of good; Jin

Guangyao assassinating the Wen Clan leader Wen Ruohan; the sworn brotherhood vow of the Three Zun; and Jin Guangyao ascending to the position of Cultivation Chief and issuing his commands. The artist was skilled at capturing the subject's essence. The pieces seemed polished yet ordinary at first glance, but upon closer examination one would discover that even when the relief on the spirit wall was stabbing a person in the back, his face splashed with blood, his eyes nonetheless still crinkled with a gentle smile. It was an eerie sight.

Immediately following Jin Guangyao were murals of Jin Zixuan. Usually, in order to emphasize their absolute authority and ensure they were not overshadowed, family heads deliberately had fewer murals depicting distinguished cultivators of their own generation or employed a lesser artist for them. Everyone tacitly considered such behavior understandable. However, Jin Zixuan was also the subject of four scenes, giving him equal standing with the current family head, Jin Guangyao. The handsome man depicted in those paintings was spirited and proud.

When Wei Wuxian dismounted the carriage, he stopped in front of the murals and looked for a while. Lan Wangji also stopped and waited for him quietly.

A sect disciple beckoned them from not far away. "Lan Clan of Gusu, please enter from this side."

"Let us go," Lan Wangji said.

Wei Wuxian said nothing and walked with him.

Upon reaching the apex of Golden Carp Tower's towering stairs, the view opened up to a spacious square finely paved with bricks. It bustled with people going hither and thither. The Jin Clan of Lanling had probably expanded and renovated a number of times in the intervening years. It was certainly much more extravagant than what Wei Wuxian had seen in the past.

At the far end of the square was a Sumeru throne-styled palace base made of white marble, raised by nine broad stone steps. The palace itself was Han-styled with double-eaved saddle roofs, magnificent in its grandeur as it looked down upon a vast sea of Sparks Amidst Snow peonies.

Sparks Amidst Snow was the flower upon the family insignia of the Jin Clan of Lanling, a white peony cultivar of exceptional beauty. The flower was as marvelous as its name suggested. Its petals came in two layers: the outer layer consisting of giant petals, whirling in on themselves with folds upon folds, like waves of snow overturning, and an inner layer consisting of smaller, more slender and beautiful petals, threaded with wispy stamens that shimmered like gold. A single bloom was already sumptuous beyond compare. And to have thousands blossoming in unison—how could such majestic scenery be described in mere words?

The front of the square was divided into a number of long queues. There were clans entering the square nonstop, but everything was orderly and organized.

"Su Clan of Moling, please enter from this side."

"Nie Clan of Qinghe, please enter from this side."

As soon as Jiang Cheng showed up, he shot them a look as sharp as knives and walked over. "Zewu-jun, Hanguang-jun," he greeted in a tepid tone.

Lan Xichen also nodded. "Sect Leader Jiang."

They absentmindedly exchanged pleasantries. Jiang Cheng commented, "Hanguang-jun has never attended symposiums at Golden Carp Tower before. What brings him here this time?"

Neither Lan Xichen nor Lan Wangji responded, but fortunately, that wasn't the question Jiang Cheng really wanted to ask as his gaze landed on Wei Wuxian. In a tone fit to spit out a flying sword and kill him on the spot, he said, "I had thought neither of you cared for bringing irrelevant individuals along on official visits, so this is unprecedented. What's going on? Who is this almighty, distinguished cultivator? Might you introduce me?"

Just then, a smiling voice was heard. "Er-ge, why didn't you tell me beforehand that Wangji was coming too?"

The master of Golden Carp Tower—Lianfang-zun, Jin Guangyao—had personally come to welcome them.

Lan Xichen returned the smile, and Lan Wangji nodded in greeting. Wei Wuxian, meanwhile, was carefully scrutinizing this Cultivation Chief, the man who commanded the cultivation world.

Jin Guangyao had a very advantageous face. He was fair of skin, with a single dot of red cinnabar between his brows. His eyes were clear, full of wit but not frivolity, and his features were clean and astute—seven parts handsome, and three parts resourceful. A faint smile forever hung upon his lips and creased his brow. He was the very image of an ingenious, perceptive man.

A face like his could charm the women without making men feel repulsed or threatened. Elders thought him adorable, and the young thought him approachable. Even if they didn't like him, they didn't hate him either—hence the "advantageous" nature of his face. While his build was a little on the short side, it was more than compensated for by his calm and deliberate demeanor. He wore a soft, black gauze cap and was dressed in the Jin Clan of Lanling's formal event attire—the full bloom of the Spark Amidst Snow family insignia embroidered on the chest of his round-collar robe, matched with a nine-ringed belt and a pair of tall boots. Resting his right hand heavily upon the sword at his waist, he gave off a surprising air of inviolable authority.

Jin Ling trailed out after Jin Guangyao, still not daring to see Jiang Cheng on his own. He hid behind Jin Guangyao and mumbled a greeting. "Jiujiu."

"You still know to call me jiujiu?!" Jiang Cheng reprimanded sharply.

Jin Ling hurriedly tugged the back of Jin Guangyao's jacket. Jin Guangyao, who seemed born to resolve conflicts, appeased Jiang Cheng thusly. "*Aiyah*, Sect Leader Jiang, A-Ling already knows he was wrong. He's been fretting so much about you punishing him that he hasn't been able to eat these past few days. Children are mischievous. You dote on him the most out of us all, so don't be so hard on him, okay?"

Jin Ling hurriedly added, "Yes, yes, that's right! Xiao-shushu can back me up, my appetite has been terrible!"

"Terrible?" Jiang Cheng scoffed. "You look fine enough; I doubt you've missed any meals!"

Jin Ling was about to talk back again when he noticed Wei Wuxian behind Lan Wangji and was instantly stunned. "Why are you here?!" he blurted.

"For the free food," Wei Wuxian stated.

Jin Ling huffed. "I can't believe you still dared to come! Didn't I warn..."

Jin Guangyao ruffled Jin Ling's hair and ushered him to stand behind him. He smiled. "How lovely. Anyone who comes to the symposium is a welcome guest. Golden Carp Tower boasts nothing if not enough food to go around." He turned to Lan Xichen. "Er-ge, sit for a bit. I need to check things over there and tell them to make arrangements for Wangji."

Lan Xichen nodded. "Please don't go to too much trouble."

"How can this be called trouble?" Jin Guangyao assured. "Really now, there's no need to hold back when you're at my home, er-ge."

Jin Guangyao could remember someone's face, name, title, and age after meeting them only once. It didn't matter how many years had passed; he could still accurately identify them and warmly approach to ask after their well-being. If he'd met them more than twice, he would remember their every like and dislike, no matter how trivial, and cater to their fancies while avoiding their distastes. Since Lan Wangji had so suddenly come to Golden Carp Tower, Jin Guangyao hadn't specifically prepared a seat for him, so he immediately went off to make preparations now.

They entered Pageantry Hall and strolled down the vibrantly red carpet. Next to the small sandalwood tables on either side of the wall stood beautiful maids, each accented with rings and accessories of emerald-green jade, all smiling graciously and abundantly. Their bosoms were as full as their waists were meek and dainty, and the similarity of their figures made for a sight that was both harmonious and pleasing to the eye.

Wei Wuxian could never help taking a second look when he encountered beautiful girls. Once they were seated and a maid poured him wine, he slipped her a smile.

"Thanks."

Unexpectedly, however, the girl seemed to take fright at this. She stole a glance at him before swiftly moving her eyes away. Wei Wuxian was a little puzzled at first but quickly realized, as he casually scanned his surroundings, that she wasn't the only one giving him weird looks. Almost half of the Jin Clan sect disciples were eyeing him askance.

He'd forgotten for a moment that this was Golden Carp Tower—the place Mo Xuanyu had been expelled from after harassing his peers. Who would've thought he'd shamelessly swagger back in, following the Twin Jades of the Lan Clan of Gusu? And he'd somehow even been given a first-class seat...

Wei Wuxian nudged closer to Lan Wangji and whispered, "Hanguang-jun, Hanguang-jun."

"What is it?" Lan Wangji asked.

"You can't leave my side, okay?" Wei Wuxian implored him. "There's sure to be plenty of people here who know Mo Xuanyu. If anyone wants to catch up with me, I'll have no choice but to keep up the crazy act. When that happens, please don't get mad if I embarrass you."

Lan Wangji cast him a look and said impassively, "Provided you do not provoke others."

Just then, Jin Guangyao entered the hall with an extravagantly dressed woman on his arm. She was composed, but her expression carried a sense of simple innocence and childish grace. This was Jin Guangyao's wife, the mistress of Golden Carp Tower, Qin Su.

For many years, the two of them had been the cultivation world's exemplar of a loving married couple. They treated each other with respect and courtesy. It was common knowledge Qin Su came from the Qin Clan of Laoling, an affiliate clan to the Jin Clan of Lanling. The family head of the Qin Clan of Laoling, Qin Cangye, was a former subordinate of Jin Guangshan's and had followed him for years. While Jin Guangyao was Jin Guangshan's son, his mother's background meant he and Qin Su were not of equal social standing.

However, Qin Su was rescued by Jin Guangyao during the Sunshot Campaign and fell in love with him. She refused to give up, adamant she would marry the man, until they finally tied the knot in a beautiful tale of love. Jin Guangyao had never been unfaithful either—while he held the same important seat as Cultivation Chief, his approach was the complete opposite of his father's. He never took any concubines, nor did he have affairs with other women, and that alone made plenty of the wives of other sect leaders genuinely envious.

As Wei Wuxian watched Jin Guangyao hold his wife's hand to

lead her the entire way, the very picture of gentleness and consideration—even being careful to ensure she did not trip on the jade steps while she walked—he thought the rumors were true.

Once the two were seated, the banquet formally began. Seated directly below them was Jin Ling, his head held high and chest puffed out. When his eyes landed on Wei Wuxian, he glared vehemently at him. Wei Wuxian, used to being a spectacle, didn't appear the slightest bit flustered. Between the merry clinking of wine cups and conversation, he ate and drank as he should, and while he was at it, listened to the praises being sung all over Pageantry Hall. An excellent event, indeed.

It was evening when the banquet finally ended. The symposium didn't formally begin until the next day, and the crowd made their way out of Pageantry Hall in groups of twos and threes as the sect disciples guided the clan leaders and distinguished cultivators to their guest houses.

Lan Xichen still appeared weighed down by his thoughts, and Jin Guangyao seemed to want to ask him what was wrong. He approached him, but had only just managed to call out "Er-ge," when someone else came charging over with a heart-rending wail.

"San-ge!!"

Jin Guangyao almost stumbled backward as he was tackled. Hastily taking hold of his cap to keep it upon his head, he asked, "What's wrong, Huaisang? If something's the matter, use your words."

Such an undignified family head could only be the Head-Shaker of the Nie Clan of Qinghe—even better, a *drunk* Head-Shaker. Nie Huaisang's face was bright red, and he refused to let go of Jin Guangyao.

"Oh, san-ge!! What should I do?! Can't you help me just this one last time?! I promise it'll be just this one last time!!"

"Didn't I already arrange to have that last incident resolved?" Jin Guangyao asked.

"The last incident got resolved, but now there's new problems!" Nie Huaisang wailed. "San-ge, what should I do?! I don't wanna live anymore!"

Seeing how incoherent he was, Jin Guangyao could only say, "A-Su, why don't you head back first? Huaisang, walk this way. Let's find a place to sit down and talk. Don't be so anxious..."

He helped Nie Huaisang out the door. Lan Xichen, who had also gone to see what was happening, was consequently seized along the way by the drunken disaster that was Nie Huaisang.

Qin Su bowed courteously to Lan Wangji.

"Hanguang-jun, it seems you have not attended symposiums at Lanling for many years. Please do forgive us, should there be any inadequacies in our hospitality."

Her voice was sweet and meek; truly a beauty who inspired the tenderest of affections. Lan Wangji nodded to return the courtesy. Qin Su's eyes landed on Wei Wuxian.

After a moment of hesitation, she said softly, "Then, please excuse me," and left with her maids.

Wei Wuxian was confused. "Everyone in Golden Carp Tower looks at me so weirdly, huh? What exactly did Mo Xuanyu do? Confess his love buck naked? What's so special about that? The people of the Jin Clan have seen too little of the world's vast oddities."

Lan Wangji listened to him chatter away, postulating nonsense, and shook his head.

"I'm gonna go find someone to wheedle info out of," Wei Wuxian continued. "Hanguang-jun, keep an eye on Jiang Cheng for me. If he doesn't come find me, great. If he does, help me stop him."

"Do not go too far," was all Lan Wangji asked of him.

"Sure," Wei Wuxian replied. "If I go too far, then we'll meet in the bedroom at night."

His eyes searched Pageantry Hall inside and out, but he didn't see the one he wanted. *That's weird,* he thought to himself. After leaving Lan Wangji's side, he searched the grounds. As he passed by a gazebo, someone suddenly emerged from one of the garden's rock formations.

"Hey!"

Ha! Found you! Wei Wuxian thought as he turned around. He whined softly, and with deliberate petulance, "What do you mean *hey*? So rude. Weren't we so chummy when we last parted? So heartless now that we've reunited, I'm heartbroken."

Jin Ling sprouted goosebumps all over his body. "Shut up right now! Who's all chummy with you?! Didn't I already warn you not to bother our families? Why are you back?!"

"Heaven be my witness, I've been following Hanguang-jun properly, not a toe out of line. I was *this* close to having him physically tie me to him. Which of your eyes saw me bothering your family? Or bothering your uncle? *Clearly*, he's the one bothering me, okay?"

Jin Ling flew into a rage. "Get outta here! That was my uncle being *suspicious* of you! Enough with your nonsense. Don't think I don't know you still haven't given up on..."

Just then, there was shouting from all around. Seven or eight boys dressed in the Jin Clan uniform suddenly leapt from the garden, and Jin Ling abruptly stopped.

The boys slowly encircled them. The one leading them was around Jin Ling's age, but much beefier. "And here I thought I was mistaken. It really is him."

Wei Wuxian pointed at himself. "Me?"

"Who else?" that boy spat. "Mo Xuanyu, I can't believe you have the face to return!"

Jin Ling's brow creased. "Jin Chan, what are you doing? You've no business here."

Oh, I see. This is probably a kiddo from the same generation as Jin Ling, Wei Wuxian thought. *And by the look of things, they don't get along.*

"I've no business here? What, do *you* have business here? What do you care what I do?"

Several boys were already making a move while they spoke, looking like they were going to pin Wei Wuxian down. Jin Ling shifted and stood in front of Wei Wuxian.

"Stop messing around!"

"What do you mean, 'messing around'? So what if I wanna teach our misbehaving sect disciple a little lesson?" Jin Chan argued.

Jin Ling humphed. "Wake up! He's already been booted out the door! He's not our clan's sect disciple anymore."

"So what?" Jin Chan demanded.

That "so what" was uttered so confidently that Wei Wuxian was stunned. Jin Ling rebutted, "So what? Did you forget who he came with today? If you plan on teaching him a lesson, why don't you go ask Hanguang-jun for permission?"

As soon as the name "Hanguang-jun" was dropped, all the boys grew apprehensive. Even if Lan Wangji wasn't present, none of them were arrogant enough to proclaim "I'm not afraid of Hanguang-jun." They held back for a moment and then Jin Chan sneered.

"Jin Ling, didn't you use to hate him? Why the change of attitude today?"

"Why do you talk so much? What's this got to do with you?" Jin Ling said.

"That guy shamelessly harassed Lianfang-zun, and yet you're taking his side?"

It was as if Wei Wuxian had been struck by lightning. He harassed *who*? Lianfang-zun? Lianfang-zun, who? Jin Guangyao?

He had never imagined that the one Mo Xuanyu harassed was... Lianfang-zun, Jin Guangyao?!

While he struggled to wrap his head around this, Jin Chan and Jin Ling exchanged heated words until they were raising fists to exchange instead. Neither of them could stand the other, so this was all it took to make them flare up.

Jin Ling yelled, "If you wanna throw hands, let's go! Like I'm scared of you!"

Another boy yelled, "Come, then! The only thing he knows how to do in a fight is call his dog to help!"

Jin Ling was just about to whistle, but when he heard this, he forcibly bit down on his tongue. He roared, "I can beat you all with my bare hands, even if I don't call Fairy!!"

Despite the gusto with which he shouted that, he was outnumbered. It seemed his skill fell short of the mark too, for it wasn't long until he was forcibly beaten back to Wei Wuxian's side. Jin Ling was furious seeing him still hanging around.

"What are you still standing there for?!"

Wei Wuxian suddenly grabbed one of his hands. Jin Ling didn't have time to yell before he felt an overpowering force on his wrist. He couldn't help but fall to his knees and topple over.

He yelled in anger, "You lookin' to die?!"

Jin Chan and his little friends were all startled to a stop at the sight of Wei Wuxian bringing Jin Ling to the ground, considering Jin Ling had been shielding him.

However, Wei Wuxian simply asked him, "You get it?"

Jin Ling was also startled. "What?"

Wei Wuxian twisted his wrist again. "Have you learned?"

Jin Ling felt a wave of numbing pain course from his wrist through his entire body. He yelled again, but that incredibly swift and incredibly minor action stuck in his mind.

"One more time," Wei Wuxian instructed again. "Watch closely."

Conveniently, another boy came rushing at them just then. With one hand behind his back, Wei Wuxian caught the boy's wrist with deadly accuracy. In the space of a breath, he'd laid that boy out on the ground. Jin Ling had seen everything clearly this time, and the vaguely throbbing place on his wrist told him which acupoint to force a burst of spiritual energy into. He leapt to his feet in high spirits.

"I got it!"

The tables turned in an instant. Before long, the garden resounded with boys yelling and shouting in frustration and anger.

Finally, Jin Chan cried, "Jin Ling, just you wait!!"

That group of boys fled in defeat, cursing as they ran. Jin Ling laughed maniacally behind them. Once he seemed to be done, Wei Wuxian spoke up.

"Look at you, so happy. First time winning?"

"Bah!" Jin Ling spat. "I always win one-on-one fights, but that Jin Chan always comes along with a bunch of helpers. Utterly shameless."

Wei Wuxian was just about to comment that he could find a bunch of people to come help him too. There were no rules saying these scuffles had to be one-on-one. Sometimes, it really did come down to who had more hands at their disposal. But he stopped himself from voicing the thought. In the many times he'd seen Jin Ling go out, he'd done so alone, without any clan juniors of the same age. He probably had no helpers he *could* call upon in the first place.

"Hey. Where did you learn that move?" Jin Ling asked.

Wei Wuxian dumped the blame directly in Lan Wangji's lap without a shred of guilt. "Hanguang-jun taught me."

Jin Ling didn't question this in the least. Since he had already seen Lan Wangji's forehead ribbon tied around Wei Wuxian's wrists, all he did was grumble. "He taught you this kinda thing too?"

"Why not?" Wei Wuxian said. "But this is just a little trick. It was effective because it was your first time using it and they'd never seen it before. If you use it too much, they'll figure it out, and it won't be so easy next time. How about it? Want to learn a few more moves with me?"

Jin Ling gave him a look and said in spite of himself, "Why are you like this? My little uncle has always tried to advise me, but you're trying to incite me."

"Advise you?" Wei Wuxian asked. "Advise you to what? To not fight and to get along with people?"

"Pretty much," Jin Ling admitted.

"Don't listen to him," Wei Wuxian said. "Let me tell you—once you're older, you'll discover that there are so many people out there you still want to beat up, but you'll have to force yourself to get along with them. So hit whoever you want to, to your heart's content, while you're still young. If you don't get into at least a few spectacular brawls, your life will be incomplete."

There seemed to be some yearning on Jin Ling's face, but he still sounded disdainful. "What nonsense are you spewing? My little uncle is always thinking of my best interests."

Jin Ling suddenly recalled that Mo Xuanyu had regarded Jin Guangyao as a god in the past. He would never have claimed the man was wrong about anything, but now, he'd just said "don't listen to him." Could he really have gotten over his presumptuous desire for Jin Guangyao?

Wei Wuxian could pretty much guess what Jin Ling was thinking by the look in his eyes. "Seems like I can't deceive you any longer," he proclaimed directly. "That's right, I've already moved on."

"..."

Wei Wuxian continued, deeply emotional, "In these intervening days, I've pondered deeply and seriously, and finally discovered that Lianfang-zun is not, in fact, my type. And he's not suitable for me either."

Jin Ling backed a couple of steps away.

"In the past, I didn't know my own heart. But after meeting Hanguang-jun, I'm now certain." Wei Wuxian drew in a deep breath and continued, "I cannot leave him anymore. I don't want anyone besides Hanguang-jun... Wait, where are you running off to, I'm not done! Jin Ling. Jin Ling!"

Jin Ling had turned around and bolted. Wei Wuxian called after him a few times, but the boy didn't turn to look even once.

Now he'll no longer suspect I still hold some sort of unspeakable flame for Jin Guangyao, he thought, feeling pleased with himself. When he turned his head, however, the white robes that were like frost and that man who was like snow stood less than a dozen meters away. Beneath the moonlight, Lan Wangji gazed at him, still and tranquil.

Wei Wuxian was struck speechless. "..."

In the days right after his resurrection, he would have said things ten times as scandalous to Lan Wangji. Yet now, under that gaze, he shockingly—and for the first time—sprouted a subtle sense of shame, one he'd never experienced in two lifetimes.

Wei Wuxian rapidly suppressed this rare emotion and walked over, completely at ease. "Hanguang-jun, you're here! Did you know Mo Xuanyu was actually driven out of Golden Carp Tower because he was harassing Jin Guangyao? No wonder everyone was shooting me complicated looks!"

Lan Wangji didn't say anything. He turned around and walked with Wei Wuxian, side by side.

Wei Wuxian continued, "You and Zewu-jun didn't know about this, and you didn't know Mo Xuanyu at all. It seems the Jin Clan of Lanling was keeping the affair under wraps from beginning to end. It makes sense—the sect leader's blood flows in Mo Xuanyu, after all. If Jin Guangshan didn't want this son of his, he wouldn't have brought him back. If all he was doing was harassing his peers, Mo Xuanyu should've been disciplined, at most. It wouldn't have warranted expulsion. But if the one he harassed was Jin Guangyao, then that's different. This was not simply Lianfang-zun. This was also Mo Xuanyu's brother from another mother. Truly, what..."

Truly, what a wholly unseemly affair! One that simply had to be cut at the roots. And Lianfang-zun would never be the one cut out, of course, so Mo Xuanyu had to go.

Wei Wuxian recalled how Jin Guangyao had looked as though nothing was the matter when they first came face-to-face at the square. The way he laughed and joked, like he didn't recognize Mo Xuanyu at all. *That man really is quite something.*

Jin Ling, however, couldn't hide how he felt. He particularly detested Mo Xuanyu, not just because he detested cut-sleeves, but because the one Mo Xuanyu was harassing was his own little uncle.

Having thought of Jin Ling, Wei Wuxian soundlessly heaved a sigh.

"What is the matter?" Lan Wangji asked.

"Hanguang-jun, have you noticed that every time Jin Ling goes out to a Night Hunt, he's always on his own?" Wei Wuxian asked. "Don't tell me that Jiang Cheng goes with him, his uncle doesn't count. He's in his teens, but I can't believe he doesn't have anyone his age attending him, any retinues escorting him. When we were younger..."

Lan Wangji's brows arched just slightly. On seeing this, Wei Wuxian changed his tune.

"All right, fine. Me. When *I* was younger. It wasn't like that for me when I was younger."

Lan Wangji replied impassively, "That was you. Not everyone is as you were."

"But all children love excitement, they like crowds, y'know," Wei Wuxian said. "Hanguang-jun, what do you think? Could Jin Ling be particularly unsociable? Does he not have a single friend in the clan? I don't know about the Jiang Clan of Yunmeng, but I don't think any juniors in the Jin Clan get along with him. They even had a fight earlier. Does Jin Guangyao not have a son or a daughter his age who's close to him?"

Lan Wangji replied, "Jin Guangyao once had a son. He was murdered at a young age."

Wei Wuxian was amazed. "That was the little young master of Golden Carp Tower! Who could've harmed him?"

"It was due to the watchtowers," Lan Wangji explained.

"What do you mean?" Wei Wuxian asked.

As it turned out, back when Jin Guangyao was first constructing the watchtowers he'd faced considerable opposition. He'd also offended some clans in the process—among them was a clan leader who lost both an argument and his senses, leading him to kill the only son of Jin Guangyao and his wife Qin Su. Their son was docile in character and dearly loved by his parents. In his grief and fury, Jin Guangyao uprooted that entire clan to avenge his son. But Qin Su was heartbroken, and ever since then, she had been unable to bear another child.

They were quiet for a moment. Then, Wei Wuxian continued, "That temper of Jin Ling's—the moment he opens his mouth, he offends people. Every action he takes kicks a hornet's nest. If it wasn't for you and I protecting him these past few occasions, how would he even be alive? Jiang Cheng doesn't know how to raise kids at all. And as for Jin Guangyao..."

Remembering why they'd come to Golden Carp Tower, he felt his head throb and rubbed his temples. Lan Wangji had been watching quietly beside him. He offered no words of consolation, but he listened all the while and answered every question posed to him.

"Let's stop talking about this," Wei Wuxian decided. "Let's go back to our room first."

The two returned to the guest house that the Jin Clan of Lanling had arranged for them. The room was exceptionally spacious and sumptuous, and even had a set of exquisite white porcelain wine cups. Wei Wuxian sat down and admired these. He fondled the set, playing around with them for a while. It wasn't until the middle of the night that he took action.

He rummaged through the chests and drawers, found a stack of white paper and a pair of scissors, and then cut out a paper doll in no time. This paper effigy was only about the size of a grown man's finger. It had a round head and sleeves cut to be abnormally large, making them look like the wings of a butterfly. Wei Wuxian took a brush from the table and drew something before tossing the brush back down. He exchanged it for a cup of wine, took a large swig, then put his head back and lay down on the bed.

The paper effigy suddenly jerked, then gave a couple of shakes. The two expansive, wing-like sleeves flew up, bringing the light body with it, fluttering as it landed on Lan Wangji's shoulder.

Lan Wangji turned his head to the side to see his own shoulder, and the paper effigy pounced on his cheek at once, climbing the contours of his face until it reached the forehead ribbon. It pulled and yanked at that ribbon, as if too fond of it to let go. Lan Wangji let the effigy twist around for a bit before reaching to pluck it off. At the sight of this, it hastily slid down with a crinkle. Whether intentionally or not, its head bumped against his lips.

Lan Wangji's movements faltered for a moment, but he finally caught the paper effigy between two fingers. "Stop playing around."

The effigy bonelessly rolled its body around his long, slender finger.

"Please take the utmost care," Lan Wangji said.

The paper effigy nodded. It flapped its wings, then pressed flat to the ground to crawl under the door and furtively slip out of the guest house.

Security at Golden Carp Tower was high, and a full-sized, living person obviously couldn't come and go as they wished. Fortunately, Wei Wuxian had studied a particular kind of black magic known as the Papercut Incarnation.

The spell was useful, yes, but also had quite a number of restrictions. Not only did it come with a strict time limit, but once the paper effigy was sent out, it had to return in the same state, without the slightest bit of damage. If it was ripped or damaged in any way, the soul of the caster would sustain the same degree of injury. The lightest consequence would be losing consciousness for a half or full year. Graver consequences might include a lifetime of stupor. As such, it called for the utmost caution.

While possessing this paper effigy, Wei Wuxian was at times stuck to the bottom hems of a cultivator's robes, at times flattening himself to slip past door cracks, at times opening his sleeves and dancing in the night like a butterfly, pretending to be a piece of waste paper. Suddenly, still in midair, he heard the faint sound of weeping from below. He looked down to see one of Jin Guangyao's guest accommodation houses, Blooming Garden.

Wei Wuxian flew under the eaves and saw three people sitting in the reception hall. Nie Huaisang had one hand clutching Lan Xichen while the other gripped Jin Guangyao, tearfully complaining about something while still in a drunken stupor. Behind the reception hall was a study. Since no one was in here, Wei Wuxian went in to take a look.

The table inside was covered with drawings annotated in red, and upon the walls there hung four paintings of the four seasons. He wasn't going to examine those at first, but when his eyes swept past, he couldn't help but want to express his admiration for the artistry. The use of color was infinitely gentle, but the subjects still came across as appropriately vast; it was clearly a singular landscape illustrated on paper, yet it seemed to span thousands of mountains and rivers. Wei Wuxian thought such skill with the brush could rival Lan Xichen's. He took a few more looks despite himself, and it was this that led him to discover that the artist of these four paintings *was* in fact Lan Xichen.

Flying out of Blooming Garden, Wei Wuxian saw a grand, five-ridged palace in the distance. The roof was laid with luminous golden glazed tiles, and outside it stood thirty-two golden pillars—a magnificent structure to behold. This had to be one of the most heavily guarded buildings within Golden Carp Tower, the place where all the family heads of the Jin Clan of Lanling through the generations slept. Fragrance Palace.

Aside from the cultivator guards dressed in Sparks Amidst Snow uniforms, Wei Wuxian could sense Fragrance Palace was densely covered with array magic from the ground all the way to the skies. He flew to a plinth carved with high reliefs of Sparks Amidst Snow to rest for a moment, then exerted some strength and squeezed through the crack of the door, crinkling all the way.

Unlike Blooming Garden, Fragrance Palace was the quintessential Golden Carp Tower structure: a majestic, sumptuous edifice with engraved beams and sculpted columns. Inside the sleeping palace were layers upon layers of gauze curtains draping to the floor. An incense burner carved in the shape of an auspicious beast sat atop the incense table, softly diffusing orchid-scented smoke. Amidst the extravagance was a lazy, overly sweet sense of decadence.

Jin Guangyao was meeting Lan Xichen and Nie Huaisang in Blooming Garden. There was no one inside Fragrance Palace, which just so happened to make it easier for Wei Wuxian to investigate. The paper effigy flew hither and thither, searching for anything suspicious. Suddenly, he spotted a letter underneath the agate paperweight on the table.

This letter had already been opened. There was no name on the envelope, nor was there any seal-stamp. Judging by the thickness though, it was clearly not empty. Wei Wuxian fluttered his sleeves and landed by the table, curious to see exactly what was inside. However, when his "hands" caught the edges of the letter and tried to pull it outward, for all his struggles it didn't move at all. His current body was a flimsy piece of paper—there was no way he could move this hefty agate paperweight.

Paperman Wei circled the agate paperweight a number of times, pushing and kicking, hopping and jumping, but unfortunately, it remained immovable. He had no choice but to leave it be and see if he could find any other areas of suspicion.

Just then, a side door to the sleeping palace was pushed open a crack. Wei Wuxian swooped down and pressed himself against a table leg, staying still.

The one who had entered was Qin Su. It seemed it wasn't that

Fragrance Palace was absent of people but rather that Qin Su had been silently present within an inner chamber.

It was perfectly normal for the mistress of Golden Carp Tower to appear inside Fragrance Palace. However, it was her current appearance that was extremely abnormal. Her face was blanched of all blood, and she wobbled like she had suffered a heavy blow and had only just woken from unconsciousness, ready to faint again at any time.

What's going on? She looked fine earlier at the banquet hall, Wei Wuxian thought.

Qin Su was leaning against the door, lost in thought. It was a while before she slowly moved toward the table, supporting herself against the wall. She stared at the letter under the agate paperweight and reached out, seeming to want to pick it up but in the end withdrawing. Under the lamplight, he could see her lips were quivering uncontrollably. What had once been a dignified, beautiful face was now practically contorted.

Suddenly, she screamed. She grabbed that letter and hurled it to the ground, her other hand clutching the fabric at her chest, shivering. Wei Wuxian lit up on seeing the letter but suppressed the urge to immediately fly over. He could handle only Qin Su discovering him, but if she screamed and called over others...his soul would be affected by any damage this paper took.

All of a sudden, a voice sounded inside the sleeping palace. "A-Su, what are you doing?"

Qin Su whipped her head around and saw a familiar figure standing just a few steps behind. The familiar face was smiling at her, as it always did.

She immediately threw herself to the ground and grabbed the letter. Wei Wuxian could only stay firmly pressed against the table leg and watch helplessly as the letter escaped his line of sight.

Jin Guangyao seemed to have taken another step closer. "What's that in your hand?"

His voice was gentle and genial—like he hadn't noticed anything amiss, hadn't noticed the odd letter in Qin Su's hands or her contorted face, but was simply inquiring about something trivial, like bidding her to put on a warmer robe or have a second helping of a dish. Qin Su clutched the letter and didn't respond.

Jin Guangyao tried again, "You don't look well, what's wrong?"

His voice was full of concern. Qin Su raised the letter, her voice shuddering as she spoke.

"I...met with someone."

"Who?" Jin Guangyao asked.

It was as though Qin Su hadn't heard him, and she continued, "That person told me some things and gave me this letter."

Jin Guangyao laughed in spite of himself. "Just who is it that you saw? And would you believe anything they tell you?"

"...wouldn't lie to me," Qin Su insisted. "Absolutely not."

Who? Wei Wuxian wondered. He didn't quite catch the pronoun, so he couldn't tell whether it was a man or a woman.

"Is everything written here true?" Qin Su demanded.

"A-Su, if you don't show me the letter, how can I know what's written in it?" Jin Guangyao reasoned.

"Fine then, take a look!"

Qin Su displayed the letter clutched in her hands. Jin Guangyao took another step forward to read it. His eyes flew past the lines and finished skimming it in a flash. There was no change in his expression, not even the shadow of a frown.

Qin Su, however, was practically shrieking.

"Say something, *speak*! Tell me that it's not true! That it's nothing but lies!"

"It's not true," Jin Guangyao assured her with conviction. "It's nothing but lies. Absurd, false charges."

Qin Su burst into tears. "You're lying! You're still trying to lie to me, even now. I don't believe you!"

Jin Guangyao sighed. "A-Su, you're the one who told me to say those words, but when I say them, you refuse to believe me. That makes it really difficult for me."

Qin Su threw the letter at him, then covered her face. "My god! My god, my god, my god! You... You really are... You really are terrifying! How could you...how *could* you?!"

She couldn't continue any further. Still holding her face in her hands, she retreated to the side. Then, holding herself up with a hand placed against a column, she suddenly began to heave. She retched so heartrendingly she seemed she might throw up her insides.

Wei Wuxian was shocked by the violence of her reaction. *She was probably vomiting in the inner chamber earlier too. What in the world is in that letter? Tales of Jin Guangyao killing and dismembering people? But Jin Guangyao killed countless people during the Sunshot Campaign. Everyone knows that, and there's no less blood on Qin Su's own father's hands. Could this be about Mo Xuanyu? No, it's impossible that Jin Guangyao and Mo Xuanyu had anything going on—in fact, Jin Guangyao was probably the one who had Mo Xuanyu thrown out of Golden Carp Tower. No matter what that letter says, her reaction shouldn't be so extreme as to make her vomit in disgust.*

Although he wasn't well acquainted with Qin Su, they had met a few times before, both being descendants of prominent clans. Qin Su was Qin Cangye's beloved daughter. She was a naive and innocent woman, but she'd been raised in privilege and had an excellent upbringing. She had never exhibited such heartrending madness before. Nothing about this felt normal.

Listening to her heave, Jin Guangyao silently crouched down and collected the papers that had scattered to the floor. He then casually raised them to a nine-layered lamp in the shape of a lotus and set them alight, letting them burn.

Watching ashes drop bit by bit to the ground, he spoke, sounding saddened. "A-Su, you and I have been husband and wife for many years. We have always had a harmonious and respectful relationship. I know I've treated you very well as a husband, so your behavior right now genuinely hurts me."

Qin Su had nothing left within her stomach to expel. She crouched on the ground on all fours, sobbing. "It's true, you've treated me well... But I... I'd rather I'd never known you! No wonder that, ever since... That ever since, there was never... Rather than do that, you should've just killed me!"

"A-Su, weren't we doing just fine before you learned about this?" Jin Guangyao reasoned. "Today, the day you found out, is the only day you've felt such nausea, and it's only because the knowledge troubles you. Which just goes to show that it doesn't *really* matter. It didn't substantially affect you in any other way. It's just your own mind causing you grief."

Qin Su shook her head, her face ashen. "...Tell me the truth. A-Song... How did A-Song die?"

Who's A-Song?

Jin Guangyao was taken aback. "A-Song? Why are you asking me this? Don't you know already? A-Song was murdered, and I've long since disposed of his murderer to avenge him. Why are you suddenly bringing him up now?"

"I did know," Qin Su stated. "But now I'm beginning to wonder whether everything I know is false."

Jin Guangyao seemed tired. "A-Su, what are you thinking?

A-Song was my son. What do you think I would do? You would rather trust someone who hides their head and tail, a letter of unknown origins, than me?"

Qin Su was crumbling. She pulled at her own hair and screamed, "It's precisely *because* he was your son that it terrifies me! What do I think you would do? If you can do even that, what *wouldn't* you do? And you still want me to trust you?! God!"

"Stop letting your mind run wild," Jin Guangyao pleaded. "Tell me, who did you see today? And who gave you this letter?"

Qin Su pulled at her hair again. "What...are you going to do?"

"If that person can tell you, they can tell others. If they can write one letter, they can write a second, a third. What are *you* going to do? Let this be exposed? A-Su, I'm begging you, no matter the circumstances, no matter the reasons, just tell me where the author of that letter is. Who told you to come back here and read that letter?"

Who is it? Wei Wuxian also really wanted to hear Qin Su say the name. Someone who could approach the Cultivation Chief's madam. Someone she'd trust. Someone who had uncovered some unspeakable secret of Jin Guangyao's. Whatever was in the letter definitely wasn't any simple crime of murder or arson—it had disgusted or horrified Qin Su to the point of vomiting. Even though only the two of them were present, she still couldn't bring herself to speak it aloud. Their discussion was vague and disjointed, without a single clear word passing between them.

But if Qin Su really did give up the name of the letter's sender, then she would be foolish indeed. If she gave up the name, not only would Jin Guangyao dispose of that person, but he would seal Qin Su's own mouth at all costs.

Thankfully, while Qin Su had been naive and ignorant of the world since she was a child, and even a little foolish at times, she no longer trusted Jin Guangyao. He sat poised and upright by the table, and she stared at him with empty eyes. The Chief Cultivator who stood above millions, her husband...he was still calm and collected in the candlelight, his face like a portrait. He rose to his feet, moving to help her up, but Qin Su violently slapped his hand away and then fell back to the floor, helplessly overtaken by another violent bout of dry heaving.

Jin Guangyao's brows twitched. "Am I really that disgusting?"

"You're not a man... You're a madman!" Qin Su cried.

Jin Guangyao's eyes were filled with grief-stricken tenderness. "A-Su, I really had no other choice. I wanted to lie to you for the rest of your life, to keep you in the dark, but that hope has been thoroughly dashed by the one who told you this today. You think me filthy, you think me disgusting, that's fine. But if this gets out—you are my wife, what would others say? What would they think of you?"

Qin Su clutched her head. "Stop talking! Don't say any more, stop reminding me!! I wish I never knew you! I wish I had nothing to do with you! Why did you draw so close to me back then?!"

After some silence, Jin Guangyao replied, "I know you won't believe anything I say now, but back then, my heart was true."

Qin Su sobbed. "...You're still trying to sweet-talk me!"

"What I said is the truth," Jin Guangyao stated. "I will always remember that you never said a single bad word about my background or my mother. I am thankful for you, and will be for my whole life. I wanted to respect you, cherish you, and love you. But you have to know—even if no one murdered A-Song, he still had to die. His only path was death. If we allowed him to grow up, you and I..."

With the subject of her son being raised, Qin Su could no longer endure this. She raised her hand to deal him a resounding slap. "Then who caused all this?! What would you *not* do for the sake of your position?!"

Jin Guangyao didn't dodge and accepted the slap, a bright red handprint surfacing on his fair cheek. He closed his eyes. A moment later, he said, "A-Su, you really won't tell me?"

Qin Su shook her head. "...Tell you, so you can go kill them and seal their mouth?"

"What are you saying? It looks like your sudden illness has muddled your head," Jin Guangyao said. "Father-in-law has departed for an ascetic cultivation retreat. I will send you to join him for a while so you can recover while enjoying your family's company. But let us finish this quickly—there are still many guests here, not to mention a symposium tomorrow."

Even now, the guests and tomorrow's symposium were still on his mind!

Though his lips said he would send Qin Su away for rest and recuperation, his hands were ignoring her pushes and blows and refusal as he helped her to her feet. He did something, and Qin Su instantly fell limp. He then calmly and unhurriedly half-carried, half-hauled his wife behind the layers of gauze curtains.

Paperman Wei tiptoed out from underneath the table and followed them. He saw Jin Guangyao place his palm on a giant bronze floor mirror. A moment later, his fingers actually plunged into the surface of the mirror like it was water. Qin Su's eyes widened. Still in tears, she watched helplessly, unable to speak or shout as her husband dragged her into the mirror.

Wei Wuxian knew only Jin Guangyao himself could open this mirror. Never one to let an opportunity slip by, he roughly calculated the timing and darted in after them.

Behind the bronze mirror was a secret chamber. Once Jin Guangyao entered, the lamps on the wall lit automatically, faintly illuminating the many lattice shelves stacked with treasures. Upon the shelves were stacks of books, scrolls, gems, weapons, and even several torture devices—black iron rings, sharp barbs, silver hooks of peculiar make. The sight alone was morbid.

Wei Wuxian knew these were mostly designed by Jin Guangyao. The leader of the Wen Clan of Qishan, Wen Ruohan, was unpredictable in temper and bloodthirsty to boot. He liked to torture people for pleasure, and Jin Guangyao had once catered to this interest of his by crafting all manner of cruel and interesting torture devices. It was how he'd managed to earn Wen Ruohan's favor, gradually climbing higher until he became a trusted aide.

Any cultivation clan had two or three secret treasure rooms. It wasn't unusual for Fragrance Palace to have such a chamber. Aside from a desk, the room also had a long, cold, black iron table large enough for a person to lie upon. There were residual dried black blotches on its surface. *That table would be perfect for butchering someone,* Wei Wuxian thought.

Jin Guangyao gently helped Qin Su to this table and laid her down. Qin Su's face was drained of life. Jin Guangyao combed back her slightly mussed hair.

"Don't be scared," he coaxed. "You shouldn't be running about in such a state. The crowds will only grow over the next few days, so rest here for now. You can join us as soon as you tell me who that person is. Nod your head if you're willing to speak with your husband. I didn't seal every meridian in your body, so you can still nod."

Qin Su's eyes rolled toward her still gentle and considerate husband. Those eyes were filled with terror, pain, and despair.

Just then, Wei Wuxian suddenly noticed a lattice shelf that was blocked off by a drape. The drape, which had blood-red, savage-looking spells drawn upon it, completely covered the shelf. It was an incredibly powerful, domineering array meant to seal something.

The paper effigy clung to the foot of the wall and slowly climbed at an agonizing pace, a centimeter at a time. At the other end of the room, Jin Guangyao was still gently pleading with Qin Su. Abruptly, like he had sensed something, he whirled his head back in alarm.

There was no one but him and Qin Su inside this secret chamber. He rose to his feet and carefully scrutinized his surroundings, only returning when he saw nothing out of place.

Of course, he couldn't have known that when he turned his head, Wei Wuxian had just reached a shelf holding books. The moment he detected movement from Jin Guangyao, he swiftly squeezed his thin body between the pages of a book and lay flat against them like a bookmark, his eyes firmly pressed to the paper. Thankfully, Jin Guangyao was abnormally vigilant but not enough so that he'd flip through books to see if there was anyone hiding inside.

All of a sudden, Wei Wuxian thought the words he was looking at seemed quite familiar. He stared hard for a long while, then cursed under his breath. How could it not be familiar? It was his own writing!

Jiang Fengmian's comments on his writing were: "frivolously scribbled, but with a certain elegance of character." This was most definitely his writing. Wei Wuxian examined it further and discerned a few bits and pieces between all the damaged and smeared spots: "*...different from possession...*", "*...revenge...*", "*...forced contract...*"

He could finally be certain. This book he had squeezed himself into was one of his own manuscripts. An essay on the forbidden magic of possession. He'd scouted everywhere for sources and organized his findings into a dissertation, along with his own added extrapolations.

He had written plenty of these manuscripts back then, all penned on a whim and tossed aside just as easily, scattered all around the cave where he slept in the Yiling Burial Mounds. Some of these manuscripts had been destroyed in the fires during the siege, while others were treated like his sword had been—taken as spoils of victory and hidden away.

He'd wondered where Mo Xuanyu had learned such forbidden magic. Now he knew. Never in a million years would Jin Guangyao have allowed unimportant people to glimpse the remains of a manuscript on forbidden magic. It seemed that even if Jin Guangyao and Mo Xuanyu weren't in *that* kind of relationship, what they shared was definitely not too different.

As he was thinking this, Jin Guangyao's voice came. "A-Su, my time is up. I have to go host the event now. I'll come and see you after."

Wei Wuxian had already twisted himself bit by bit out of the stack of his own manuscripts. At the sound of Jin Guangyao's voice, he rapidly stuffed himself back. This time, what he saw wasn't a manuscript but...a property deed and a land deed?

He thought this mightily strange. What was so special about property and land deeds that they should be shelved next to the Yiling Patriarch's manuscripts? Yet no matter how he looked, they were indeed two entirely ordinary deeds, written up correctly, with no ciphers or codes. The sheets were yellowing on the edges, and even ink-stained. He still didn't believe Jin Guangyao had casually placed them here, so he memorized the address, which was located in Yunping City of Yunmeng. If he had a chance to visit it in the future, maybe he'd unearth something there.

Only after there had been no sounds outside for a while did Wei Wuxian continue to crawl upward, still clinging to the wall. He finally made it to the lattice that was sealed behind the drape, but before he could see what exactly was behind it, light suddenly poured in.

Jin Guangyao had come over and lifted the drapes.

In that instant, Wei Wuxian thought he had been discovered. However, once the faint firelight permeated through the drapes, he discovered he was shrouded in a shadow. There was something round in front of him that just so happened to block him from view.

Jin Guangyao stood there, rooted in place, and seemed to be staring at something placed in this lattice.

It was a good moment before he asked, "Was it you watching me earlier?"

Of course, there was no response. After a moment of silence, Jin Guangyao lowered the drapes.

Wei Wuxian soundlessly clung to the object, which was cold and hard, like a helmet. When he circled to the front, he saw a ghastly pale face. Just as he'd expected. The one who placed the seal on this head wanted it to be unseeing, unhearing, and unspeaking. Thus, the skin of the pale, ghastly face was scrawled densely with spells, firmly sealing the eyes, ears, and mouth.

I've heard much about you, Chifeng-zun, Wei Wuxian greeted solemnly in his head.

As expected, the last of Nie Mingjue's body parts—the head—was here with Jin Guangyao.

Nie Mingjue, the fiery-tempered Chifeng-zun, who seemed so invincible in the Sunshot Campaign of years past, was now heavily sealed up in this dark, gloomy, and cramped secret chamber, never to see the light of day.

Wei Wuxian had only to unravel the seal, and the rest of Chifeng-zun's corpse would sense it and come seeking it on its own. He scrutinized the seal on the helmet for a moment. Just as he was thinking about how to go about removing it, an unusually strong force sucked him forward, powerfully yanking his light paper body against Nie Mingjue's forehead.

— PART 2 —

AT THE OTHER END of Golden Carp Tower, Lan Wangji gazed at Wei Wuxian as he sat beside him. He watched for a while. Then his fingers twitched, and with lowered lashes, he raised a hand to lightly touch his own lips.

Very, very lightly—just like the paper effigy had bumped into them earlier.

All of a sudden, both of Wei Wuxian's hands clenched into tight fists. Lan Wangji's attention focused. He took him into his arms and lifted his face. Wei Wuxian's eyes were still closed, but deep creases were starting to form between his brows.

In the secret chamber, Wei Wuxian had no time to react at all. Those who died filled with intense resentment ceaselessly radiated that resentment and hatred from their corpses, infecting others with negative energy to appease their rage. The phenomenon was the cause of many hauntings. In fact, it was also the principle on which the technique of Empathy worked.

The physical body was a line of defense for the soul. If Wei Wuxian had been in his physical body right now, the resentful energy could not have infected him against his will. But given that he was presently possessing a flimsy piece of paper, his defenses were greatly and unavoidably diminished. Furthermore, he was too close to Nie Mingjue, and the force of the man's resentment was too powerful to resist. In a brief moment of carelessness, it had affected him.

The thought *oh no!* had barely registered in his mind when, the next second, he caught the scent of blood.

It had been many years since he'd last been surrounded by such a thick stench of it. Something in his bones awakened, clamored, started boiling. As soon as he opened his eyes, there was the flash of a blade, a splash of blood, a head flying through the air, and the sight of its fallen body toppling over.

Emblazoned on the back of the beheaded man's family uniform was a blazing sun. Wei Wuxian watched "himself" sheathe his blade as a deep voice came from his mouth.

"Collect the head and hang it where the Wen dogs can see."

Someone behind him answered, "Yessir!"

Wei Wuxian knew who the beheaded man was now. It was Wen Xu, the eldest son of Wen Ruohan, the head of the Wen Clan of Qishan. He'd been ambushed and killed by Nie Mingjue at Hejian. Severed by one slash of Nie Mingjue's saber, Wen Xu's head was put on display before the Wen Clan cultivators' formation as a show of might. His body, on the other hand, was cut to pieces and crushed into mangled meat. This bloody paste was then used by enraged Nie Clan cultivators to paint the ground of the battlefield red.

Nie Mingjue swept the barest glance over the corpse on the ground and kicked it away. With his hand pressing down on the hilt of his blade, he slowly surveyed his surroundings.

Chifeng-zun was a very tall man. When Wei Wuxian had his session of Empathy with A-Qing, his field of vision was quite low. Now, it was much higher than his usual line of sight. A scan of the area revealed countless casualties. Some wore the blazing sun Wen Clan robes, while others had the beast head family insignia of the Nie Clan of Qinghe on their backs. There were also some without a family emblem at all. Each of these accounted for around thirty percent of the bloody total.

It was a tragic scene to behold, the stench of blood reeking to the high heavens. He swept his eyes across the area, then strode forward as if to check if there were any cultivators of the Wen Clan still breathing.

Suddenly, a strange clang rang out from a nearby tile-roofed house. Nie Mingjue brandished his saber, and the ensuing wind from his blade swiftly swept over to cleave open the house's simple door, exposing the terrified mother and daughter hiding inside.

The house was dilapidated and bare. With nowhere else to hide themselves, the mother and daughter huddled under the table in each other's arms, not daring to breathe too hard. The young mother's round, wide eyes reflected Nie Mingjue's blood-soaked, murderous appearance, and her tears began to flow. The girl in her arms froze in fear, her mouth agape.

Nie Mingjue's tightly furrowed brows relaxed on seeing they were ordinary people, likely commoners who had not fled in time when the battle broke out. A subordinate came up behind him. Not knowing what was going on, he addressed him.

"Sect leader?"

All the mother and daughter knew was that a bunch of cultivator factions had swarmed in out of nowhere and started killing each other, all while they were just trying to live their ordinary lives. They didn't know who the good guys were or who were the villains. The sight of sabers and swords alone was enough to terrify them into assuming they were surely going to die. They looked more and more terror-stricken with each passing moment.

Nie Mingjue cast a glance at them and reined in his murderous aura.

"Everything's all right," he answered.

He lowered the hand that grasped his blade and strode to the side of the battlefield with steady steps. The young married woman instantly slumped to the ground with her daughter in her arms. After a moment, she could not help but weep in a small, desperate voice.

After walking a few steps, Nie Mingjue suddenly halted in his tracks to ask something of the subordinate behind him. "The rear

personnel who was last to leave during the previous battlefield cleanup, who was he?"

That subordinate gave a slight start and then answered, "The one who was last to leave? I...don't really remember..."

"Tell me when you do," Nie Mingjue said with a frown.

He continued on his way while that particular subordinate hurried to ask the others milling around. Not long later, he caught up to Nie Mingjue.

"Sect leader! I've asked around, and the rear personnel who was the last to leave during cleanup on the previous battlefield is known as Meng Yao."

Nie Mingjue raised his brows at hearing this name, as if astonished.

Wei Wuxian knew why. Before Jin Guangyao was acknowledged by the Jin Clan, he used his mother's surname, going by the name of Meng Yao. This was no secret—indeed, that name had once been just as famous.

Although not many personally witnessed Jin Guangyao's first time ascending Golden Carp Tower—the same tower he would one day climb to the very peak of, as the all-powerful Lianfang-zun—the rumors around the event were extremely detailed. Jin Guangyao's mother was a famous courtesan in Yunmeng, renowned for her talent in the fine arts. It was said she was skilled at the guqin and in calligraphy, and she was well educated with a good head on her shoulders. Though not from a renowned family, she still far surpassed the ladies of said families.

Even so, in the mouths of others, a prostitute was still a prostitute. Jin Guangshan occasionally passed through Yunmeng, and naturally, he couldn't miss the famous prostitute who was the talk of the town back then. After several days spent dallying with her, he gave her a love token and departed, sated and content. Of course, once he made it back home, he forgot all about the woman with whom he had rolled about—just as he had countless times before.

Mo Xuanyu and his mother could be considered favored, by comparison. At least Jin Guangshan had *remembered* at some point that he'd sired a son and summoned him to Golden Carp Tower. Meng Yao was not so lucky. The son of a prostitute could hardly be compared to the descendant of a decent family, and so, Lady Meng bore Jin Guangshan a son all by her lonesome. Like Second Lady Mo, she waited and waited, yearning and hoping for this head of the cultivators to return and take her and their child away. She devoted her heart and soul to preparing Meng Yao for his future in a cultivation sect.

But even as the boy became a youth, there was still no news from that father of his. Lady Meng, however, fell critically ill. Before she breathed her last, she gave her son the love token Jin Guangshan left her, telling him to head for Golden Carp Tower and seek a way out of this life.

Thus, Meng Yao packed his things and set off from Yunmeng. He trekked across mountains and rivers before finally arriving at Lanling, approaching the foot of Golden Carp Tower. He was stopped at the entrance, so he took out the love token and asked them to notify Jin Guangshan of his arrival.

The love token Jin Guangshan had left was a pearl button, which was nothing special to the Jin Clan of Lanling. They were so abundant, in fact, that you could fling out a hand at random and come away with a fistful. Their most common use was to be given as gifts to the beautiful women Jin Guangshan dallied with when away from home. He would pass these pretty little baubles off as rare treasures and top them off with a pledge of undying and eternal love. He gave them out as he pleased and forgot all about them after the fact.

The timing of Meng Yao's arrival was truly unfortunate. It happened to be Jin Zixuan's birthday, and Jin Guangshan and Madam Jin were hosting a banquet to celebrate their precious son, with many family members present. Six hours later, when evening came, they set out together to release lanterns with their prayers for blessings. That was when the servant saw an opening to step forward and inform them.

When Madam Jin saw the pearl button, she recalled all of Jin Guangshan's past indiscretions. Her face immediately darkened. Jin Guangshan hurriedly crushed the pearl to dust and rebuked the servant loudly, instructing him to chase off the person so they wouldn't bump into him when they stepped out to release the lanterns.

And thus, Meng Yao was kicked off Golden Carp Tower, rolling from the topmost stair to the bottommost one.

As the story went, he said nothing after he climbed to his feet. He simply wiped the blood from his forehead, patted the dust from his body, and left with his bag on his back.

After the Sunshot Campaign began, Meng Yao joined a sect under the banner of the Nie Clan of Qinghe.

The Nie Clan cultivators under Nie Mingjue's command, as well as the recruited rogue cultivators, were stationed across several locations—one of which was located in a nameless mountain range in Hejian. Nie Mingjue hiked up the mountain on foot, but before he could get close to camp, he saw a youth in cloth robes leaving the emerald forest, a bamboo tube in hand.

The youth seemed to have just returned from retrieving water. Moving with slightly tired steps, he was just about to enter the cave when he suddenly stopped outside and listened intently for a while. He seemed to be debating whether to go in or not. Eventually, he silently walked off in another direction, bamboo tube and all.

After walking for a distance, he found a spot at the side of the road and squatted down. He fished out a small piece of dry, white rations from the fold of his robes and slowly ate it with plain water.

Nie Mingjue walked over to him. The youth had his head down as he ate his food but found that a tall shadow had suddenly enveloped him. He looked up and hastily tucked his rations away, then stood to greet him.

"Sect Leader Nie."

This youth's stature was comparatively small. He was fair-faced, with delicate brows—the very same gainfully lovable face of Jin Guangyao. He had yet to be accepted by Golden Carp Tower at this time, so he naturally lacked the cinnabar mark on his forehead.

Nie Mingjue obviously had some recollection of this face, as he asked, "Meng Yao?"

"I am," Meng Yao answered respectfully.

"Why aren't you resting inside the cave with the others?" Nie Mingjue asked.

Meng Yao opened his mouth but could only manage a slightly awkward smile, as if he did not know what to say. At the sight of this, Nie Mingjue walked past him and headed over to the cave. Meng Yao looked like he wanted to stop him but did not dare.

Nie Mingjue concealed the sound of his approach, so no one noticed even when he was right outside the cave. The people inside were still having a merry time chatting and gossiping.

"...Right, that's him."

"No way! Jin Guangshan's son? How could Jin Guangshan's son slum it with the likes of us? Why doesn't he go back and find his father? All it'd take is one word from his father and he wouldn't have to work like a dog."

"You think he doesn't want to? Didn't he travel to Lanling with that little token, all the way from Yunmeng, all just to try and get his father to take him in?"

"Bad decision. Jin Guangshan's woman is a formidable one."

"Not to rub salt in the wound, but Jin Guangshan has sired so many children. He has at least a dozen bastard sons and daughters out there, but have you ever seen him acknowledge a single one? He's just disgracing himself, making a scene like that."

"See, this is why people shouldn't dream about what's outta their league. Who can he blame but himself for getting tumbled bloody? No one. He asked for it."

"What a fool! Why would Jin Guangshan give a damn about other sons when he has Jin Zixuan? What's more, his mother was a whore who was bedded by thousands of men. Hell knows whose bastard he really is. The way I see it, Jin Guangshan probably didn't dare acknowledge him because he had doubts of his own! Ha ha ha ha..."

"Please! I don't think he even remembers having an encounter with the woman."

"Now that I think about it, I actually like the idea of Jin Guangshan's son resigning himself to his fate and fetching water for us. Ha ha ha..."

"Resigning, my ass. He's doing his best to perform. Don't you see how hard he's working, running around all day doing this and that? He's so eager to please, hoping so hard to make a name for himself so his father will be willing to acknowledge him and take him back."

Fury blazed in Nie Mingjue's chest, so searing that it burned its way into Wei Wuxian's own. His hand pushed down on the hilt of his saber. Meng Yao hurriedly reached out to stop him but didn't succeed. The saber was already drawn.

A rock before the cave dropped to the ground with a thunderous crash. Dozens of cultivators who were sitting inside the cave taking a break were so startled by its collapse that they sprang up and drew their swords in unison. The bamboo drinking tubes they were holding in their hands fell to the ground in a clattering chorus.

Without delay, Nie Mingjue bellowed, "Drinking water that others fetched for you while spewing such malicious words! Did you all pledge yourselves to my command to gossip instead of slaying those Wen dogs?!"

A flurry of commotion broke out inside the cave. Everyone knew Chifeng-zun's temperament—the more they tried to explain, the more furious he would get. None of them were likely to escape punishment today. All they could do was admit fault without putting up a resistance, and so, no one dared speak.

Nie Mingjue sneered but didn't enter the cave. He said to Meng Yao, "Come with me."

He turned around and walked down the mountain. Sure enough, Meng Yao followed. Both of them walked for a distance, but Meng Yao's head hung lower and lower as they went, and his steps grew increasingly heavy. It was a long time before he managed to speak.

"Thank you, Sect Leader Nie."

Nie Mingjue said, "A man stands upright and moves with principle. There's no need for you to take that idle gossip to heart."

Meng Yao nodded and answered, "Yes, sir."

Though he said that, his face still showed a hint of worry. Nie Mingjue standing up for him today would keep the cultivators in check for a while, but the men would definitely take their frustrations out on him a hundredfold in the future. How could he not worry?

Nie Mingjue, however, said, "The more those fools talk behind your back, the more you have to prove yourself and render them speechless. I've seen you in battle before. Every time, you were at the fore, and every time, you stayed until the end to guide and settle the common people. You've done well. Keep it up."

Meng Yao froze on hearing this praise from him. He lifted his head slightly.

Nie Mingjue continued, "Your swordplay is very agile but not decisive enough. You still need practice."

This was already an explicit encouragement. Meng Yao hurriedly said, "Thank you, Sect Leader Nie, for your guidance."

But Wei Wuxian understood that no amount of practice would help. Jin Guangyao wasn't like the other clan juniors. His cultivation foundation was too poor for him to scale new heights. He could only seek breadth of knowledge in his cultivation, not depth or proficiency. This was also why he sought to consolidate the strengths of the various clans, and to learn of the unique skills of each, leading him to once be denounced as a "thief of skills."

Hejian was a key stronghold of the Sunshot Campaign. It was also Nie Mingjue's main battleground, an iron bastion that straddled the western side of the Wen Clan's territory at Qishan, leaving them no choice but to invade east and march south. The Nie Clan of Qinghe and the Wen Clan of Qishan had old grudges to begin with, which they had previously managed to hold back. But when the war broke out, both sides burst into action, waging dozens of battles of varying scale to the bitter end, taking heavy casualties each time. The commoners in Hejian suffered as a result, and while the unscrupulous Wen Clan of Qishan would stop at nothing to win, the Nie Clan of Qinghe could not do the same.

Under these circumstances, Meng Yao, who always went out of his way to clear the battlefield and guide and reassure commoners, began to gain more and more attention from Nie Mingjue. After a few such engagements, Nie Mingjue directly promoted him to be at his side as a deputy envoy. Meng Yao seized this opportunity, reliably executing the tasks he was given every time. Thus, the Jin Guangyao of this period was not harshly lectured by Nie Mingjue but rather appreciated and well regarded. Wei Wuxian had heard so many jokes along the lines of "Lianfang-zun fled every time he heard Chifeng-zun approach," that he found it surreal to see Meng Yao getting along so easily and harmoniously with Nie Mingjue.

On this day, the Hejian battleground welcomed a guest.

During the Sunshot Campaign, tales of the heroic deeds of the Three Zun were told across the land. Chifeng-zun—Nie Mingjue—was the invincible one, who swept clean all the lands he passed, destroying all Wen dogs in his path. Zewu-jun—Lan Xichen—was different. Lan Qiren was able to defend Gusu once the situation there stabilized, so Lan Xichen often ventured forth to offer assistance and deliver the people from despair and misery, as well as recover lost territory. During the Sunshot Campaign, he snatched countless lives from the jaws of death on an innumerable number of occasions. As such, people rejoiced at the sound of his name, as if his very existence was a glimmer of hope, a guarantee of their survival.

Every time Lan Xichen escorted cultivators from other clans through Hejian, he would stop to rest, using it as a sort of transit station. This time was no different. Nie Mingjue personally led him into a bright and spacious hall with several other cultivators already sitting at its head.

Although Lan Xichen's appearance was almost identical to Lan Wangji's, Wei Wuxian could distinguish one from the other with a single glance. But when he saw his face, his heart couldn't help but skip a beat. *I wonder how my body's holding up?* he thought. *With this paper one being assaulted by resentment, will something go awry with my physical body? Will Lan Zhan notice that something's amiss?*

After a few pleasantries, Meng Yao, who had been standing at attention behind Nie Mingjue, came out to serve tea to each of the guests. On the battlefield, one person did the work of six; there was simply no room for dedicated errand-runners or maidservants. And so, Jin Guangyao, the deputy envoy, took the initiative to undertake all such daily sundries.

The cultivators were taken aback when they got a clear look at his face, each reacting with different expressions. Jin Guangshan's amorous anecdotes had always been a hot topic of conversation, and since Meng Yao had been a famous laughingstock for a while, a few of them recognized him. Probably thinking the son of a prostitute was perhaps unclean as well, these cultivators did not drink the tea he served them with both hands. They accepted the teacups but then set them aside, looking ill, and took out snow-white handkerchiefs to repeatedly scrub the fingers that had just touched the cups.

Nie Mingjue was not a mindful person by nature and did not notice. Wei Wuxian, on the other hand, caught a glimpse out of the corner of his eyes. Meng Yao continued to serve the tea, his smile unflagging, as if he hadn't seen it.

When Lan Xichen accepted the tea, he looked up at him and smiled. "Thank you."

He promptly lowered his head to take a sip, then continued his discussion with Nie Mingjue after having done so. The other cultivators felt somewhat uncomfortable at the sight of this.

Nie Mingjue was a serious man of few words, but even his expression would soften when he was in Lan Xichen's presence. "How long are you staying?"

"I'll stay the night at Mingjue-xiong's place and set off tomorrow to meet up with Wangji," Lan Xichen replied.

"Where are you heading?" Nie Mingjue asked.

"Jiangling," Lan Xichen answered.

Nie Mingjue frowned. "Isn't Jiangling still in the hands of the Wen dogs?"

"Not since two days ago," Lan Xichen replied. "It is now held by the Jiang Clan of Yunmeng."

One of the clan heads spoke up. "Sect Leader Nie may not be aware of this, but Sect Leader Jiang of Yunmeng's influence in the area is quite impressive, now."

"And why wouldn't it be?" another person said. "Wei Wuxian can take on an army of a million all by himself. What does he have to fear? He doesn't need to kill himself running around the way we do, he's in total control of that area. What luck..."

Someone else, sensing his tone wasn't quite right, hurriedly added, "Thank goodness for Zewu-jun and Hanguang-jun's assistance everywhere—if not for them, who knows how many prominent clans and innocent commoners would meet their end at the hands of the Wen dogs?"

"Your younger brother is there?" Nie Mingjue asked.

Lan Xichen nodded. "He escorted some men there earlier this month."

"Your younger brother's cultivation level is high," Nie Mingjue commented. "He alone is enough, so why are you still going?"

For some reason, Wei Wuxian was happy to hear him praise Lan Wangji. *You've got a good eye there, Chifeng-zun.*

"It's embarrassing to speak of," Lan Xichen said with a sigh, "but after Wangji arrived, it seems he had an unpleasant encounter with Wei-gongzi from the Jiang Clan of Yunmeng. I think I'd better go take a look."

Nie Mingjue asked, "What happened?"

"It seems it was because Wei Wuxian's methods were too dark and grotesque," someone said. "They got into an argument. Apparently, Lan Wangji severely rebuked Wei Wuxian—something about him demeaning corpses, being cruel and bloodthirsty, losing sight of his nature and whatnot. But rumors of the battle at Jiangling are spreading, making Wei Wuxian out to be a legend. I'll have to take a look for myself, should the chance arise."

What this man recounted was actually one of the better versions of the story. The exaggerated versions had him and Lan Wangji fighting each other at the same time they were killing Wen dogs on the battlefield, but in truth, their relationship at the time wasn't as irreconcilable or antagonistic as the rumors made them out to be. Still, they did have some minor, unhappy disagreements. At the time, Wei Wuxian had been out digging up graves every day. Lan Wangji never had anything good to say about this, and even actively tried to stop him. Something, something, "harming the body and mind is not the right path," and so forth. Since they were clashing with the Wen dogs every few days, either by staging ambushes or meeting them head-on, tempers ran hot all the time and they often parted on bad terms. It all felt like a lifetime ago as Wei Wuxian listened to the others discuss this.

Not as if, he suddenly remembered. *It really was a lifetime ago.*

"If you ask me, there's no need for Hanguang-jun to fuss so much," someone else said. "The living are already on the verge of death. Who cares about the bodies of the dead?"

"Yeah, these are desperate times," another chimed in. "Sect Leader Jiang is right. Who can beat the Wen dogs when it comes to evil? In any case, he's on our side. It's all good as long as it's the Wen dogs he's killing."

That's not what you people said later, when you all joined forces to kill me, Wei Wuxian thought.

Not long later, Lan Xichen rose with his men and let Meng Yao lead them to the rest area while Nie Mingjue returned to his own room. He retrieved a long, slender saber and took it with him to find Lan Xichen. But before he got close, he heard the two talking inside the rest area.

Lan Xichen said, "Such a coincidence. To think you joined Mingjue-xiong's command and became his deputy envoy."

"It's all thanks to Chifeng-zun's appreciation and decision to promote me," Meng Yao said.

"Mingjue-xiong has a personality that blazes like fire," Lan Xichen said with a smile. "It cannot have been easy for you to earn his appreciation and have him promote you." After a moment's pause, he continued, "Recently, Sect Leader Jin of Lanling has been having a difficult time holding the line at Langye. They are currently recruiting talent from all over."

Meng Yao was slightly taken aback. "Zewu-jun, you mean..."

Lan Xichen said, "No need to sound so cautious. I remember you telling me how you hoped to earn a place at the Jin Clan of Lanling and win your father's approval. Now that you have established yourself under Mingjue-xiong's command and had the opportunity to put your talents to good use here, does your old wish still hold true?"

Meng Yao seemed to hold his breath, his brows knitting. After a long silence, he answered, "Yes."

"I imagined so," Lan Xichen said.

"But I'm already the deputy envoy for Sect Leader Nie," Meng Yao protested. "I owe him a debt of gratitude for his recognition and appreciation. Whether or not I still wish for it, I can't leave Hejian."

Lan Xichen pondered this for a moment. "Indeed. Even if you desire to leave, it might be difficult to broach the subject. But I trust that if you ask, Mingjue-xiong will respect your wishes. In the event he refuses to let you go, I can help persuade him a little."

Nie Mingjue suddenly spoke up. "Why would I refuse?"

He pushed the door open and entered the room. Lan Xichen and Meng Yao, who sat facing each other with solemn expressions, were surprised by his sudden entry. Meng Yao jolted to his feet, but before he could say a word, Nie Mingjue gave an order.

"Sit."

Meng Yao did not move.

Nie Mingjue continued, "I'll write you a letter of recommendation tomorrow."

"Sect Leader Nie?" Meng Yao said tentatively.

Nie Mingjue stated, "You can take this letter to Langye and look for your father."

Meng Yao hurriedly said, "Sect Leader Nie, if you heard all of that, then you should also have heard me say..."

"I did not promote you because I wanted you to repay my kindness," Nie Mingjue interrupted. "I merely think you are capable and that your character is very much to my liking, which is why you deserve this position. If you genuinely wish to repay me, kill more of the Wen dogs on the battlefields!"

These words stumped the ever-eloquent Meng Yao. Lan Xichen smiled. "You see? I told you Mingjue-xiong will respect your choice."

Meng Yao's eyes reddened. "Sect Leader Nie, Zewu-jun... I..." He bowed his head. "...I really don't know what to say."

Nie Mingjue sat down. "Then don't say a word."

He set the other saber in his hand on the table. Seeing this, Lan Xichen smiled.

"Huaisang's saber?"

"Although he is safe at your home, he mustn't neglect his studies,"

Nie Mingjue said. "Have someone supervise him when they are free. The next time we meet, I want to evaluate his saber techniques and understanding of cultivation scripture."

Lan Xichen tucked the saber away in his qiankun sleeve. "Huaisang was initially pleased to be excused from training, saying he left his saber at home. Now he has no more reason to slack off."

"Come to think of it, have the two of you met before?" Nie Mingjue wondered.

"Yes, I've met Zewu-jun before."

"Where? When?" Nie Mingjue probed.

Lan Xichen shook his head with a smile. "Let's not bring it up. It's the greatest disgrace of my life, so please don't probe further, Mingjue-xiong."

"Why would you worry about losing face in front of me?" Nie Mingjue said. "Meng Yao, you tell me."

But Meng Yao said, "Since Zewu-jun is unwilling to say, I cannot reveal it."

The three chatted, talking business one moment and making idle conversation the next, their manner more relaxed and casual than it had been in the hall earlier. Wei Wuxian kept wanting to butt in as he listened, but he couldn't, so he let his thoughts wander.

Their relationship isn't bad at all, right now. Why is Lan Zhan so bad at making conversation when Zewu-jun is this chatty? Well, it's okay. It's fine if he keeps his mouth shut. Since I already talk enough for the two of us, he can just listen and acknowledge me with his "mn"s. That's nice too. What do you call that again...?

A few days later, Meng Yao left Hejian for Langye with the letter of recommendation from Nie Mingjue.

After he left, Nie Mingjue had a change of deputy envoys, but Wei Wuxian felt that the replacement was always somehow half a beat slower. Meng Yao was a rare talent, resourceful and quick-witted, able to understand what was left unsaid, complete a task in its entirety even when only a fraction of it was described to him. Always efficient, never sloppy—it was hard not to compare the work of others when you'd grown accustomed to someone like him.

After some time, the Jin Clan of Lanling—which had already been struggling to hold the line at Langye—was nearly at their breaking point. Lan Xichen happened to be assisting another afflicted area, so Jin Guangshan sought help from Hejian instead, and Nie Mingjue answered the call.

After the battle was over, a frazzled Jin Guangshan came over to express his gratitude. Nie Mingjue exchanged a few curt words with him before asking after Meng Yao.

"Sect Leader Jin, what is Meng Yao's position now?"

Jin Guangshan was confused to hear the name. "Meng Yao? Um... meaning no offense to Sect Leader Nie, of course, but who's that again?"

Nie Mingjue immediately frowned. The incident in which Meng Yao was kicked down Golden Carp Tower had been a popular anecdote for some time now. Even bystanders knew all about the farce, meaning there was no way one of the main people involved didn't remember the name. Anyone with less face would have been embarrassed to play dumb, but as it turned out, Jin Guangshan's skin was as thick as they came.

"Meng Yao was my former deputy envoy," Nie Mingjue explained frostily. "I wrote a letter and had him bring it to you."

Jin Guangshan continued to play dumb. "Is that so? But I've never seen any letters nor met any such person. Alas, if I had known Sect Leader Nie had sent his deputy envoy over, I'd have given him a proper reception. Perhaps something went amiss along the way?"

Nie Mingjue's expression grew increasingly cold at these perfunctory excuses of not remembering and never hearing of such a person. Thinking there must be something more to the situation, he unceremoniously took his leave. He asked the other cultivators but came up with nothing. He was striding about at random when he came upon a small patch of woods.

These woods were very secluded. An ambush attack and subsequent massacre had just occurred, and the battlefield had yet to be cleaned up. As Nie Mingjue walked through the trees, the ground was strewn with the corpses of cultivators dressed in various attire: some from the Wen Clan, some from the Jin Clan, and some from other clans.

Suddenly, a ripping sound tore through the air ahead.

Nie Mingjue put his hand on the hilt of his saber and crept over stealthily. He quietly brushed aside the leaves, only to see Meng Yao standing among the pile of corpses.

With a twist of his wrist, Meng Yao pulled a long sword out of a cultivator's chest. He looked extremely calm. His strike was steady, swift, and so careful that there wasn't so much as a drop of blood on him.

The sword was not his own. Its hilt had flame-like iron ornamentation—it was the sword of a cultivator from the Wen Clan.

His sword technique was also of the Wen Clan.

As for the man he'd killed, he was wearing a robe depicting the peony Sparks Amidst Snow. He was a cultivator of the Jin Clan of Lanling.

Nie Mingjue took this scene in and said nothing. His saber left its sheath an inch, emitting a sharp, jarring noise. The familiar sound of a blade leaving its sheath made Meng Yao shiver, and he whirled his head back, almost scared out of his wits.

"...Sect Leader Nie?"

Nie Mingjue drew his saber out of its sheath in its entirety. Its glint flashed bright, but the blade itself was tinged slightly blood-red. Wei Wuxian could feel the monstrous fury boiling from him, as well as the bitter disappointment.

Meng Yao, well acquainted with Nie Mingjue's personality, threw away his sword with a clatter. "Sect Leader Nie, Sect Leader Nie! Wait, please wait! Let me explain!"

Nie Mingjue bellowed, "What is there for you to explain?!"

Meng Yao scrambled over. "I had no choice! I was forced to do it!"

Nie Mingjue fumed. "What do you mean, no choice?! What did I say when I sent you over?!"

Meng Yao prostrated himself at Nie Mingjue's feet. "Sect Leader Nie, Sect Leader Nie, hear me out! I joined the Jin Clan of Lanling, and this man was my superior. He belittles me, always humiliates and reprimands me in every possible way..."

"So you killed him?" Nie Mingjue curtly asked.

"No! It wasn't because of this!" Meng Yao cried out. "What humiliation is there that I cannot endure? Beatings and insults are nothing to me! But with every stronghold we won over—all the pain and effort I put into strategizing, planning our approach—he only needed to say a few breezy words, make a few brushstrokes, and claim all credit for himself, saying I had nothing to do with it! This wasn't the first time. He did it every time, every single time! I tried to reason with him, but he didn't care at all, and when I went to the others, no one was willing to listen. He even said earlier that my mother...my mother was a... It was really more than I could bear. In a moment of rage, I lost my head. I made a misstep."

Meng Yao spoke rapidly in his panic, scared that Nie Mingjue would bring his blade down on him without letting him finish, but his account was as clear and methodical as ever—every word emphasizing how others were so loathsome and how innocent he was.

Nie Mingjue grabbed him by his collar and lifted him up. "You're lying!"

Meng Yao shuddered. Nie Mingjue stared directly into his eyes and enunciated his response word by word.

"You couldn't bear it anymore? Lost your head in a moment of rage and made a misstep? Would someone who lost his head in a moment of rage have worn the kind of expression you did when killing a man? Would he have so deliberately chosen a secluded, hidden forest where a massacre had just taken place? Would he specifically use a Wen sword and Wen techniques to kill? Would he disguise himself as a Wen dog to launch a sneak attack, so as to frame them? You've clearly been planning this for a long time!"

Meng Yao raised his hand to swear it. "I'm telling the truth! Every word of it is true!"

"Even so, you can't just kill him!" Nie Mingjue raged. "It's only a bit of military merit! You care that much about this tiny bit of trivial glory?!"

"...a tiny bit?" Meng Yao muttered. His voice trembled as he continued. "...what do you mean, a tiny bit of military merit? Chifeng-zun, do you know how much effort I've put in to earn this tiny bit of military merit? How much hardship I've suffered? Trivial glory? Without this tiny bit of trivial glory, I would have nothing!"

Nie Mingjue sized up his tearful and trembling face. The contrast with his cold-blooded act of murder earlier was far too intense. The shock of it had yet to fade from his mind.

"Meng Yao, let me ask you—the first time I met you, did you deliberately put on that weak, bullied act for my benefit? All so that

I'd stand up for you? If I hadn't, would you have killed those people like you did this man today?"

Meng Yao's throat bobbed. A drop of cold sweat slid down his face. He was just about to answer when Nie Mingjue bellowed at him.

"Do not lie to me!"

Meng Yao gave a start and swallowed his words. He kneeled on the ground, his entire body trembling as the fingers of his right hand dug deep into the earth.

After a while, Nie Mingjue slowly returned his saber to its sheath. "I will not lay a hand on you."

Meng Yao's head shot up.

Nie Mingjue continued, "Go confess your crime to the Jin Clan of Lanling and receive your punishment, whatever it may be."

After a moment of stupefaction, Meng Yao said, "...Chifeng-zun, I can't die at this step."

"With this step, you've strayed from the proper path," Nie Mingjue stated.

"You're asking me to pay with my life."

"A price that needn't be paid if everything you've said is the truth," replied Nie Mingjue. "Go. Repent and turn over a new leaf."

Meng Yao murmured under his breath. "...My father hasn't seen me yet."

It wasn't that Jin Guangshan had not seen him. He was merely pretending to be unaware of his existence.

Eventually, under pressure from Nie Mingjue, Meng Yao arduously uttered a "yessir." After a moment of silence, Nie Mingjue said, "Get up."

Meng Yao stood up from the ground in a trance, as if drained, and staggered a few steps. Seeing he was about to fall, Nie Mingjue steadied him.

Meng Yao mumbled, "...thank you, Sect Leader Nie."

At the sight of his despondent look, Nie Mingjue turned around. But suddenly, he heard Meng Yao say, "...still can't do it."

Nie Mingjue jerked his head back. A longsword had somehow found its way into Meng Yao's hand. He was already aiming the sword at his own stomach.

His expression was one of despair. "Sect Leader Nie, I've proven unworthy of your great kindness."

With that, he stabbed down hard. Nie Mingjue's pupils shrank as he swiftly made a grab for the sword, but it was already too late. The sword in Meng Yao's hand pierced his abdomen and jutted out through his back. He slumped in the pool of blood that was not his own.

Nie Mingjue was momentarily stunned before he rushed over and half kneeled on the ground to turn over Meng Yao's body. "You...!!"

Meng Yao's ghastly pale face looked up at him feebly as he said with a forced, wry smile, "Sect Leader Nie, I..."

He had yet to finish his words when his head slowly drooped. Nie Mingjue lifted his body and, avoiding the blade, pressed his palm to his chest to transfer a burst of spiritual energy. But unexpectedly, his own body suddenly gave a slight jolt as a cold, ceaseless flow of spiritual current spread through his abdomen.

Wei Wuxian, having long expected there to be an underhanded trick in store, wasn't surprised. But Nie Mingjue had never expected Meng Yao to attack him so viciously. As such, even when he found himself unable to move, his shock still far outweighed his fury as he watched Meng Yao slowly crawl back to his feet.

Meng Yao had likely calculated beforehand how to avoid his vitals. He calmly and carefully pulled the sword from his abdomen, bringing a small spray of crimson along with the bright red blade. Then he compressed the wound and seemed to consider it taken care of. Meanwhile, Nie Mingjue was still frozen in his pose of going to Meng Yao's aid. Half kneeling on the ground, he raised his head slightly to meet Meng Yao's eyes.

Nie Mingjue said nothing. Neither did Meng Yao. He inserted his sword back into its sheath, bowed, and darted away without sparing a backward glance.

Moments ago, he had obediently admitted his mistake and agreed to receive his punishment. Then, in the blink of an eye, he resorted to trickery and pretended to commit suicide only to stab Nie Mingjue in the back. Now he had fled without a trace. Nie Mingjue had probably never met a more shameless man. Worse, the man had once been a trusted aide whom he'd promoted himself.

Consequently, he flew into a rage and was particularly savage when he faced the Wen Clan's cultivators. When Lan Xichen found time to head to Langye and assist with the battle a few days later, Nie Mingjue's fury had still not subsided.

The moment Lan Xichen arrived, he said with a smile, "That's quite the rage Mingjue-xiong is in. Where's Meng Yao? Why isn't he here to douse those flames of yours?"

"Don't mention that name!" Nie Mingjue barked.

He relayed the incident where Meng Yao committed murder, framed another, feigned death, and fled in its entirety to Lan Xichen, who was also stunned to hear it.

"How could this be? Is there some kind of misunderstanding?"

"I caught him red-handed." Nie Mingjue said, "What misunderstanding can there be?"

Lan Xichen thought for a moment. "Going by what he said, the man he killed was indeed at fault, but he really should not have killed him. It is hard to judge what is correct in such desperate times. I wonder where he is now."

"He'd better not let me catch him, or I'll sacrifice him to my blade!" Nie Mingjue replied sharply.

Unexpectedly, the remark proved to be prophetic. In the years that followed, Meng Yao seemed to have vanished entirely, like a stone sunk into the sea, never to be seen or heard from again. There was not a single trace of him to be found.

Nie Mingjue detested Meng Yao with the same fervor he had initially admired and valued him. He would grow enraged every time Meng Yao was mentioned and be unable to explain why. Once he was certain there was no news of him to be had, he refused to discuss him with anyone.

Nie Mingjue never got close to other people, and he rarely bared his heart to them. To finally have a competent, trustworthy subordinate whose capabilities and character he approved of, then discover the person's true colors were not at all what he'd initially thought—it couldn't have been easy on him. No wonder his reaction was so vehement.

Just as Wei Wuxian thought this, he was suddenly struck by a splitting headache. Every bone in his body seemed to have been run over by a war chariot. The slightest jerk made his bones creak.

He was immobile. He opened both eyes, his vision so blurred that he could barely make out the many figures sprawled on the floor tiled with icy-cold black jade. Nie Mingjue seemed to have suffered a head injury. The wound was already numb, and blood congealed over his eyes and face. He moved slightly, and warm blood trickled down his forehead again.

Wei Wuxian was astonished. Nie Mingjue was almost invincible during the Sunshot Campaign. Enemies couldn't even get close to him, let alone injure him so badly.

What's going on here?!

There was a minuscule movement to the side. Wei Wuxian swept a glance out of the corner of his eye and spied a few blurred figures. He focused his vision with some difficulty and managed to make out several cultivators dressed in blazing sun robes. They were kneeling, shuffling around the room on their knees.

Wei Wuxian refrained from comment. "..."

All of a sudden, an oppressive feeling washed over him. It spread to Wei Wuxian through Nie Mingjue's limbs and bones, making his hair stand on end. Nie Mingjue lifted his head slightly and saw a giant jade throne at the end of the black jade tiling.

A man sat on it. At this distance, and with blood obscuring his vision, Nie Mingjue couldn't get a clear look at him. But even so, he could guess who it was.

The doors to the main hall opened, and a man entered.

The disciples in the great hall all remained on the ground, moving only on their knees. But this man, other than giving a slight bow and lowering his head in greeting on entry, was not like them. With easy indifference, he walked straight down the long line of jade tiles to the end, where he appeared to bend over and listen to the man on the jade throne say a few words before turning.

Slowly pacing forward, this man quietly sized up Nie Mingjue, who was drenched in blood but still forcing himself upright. He seemed to smile as he greeted him.

"It's been a while, Sect Leader Nie."

That voice—who else could it be, if not Meng Yao?

Wei Wuxian was finally certain what he was seeing.

This was the year Nie Mingjue received intelligence that led him to launch a surprise attack in Yangquan. Chifeng-zun always secured victory whenever he took the initiative to lead an offensive. But this time, whether because of a flaw in their intel, their plans being leaked, or a simple case of "man proposes, god disposes," they ran unexpectedly into Wen Ruohan, head of the Wen Clan of Qishan. Their erroneous estimate of the enemy's strength allowed the Wen Clan of Qishan to turn the tables on them. In one fell swoop, they rounded up all the attacking cultivators and brought them back to Nightless City as prisoners.

Meng Yao half kneeled beside Nie Mingjue. "I really never thought there'd be a day I'd see you in such a sorry state."

Nie Mingjue only said, "Get lost."

Meng Yao's chuckle was laced with pity. "Do you still think you're the King of Hejian? Look carefully. This is the Scorching Sun Palace."

A cultivator at the side spat. "What 'Scorching Sun Palace'? It's merely a den of Wen dogs!"

Meng Yao's expression changed. He drew his longsword.

In an instant, a streak of blood spewed from the cultivator's neck, who toppled over without so much as a grunt. His fellow sect members screamed and lunged forward.

Nie Mingjue was furious. "You!"

Another cultivator roared in rage, "Wen dog! Kill me too, if you're so capable..."

Meng Yao's brows didn't so much as twitch. With a backhanded swing, his sword cut that cultivator's throat as well, spattering blood.

"Certainly," he answered with a smile.

Sword in hand, he stood before a pool of blood, the corpses of the two cultivators in white toppled at his feet. He grinned.

"Who else wants to repeat those two words?"

Nie Mingjue answered coldly, "Wen dog."

He knew perfectly well that falling into the hands of Wen Ruohan meant certain death, and so he felt no fear. If Wei Wuxian had been in his shoes, he would also have cussed to his heart's content—to hell with everything, he was going to die anyway. But instead of flying into a rage, Meng Yao merely smiled. He snapped his fingers, and a Wen Clan cultivator came up to him on his knees, both hands held over his head to present a long box. Meng Yao opened the box.

"Sect Leader Nie, why don't you take a look at what this is?"

It was Nie Mingjue's saber, Baxia!

"Get out of my sight!" Nie Mingjue raged.

But Meng Yao had already taken Baxia out of the box. "Sect Leader Nie, Baxia has passed through my hands a number of times at this point. Isn't it a bit too late for you to be angry now?"

Nie Mingjue enunciated each word: "Remove. Your. Hands!"

However, it was as though Meng Yao was purposely trying to incense him. He weighed the saber in his hand, commenting, "Sect Leader Nie, one could begrudgingly consider this saber of yours to be a first-rate spiritual weapon, no? But it's still slightly inferior to the saber of your father—the former Sect Leader Nie. Why don't you make a wager on how many times Sect Leader Wen needs to slap it to break it this time around?"

In that instant, every drop of blood in Nie Mingjue's body surged to his head. His sudden burst of rage sent a chill down Wei Wuxian's spine as he thought, *How vicious.*

The one thing Nie Mingjue hated most in his life—the one thing he could not move past—was the death of his father.

It had happened when Nie Mingjue was only in his teens and his father was still the head of the Nie Clan of Qinghe. Someone paid tribute to Wen Ruohan with a treasured saber, which delighted him for several days. He asked the guest cultivators at his side, *What do you think of this saber of mine?*

He had always been an unpredictable, capricious man who turned hostile and fell out with people at the drop of a hat. And so the guest cultivators naturally went along with him, vigorously praising the saber as having no equal. But one of them, whether out of animosity for the former Sect Leader Nie or the desire to stand out by giving a different answer, said, *This saber of yours is incomparable, of course. But, well, I'm afraid there's someone who wouldn't agree.*

That made Wen Ruohan unhappy, and he demanded, *Who?*

The clan head of the Nie Clan of Qinghe, of course, the guest cultivator answered. *His family has been renowned through the ages for their saber cultivation. He boasts at every opportunity that his own precious saber is invincible and unrivaled, that not a single saber forged in the past few centuries can ever compare to his. His arrogance is extreme. No matter how great your saber is, he will never admit as much. Even if he does so aloud, it'll be a different story deep down in his heart.*

Wen Ruohan roared with laughter, saying he had to see this for himself. Thus, he immediately summoned the former Sect Leader Nie over from Qinghe. He took his saber and looked it over, seated on his throne. Eventually, he said, *Yes. A fine saber, as I thought.* He idly slapped it a few times and let the man go.

Nothing appeared odd at the time. The former Sect Leader Nie was puzzled, of course, and also quite displeased by the man's audacity at summoning and dismissing him on a whim. But unexpectedly, several days after he returned home, his saber suddenly shattered into several pieces when he brought it down upon a demonic beast during a Night Hunt. The beast seized the opportunity to charge and severely gored him with its horns.

And Nie Mingjue, who had been Night Hunting with his father, witnessed this scene with his very own eyes.

Although the previous Sect Leader Nie was saved from immediate death, the injustice of it all was too much for him to swallow. His injuries never did heal, and he lingered in ill health for half a year before finally passing away. No one knew if he died of anger or of illness. This was why Nie Mingjue and the entire Nie Clan of Qinghe loathed the Wen Clan of Qishan with such intensity.

And now Meng Yao was holding his saber in Wen Ruohan's presence, all the while dredging up his lifelong regrets around his father's shattered saber and death. Meng Yao was simply malicious to the core!

Nie Mingjue struck out with a palm, and Meng Yao staggered back and coughed out a mouthful of blood. At this, the figure on the jade throne leaned slightly forward, as if poised to move. Meng Yao promptly climbed to his feet and charged over to kick Nie Mingjue in the chest. Nie Mingjue had expended too much energy on that one strike, and the kick knocked him heavily to the ground. The blood that was burning in his veins finally boiled over and spewed from his mouth. Wei Wuxian, on the other hand, was struck dumb.

There were so many versions of this story floating around. He could never have imagined so entertaining a detail as Lianfang-zun taking a flying kick at Chifeng-zun!

Meng Yao stomped down firmly on Nie Mingjue's chest and shouted, "You dare behave so atrociously before Sect Leader Wen?!"

He stabbed downward with his sword. Nie Mingjue struck out a palm, breaking the sword in Meng Yao's hands into pieces. The blow also knocked Meng Yao over, but just as Nie Mingjue was about to land a second strike on his head, a strange force suddenly yanked his body in the direction of Wen Ruohan's jade throne.

Nie Mingjue was hauled across the jade tiles with such speed that he left a trail of blood nine meters long and growing.

He reached out to grab a Wen Clan disciple who was kneeling on the ground and tossed him in the direction of the jade throne. With a *bang*, blood exploded through the air like a watermelon being blown apart, splattering pulp all over the ground. To think Wen Ruohan had actually cleaved a disciple's skull to pieces by simply striking his palm at the air!

But this also bought time for Nie Mingjue. Fury gave him a sudden boost of inexhaustible power, and he sprang up and brandished his hand to form a seal. Baxia came flying toward him.

"Sect Leader, watch out!" Meng Yao yelled.

A voice laughed maniacally. "No harm done!"

Wei Wuxian was not in the least bit surprised by how youthful the voice sounded. Wen Ruohan's cultivation level was high, and thus, his physical body was naturally maintained at its prime.

As soon as Nie Mingjue grabbed Baxia's hilt, he swung out and cleaved the dozens of Wen Clan cultivators who had come to surround him in half.

The black jade path was strewn with mutilated corpses. All of a sudden, a shiver ran down Wei Wuxian's back.

A figure materialized behind him. Nie Mingjue slashed out horizontally, and his spiritual energy shattered a long strip of the floor to pieces. His strike missed its target, but he received a heavy kick to the chest for his trouble, crashing into the golden pillar in the hall. He coughed out another mouthful of blood. Fresh blood trickled down his forehead. His gradually blurring vision sensed someone approaching. He raised his saber again and, this time, was punched right in the chest. At this strike, his entire body sank nearly a meter into the jade floor!

Wei Wuxian, whose five senses were connected to Nie Mingjue's, was left stunned even as he was brutally battered.

Wen Ruohan's strength really was unimaginably terrifying!

Never having dueled Nie Mingjue before, Wei Wuxian had no clue who might win or lose. But based on his observations, as far as power and skill went, Nie Mingjue was in the top three of all the cultivators he had ever seen. And even so, he was entirely unable to counterattack when faced with Wen Ruohan! In fact, Wei Wuxian would have been hard-pressed to claim he'd do any better if he were in Nie Mingjue's place.

Wen Ruohan stepped on Nie Mingjue's chest. Wei Wuxian's vision was going black, and the stench of blood was surging straight up his throat.

Meng Yao's voice gradually approached. "I am an incompetent subordinate, to have troubled Sect Leader to make a personal appearance."

"Trash," Wen Ruohan said with a laugh.

Meng Yao chuckled too.

"He's the one who killed Wen Xu?" Wen Ruohan asked.

"That's right," Meng Yao answered. "The very one. Sect Leader, will you be killing him with your own hands or dragging him off to Inferno Palace? My personal suggestion is that he'd be best suited for Inferno Palace."

The Inferno Palace was Wen Ruohan's playground. It was where he stored his collection of thousands of torture devices, with the specific intent to inflict them on others. This meant that Meng Yao was unwilling to give Nie Mingjue a swift and straightforward death. He wanted to drag him to Wen Ruohan's torture chamber and use the devices he had personally made to slowly and methodically grind him into the grave.

As Nie Mingjue listened to these two men merrily discussing what to do with him, his fury blazed, and the blood in his chest churned.

"What pleasure is there in toying with the life of someone already half-dead?" Wen Ruohan commented.

"Well, now," Meng Yao replied. "Given Sect Leader Nie's strong and healthy physique, who knows if he will return to his awe-inspiring self after a few days of recuperation?"

"Do as you will," Wen Ruohan said.

"Yes, sir," Meng Yao answered.

However, at the same time he spoke, an extremely thin flash of cold light swept across Wei Wuxian's vision.

Wen Ruohan suddenly went dead silent.

Warm blood splashed onto Nie Mingjue's face. As if sensing something, he strained to raise his head to see what was going on but was ultimately too severely injured to hold on any longer. His head fell heavily, and he closed his eyes.

An unknown amount of time passed before Wei Wuxian felt a glimmer of light before him. Nie Mingjue was gradually opening his eyes.

The moment he came to, he discovered that he was being supported by Meng Yao. With one of Nie Mingjue's arms draped over his shoulder, Meng Yao strained to move forward while half-dragging and half-carrying him on his back.

"Sect Leader Nie?" Meng Yao called to him.

"Wen Ruohan is dead?" Nie Mingjue asked.

Meng Yao seemed to have slipped for a moment. He answered in a trembling voice, "He...should be."

He was still holding something in his hand.

Nie Mingjue said darkly, "Give me the saber."

Wei Wuxian couldn't see the expression on Meng Yao's face but could hear the wry smile in his voice. "Sect Leader Nie, let's not think about chopping me up at a time like this..."

Nie Mingjue was silent for a moment. After he had mustered up enough energy, he made a grab for the saber. Although Meng Yao was nimble and quick-witted, raw power and strength still won in such situations. Unable to defend himself, he hastily leapt away.

"Sect Leader Nie, you're still injured."

With the long saber in hand, Nie Mingjue said coldly, "You killed them."

Referring, of course, to the cultivators who had been captured alongside him.

Meng Yao said, "Sect Leader Nie, you should know that under the circumstances earlier...I had no choice."

This was exactly the kind of excuse Nie Mingjue hated most. His chest burned with anger as he swept his saber down in rage. "What do you mean, no choice?! It was up to you whether to do it!"

Meng Yao dodged the blow and defended himself. "Was it really up to me? Sect Leader Nie, if you were in my shoes..."

Nie Mingjue anticipated what he was going to say and cut him off. "I would not!"

Meng Yao seemed utterly exhausted as he repeatedly dodged the blows. Unable to react in time, he nearly tripped, looking rather unkempt as he panted for breath. All of a sudden, he shouted in what seemed to be an outburst of anger, "*Chifeng-zun!!* Do you not understand that if I didn't kill them, it would've been *your* corpse lying there?!"

This was no different from saying *"Since I saved your life, you can't kill me or you'll be in the wrong."* But Jin Guangyao, being Jin Guangyao, had a way with words. His plea was heavy with reserved sorrow and a kind of implicit grievance.

Sure enough, Nie Mingjue's movement faltered. He stood rigidly in place, veins bulging on his forehead. Gripping the hilt of his saber, he bellowed his response.

"*Fine!* I'll hack you to death, then take my own life!"

Meng Yao cowered back as soon as he shouted. And when Baxia came sweeping down, he was scared out of his wits and took to his heels. Both men, drenched in blood, staggered and stumbled along, one of them hacking and one of them fleeing. Wei Wuxian was laughing himself half to death while Nie Mingjue hacked away at the future Cultivation Chief, thinking that if not for Nie Mingjue's severe injuries and depleted spiritual energy, Meng Yao would have long been dead.

Amidst this ridiculous display, an astonished voice suddenly rang out.

"Mingjue-xiong!"

In a flash, a figure in a radiantly white robe darted out of the forest. It was like Meng Yao had laid eyes on a god. He immediately scrambled over behind him.

"Zewu-jun!! *Zewu-jun!!*"

Nie Mingjue was so overwhelmed with rage that he didn't even ask why Lan Xichen was suddenly here. He bellowed, "Xichen, get out of the way!"

Baxia bore down on them so menacingly that Shuoyue had no choice but to leave its sheath. Lan Xichen moved to meet him, partly to support him and partly to stop him.

"Mingjue-xiong, peace! Why be like this?"

"Why don't you ask him what he has done?!" Nie Mingjue retorted.

Lan Xichen looked back at Meng Yao, who stammered, looking panic-stricken and too afraid to speak.

"No wonder I couldn't find him anywhere after he fled Langye!" Nie Mingjue spat. "Turns out he ran off to be a lackey of the Wen dogs and aid that tyrant in perpetuating his evil from Nightless City!"

Lan Xichen called out, "Mingjue-xiong."

He rarely interrupted others, so Nie Mingjue was slightly taken aback. Lan Xichen continued, "Do you know who slipped us the Wen Clan's tactical deployment maps in these last few engagements?"

"You," Nie Mingjue answered.

"I was merely passing them on," Lan Xichen replied. "Do you know who the real source of that information was, all this time?"

The meaning of his words could not be more obvious. Nie Mingjue looked at Meng Yao, who had his head bowed behind Lan Xichen. Nie Mingjue's brows were twitching incessantly, obviously in disbelief.

"There's no need to doubt it," Lan Xichen said. "The very reason I am here at this moment to assist is because he sent me a message asking me to come. By what other coincidence would I be here?"

Nie Mingjue was speechless.

Lan Xichen added, "A-Yao regrets the incident at Langye, but he did not dare encounter you. All he could think to do was infiltrate the Wen Clan of Qishan and get close to Wen Ruohan before sending letters to me in secret. I didn't know the identity of the sender at first. It was only by coincidence that I found out and recognized him." He turned to Meng Yao and said in a low voice, "Didn't you tell Mingjue-xiong about this?"

"..." Meng Yao covered the wound on his arm and said with a wry smile, "Zewu-jun, you saw it too. Even if I told him, Sect Leader Nie would not believe me."

Nie Mingjue kept silent. Baxia and Shuoyue were still at an impasse. Meng Yao only had to cast a glance at the glare of clashing saber and sword for terror to brim in his eyes. After a moment, however, he kneeled before Nie Mingjue.

"Meng Yao?" Lan Xichen called out tentatively.

"Sect Leader Nie," Meng Yao said softly. "I did injure you at Scorching Sun Palace, though I did it to gain Wen Ruohan's trust, so he wouldn't sense something was amiss. And I did speak insolently to you. I knew what happened to the former Sect Leader Nie sorely grieves you, but I still intentionally twisted the knife in that wound... While it might have been a last resort, I really am truly sorry."

Nie Mingjue replied, "You should not kneel to me, but instead to all those cultivators you killed with your own hands."

"Wen Ruohan was a brutal man who went berserk at the slightest hint of defiance," Meng Yao said. "I had to pretend to be his trusted aide. How could I stand by and do nothing when others insulted him? That was why..."

"Good," Nie Mingjue observed. "Seems like you've done your fair share of such deeds before this too."

Meng Yao sighed. "When in Qishan..."

Lan Xichen sighed, still holding his sword in place. "Mingjue-xiong, it...was unavoidable that he would have to do certain things while undercover in Qishan. When he did them, he also felt..."

Wei Wuxian shook his head. *Zewu-jun really is far too pure and kind.*

Then again, he was only able to see through Jin Guangyao because he was already deeply suspicious of him. The Meng Yao currently standing before Lan Xichen, on the other hand, was an undercover agent who endured endless humiliation to carry out his mission alone, left with no choice but to put himself in danger. With such different perspectives, how could their feelings be compared?

After a long moment, Nie Mingjue abruptly raised his saber.

"Mingjue-xiong!" Lan Xichen called out.

Meng Yao closed his eyes. Lan Xichen tightened his grip on Shuoyue as well and said, "Please pardon..."

Before he could finish his words, the silver glint of the saber slashed down—landing on a large boulder next to them.

Meng Yao cowered at the thunderous sound of cracking rock. He turned to look and found the massive stone had been split in half.

In the end, Nie Mingjue could not make himself bring his saber down on Meng Yao. Returning Baxia to its sheath, he turned around and left without sparing them a single backward glance.

Wen Ruohan was dead. Although there were still surviving members of the Wen Clan of Qishan, their forces no longer posed a threat. Their defeat was already set in stone.

And Meng Yao, the brave warrior who went undercover at Nightless City for several years and was willing to give his life for the cause, won acclaim in one battle.

Ever since Meng Yao betrayed and defected from the Nie Clan of Qinghe, his relationship with Nie Mingjue had never been the same again. So, Wei Wuxian had wondered, how did they go on to become sworn brothers later?

Based on his observations, it could be presumed that—aside from Lan Xichen taking the initiative to suggest it, in hopes that they would reconcile—the most important factor was the debt of gratitude Nie Mingjue owed Meng Yao for saving his life and for delivering them intelligence. The information Meng Yao had passed them through Lan Xichen had been of crucial aid to Nie Mingjue in all the battles he waged. He still considered Jin Guangyao a rare talent, and had the mind to guide him back onto the right path, but the man was no longer his subordinate. It was only by becoming sworn brothers that he could regain the right and the status to supervise him, the same way he supervised and disciplined his younger brother Nie Huaisang.

After the Sunshot Campaign concluded, the Jin Clan of Lanling organized a days-long flower-viewing banquet and invited countless cultivators and clans to celebrate with them.

All this pomp, Wei Wuxian thought. *It's like he's ascending to the heavens. These people both fear and respect Nie Mingjue. There were plenty who feared me, but those who respected me were few and far between.*

Jin Guangyao stood at the side of the Sumeru throne-styled palace base. After becoming sworn brothers with Nie Mingjue and Lan Xichen, and being recognized by his clan, he now had a cinnabar mark in between his brows. Dressed in a Sparks Amidst Snow robe with a white base and gold trimmings and a black gauze cap, he had an entirely different air about him, something radiant and refined. He was still as quick-witted as ever, but his bearing was calm and composed, a far cry from how he'd been in the past.

Wei Wuxian was surprised to see a familiar figure at his side.

Xue Yang.

Xue Yang was extremely young at this point in time. Although his face still had a boyish cast to it, he was already very tall. He also wore a Sparks Amidst Snow robe, the very picture of carefree youth as he stood beside Jin Guangyao, like a spring breeze caressing the willow.

They seemed to be talking about something interesting. Jin Guangyao grinned and gestured with his hand. Both men traded glances, and Xue Yang burst out laughing. He nonchalantly swept his eyes across the milling cultivators with a tinge of contempt and apathy in his gaze, as if they were all walking piles of refuse. When he saw Nie Mingjue, he showed no fear, as the others had. Instead, he grinned widely, baring his canine teeth in his direction.

Noticing Nie Mingjue's hostile expression, Jin Guangyao hurriedly curbed his smile and lowered his voice to say a word to Xue Yang, who waved his hand and swaggered off elsewhere.

Jin Guangyao walked over and greeted respectfully, "Da-ge."

"Who is that?" Nie Mingjue asked.

Jin Guangyao hesitated for a moment, then replied very carefully, "Xue Yang."

Nie Mingjue frowned. "Xue Yang from Kui Prefecture?"

Jin Guangyao nodded. Xue Yang was already infamous at a young age. Wei Wuxian could clearly sense Nie Mingjue's frown deepening.

"What are you doing, mingling with the likes of him?" he asked.

"The Jin Clan of Lanling recruited him," Jin Guangyao answered.

He did not dare explain himself further but hastily fled to the other side of the square under the pretext of receiving incoming guests. Nie Mingjue shook his head and turned around. Wei Wuxian's eyes lit up—Lan Xichen and Lan Wangji walked side by side as they made their way over. The sight of them strolling down the hall, bathed in moonlight, was like a vision of frost and snow drifting down from the heavens.

The Twin Jades of the Lan Clan stood together: one with his xiao and one with his guqin, one gentle and refined and one cold and cheerless. They were both beautiful in appearance and elegant in demeanor, both truly of a singular color, but each had a different kind of charm. It was no wonder they drew attention and endless admiration wherever they went.

The Lan Wangji of this time still had a trace of youthful innocence in the contours of his face, but his expression remained aloof, keeping others at arm's length. Wei Wuxian's eyes were immediately glued to him, unable to look away. Not caring whether or not Lan

Wangji could hear him, he gave in to impulse and hollered happily in his mind, *Lan Zhan! I miss you so much! Ha ha ha ha ha ha ha!!*

Suddenly, a voice spoke up. "Sect Leader Nie, Sect Leader Lan."

Wei Wuxian's heart skipped a beat when he heard this familiar voice. Nie Mingjue turned around again to take a look. Jiang Cheng, dressed all in purple, was walking over with his hand resting on his sword.

And the man standing beside Jiang Cheng was none other than Wei Wuxian himself.

He saw himself, dressed all in black, standing with his hands clasped behind his back. A black flute with a bright red tassel hung at his waist. He was not carrying his sword with him. He stood side by side with Jiang Cheng and nodded in greeting. His body language was arrogant, his demeanor so awfully enigmatic and disdainful of everyone present. Seeing this cringe-worthy posturing, Wei Wuxian had the sudden urge to charge up to his younger self and beat the hell out of him.

Lan Wangji had also noticed Wei Wuxian standing beside Jiang Cheng. His eyebrows twitched, but his light eyes soon turned back to stare straight ahead once more, expression still dignified. Jiang Cheng and Nie Mingjue met each other's gaze, straight-faced, and nodded. They had nothing superfluous to say to one another, so they said a hasty greeting and each went their separate ways.

Wei Wuxian saw his black-clad past self glancing left and right until his eyes fell upon Lan Wangji. He was just about to say something when Jiang Cheng walked over to stand beside him. Both men lowered their heads and exchanged words with solemn expressions. Wei Wuxian burst out laughing and walked shoulder to shoulder with Jiang Cheng to the other side. The people coming and going around them also automatically made way, giving them a wide berth.

Wei Wuxian thought back carefully, trying to remember what they'd been talking about at the time. He couldn't recall at first, but then he saw the movement of their lips through Nie Mingjue's eyes and it came to him. He'd said, *"Jiang Cheng, Chifeng-zun's so much taller than you, ha ha."*

And Jiang Cheng had said, *"Screw off. You wanna die?"*

Nie Mingjue's attention turned back to the Lans. "Why does Wei Ying not have a sword?" he asked.

Carrying a sword was akin to dressing in formal attire. It was a necessary symbol of etiquette during grand gatherings, and those born to prominent clans attached great importance to it.

"He has probably forgotten," Lan Wangji answered impassively.

Nie Mingjue arched his brows. "He can forget something like that?"

"It is not surprising," Lan Wangji said.

Well, well! Wei Wuxian thought. *Bad-mouthing me behind my back! I caught you red-handed.*

Lan Xichen chuckled. "Young Master Wei said he didn't want to bother with such convoluted formalities. Never mind neglecting to carry his sword—even if he chose not to bother with wearing clothes, what could anyone do to stop him? Ah, to be young."

It really was an indescribable feeling to hear his own arrogant words repeated from the mouth of another. Wei Wuxian felt a little embarrassed, but there was nothing he could do. Suddenly, he heard Lan Wangji muttering under his breath.

"...Irreverent."

He said it very softly, as if only for his own benefit. The word drummed in Wei Wuxian's ears, causing his heart to inexplicably skip a beat.

Lan Xichen looked at him. "Hmm? Why are you still here?"

"Xiongzhang is here, so naturally I am as well," Lan Wangji replied, slightly puzzled though still serious-faced.

"Why aren't you going over to talk to him?" Lan Xichen clarified. "They're going away."

Wei Wuxian found this curious. *Why did Zewu-jun say that? Don't tell me Lan Zhan had something to say to me?*

Before he could get a clear look at Lan Wangji's reaction, a commotion suddenly broke out at the other end of the area. Wei Wuxian heard his own furious shouting.

"Jin Zixuan! Don't you *ever* forget what you said and did! What do you mean by this?!"

Wei Wuxian remembered, now. *Ah, so it was this incident!*

On the other end, Jin Zixuan was also furious. "I'm asking Sect Leader Jiang, not you! And I'm asking about Miss Jiang. What's it got to do with you?!"

Wei Wuxian snapped back at him, "Well said! What *does* my shijie have to do with you? Who was the one so proud his eyes grew on top of his head, too uppity to see her in the first place?"

"Sect Leader Jiang," Jin Zixuan complained, "this is my clan's flower-viewing banquet, and he is from your clan! Are you going to do something about this?!"

"Why are they quarreling, again?" Lan Xichen wondered.

Lan Wangji looked over at them, but his feet remained glued to the ground. A moment later, he took a step forward, as if he'd made up his mind and was about to walk over. But just then, Jiang Cheng's voice rang out.

"Wei Wuxian, you shut up. Jin-gongzi, I'm sorry about this. My elder sister is fine, thank you for your concern. We can discuss this matter next time."

Wei Wuxian sneered. "Next time? There is no next time! There is no need for him to worry about whether she's fine or not! Who does he think he is?!"

Having said that, he spun on his heel and stalked away. Jiang Cheng hollered after him, "Come back here! Where are you going?"

Wei Wuxian waved his hand. "Anywhere is fine! Just don't let me see his face. I didn't want to come in the first place. You can deal with this yourself."

Having been left behind, Jiang Cheng's face grew gradually stormy. Jin Guangyao had initially been busying and bustling about, with a smile for every guest and a solution for every problem. Seeing this disturbance, he popped up again and called out to him.

"Wei-gongzi, please stay!"

Wei Wuxian walked swiftly with his hands clasped behind his back. His expression was sullen, and he paid no notice to anyone. Lan Wangji took a step toward him, but before he could open his mouth, both men had already brushed past each other.

Jin Guangyao, unable to catch up with Wei Wuxian, kicked at the ground and sighed. "Well, he's gone. Sect Leader Jiang, what... what should we do?"

Jiang Cheng reined in his gloomy expression. "Leave him. He's used to getting his own way at home. No manners." Then he started to converse with Jin Zixuan.

Watching this, Wei Wuxian inwardly heaved a long sigh. Fortunately, Nie Mingjue seemed uninterested. He quickly shifted his gaze away, and Wei Wuxian couldn't see them anymore.

The three Zun were at the Impure Realm, residence of the Nie Clan of Qinghe.

Nie Mingjue was in his seat, while Lan Xichen played a guqin that lay horizontally before him. The tune came to an end, and he placed his hand over the strings, calming its vibrations.

Jin Guangyao smiled. "All right. Now that I've heard er-ge's playing, I'll be sure to smash my guqin as soon as I get home."

"San-di's playing would be considered very good, outside of Gusu," Lan Xichen assured him. "Was your mother the one who taught you?"

"No, I taught myself through observation. She never taught me these sorts of things, only how to read and write. She also bought some expensive swordplay and cultivation manuals for me to study."

Lan Xichen was astonished. "Swordplay and cultivation manuals?"

"Er-ge, you've never seen those before, have you?" Jin Guangyao explained. "They're small booklets sold by common folk, with random figure drawings and a lot of fanciful text."

Lan Xichen shook his head with a smile. Jin Guangyao shook his head too.

"They're all scams. Fraudulent scraps meant specifically to deceive women like my mother, and ignorant children. Practicing their 'teachings' will do you no harm, but it won't benefit you either." He then lamented, "But how could my mother know that? She just bought them all, regardless of price. She said that when I returned to see my father someday, I had to meet him as a skilled and capable man. I couldn't allow myself to fall behind. And so, all our money went to such things."

Lan Xichen plucked a couple of times at the strings. "You are very talented, to have learned so much simply through observation. With the guidance of a renowned master, you'd no doubt improve by leaps and bounds."

Jin Guangyao laughed. "Such a renowned master is right before me, but I wouldn't dare impose on him."

"Why not?" Lan Xichen said. "Please take a seat, gongzi."

Jin Guangyao sat opposite him, prim and proper, and made to listen humbly. "What does Lan-xiansheng wish to teach me?"

"How about the Purification Tone?" Lan Xichen proposed.

Jin Guangyao's eyes lit up, but before he could say a word, Nie Mingjue looked up.

"Er-di, the Purification Tone is one of the unique arts of your Lan Clan of Gusu. Don't divulge it to outsiders."

Lan Xichen didn't seem to consider this an issue. He said with a smile, "The Purification Tone is unlike the Eradication Tone. Its purpose is to clear the heart and calm the mind. Why keep such a helpful healing art all to ourselves? Besides, how could teaching it to san-di be considered divulging to an outsider?"

Since he knew what he was doing, Nie Mingjue said nothing more on the matter.

One day, upon returning to the Impure Realm, he entered the main hall to see a dozen or so gold-edged folding fans unfurled and lined up before Nie Huaisang. Nie Huaisang was fondly stroking them one at a time, mumbling to himself as he compared the inscriptions on each fan. Veins instantly popped on Nie Mingjue's forehead.

"Nie Huaisang!"

Nie Huaisang immediately dropped to the ground, startled into a kneeling position. He clambered to his feet afterward in trepidation and stuttered a greeting. "Da-da-da-da-ge!"

Nie Mingjue demanded, "Where is your saber?"

Nie Huaisang stammered, "In...in my room. Wait, no. At the drilling grounds. No, I... Let me think..."

Wei Wuxian could sense Nie Mingjue's desire to hack him to bits right where he stood. "You carry dozens of fans with you, but you don't even know where your own saber is?!"

"I'll go look for it right now!" Nie Huaisang said hastily.

"Forget it!" Nie Mingjue barked. "You can't learn anything with it, even if you find it. Burn all of these!"

The color drastically drained from Nie Huaisang's face. He scooped all the fans into his arms in a panic, saying, "Da-ge, please don't! These are all gifts from someone!"

Nie Mingjue cracked the table with one slam of his palm. "Who was it? Tell him to get the hell over here!"

"It was me," a voice answered.

Jin Guangyao strode into the hall. Nie Huaisang exclaimed in delight, as if he'd just sighted his savior. "San-ge, you came!"

It wasn't that Jin Guangyao could appease Nie Mingjue's fury—just that that fury was immediately transferred to him as soon as he showed up, leaving Nie Mingjue too preoccupied to scold anyone else. So it really wasn't much of a stretch to call him Nie Huaisang's savior. Overjoyed, Nie Huaisang repeatedly greeted, *"Hello, san-ge!"* as he hurriedly scooped the tableful of fans into his arms. Seeing his younger brother like this, Nie Mingjue was so angry that he now found it faintly ludicrous.

He snapped at Jin Guangyao, "Stop sending him such nonsensical trinkets!"

Nie Huaisang dropped two fans onto the ground in his rush, and Jin Guangyao helped pick them up, tucking them back into his arms. "Huaisang is passionate about the arts and studies paintings and calligraphy with rapture. These are not bad habits. How can you call it nonsense?"

Nie Huaisang nodded enthusiastically. "Yeah! San-ge is right!"

"It's not like you can use those things when you are head of the clan," Nie Mingjue said.

Nie Huaisang retorted, "I'm not *going* to be the head of the clan. Da-ge can have the position. I'm not doing it!"

He immediately shut up when his elder brother shot him a glare. Nie Mingjue then turned to Jin Guangyao.

"What are you doing here?"

"Er-ge said he gifted you a guqin." Jin Guangyao replied.

It was the same one Lan Xichen had brought along from before to play the Purification Tone for Nie Mingjue. He'd gifted it to him to help soothe him.

Jin Guangyao added, "Since the Lan Clan of Gusu has been busy lately with the urgent matter of reconstructing the Cloud Recesses, da-ge has forbidden him to come. So er-ge taught me the Purification Tone. Even if I cannot match er-ge's superb playing, I can still help da-ge calm down."

"You should just focus on your own matters," Nie Mingjue said.

Nie Huaisang, however, had his interest piqued. "San-ge, what song is that? Can I listen? Let me tell you, that out-of-print book you found for me last time..."

"Return to your room!" Nie Mingjue barked.

Nie Huaisang quickly fled with his tail between his legs. Of course, he didn't go back to his room—rather, he scurried to the parlor to paw through the other gifts Jin Guangyao had brought for him.

After being interrupted several times, Nie Mingjue's fury had mostly subsided. He looked back at the slightly tired-looking Jin Guangyao, whose Sparks Amidst Snow robe was dusty and travel-worn. Presumably, he'd hurried here from Golden Carp Tower.

After a moment's pause, Nie Mingjue said, "Have a seat."

Jin Guangyao gave a slight nod and sat down as instructed. "If da-ge is concerned about Huaisang, a softer approach wouldn't hurt. Why be so harsh?"

"He'd still be like this with a saber held to his neck." Nie Mingjue said, "Seems he'll always be a good-for-nothing, even if I beat him to death."

"It's not that Huaisang is worthless but just that his ambitions don't lie here," Jin Guangyao advised him.

"And you've figured out exactly where his ambitions *do* lie?" Nie Mingjue said.

Jin Guangyao smiled. "Of course. Is this not my forte? The only one I can't figure out is da-ge."

Knowing a person's likes and dislikes, and then catering to them accordingly, made getting things done easier. You could accomplish your goals with half as much effort. As such, the ability to discern people's desires truly was Jin Guangyao's forte. The only person he could never seem to pry any useful information out of was Nie Mingjue.

Wei Wuxian had seen this firsthand, back when Meng Yao worked under Nie Mingjue's command. The man never laid his hands on women, alcohol, or material wealth; paintings, calligraphy, and antiques were all piles of ink and mud in his eyes. Top-grade premium tea tasted the same to him as dregs from a roadside stall. Meng Yao had racked his brain and still failed to identify anything Nie Mingjue might have a taste for, other than training with his saber every day and killing Wen dogs. He was truly an iron bastion, with no weaknesses to exploit.

Hearing him speak so self-deprecatingly, Nie Mingjue did not feel as repelled as usual. "Don't encourage that disgraceful behavior of his."

Jin Guangyao smiled and asked again, "Da-ge, where is er-ge's guqin?"

Nie Mingjue pointed it out for him.

From that point onward, Jin Guangyao would rush from Lanling to Qinghe every few days and play the Purification Tone to help Nie Mingjue purify his mind. He did this to the best of his ability, without a single word of complaint. The Purification Tone was indeed mysterious and effective. Wei Wuxian could clearly sense the resentful energy lurking within Nie Mingjue's heart being suppressed, and the conversations and interactions they had while the guqin played were like those they'd shared in the peaceful past, when they had yet to fall out with one another.

Perhaps being unable to get away from the reconstruction of the Cloud Recesses was merely an excuse on Lan Xichen's part. Perhaps he only wanted to give Nie Mingjue and Jin Guangyao an opportunity to ease the tension in their relationship.

But the thought had only just occurred to Wei Wuxian when an even more maniacal fury surged up within Nie Mingjue.

He threw off two disciples, who didn't dare try to stop him again, and barged straight into Blooming Garden. Lan Xichen and Jin Guangyao were solemnly discussing something in the study, with several blueprints marked in various colors spread out on the table before them. Lan Xichen was slightly taken aback by his intrusion.

"Da-ge?"

"You stay right there," Nie Mingjue said to Lan Xichen. Then he said coldly to Jin Guangyao, "You. Come out."

Jin Guangyao looked at him, then looked at Lan Xichen. He smiled. "Er-ge, might I trouble you to help me sort these plans out? I must go discuss some private matters with da-ge first. I'll beg your thoughts after."

Lan Xichen looked worried, but Jin Guangyao followed Nie Mingjue out. They had only just arrived at the edge of Golden Carp Tower when Nie Mingjue struck out at him.

Several nearby disciples looked alarmed, but Jin Guangyao nimbly dodged the blow and motioned for them not to make any rash moves. He turned to Nie Mingjue.

"Da-ge, why do this? If something's the matter, we can talk it over."

"Where's Xue Yang?" Nie Mingjue demanded.

"He's been sent to the dungeons, sentenced for life..."

"What was it that you said to me back then?" Nie Mingjue demanded.

Jin Guangyao fell silent.

Nie Mingjue continued, "I wanted him to pay in blood, pay with his life. And you merely gave him a life sentence instead?!"

Jin Guangyao replied cautiously, "As long as he is punished and cannot commit such crimes again, does it truly matter if he pays with his life...?"

"The fine guest cultivator you recommended did such a fine thing!" Nie Mingjue rebuked sharply. "And yet you still dare shield him, even now!"

"I'm not shielding him," Jin Guangyao defended himself. "The incident with the Chang Clan of Yueyang shocked me greatly as well. How could I have anticipated Xue Yang would slaughter a family of over fifty people? But my father insists on keeping him..."

"Shocked?" Nie Mingjue exclaimed. "Who was the one to recruit him? The one who recommended him? Gave him an important position? Stop using your father as a cover. How could you not have known what Xue Yang was doing?!"

Jin Guangyao sighed. "Da-ge, it really was on my father's orders, I couldn't refuse. You're demanding that I dispose of Xue Yang, but how would you have me explain my actions to my father afterward?"

"No excuses," Nie Mingjue said. "Bring me Xue Yang's head."

It seemed Jin Guangyao still had more to say, but Nie Mingjue's patience was already exhausted. "Meng Yao, don't you dare play games with me. Those tricks of yours no longer work!"

For an instant, Jin Guangyao's expression showed a hint of embarrassment—as though some unspeakable affliction of his had been exposed in full view of the public, with nowhere to hide and no hole to crawl into.

"Those 'tricks' of mine?" he countered. "Which ones? Da-ge, you constantly castigate me for being calculating, for being unorthodox. You say you stand tall and straight, that you are daunted by nothing, that a real man has no need to resort to underhanded means. Fine. You come from a distinguished background, and your cultivation level is high. But what about me? Am I the same? To begin with, unlike you, I don't have a high level of cultivation and a stable foundation. In all my life, no one ever taught me those things. Furthermore, I don't have a prominent family background. You think my place in the Jin Clan of Lanling is stable? Did you think that I would rise in position with Jin Zixuan's death? Jin Guangshan would rather bring back another illegitimate son than have me succeed him! You tell me not to fear heaven and earth? But I do fear, and I fear people too! It's easy for you to say such things because you're not in my shoes, just like those who have never known hunger can never imagine how it feels to starve!"

Nie Mingjue said coldly, "At the end of the day, what you really mean is that you do not want to kill Xue Yang and do not want to jeopardize your status in the Jin Clan of Lanling."

"Of course I don't!" Jin Guangyao shot back.

He raised his head, his eyes blazing with indiscernible flames. "But da-ge, I've been meaning to ask you one thing. You've taken far more lives than I have. So why is it that, when I was forced by circumstance to kill a few cultivators so long ago, I must still endure you constantly nagging me about it, even to this day?"

Nie Mingjue laughed out of sheer anger. "Fine! I'll answer you. Countless people have perished by my saber, but I've never killed for my own selfish desires—or worse, killed for the sake of climbing to the top!"

"Da-ge, I understand what you mean now," Jin Guangyao said. "Are you trying to say that everyone you killed deserved it?"

He chuckled and, with an inexplicable burst of courage, took a few steps toward Nie Mingjue. His voice raised as he continued, forcefully.

"Then, may I presume to ask *how* you determine whether a person deserves death? Are your standards the only correct ones? Let's say that I killed one person and saved the lives of a hundred others in doing so—does the merit outweigh the misdeed, or am I culpable of wrongdoing? To achieve great things, one must make sacrifices."

Nie Mingjue retorted, "Then why don't you sacrifice yourself? Are you more distinguished than them? Are you different from them?"

Jin Guangyao looked steadily at him. Then, as if he'd finally made up his mind—and in the same moment, given up on something—he calmly replied, "Yes."

He raised his head high, his expression proud, frank, and faintly insane in equal proportion.

"I am, of course, different from them!"

His words and expression enraged Nie Mingjue.

He lifted a leg, and Jin Guangyao, caught completely off guard, did not dodge. He took the full force of the kick and tumbled down Golden Carp Tower once more.

Nie Mingjue lowered his head and bellowed down at him. "As expected of the son of a prostitute!"

Jin Guangyao rolled for over fifty steps before he landed on solid ground. He didn't lie sprawled there for even a moment but crawled immediately to his feet. He waved away the servants and sect disciples gathering around him and brushed the dust off his Sparks Amidst Snow robe. Then, very slowly, he raised his head to meet Nie Mingjue's eyes with a gaze that was calm and even somewhat apathetic.

Nie Mingjue drew his saber—just as a worried Lan Xichen, who'd been waiting in vain for them to return, walked out of the inner hall to see what was happening. At the scene before him, he immediately drew Shuoyue too.

"What happened between the two of you this time?"

"It's nothing," Jin Guangyao said. "Many thanks to da-ge for your lesson."

"Do not stop me!" Nie Mingjue snapped.

"Put your saber away first, da-ge," Lan Xichen pleaded. "Your mind is in turmoil!"

"No, it is not. I know very well what I am doing," Nie Mingjue argued. "He's incorrigible. If this goes on, he will be a scourge upon the world. The sooner I kill him, the sooner we can live in peace!"

Lan Xichen froze. "Da-ge, what are you saying? Don't tell me all he gets in return for constantly rushing back and forth between Qinghe and Lanling these days is being called 'incorrigible'?"

When dealing with someone like Nie Mingjue, the optimal strategy was to mention debts owed, both of kindness and enmity. Sure enough, Nie Mingjue faltered a little as he cast a glance down at Jin Guangyao, whose forehead was bleeding. As well as the new wound from the fall, he sported an older, bandaged injury that had been concealed by the black gauze cap he was wearing. Wounds both old and new had been torn open, so Jin Guangyao tugged off the bandage and dabbed it against his head, wiping away the fresh blood so it would not stain his clothes. He then tossed it to the ground and stood there unspeaking, his thoughts indiscernible.

Lan Xichen looked back and said, "San-di, why don't you go back first. I'll talk to da-ge."

Jin Guangyao bowed in their direction, then turned on his heel and left. Noticing Nie Mingjue had slackened his grip, Lan Xichen withdrew his blade as well and patted his shoulder to lead him over to the side.

"Da-ge," he said as they walked. "You probably don't know, but san-di's situation really is not good."

"The way he puts it, one would think he lives forever in abject misery," Nie Mingjue said frostily.

Despite saying so, he slowly sheathed his saber.

"Who says he's not?" Lan Xichen said. "He talked back to you earlier, didn't he? Would he have done so in the past?"

Indeed, he would not. It was certainly unusual behavior for Jin Guangyao, who wasn't the kind to lash out. He knew very well that the best way to deal with Nie Mingjue was for him to make concessions. The outburst of defiance earlier was quite out of character for him.

"His stepmother, Jin Guangshan's wife, was never fond of him to begin with," Lan Xichen explained. "She already beat and scolded him, and after Zixuan-xiong passed away, those beatings and scoldings have only grown harsher and more frequent. His father has also refused to listen to his words of late, rejecting all the proposals he submits."

Wei Wuxian recalled the stack of blueprints on the table earlier, and understanding dawned on him. *The watchtowers.*

Finally, Lan Xichen said, "Don't push him too hard, for now. I trust that he knows what he should do. Just give him a little more time."

"I hope so," Nie Mingjue said.

After the kick Nie Mingjue gave him, Wei Wuxian had thought Jin Guangyao would keep to himself for a while. But, unexpectedly, he still showed up at the Impure Realm as usual a few days later. Nie Mingjue was at the drilling grounds, personally supervising and instructing Nie Huaisang in his saber practice. He paid no attention to Jin Guangyao, who waited respectfully at the edge of the inner drilling grounds.

Nie Huaisang was unenthusiastic about his practice, especially given the scorching sun, so his efforts were half-hearted at best. He only took a couple more swings before claiming he was tired and joyfully trotting over to see what gifts Jin Guangyao had come bearing this time. In the past, the most Nie Mingjue would have done was frown at this. But this time, he was enraged.

"Nie Huaisang, do you want me to cleave your head with this saber?! Get the hell back here!"

If only Nie Huaisang could feel, as Wei Wuxian did, the force with which Nie Mingjue's anger blazed at that moment—then he would not grin as cheekily. "Da-ge, it's time for a break!"

"You only just took a break one incense time ago," Nie Mingjue scolded. "Continue until you master this."

Nie Huaisang was still feeling complacent. "I'm never going to master it anyway. I'm not training anymore today!"

This was something Nie Huaisang always used to say. But Nie Mingjue's reaction was unexpectedly completely different from what it had been before. He bellowed, "Even a pig would have already mastered it under my watch, so why are you not getting it?!"

Not expecting this sudden outburst, Nie Huaisang cowered toward Jin Guangyao, dumbstruck. At the sight of the two together, Nie Mingjue's anger surged even higher.

"It's been a year, and you still haven't mastered a single set of saber techniques. Complaining after spending a single incense time in the drilling grounds—I'm not asking you to be outstanding, but you can't even defend yourself! How did the Nie Clan of Qinghe produce such a good-for-nothing?! The two of you ought to be tied up and beaten every day! Fetch all those things from his room!"

This last sentence was directed at the sect disciples standing by the side of the drilling grounds. Nie Huaisang was on tenterhooks as he watched them leave. A short while later, the disciples returned, having really fetched all the calligraphy, paintings, porcelain wares, and folding fans from his room.

Nie Mingjue had always gone on about burning his things in the past but had never actually done it. This time, however, he meant business.

Nie Huaisang panicked and lunged over. "Da-ge! You can't burn them!"

Seeing this did not bode well, Jin Guangyao piped up too. "Don't be rash, da-ge."

But Nie Mingjue had already swung out his saber, engulfing the pile of exquisite things at the center of the drilling grounds in a towering, raging fire. Nie Huaisang let out a tragic wail and pounced into the fire to save them. Jin Guangyao hurriedly pulled him back to stop him.

"Huaisang, careful!"

Nie Mingjue struck out, and the two items of white porcelain Nie Huaisang had grabbed from the fire shattered to pieces in his hands. The scrolls of calligraphy and paintings had already turned to ash. Nie Huaisang watched, speechless and helpless, as all the beloved objects he had collected over the years, from all around the world, were consumed by the flames.

Jin Guangyao grabbed his palms to inspect them. "Were you burned?" He turned to the other sect disciples. "Might I trouble you to go prepare some medicine?"

The sect disciples acknowledged him and left to do so. Nie Huaisang stood rooted to the ground, his whole body shaking as he looked at Nie Mingjue with eyes that were gradually growing bloodshot. Jin Guangyao, noticing this, put his arm around his shoulders.

He said softly, "Huaisang, how are you? Don't watch this anymore. Let's go inside to rest."

Nie Huaisang's eyes continued to redden. He remained silent. Jin Guangyao continued, "It's no big deal if they're gone. San-ge will find more for you in the future..."

"He brings those things into the house again, and I'll burn them all too," Nie Mingjue said coldly.

Indignation and exhaustion flashed across Nie Huaisang's face. He flung his saber to the ground and yelled, "Go ahead, then!!"

Jin Guangyao hurriedly said, "Huaisang! Your da-ge is just angry right now, don't..."

Nie Huaisang bellowed back at Nie Mingjue, "Saber, saber, saber! Who the fuck wants to practice this crap?! What if I'm happy being a good-for-nothing?! Whoever else wants to be clan leader can go right ahead! If I can't do it, I can't do it. If I don't like it, that's what it means! What's the point of forcing me?!"

He kicked his saber away and dashed out of the grounds. Jin Guangyao called after him.

"Huaisang! Huaisang!"

But just as he was about to give chase, Nie Mingjue ordered coldly, "Hold it!"

Jin Guangyao paused and turned around.

Nie Mingjue shot him a look and demanded with barely suppressed anger, "You still dare come?"

"To admit fault," Jin Guangyao replied in a small voice.

That skin of his really is way thicker than mine, Wei Wuxian thought.

"You know how to do that?" Nie Mingjue said derisively.

Jin Guangyao was about to speak when the sect disciples who'd gone to retrieve medicine returned. "Sect Leader, Lianfang-zun, er-gongzi locked the door and is refusing to let anyone inside."

"Let's see how long he lasts. The nerve of him!"

"Thanks for the trouble," Jin Guangyao said pleasantly to the sect disciple. "Why don't you give me the medicine? I'll deliver it to him in a bit."

He took the medicine bottle. When the others had left, Nie Mingjue demanded, "Why exactly are you here?"

"Has da-ge forgotten? Today is guqin day," Jin Guangyao replied.

"The matter of Xue Yang is non-negotiable," Nie Mingjue said, point-blank. "There's no need for you to curry my favor. It's futile."

"First, I'm not trying to curry your favor," Jin Guangyao said, "Second, if it's futile, why does da-ge dread it so?"

Nie Mingjue didn't answer.

"Da-ge, you've been putting more and more pressure on Huaisang lately," Jin Guangyao continued. "Could the saber spirit be..." He paused briefly, then asked, "Does Huaisang still not know about the saber spirits?"

"Why tell him so soon?" Nie Mingjue said.

Jin Guangyao heaved a sigh. "Huaisang may be spoiled rotten, but he can't stay the idle second young master of Qinghe forever. There will come a day when he learns da-ge has his best interests at heart, just as I've come to know that da-ge has *my* best interests at heart."

Really gotta hand it to him, Wei Wuxian thought. *I could never say something like that in two lifetimes, but he controlled his tone so well that it sounded totally natural. Sincere, even.*

Nie Mingjue said, "If you really think that, then bring me Xue Yang's head."

Unexpectedly, Jin Guangyao immediately replied, "Done."

Nie Mingjue regarded him. Jin Guangyao matched his stare squarely and repeated again, "It will be done. As long as da-ge gives me one last chance, then within two months, I will personally bring you Xue Yang's head."

"And if you don't?" Nie Mingjue asked.

Jin Guangyao spoke with conviction. "Then da-ge can do with me as he sees fit!"

Wei Wuxian found Jin Guangyao almost admirable at this point. Although the man lived in constant fear of Nie Mingjue, he still found a hundred thousand ways and words to wheedle another chance out of him. When night fell, Jin Guangyao was back to playing the Purification Tone inside the Impure Realm as if nothing had happened.

Despite the solemnity of the vow Jin Guangyao had made him, Nie Mingjue never saw those two months pass.

One day, the Nie Clan of Qinghe hosted a martial arts drill. Nie Mingjue was passing by a guest accommodation house when he suddenly heard hushed voices inside. One sounded like Jin Guangyao. Moments later, there came another unexpectedly familiar voice.

"Da-ge swore an oath of brotherhood with you," Lan Xichen said. "That means he acknowledges you."

Jin Guangyao sounded dejected, "But, er-ge, did you not hear what he vowed? Every word was an implication—'Incite universal condemnation and be executed by way of dismemberment' He was clearly warning me. I…have never heard vows like that in an oath of sworn brotherhood…"

"He said 'should you stray in loyalty,'" Lan Xichen replied gently. "Have you done so? If not, then why brood?"

"I haven't," Jin Guangyao protested. "But da-ge is already convinced that I have. What can I do?"

"He's always treasured your talent and hoped you would walk the right path," Lan Xichen said.

"It's not as though I don't know right from wrong. It's just that there are times when I really don't have a choice," Jin Guangyao said. "I'm beset with difficulties everywhere I go, and I must bear the brunt of everyone's temper. The others, I can deal with, but what have I done to let da-ge down? Er-ge, you heard how he insulted me last time."

Lan Xichen sighed. "It was simply a poor choice of words in a moment of anger. Da-ge's disposition is no longer as it once was. It would be best if you never provoke his ire again. He's been deeply afflicted by the saber spirit's torment of late, and still quarreling with Huaisang… They have yet to reconcile."

Jin Guangyao's voice was choked with sobs. "If he can say such things in a fit of anger, then what does he usually think of me? I didn't choose my background. My mother couldn't choose her fate. Must I expect to be degraded my whole life? If that's the case, then how is da-ge different from all the others who look down on me? No matter what I do, in the end, he still dismisses me with a single 'son of a prostitute.'"

Last night, Jin Guangyao had been having a heart-to-heart with Nie Mingjue as he played the guqin, with none of these complaints.

But now here he was, pouring out his woes to Lan Xichen. The moment Nie Mingjue realized he was sowing such discord behind his back, he flew into a rage and kicked in the door. The raging flames in his head spread throughout his body, and he roared at Jin Guangyao like thunder crashing in his ears.

"You wretch!"

The moment Jin Guangyao saw him enter, he dodged behind Lan Xichen, scared out of his wits. Sandwiched between the two of them, Lan Xichen couldn't get a word out before Nie Mingjue was already lunging with his saber drawn.

Lan Xichen drew his sword to parry and cried to Jin Guangyao, "Run!"

Jin Guangyao bolted out the door. Nie Mingjue shook off Lan Xichen and snarled at him, "Don't stop me!!"

He chased after Jin Guangyao. As he rounded a long corridor, he suddenly saw Jin Guangyao leisurely walking toward him. He struck with his saber, and blood spurted forth, painting his surroundings red in an instant. But Jin Guangyao had clearly just been running for his life—why would he be doubling back in so leisurely a manner?!

Once Nie Mingjue had struck, he staggered for a stretch and then charged to the square. He looked up, panting, and Wei Wuxian could hear the loud thumping of his heart.

Jin Guangyao!

In the square, all around, every person going to and fro—they all bore the appearance of Jin Guangyao!

Nie Mingjue had qi-deviated!

His mind was lost to him. He only knew to kill, to kill, kill, kill, kill, kill Jin Guangyao. He hacked at everyone around him, filling the air with screams. Suddenly, Wei Wuxian heard a cry.

"Da-ge!!"

Nie Mingjue jolted at the sound of that voice. Calming down somewhat, he turned his head to look, and finally, blearily, saw a different face from the field of Jin Guangyaos.

Nie Huaisang was clutching his arm, which had been wounded by Nie Mingjue's saber. He shuffled arduously toward him, dragging one leg, moved to tears of joy upon seeing that his brother had suddenly stilled.

"Da-ge! Da-ge! It's me, put down your saber, it's me!"

But Nie Huaisang didn't make it to his side before Nie Mingjue collapsed to the ground.

Before he fell, clarity finally returned to his eyes, and he saw the real Jin Guangyao.

He stood at the end of a long corridor without a spot of blood on him. He was staring at Nie Mingjue, twin streams of tears pouring from his eyes. Sparks Amidst Snow bloomed wildly from his chest, seeming to smile on his behalf.

All of a sudden, Wei Wuxian heard a voice calling him from a distance. The voice was cool and deep, but hazy at first, very far away, almost surreal. The second call was much clearer. He could even detect a barely perceptible distress.

The third time, he heard it loud and clear.

"Wei Ying!"

At that voice, Wei Wuxian forcibly pulled himself out!

He was still a flimsy paper effigy, stuck to the helmet that sealed Nie Mingjue's head. He'd already pulled loose the strings of the visor blocking Nie Mingjue's vision, revealing a pair of bulging, furious eyes that crawled with red veins.

There wasn't much time left—he had to return to his physical body!

— PART 3 —

PAPERMAN WEI shook his sleeves and fluttered forth like a butterfly. Unexpectedly, the moment he charged out from behind the drapes, he saw someone standing in the shadowed corner of the secret chamber. Jin Guangyao gave an easy smile and soundlessly drew the softsword[4] hung at his waist.

This was the famous Hensheng. Back when Jin Guangyao was undercover at Wen Ruohan's side, he often hid this softsword around his waist or his wrist for use in dire situations. Hensheng's blade was so soft and so flexible that one might almost believe the sword itself was equally quick to concede and yield—when in fact, it was vicious, sharp, and unrelenting. Once Hensheng was wrapped around its prey, Jin Guangyao would release into it a current of strange spiritual power, and the softsword, which seemed so much like gentle spring waters, would wring its prey to pieces. It had destroyed many famous swords in exactly this way, reducing them to nothing but piles of scrap metal.

Hensheng was currently like a venomous snake with glimmering silver scales, chasing and biting at the paper effigy. If Wei Wuxian was even slightly careless, he would be caught between those fangs!

Paperman Wei flapped his sleeves and agilely evaded the sword, dodging left and right. All the same, this wasn't his own body. He nearly caught a bite from Hensheng's tip, and if this went on much longer, he'd be pierced through for sure.

Suddenly, he spotted a longsword lying quietly on one of the lattice shelves. It had clearly been neglected for many years, as layers of dust covered it and the surrounding shelf.

---

4 *A softsword (軟劍 / ruan jian) is a type of sword with a highly flexible blade. While it is not suitable for stabbing and slicing, its sheer attack speed and unpredictable movements make it a formidable weapon to face in battle—it can easily bend around an enemy's guard and sever arteries in the neck or strike the side or back. It is extremely hard to master and equally difficult to defend against.*

Amazingly, it was his old sword—Suibian!

Paperman Wei pounced onto the lattice shelf and stomped on the hilt of Suibian. *Sching!* It heeded his call, and the blade sprung from its sheath!

Suibian shot forth and began tangling with Hensheng's eerie sword glare. Once the shock on Jin Guangyao's face subsided, he quickly smoothed out his expression. He nimbly twisted his wrist a few times, causing Hensheng to wrap itself around Suibian's snow-white blade like a tangling vine, then released it to let the two swords fight on their own. Meanwhile, he hurled a talisman in Wei Wuxian's direction.

The talisman ignited into blazing flame as it sailed through the air. Wei Wuxian felt the scorching heat blast toward him. While the two battling blades blinded the room with their flashing glares, he used this opportunity to fervently flap his paper sleeves and shoot out of the secret chamber!

He was almost out of time. Wei Wuxian couldn't afford to take it slow and ensure he wasn't spotted. He flapped all the way back to the guest house, incidentally arriving just as Lan Wangji opened the door. He flapped hard one last time, pouncing right onto Lan Wangji's face, where he clung tightly, seeming to shake, tremble, shiver.

Lan Wangji's eyes were covered by the paper effigy's expansive sleeves. He let him tremble there for a bit before he gently plucked him off.

A brief moment later, Wei Wuxian successfully returned to his body. He immediately drew in a deep breath, lifted his head and opened his eyes, then shot to his feet. However, his body hadn't adjusted yet. His head spun, and he swooned forward. Seeing this, Lan Wangji immediately caught him, but Wei Wuxian's head unexpectedly shot up at the same time, colliding with Lan Wangji's chin. They both grunted.

Wei Wuxian felt his head with one hand while his other rubbed Lan Wangji's chin. "Oops! Sorry. Are you okay, Lan Zhan?"

After letting him rub a few more times, Lan Wangji gently moved his hand away and shook his head. Wei Wuxian tugged at him.

"Let's go!"

Lan Wangji rose to his feet without question. They were already on their way before he asked, "Where to?"

"Fragrance Palace!" Wei Wuxian replied. "The bronze mirror inside the palace is the entrance to a secret chamber. His wife accidentally uncovered some secret of his and got dragged inside, so she should still be in there! Chifeng-zun's head is in there too!"

Jin Guangyao would definitely lose no time strengthening the seal on Nie Mingjue's head and moving it elsewhere. However, he could move a head but not his wife! Qin Su was the first lady of Golden Carp Tower and had very recently been seen at the banquet. To have someone of such honorable status vanish so suddenly—people would surely have questions.

He had to use this opportunity to barge in and take care of this in the fastest way possible, leaving Jin Guangyao no time to fabricate lies and seal lips!

The two moved with earth-shaking momentum, kicking aside anyone who blocked their path. The sect disciples Jin Guangyao had planted near Fragrance Palace were all trained to be exceptionally vigilant. If they sensed an intruder and were unable to stop them, they immediately cried out to sound the alarm and alert the master of the palace inside. But this backfired—the more they raised the alarm, the more disadvantageous the situation got for Jin Guangyao. Since countless cultivation sects and clans had gathered here today, while the disciples' cries did alert him to be on his guard, they also attracted dozens of people!

The first to arrive was Jin Ling, with his sword already in hand. He asked, puzzled, "Why are you two here?"

While he asked that question, Lan Wangji had already ascended three of the jade stairs and drawn Bichen. Jin Ling was alarmed.

"These are my little uncle's sleeping quarters! You guys got lost, right? No wait, you barged in. What are you doing?"

Everyone who had gathered at Golden Carp Tower, from the heads of various clans to individual cultivators, rushed over curiously.

"What's going on?"

"Why is there such a commotion here?"

"This is Fragrance Palace, is it all right for us to be here...?"

"I heard the alarm blare just now..."

They were either unnerved or frowning in silence. No sound came from inside the sleeping palace. Wei Wuxian gave a casual knock.

"Sect Leader Jin? Cultivation Chief Jin?"

Jin Ling was furious. "What are you trying to do? You've dragged everyone here! These are my little uncle's sleeping quarters, *sleeping quarters*, do you understand?! Didn't I tell you not to..."

Lan Xichen walked up the steps, and Lan Wangji regarded him. The two locked eyes. At first Lan Xichen looked taken aback, then his expression instantly grew complicated, like he was still in disbelief. But it seemed he understood.

Nie Mingjue's head was inside Fragrance Palace.

Just then, a smiling voice addressed them. "What's going on? Could my hospitality have been so inadequate during the day that everyone has come here to continue feasting into the night?"

Jin Guangyao strolled out from behind the crowd.

"Right on time, Lianfang-zun," Wei Wuxian said. "If you'd come out any later, we wouldn't have been able to see the thing inside the secret chamber of your Fragrance Palace, huh?"

Jin Guangyao looked taken aback. "Secret chamber?"

The crowd was doubtful, unsure what was happening.

Jin Guangyao remained slightly confused. "What is it? Secret chambers aren't that strange, are they? As long as they possess rare spiritual weapons, who *doesn't* have some secret chambers to serve as vaults in their homes?"

Lan Wangji was about to speak, but Lan Xichen beat him to it.

"A-Yao," he said. "Might you open the door for us and allow us to view this secret chamber?"

Jin Guangyao seemed to find this request strange and was hesitant to grant it. "Er-ge, it's called a secret chamber because the things stored in there are meant to be hidden. Asking me to open it so suddenly is..."

He couldn't possibly have moved Qin Su elsewhere in such a short period of time without anyone noticing. A transportation talisman could only transport the caster, and based on Qin Su's current state, she definitely had neither the spiritual power to fuel it nor the desire to use it. Which meant she must still be inside—either alive or dead. Either way, her presence would prove fatal to Jin Guangyao.

Though cornered, Jin Guangyao continued to calmly make excuses. But the more he declined, the firmer Lan Xichen's tone grew.

"Open it."

Jin Guangyao stared him straight in the eyes, then suddenly beamed. "If er-ge says so, I have no choice but to open it for everyone to see."

He stood in front of the entrance, waved, and the doors to the sleeping palace swung open.

Someone in the crowd suddenly said, his tone cold, "They say the Lan Clan of Gusu holds propriety in the highest regard, but it seems that was merely a rumor. Forcing his way into the master of the household's bedroom—propriety, indeed."

Wei Wuxian had heard the Jin sect disciples respectfully greet this man earlier in the square, addressing him as "Sect Leader Su." This was Su She, leader of the Su Clan of Moling, which had been enjoying some fame in recent years. He was dressed all in white, thin-browed and thin-lipped. Though his features were clean and handsome, he exuded quite a bit of haughtiness. His appearance and bearing were fine, but unfortunately, not quite fine enough to make him noteworthy.

"Never mind," Jin Guangyao assured. "It's fine, it's not like there's anything unfit to be seen."

He controlled his tone expertly, making himself sound even-tempered while adding just the right amount of uneasiness to his response. Jin Ling followed him, feeling indignant on behalf of his little uncle, who'd gotten his door kicked in out of the blue. He shot several death glares at Wei Wuxian.

"You wanted to take a look at the secret chamber, right?" Jin Guangyao asked again.

He placed his hand on the bronze mirror and drew a formless spell over its surface before entering. Wei Wuxian was right on his heels. He re-entered the secret chamber, seeing the spell-covered drape on the lattice and the iron table for butchering corpses.

He even saw Qin Su. She stood beside the iron table, her back to them. Lan Xichen was stunned.

"Why is Madam Jin in here?"

"We share everything we own," Jin Guangyao explained. "A-Su often comes in here to look around."

Wei Wuxian was shocked to see Qin Su. *Jin Guangyao didn't move her or kill her? Is he not scared of what she might say?*

Not reassured, he moved next to Qin Su, carefully examining her profile. She was still alive and well. Although her expression was wooden, Wei Wuxian was certain there were no evil spells cast upon her, nor any strange poisons affecting her. Her mind was clear.

But the fact that she was conscious made the situation even stranger. He had seen with his own eyes how emotional Qin Su had become and how strongly she'd resisted Jin Guangyao. How had he managed, in such a short period of time, to come to an agreement with her that would make her seal her lips?

Wei Wuxian had a bad feeling about this. Things weren't going as smoothly as he'd thought.

He walked to the lattice shelf and lifted the drapes at once.

There was no helmet behind the drapes, and definitely no head. There was only a dagger.

This dagger emitted an eerie, frigid glint, roiling with a murderous aura. Lan Xichen had been staring at those drapes too, unable to decide whether to lift the fabric for the longest time. Seeing they did not conceal something he'd dreaded discovering, he seemed to breathe a sigh of relief.

"What is that?"

"This?" Jin Guangyao went to the shelf and turned the dagger over in his hand. "A rare weapon indeed. This dagger was the weapon of an assassin. It has killed countless people and is incomparably sharp. Take a look at the blade. Look closely. You'll see the reflection is not your own, but sometimes a man, sometimes a woman, sometimes an elder. Each is a soul that died at the assassin's hand. The blade is heavy with yin energy, so I added drapes to seal it off."

Lan Xichen knitted his brows. "Could this be..."

"Yes," Jin Guangyao replied easily. "It was Wen Ruohan's."

Jin Guangyao was clever, indeed. Anticipating that his secret chamber might be discovered some day, he had stored a number of things in here besides Nie Mingjue's head. Swords, talismans, fragments of ancient tablets, spiritual weapons—there was no shortage of rare items here, making the secret chamber look like an ordinary vault. As for the dagger—as he'd said, it was a rare item laden with yin energy. Plenty of cultivation clans enjoyed collecting rare weapons for sport. Not to mention the fact that he'd killed the leader of the Wen Clan of Qishan, making this his trophy.

It was all, in short, perfectly normal.

Qin Su stood by Jin Guangyao's side, watching as he fiddled with the dagger. Suddenly, she snatched it from him! Her face started to twist and tremble. The others didn't understand her expression, but Wei Wuxian, who had just spied on her dispute with Jin Guangyao could easily read the pain, anger, and humiliation written there.

Jin Guangyao's smile froze. "A-Su?"

Lan Wangji and Wei Wuxian both struck out to grab the dagger, but Qin Su dodged. The sharp glint of that dagger was already wholly buried in her belly.

"A-Su!" Jin Guangyao cried out in spite of himself.

He rushed to embrace her limp body, while Lan Xichen immediately retrieved medicine to apply emergency aid. But the dagger was both extremely sharp and laden with resentment and yin energy—in the blink of an eye, Qin Su was dead!

Everyone present was stunned, never having expected such a turn of events. Jin Guangyao mournfully cried his wife's name again and again, a hand cupping her face. His eyes were wide, and his tears fell like rain onto her cheeks.

Lan Xichen said, "A-Yao, Madam Jin, she... I'm so sorry."

Jin Guangyao looked up. "Er-ge, what is going on? Why would A-Su suddenly kill herself? And why would you all suddenly gather before Fragrance Palace to make me open the secret chamber? Is there something you're not telling me?"

Jiang Cheng, who had arrived late to this impromptu gathering, said coldly, "Zewu-jun, please provide an explanation. We are all in the dark as well."

The crowd all agreed, so Lan Xichen had no choice but to explain. "A while ago, a number of juniors from our Lan Clan passed by the Mo Estate during a Night Hunt and were attacked by a disembodied left arm. The arm was heavy with resentment and had a significant murderous aura, so Wangji investigated, following the direction in which it pointed. However, once enough dismembered pieces were collected, we discovered that the fierce corpse they belonged to was... da-ge."

An uproar erupted both inside the treasure room and out.

Jin Guangyao was utterly stunned. "Da-ge? Wasn't da-ge buried? I saw it myself!"

Nie Huaisang thought he had misheard too. "Da-ge?" he asked incoherently. "Xicheng-ge? You said it's my da-ge? And your da-ge too?"

Lan Xichen nodded gravely. Nie Huaisang's eyes rolled back, and he fell forward in a heap with a thud. The circle of people shouted in panic:

"Sect Leader Nie! Sect Leader Nie!"

"Call a doctor!"

Jin Guangyao's eyes were still brimming with tears, but reddening with anger too. He clenched his fists tightly and cried in grief and indignation, "Dismemberment...dismemberment! Who would dare to do such a vile, mad thing?!"

Lan Xichen shook his head. "I do not know. The clues stopped at the head."

Jin Guangyao blinked. Then, realization suddenly dawned on him. "The clues stopped... So, you came here to look?"

Lan Xichen was silent.

"When you wanted me to open the secret chamber earlier," Jin Guangyao asked with disbelief, "it was because you suspected...that da-ge's head is here with me?"

Guilt now colored Lan Xichen's face.

Jin Guangyao hung his head and hugged Qin Su's body. He continued after a while, "...It's fine. We won't discuss it further. But, er-ge, how did Hanguang-jun know about the secret chamber in my sleeping palace? And how did he decide that da-ge's head was inside my secret chamber? Golden Carp Tower is heavily guarded. If I really did it, would da-ge's head be so easily discovered?"

Lan Xichen was actually stumped by the question. So was Wei Wuxian. Who could've imagined that Jin Guangyao wouldn't just move the head in such a short period of time but also do or say something that drove Qin Su to kill herself in public and seal her own lips?

As the gears rapidly spun in Wei Wuxian's head, Jin Guangyao sighed. "Xuanyu, was it you who told my er-ge and the others? What's the use in telling such an easily disproven lie?"

One of the clan leaders was puzzled. "Lianfang-zun, who are you talking about?"

"Who else?" another voice replied coldly. "The one standing right beside Hanguang-jun."

Everyone's eyes turned that way.

The one who'd just spoken was Su She. "Those not of the Jin Clan of Lanling might not know him," he said. "This man is Mo Xuanyu, who was expelled from the Jin Clan of Lanling for improper behavior—for harassing Lianfang-zun. Recently, there've been rumors that he somehow managed to charm Hanguang-jun. He's been following him everywhere, the two of them roaming the land together. It truly boggles the mind why Hanguang-jun, who has always been known for his elegance and righteousness, would keep such a person by his side."

Jin Ling looked incredibly upset at those words. Amidst the hushed whispers in the crowd, Jin Guangyao laid down Qin Su's body and slowly rose to his feet. He placed his hand on the hilt of Hensheng and took a threatening step toward Wei Wuxian.

"I won't mention what is now in the past, but please tell me the truth. Do you have anything to do with A-Su's inexplicable suicide?"

When Jin Guangyao lied, he did so with aplomb, playing the part of the guiltless victim to perfection. Every person who heard him naturally concluded that Mo Xuanyu had slandered Lianfang-zun out of resentment, while simultaneously manipulating Madam Jin to make her commit suicide. Even Wei Wuxian couldn't think of a counterargument in the moment. What should he say? Tell everyone about how he had seen Nie Mingjue's head or how he infiltrated the secret chamber? Talk about the person Qin Su had met, even though the witness herself was now dead? Tell everyone about the strange letter that could so easily be written off as nonexistent and fictional? He'd only dig himself deeper if he tried.

As he rapidly racked his brain for a plan, Hensheng had already left its sheath. Lan Wangji stood in front of him, and Bichen blocked the strike.

When the other cultivators saw this, they all drew their swords as well. Two swords came flying at them from the side. Wei Wuxian had no weapon in hand to parry the attacks, but when he turned his head, Suibian just so happened to be lying right there. He immediately grabbed it and drew the sword from its sheath!

Jin Guangyao's eyes sharpened, and he cried, *"Yiling Patriarch!"*

Suddenly, the whole of the Jin Clan, including Jin Ling, pointed their swords at him!

Wei Wuxian gazed at Jin Ling's confused face and then at Suihua's blade, dumbfounded to have his identity so suddenly exposed.

Jin Guangyao continued, "I wasn't aware the Yiling Patriarch had returned to the world. We are honored by your presence. Forgive me for not having come out to welcome you."

Wei Wuxian was completely lost in the mists, having no earthly idea how he'd given himself away. Nie Huaisang was dazed too.

"San-ge? What did you say just now? Is this not Mo Xuanyu?"

Jin Guangyao pointed Hensheng at Wei Wuxian. "Huaisang, A-Ling, both of you come here. Everyone, please be careful. He pulled out that sword, so he is doubtlessly the Yiling Patriarch, Wei Wuxian!"

Since Wei Wuxian's sword had an unspeakable name, people always used "this sword" or "that sword" when they referred to it. And when the name "Yiling Patriarch" was spoken, it was even more hair-raising than the revelation that Chifeng-zun had been dismembered. Even those who hadn't intended to draw their weapons now reflexively unsheathed their swords, surrounding this corner of the secret chamber. Wei Wuxian scanned the swords glimmering all around him, remaining unflustered.

"So anyone who can pull out that sword is the Yiling Patriarch?" Nie Huaisang asked. "San-ge, er-ge, Hanguang-jun, is there some kind of misunderstanding here?"

"There is no misunderstanding," Jin Guangyao said, "He must be Wei Wuxian."

"Wait!" Jin Ling suddenly called out. "Xiao-shu, wait! Jiujiu, jiujiu, didn't you lash him with Zidian back at Mount Dafan? His soul wasn't whipped out, so he's definitely not possessed, right? So he might not be Wei Wuxian?!"

Jiang Cheng looked incredibly upset, but he didn't speak. He had his hand pressed to the hilt of his sword, seeming to ponder what action to take next.

"Mount Dafan?" Jin Guangyao said. "That's right. A-Ling, you just reminded me of what else appeared on Mount Dafan. Wasn't he also the one who summoned Wen Ning?"

Jin Ling's face turned ashen as he was not only denied the reassurance he wanted but also realized he had unwittingly provided further confirmation.

"No one here knew this," Jin Guangyao continued, "but when Xuanyu was still here at Golden Carp Tower, he saw one of the Yiling Patriarch's manuscripts. This manuscript was a dissertation on a particular black magic: Sacrifice. It uses the soul and physical body as the price to summon malicious ghosts and evil spirits to seek vengeance on the caster's behalf. Sect Leader Jiang can whip him a hundred times with Zidian and nothing would come of it—because the caster willingly sacrificed their body, it cannot be considered possession!"

The explanation made perfect sense in every way. After Mo Xuanyu was chased out of Golden Carp Tower, resentment grew in his heart. He recalled the black magic he had read about, and in his desire for vengeance, begged for a malicious ghost to descend upon him. In doing so, he summoned the Yiling Patriarch. Everything Wei Wuxian had done was to avenge Mo Xuanyu, which meant Nie Mingjue's dismemberment must've been his handiwork too. In any event, before any alternate explanations proved true, the most likely story was that it was all the work of the dastardly Yiling Patriarch!

However, some people remained skeptical. "Since we can't verify this Sacrifice magic was used, you can't make such conclusions on your own judgment alone, Lianfang-zun."

Jin Guangyao replied, "Indeed, whether Sacrifice was used can't be verified, but whether he is the Yiling Patriarch can. Ever since the Yiling Patriarch was crushed to pieces from the rebound of his malicious ghosts at the Burial Mounds, the Jin Clan of Lanling kept his sword. And in no time at all, the sword sealed itself."

Wei Wuxian was taken aback. "The sword sealed itself?"

A sense of foreboding sprouted in his mind.

Jin Guangyao continued, "I'm sure I don't need to explain what a sealed sword is. The sword has a spirit. That spirit refused to allow anyone besides Wei Wuxian to wield it, and so, it sealed itself. No one other than the Yiling Patriarch himself can draw it from its sheath. But this 'Mo Xuanyu,' before your very eyes, just pulled out this sword that's been sealed for thirteen years!"

He hadn't yet finished before there were over a dozen sword glares shooting uniformly in Wei Wuxian's direction.

Lan Wangji blocked them all, and Bichen shocked away a number of men, clearing out a path.

"Wangji!" Lan Xichen exclaimed.

The clan leaders who were knocked down by the shock wave of Bichen's frigid qi cried out furiously. "Hanguang-jun! You..."

Wei Wuxian wasted no words. He pushed himself up the window lattice with his right hand and weightlessly hopped out. The moment his feet touched the ground, he dashed off. As he ran, his mind was racing as fast as lightning.

Jin Guangyao saw that strange paper effigy and saw Suibian unsheathe, so he must've guessed my identity right then. He immediately fabricated a slew of lies, talked Qin Su into suicide, and then purposely cornered me to the lattice shelf where Suibian was stored to tempt me into pulling the sword and exposing my identity. Scary, scary, scary. I never expected he'd react so fast and could lie so smoothly!

Just then, someone joined him. It was Lan Wangji, who had caught up without a word spoken. Wei Wuxian had always had an amazingly bad reputation and this wasn't the first time something like this had happened, but his mindset this time around was not the same as it had been in his previous life, and he could face this quite unperturbed. Run first and fight back if the chance presented itself in the future. If that didn't happen, that was okay too. Sticking around was completely pointless—unless he wanted the opportunity to get beaten by several hundred-some swords—and crying about injustice was even more laughable. Everyone was convinced he would return one day for revenge and massacre the cultivation world in his madness. No one would listen to his explanation, not to mention Jin Guangyao was there fanning the flames.

Lan Wangji was the complete opposite of him though. He didn't need to explain himself at all—in fact, people would do it for him, announcing that Hanguang-jun had been deceived by the Yiling Patriarch.

Wei Wuxian called to him, "Hanguang-jun, you don't have to follow me!"

Lan Wangji kept his eyes to the front and didn't answer him. They kept moving, leaving behind the cries rallying all present to strike to kill. Despite his preoccupation, Wei Wuxian pressed Lan Wangji once more.

"Are you really coming with me? You've thought this through? Once you leave this place, your reputation is done for!"

By now they had dashed down the steps of Golden Carp Tower. Lan Wangji seized one of his wrists, looking like he had something to say, when a white shadow flashed before them. Jin Ling was blocking their way.

When Wei Wuxian saw it was Jin Ling, he sighed in relief. They were about to slip around him, but Jin Ling moved, once again blocking their way.

"You're Wei Ying?!"

He was confused and unkempt, his eyes red. Furious and hateful, hesitant and uneasy, sorrowful and at a loss.

He barked again, "Are you really Wei Ying—Wei Wuxian?!"

Seeing him like this, the pain far outweighing the hatred in his voice, Wei Wuxian's heart trembled. But it would only be mere moments before his pursuers caught up. He had no more time to mind the boy but could only clench his teeth and circle around him for the third time.

Unexpectedly, he felt a coldness in his belly. When he looked down, Jin Ling had already withdrawn the snow-white blade, now dyed red.

He had never imagined Jin Ling would actually attack.

The only thought on Wei Wuxian's mind was: *Of all the people he could take after, why does it have to be his uncle? He even chooses the same spot to stab me in.*

Everything was a blur after that, and he only felt himself attacking at random. It was a chaotic mess, incredibly noisy with endless collisions and the incessant, explosive sounds of weapons and spiritual powers clashing. An unknown amount of time passed, and then Wei Wuxian fuzzily opened his eyes. Lan Wangji was mounted on Bichen, while Wei Wuxian lay on Lan Wangji's back. Half of that snow-white cheek was splashed with blood.

To be honest, the stomach injury wasn't all that painful. After all, it was just a hole in his body. He'd initially thought he could just grit his teeth and endure it, but this body had probably never weathered an injury like this before. The nonstop bleeding made him dizzy—and that, of course, was hardly anything he could control.

"...Lan Zhan," Wei Wuxian called out.

Lan Wangji's breathing wasn't as steady as it usually was—it was slightly short, probably from overexerting himself in hand-to-hand combat while carrying Wei Wuxian on his back. However, the tone with which he answered him had the same steadiness he'd always possessed, and it was still that word:

"Mn."

After that, he added, "I'm here."

Hearing those two words, a feeling Wei Wuxian had never felt before spread into his heart. It was like an ache. His heart throbbed a little, but it was also a little warm.

He still remembered back when they were in Jiangling—Lan Wangji had traveled thousands of kilometers to help him but Wei Wuxian wasn't grateful at all, and he'd constantly clashed with him and made it awfully unpleasant between the two of them.

But he really hadn't expected it to turn out like this. When everyone was praising him out of fear, Lan Wangji rebuked him to his face. When everyone spat and hated on him, Lan Wangji stood by his side.

Wei Wuxian said, all of a sudden, "Ah, I remember now."

"What did you remember?" Lan Wangji asked.

"I remembered, Lan Zhan. Just like this. I...I've carried you on my back before."

THE STORY CONTINUES IN

Grandmaster of Demonic Cultivation

VOLUME 3

Grandmaster of Demonic Cultivation
MO DAO ZU SHI
Character
&
Name Guide

Characters

The identity of certain characters may be a spoiler; use this guide with caution on your first read of the novel.

Note on the given name translations: Chinese characters may have many different readings. Each reading here is just one out of several possible readings presented for your reference and should not be considered a definitive translation.

MAIN CHARACTERS

Wei Wuxian

BIRTH NAME: Wei Ying (魏婴 / Surname Wei, "Infant")

COURTESY NAME: Wei Wuxian (魏无羡 / Surname Wei, "Having no envy")

SOBRIQUET: Yiling Patriarch

WEAPON:

Sword: Suibian (随便 / "Whatever")

Hufu/Tiger Tally: Yin Tiger Tally (阴虎符)

INSTRUMENT:

Dizi (side-blown flute): Chenqing (陈情 / "To explain one's situation in detail." This is a reference to a line in a collection of poems, *Chu Ci* [楚辞], by famous poet Qu Yuan)

Unnamed dizi (side-blown flute)

In his previous life, Wei Wuxian was the feared Yiling Patriarch. He commanded an army of the living dead with his wicked flute Chenqing and laid waste to the cultivation world in an orgy of blood that eventually resulted in his death. Thirteen years later, a troubled young man sacrifices his soul to resurrect Wei Wuxian in his own body, hoping the terrible Yiling Patriarch will enact revenge on his behalf. Awakening confused and disoriented in this new body, Wei Wuxian stumbles forth into his second chance at life. Now, he must piece together the mystery surrounding his return—and face the lingering consequences of his last life, which continue to dog him even beyond death.

Wei Wuxian is mischievous and highly intelligent. He seems physically incapable of keeping his mouth shut and also can't seem to stop himself from teasing people who catch his interest—with Lan Wangji being a perennial favorite target, even after thirteen years away from the land of the living. He has a soft spot for children and can often be found scolding junior disciples for endangering themselves during missions.

Lan Wangji

BIRTH NAME: Lan Zhan (蓝湛 / "Blue," "Clear" or "Deep")

COURTESY NAME: Lan Wangji (蓝忘机 / "Blue," "Free of worldly concerns")

SOBRIQUET: Hanguang-jun (含光君 / "Light-bringer," honorific "-jun")

WEAPON: Sword: Bichen (避尘 / "Shunning worldly affairs")

INSTRUMENT: Guqin (zither): Wangji (忘机 / "Free of worldly concerns")

Lan Wangji's perfection as a cultivator is matched by none. Shunning petty politics and social prejudices, he appears wherever there is chaos to quell it with his sword Bichen, and evildoers quake in fear at the sound of strumming guqin strings. His remarkable grace and beauty have won him renown far and wide, even though his perpetual frown makes him look like a widower.

Younger brother to the current Lan Sect leader, Lan Xichen, Lan Wangji is stern, reserved, highly principled, and an avid fan of rabbits. While he was easily affected by teasing in his youth, he seems harder to perturb these days.

SUPPORTING CHARACTERS

A-Qing

BIRTH NAME: A-Qing (阿箐 / diminutive "A-," "Bamboo")

WEAPON: Street smarts, and a bamboo pole

A teenage urchin. She was born with naturally white eyes, making most people assume she is blind when she can actually see perfectly well. She leverages this to her advantage to survive a life on the streets by playing on people's sympathy with her small stature and cute looks. She is crafty, clever, and charming, though quite foulmouthed.

Xiao Xingchen

COURTESY NAME: Xiao Xingchen (晓星尘 / "Dawn," "Stardust")

WEAPON: Sword: Shuanghua (霜华 / "Frost Flower," referring to the natural phenomenon when ice crystals form on long-stemmed plants)

A mysterious and once-highly regarded cultivator. He is close friends with Song Lan and dreamed of founding a sect with him. He lived on a remote mountaintop for most of his life, under the tutelage of his shizun, the immortal Baoshan-sanren. He descended the mountain to do good deeds for the common people of the world and was well known for his skill and sense of justice. However, just as suddenly as he appeared, he disappeared, and has not been heard from since.

Xue Yang

BIRTH NAME: Xue Yang (薛洋 / Surname Xue, "Ocean")

WEAPON: Sword: Jiangzai (降灾 / "To call forth disasters [from the heavens]")

On the surface, Xue Yang is a petty thug with a penchant for violence. Below the surface, he is still a petty thug with a penchant for violence, but with a strange knack for understanding the dark arts—a truly terrible combination. How deep would someone have to dig to find something sweet in that black heart? Once a guest cultivator with the Jin Clan of Lanling, Xue Yang later disappeared, supposedly having been taken care of as punishment for his involvement in the massacre of the Chang Clan of Yueyang.

Song Lan

BIRTH NAME: Song Lan (宋岚 / Surname Song, "Mist")

COURTESY NAME: Song Zichen (宋子琛 / Surname Song, a common male name prefix "Son," "Gem" or "Jewel")

WEAPON: Sword: Fuxue (拂雪 / "To sweep away snow")

A Daoist cultivator and close friend of Xiao Xingchen. Song Lan was raised by the priests of Baixue Temple and in turn learned the art of cultivation from them. He was known to be quiet and stern, and dreamed of founding a new sect by Xiao Xingchen's side.

Wen Ning

BIRTH NAME: Wen Ning (温宁 / "Mild" or "Warm," "Peaceful")

COURTESY NAME: Wen Qionglin (温琼林 / "Mild" or "Warm," "Beautiful" or "Fine jade," "Forest")

SOBRIQUET: Ghost General (鬼将军)

WEAPON: Fists, feet, and metal chains

A fierce corpse known as the Ghost General, thought to have been destroyed during the Siege of the Burial Mounds. One of the Yiling Patriarch's finest creations, Wen Ning retains his mind and personality. Coupled with the strength to crush steel to dust with his bare fists, it is no wonder that he was once Wei Wuxian's right-hand man. Over the years since, however, not only is he discovered to still be "alive," it seems that something (or someone) is suppressing Wen Ning's capacity for rational thought.

Lan Jingyi

COURTESY NAME: Lan Jingyi (蓝景仪 / "Blue," "Scenery," "Bearing" or "Appearance")

WEAPON: Unnamed sword

A junior disciple in the Lan Sect. He is close friends with Lan Sizhui, and appears to have a special kind of admiration for Lan Wangji. Although he was raised in such a strict sect, Lan Jingyi is distinctly un-Lan-like in his mannerisms, being loud, bluntly honest, and easily worked up into a tizzy. That being said, like any Lan, he is still very quick to spot and accuse instances of rule-breaking on the Cloud Recesses' premises.

Lan Sizhui

BIRTH NAME: Lan Yuan (蓝愿 / "Blue," "Wish")

COURTESY NAME: Lan Sizhui (蓝思追 / "Blue," "To remember and long for")

WEAPON: Unnamed sword

INSTRUMENT: Unnamed guqin

A junior disciple in the Lan Sect. He is close friends with Lan Jingyi and appears to have a special kind of admiration for Lan Wangji. Lan Sizhui is poised and quite mature for his age, and is a natural leader of his peers when the juniors are sent out on investigations. Although raised in such a strict sect, Lan Sizhui retains an air of warmth about him. He is kind, intuitive, and willing to see beyond surface appearances.

Jin Ling

BIRTH NAME: Jin Ling (金凌 / "Gold," "Tower aloft")

COURTESY NAME: Jin Rulan (金如兰 / "Gold," "Like" or "As if," "Orchid")

WEAPON:

Sword: Suihua (岁华 / "Passage of time"), previously owned by Jin Zixuan

Fairy (spirit dog)

Unnamed bow

The young heir to the Jin Clan and son of Jin Zixuan and Jiang Yanli. Jin Ling grew up a lonely child, bullied by his peers and overly doted on by his caretakers out of pity. Though Jin Ling remains quite spoiled and unmanageable in temperament, he strongly dislikes being looked down upon and seeks to prove himself as a cultivator. He is often seen squabbling with his maternal uncle and sometimes-caretaker Jiang Cheng or hurling himself headlong into mortal peril alongside his loyal spirit dog Fairy.

Jiang Cheng

BIRTH NAME: Jiang Cheng (江澄 / "River," "Clear")

COURTESY NAME: Jiang Wanyin (江晚吟 / "River," "Night," "Recitation")

SOBRIQUET: Sandu Shengshou (三毒圣手 / "Three Poisons," a reference to the Buddhist three roots of suffering: greed, anger, and ignorance, "Sage Hand"

WEAPON:

Whip: Zidian (紫电 / "Purple," "Lightning")

Sword: Sandu (三毒 / "Three Poisons")

Jiang Cheng is the leader of the Jiang Sect and Jin Ling's maternal uncle. Known to be stern and unrelenting, he possesses a long-standing grudge against Wei Wuxian even after the latter's death. This is a far cry from the way things once were—Jiang Cheng and Wei Wuxian grew up together at Lotus Pier when the homeless and orphaned Wei Wuxian was taken in by Jiang Cheng's father, and were the closest of friends as well as martial siblings. However, after Wei Wuxian's rise as the Yiling Patriarch, their friendship ended alongside the many people who died at his hands...or so it seems.

Jin Guangyao

BIRTH NAME: Meng Yao (孟瑶 / "Eldest," "Jade")

COURTESY NAME: Jin Guangyao (金光瑶 / "Gold," "Light and glory," "Jade")

SOBRIQUET: Lianfang-zun (敛芳尊 / "Hidden fragrance," honorific "-zun")

WEAPON: Softsword: Hensheng (恨生 / "To hate life/birth")

INSTRUMENT: Unnamed guqin

The current Jin Sect leader. He is half siblings with Jin Zixuan, Mo Xuanyu, and countless other children born of Jin Guangshan's wandering libido. He is also sworn brothers with Lan Xichen and Nie Mingjue, and together they are known as the Three Zun. He is particularly close to Lan Xichen and could easily be named the man's most trusted companion. However, Jin Guangyao had a considerably more troubled relationship with Nie Mingjue before the man's death, and they frequently had heated disagreements over their conflicting worldviews.

Jin Guangyao rose from humble circumstances and became not only the head of the Jin Sect but also the Cultivation Chief of the inter-sect alliance. His skill at politicking and networking is matched by none, and through restructuring and reparations he was able to largely make up for the damage done to the Jin Sect's reputation by his father's rule.

Jin Guangshan

COURTESY NAME: Jin Guangshan (金光善 / "Gold," "Light and glory," "Kindness")

The former Jin Sect head and father to Jin Zixuan, Jin Guangyao, Mo Xuanyu, and many, many more. He was a womanizer who would abandon his lovers just as quickly as he would any children born of his dalliances. Despite this ravenous appetite, he only sired one child (Jin Zixuan) with his lawful wife. Under his rule, the Jin Sect was loathed by the cultivation world for its shameless abuses, corruption, and excess. Thankfully, he eventually died of exhaustion during an orgy and was succeeded by Jin Guangyao.

Jin Zixuan

COURTESY NAME: Jin Zixuan (金子轩 / "Gold," common male prefix "Son," "Pavilion")

WEAPON: Sword: Suihua (岁华 / "Passage of time")

The Jin Clan heir and the only legitimate son of Jin Guangshan. He married Jiang Yanli and together they had a son, Jin Ling. He attended school at the Cloud Recesses in his youth and was classmates with Wei Wuxian, Jiang Cheng, and Nie Huaisang. Due to his status, his natural skill, and his good looks, Jin Zixuan was generally rather prideful and arrogant, and was disliked by his peers.

Nie Huaisang

COURTESY NAME: Nie Huaisang (聂怀桑 / "Whisper," "Cherish," "Mulberry")

SOBRIQUET: Head-Shaker (一问三不知 / "One Question, Three Don't-Knows")

WEAPON:

Unnamed saber (ostensibly)

Crying (actually)

The current Nie Sect head and Nie Mingjue's younger half brother. When they were young, he attended school at the Cloud Recesses with Wei Wuxian and Jiang Cheng. Nie Huaisang is a dilettante dandy who possesses a passionate love of fashion and the arts, but unfortunately possesses no such innate genius for politics or management. He is frequently seen looking stricken and panicked, and largely relies on the compassion and assistance of his older brother's sworn brothers (Lan Xichen and Jin Guangyao) to keep the Nie Sect struggling along.

Nie Mingjue

COURTESY NAME: Nie Mingjue (聂明玦 / "Whisper," "Bright" or "Righteousness," "Jade ring")

SOBRIQUET: Chifeng-zun (赤锋尊 / "Crimson Blade," honorific "-zun")

WEAPON: Saber: Baxia (霸下 / "To be ruled by force," also the name of one of the mythical Dragon King's nine sons.)

The former Nie Sect head and Nie Huaisang's older half brother. He is also sworn brothers with Lan Xichen and Jin Guangyao, and together they are known as the Three Zun. Nie Mingjue was a fierce man who was quick to use violence as a solution. He was unable to tolerate injustice or underhanded behavior, and was fearless in calling out even those in the highest seats of power. Unfortunately, his temperament eventually got the better of him, and he died at a young age from a qi deviation.

Baoshan-sanren

COURTESY NAME: Baoshan-sanren (抱山散人 / "To embrace," "Mountain," "Scattered One")

A mysterious immortal cultivator. She lives the life of a hermit on a secluded mountain, far removed from the chaos and pain of the outside world. She frequently takes in orphaned children to be brought up as cultivators under her tutelage and has but a single rule for her students to follow: If they ever choose to leave the mountain, they will never be allowed to return. She was the teacher of Xiao Xingchen and Cangse-sanren.

Cangse-sanren

COURTESY NAME: Cangse-sanren (藏色散人 / "Hidden," "Colors," "Scattered One")

A famous cultivator of remarkable skill and beauty who studied under Baoshan-sanren. Upon leaving her teacher's secluded mountain, she fell in love with a servant from a renowned cultivation sect, and they ran away together. They eventually perished together during a Night Hunt gone wrong, leaving behind their young son, Wei Wuxian.

Chang Ping

BIRTH NAME: Chang Ping (常平 / Surname Chang, "Average," "Usual"/ "Peace," "Flat")

The former head of the now-defunct Chang Clan of Yueyang. His clan was brutally massacred in a single night. As he was out of town that evening, Chang Ping was initially spared that grisly fate, but the lack of justice he received in the resulting official investigation was perhaps even more painful to experience. He was eventually found tortured to death, and as he had no heirs, the Chang Clan of Yueyang ended there.

Jiang Yanli

BIRTH NAME: Jiang Yanli (江厌离 / "River," "To dislike separation")

WEAPON: Love, patience, soup

The eldest daughter of the Jiang Clan, older sister to Jiang Cheng, and older martial sister to Wei Wuxian. She is Jin Zixuan's wife and Jin Ling's mother, and is warmly remembered by Wei Wuxian as being unconditionally kind and caring.

Lan Qiren

COURTESY NAME: Lan Qiren (蓝启仁 / "Blue," "Open" or "Awaken," "Benevolence")

WEAPON: Long lectures, closed-book exams

A Lan Clan elder and the paternal uncle of Lan Xichen and Lan Wangji. He is well known across the cultivation world as an exemplary (and extremely strict) teacher who consistently produces equally exemplary students. He loves his nephews deeply and is clearly extremely proud of their accomplishments and skill as cultivators and gentlemen both. However, he does not exclude them from the prescribed clan punishments on the rare occasion that such things are warranted.

Lan Xichen

BIRTH NAME: Lan Huan (蓝涣 / "Blue," "Melt" or "Dissipate")

COURTESY NAME: Lan Xichen (蓝曦臣 / "Blue," "Sunlight," "Minister" or "Subject")

SOBRIQUET: Zewu-jun (泽芜 / "Moss-shaded pool," honorific "-jun")

WEAPON: Sword: Shuoyue (朔月 / "New moon")

INSTRUMENT: Xiao (end-blown flute): Liebing (裂冰 / "Cracked," "Ice")

Unnamed guqin

The current Lan Sect head and Lan Wangji's elder brother. He is also sworn brothers with Jin Guangyao and Nie Mingjue, and together they are known as the Three Zun.

Lan Xichen possesses a warm and gentle personality and can easily get along with anyone and everyone. He possesses the unique and curious ability to understand his reticent little brother at a glance. He is as calm and undisturbed as the shaded pool from which he takes his sobriquet and will lend an ear to anyone who approaches, whatever their social standing.

Mo Xuanyu

COURTESY NAME: Mo Xuanyu (莫玄羽 / "Nothing" or "There is none who," "Mysterious" or "Black," "Feathers")

The young man who offered up his own body to bring Wei Wuxian back into the land of the living at a most horrible price: the obliteration of his own soul. He is one of the many illegitimate sons of Jin Guangshan. After he was expelled from the Jin Sect, the humiliation took a dreadful toll on his mind. He endured years of relentless abuse by the Mo household and eventually turned to demonic cultivation to exact revenge on those who tormented him.

With his soul destroyed, Mo Xuanyu himself is now but a memory, and Wei Wuxian inhabits his body.

Ouyang Zizhen

BIRTH NAME: Ouyang Zizhen (欧阳子真 / Surname Ouyang, common male prefix "Son," "Genuine," "Truth")

WEAPON: A sentimental heart

One of the junior disciples who found themselves lost in Yi City's fog. He is described by Wei Wuxian as having a sentimental outlook on the world, as evidenced by his glowing description of A-Qing's ghostly charms and his openly tearful reaction to her sad tale.

Qin Su

BIRTH NAME: Qin Su (秦愫 / Surname Qin, "Sincerity")

Jin Guangyao's wife. She is kind, naive, and innocent; all traits that are in short supply in the world of cultivation politics. Despite her high social status, she was determined enough to be allowed to marry for love and is devotedly loyal to her husband and those that she calls dear. She and Jin Guangyao had one child, Jin Rusong (金如松 / "Gold," "Like/as if," "Pine"), who died tragically at a young age.

Wen Ruohan

COURTESY NAME: Wen Ruohan (温若寒 / "Mild" or "Warm," "As though," "Cold" or "Tremble")

The leader of the Wen Clan of Qishan and an immensely powerful cultivator. He is cruel and power-hungry, and will stop at nothing to ensure that the Wen Clan crushes all other clans beneath its heel. He has an extensive collection of torture devices, and does not hesitate to use them to toy with his victims until death releases them.

Little Apple

WEAPON: Hooves, teeth, and raw fury

A spotted donkey that Wei Wuxian stole from Mo Manor as he made his escape after the ghost arm incident. Little Apple is imperious, hard to please, and very temperamental; however, it possesses a strong sense of justice and a heart brave enough to put even the most renown cultivators to shame. It also really loves apples. Little Apple's gender is never specified in the text.

Fairy

WEAPON: Claws, jaws, and the only brain in the room (usually)

INSTRUMENT: Woof!

Jin Ling's loyal spirit dog. As a spirit dog, Fairy possesses intelligence of a level above the average canine and can detect supernatural beings. Regarding the pup's name, "Fairy" could refer to the Chinese *xianzi* (仙子), a female celestial being, but it is also a common way to describe a woman with ethereal, otherworldly beauty. That being said, Fairy's gender is never specified in the text.

Locations

HUBEI

Yunmeng (云梦)

A city in the Hubei area. Its many lakes and waterways make it a prime juncture point for trade.

Lotus Pier (莲花坞)

The residence of the Jiang Clan of Yunmeng, located on the shores of a vast lake rich with blooming lotuses.

Yiling (夷陵)

A foreboding mountainous ridge, said to be the spot where an ancient and most terrible battle was waged. It is heavily ravaged by resentful energy and packed to the brim with walking corpses and vengeful ghosts. It has proven to be extremely resistant to any attempts at purification from top cultivation sects, and as such it was sealed off with magical barriers and written off as a lost cause. That is, until the dreaded Yiling Patriarch Wei Wuxian claimed it as his base of operations...

JIANGNAN

Gusu (姑苏)

A city in the Jiangnan region. Jiangnan is famous for its rich, fertile land and its abundant agricultural goods. Its hazy, drizzling weather and the soft sweet dialect make it a popular setting in Chinese romance literature.

Cloud Recesses (云深不知处)

The residence of the Lan Clan of Gusu, located on a remote mountaintop. The Cloud Recesses is a tranquil place constantly shrouded in mist. Beside the entrance there looms the Wall of Discipline, carved with the three thousand (later four thousand) rules of the Lan Clan.

The Cloud Recesses is home to the Library Pavilion where many rare and ancient texts are housed, the Tranquility Room where Lan Wangji resides, and the Orchid Room where Lan Qiren hosts lectures. There is also the Nether Room, a tower in which spirit-summoning rituals are performed, as well as a cold spring for bathing. On the back of the mountain is a secluded meadow where Lan Wangji keeps his pet rabbits.

The Cloud Recesses' name translates more literally to "Somewhere Hidden in Clouds" (云深不知处) and is a reference to a line in the poem "Failing to Find the Hermit," by Jia Dao:

I asked the young disciple beneath the pine;
"My master is gone to pick herbs," he answered.
"Though within this mountain he is,
The recesses of clouds hide his trail."

HEBEI

Qinghe (清河)

A city in the Hebei region. Qinghe is the home territory of the Nie Clan and is where their residence is located.

Impure Realm (不净世)

The residence of the Nie Clan of Qinghe. Its name may be a reference to Patikulamanasikara (in Chinese, written as 不淨觀 / Impure View), a set of Buddhist sutras meant to help overcome mortal desires. It thus serves both as a goal for the Nie Clan to aspire to and a reminder of their background as butchers.

QISHAN

Nightless City (不夜天城)

The residence of the Wen Clan of Qishan. Its name is derived from the fact that the expansive complex is vast enough to be comparable to the size of a city, as well as the brazen declaration of the Wen Clan that the sun never sets upon their domain—since it is their clan crest. The Scorching Sun Palace is the seat of Wen Ruohan's power, and the Inferno Palace is where he stores and demonstrates his vast collection of torture devices on unlucky guests.

SHAANXI

Yueyang (栎阳)

A city in the Shaanxi region. It is near Qishan, the territory the Wen Sect once controlled. It was once the home of the Chang Clan, until they were wiped out in a terrible massacre that claimed the lives of the whole family. It's said that if you venture near the cemetery, you can hear their spirits desperately banging their fists on the lids of their coffins.

SHANDONG

Lanling (兰陵)

A city in the Shandong region.

Golden Carp Tower (金麟台)

The residence of the Jin Clan of Lanling, located at the heart of the city of Lanling. The main road to the tower is only opened when events are being hosted, and this grand avenue is lavishly decorated with murals and statuary. Upon reaching the tower base, travelers must scale the numerous levels of steep staircases that lead to the tower proper. These staircases are a reference to the legend from which Golden Carp Tower derives its name—it is said that if an ordinary carp is able to leap to the top of a waterfall, it can turn into a glorious dragon.

Once the arduous journey to the top is complete, one will find themselves overlooking the city of Lanling from on high, and vast gardens of the Jin Clan of Lanling's signature flower: the cultivar peony, Sparks Amidst Snow. The Jin Sect's wealth and influence, as well as current leader Jin Guangyao's position as Cultivation Chief, sees Golden Carp Tower hosting frequent symposiums and banquets with VIP guests from the cultivation world's most powerful sects.

Shudong (蜀东)

Located in present-day Sichuan, it is a mountainous region with plentiful river valleys. This results in many areas being shrouded in year-long fog.

Yi City (义城)

A small, remote city that specializes in the production of funerary goods. The environment is foreboding and unnerving; it is fully surrounded by steep cliffs that loom overhead at severe angles, and a murky fog is ever-present. It is said that the city's residents are doomed to live short lives and are particularly prone to violent, sudden deaths. Perhaps this is a natural consequence of the unfavorable qi produced by such an inauspicious landscape, but with the city's even more fearsome reputation of late, there might be something darker and more evil lurking about its foggy streets.

Name Guide

Courtesy Names

A courtesy name is given to an individual when they come of age. Traditionally, this was at the age of twenty during one's crowning ceremony, but it can also be presented when an elder or teacher deems the recipient worthy. Generally a male-only tradition, there is historical precedent for women adopting a courtesy name after marriage. Courtesy names were a tradition reserved for the upper class.

It was considered disrespectful for one's peers of the same generation to address someone by their birth name, especially in formal or written communication. Use of one's birth name was reserved for only elders, close friends, and spouses.

This practice is no longer used in modern China but is commonly seen in wuxia and xianxia media. As such, many characters have more than one name. Its implementation in novels is irregular and is often treated malleably for the sake of storytelling. For example, in *Grandmaster of Demonic Cultivation*, characters as young as fifteen years of age are referred to only by their courtesy names, while traditionally they would not have been permitted to use them until the age of twenty.

Diminutives, Nicknames, and Name Tags

XIAO-: A diminutive meaning "little." Always a prefix.

EXAMPLE: Xiao-Pingguo (Little Apple), Xiao-mei ("little sister").

-ER: A word for "son" or "child." Added to a name, it expresses affection. Similar to calling someone "Little" or "Sonny."

A-: Friendly diminutive. Always a prefix. Usually for monosyllabic names, or one syllable out of a two-syllable name.

EXAMPLE: A-Qing, A-Yuan, A-Xian (For Wei Wuxian)

Doubling a syllable of a person's name can be a nickname, and has childish or cutesy connotations. For example: Xianxian (for Wei Wuxian, referring to himself).

FAMILY

DI: Younger brother or younger male friend. Can be used alone or as an honorific.

DIDI: Younger brother or a younger male friend. Casual.

XIAO-DI: Does not mean "little brother", and instead refers to one's lackey or subordinate, someone a leader took under their wings.

GE: Older brother or older male friend.

GEGE: Older brother or an older male friend. Casual and has a cutesier feel than "ge," so it can be used in a flirtatious manner.

JIE: Older sister or older female friend. Can be used alone or as an honorific.

JIEJIE: Older sister or an unrelated older female friend. Casual.

JIUJIU: Uncle (maternal, biological).

MEI: Younger sister or younger female friend. Can be used alone or as an honorific.

MEIMEI: Younger sister or an unrelated younger female friend. Casual.

SHUFU: Uncle (paternal, biological) Formal address for one's father's younger brother.

SHUSHU: An affectionate version of "Shufu."

XIAO-SHU OR XIAO-SHUSHU: Little (paternal) uncle; affectionate.

XIONG: Older brother. Generally used as an honorific. Formal, but also used informally between male friends of equal status.

XIONGZHANG: Eldest brother. Very formal, blood related-only.

XIANSHENG: Historically "teacher," but modern usage is "Mister." Also an affectionate way for wives to refer to their husband.

If multiple relatives in the same category are present (multiple older brothers, for example) everyone is assigned a number in order of birthdate, starting with the eldest as number one, the second oldest as number two, etc. These numbers are then used to differentiate one person from another. This goes for all of the categories above, whether it's siblings, cousins, aunts, uncles, and so on.

EXAMPLES:

If you have three older brothers, the oldest would be referred to as "da-ge," the second oldest "er-ge," and the third oldest "san-ge."

If you have two younger brothers you (as the oldest) would be number one. Your second-youngest brother would be "er-di," and the youngest of your two younger brothers would be "san-di."

Cultivation and Martial Arts

GENERAL

GONGZI: Young master of an affluent household

-JUN: A suffix meaning "lord."

-QIANBEI: A respectful suffix for someone older, more experienced, and/or more skilled in a particular discipline. Not to be used for blood relatives.

-ZUN: A suffix meaning "esteemed, venerable." More respectful than "-jun."

SECTS

SHIDI: Younger martial brother. For junior male members of one's own sect.

SHIFU: Teacher/master. For one's master in one's own sect. Gender neutral. Mostly interchangeable with Shizun, but has a slightly less formal feel.

SHIJIE: Older martial sister. For senior female members of one's own sect.

SHIMEI: Younger martial sister. For junior female members of one's own sect.

SHINIANG: The wife of a shifu/shizun.

SHISHU: The younger martial sibling of one's master. Can be male or female.

SHIXIONG: Older martial brother. For senior male members of one's own sect.

SHIZUN: Honorific address (as opposed to shifu) of one's teacher/ master.

Cultivators and Immortals

DAOREN: "Cultivator."

DAOZHANG: A polite address for cultivators. Equivalent to "Mr. Cultivator." Can be used alone as a title or attached to someone's name

EXAMPLE: referring to Xiao Xingchen as "Daozhang" or "Xiao Xingchen-daozhang."

SANREN: "Scattered One." For cultivators/immortals who are not tied to a specific sect.

Pronunciation Guide

Mandarin Chinese is the official state language of China. It is a tonal language, so correct pronunciation is vital to being understood! As many readers may not be familiar with the use and sound of tonal marks, below is a very simplified guide on the pronunciation of select character names and terms from MXTX's series to help get you started.

More resources are available at **sevenseasdanmei.com**

Series Names

SCUM VILLAIN'S SELF-SAVING SYSTEM (RÉN ZHĀ FĂN PÀI ZÌ JIÙ XÌ TŎNG):
ren jaa faan pie zzh zioh she tone

GRANDMASTER OF DEMONIC CULTIVATION (MÓ DÀO ZŬ SHĪ):
mwuh dow zoo shrr

HEAVEN OFFICIAL'S BLESSING (TIĀN GUĀN CÌ FÚ):
tee-yan gwen tsz fuu

Character Names

SHĔN QĪNGQIŪ: Shhen Ching-cheeoh
LUÒ BĪNGHÉ: Loo-uh Bing-huhh
WÈI WÚXIÀN: Way Woo-shee-ahn
LÁN WÀNGJĪ: Lahn Wong-gee
XIÈ LIÁN: Shee-yay Lee-yan
HUĀ CHÉNG: Hoo-wah Cch-yung

XIǍO-: shee-ow
-ER: ahrr
A-: ah
GŌNGZǏ: gong-zzh
DÀOZHǍNG: dow-jon
-JŪN: june
DÌDÌ: dee-dee
GĒGĒ: guh-guh
JIĚJIĚ: gee-ay-gee-ay
MÈIMEI: may-may
-XIÓNG: shong

Terms

DĀNMĚI: dann-may
WǓXIÁ: woo-sheeah
XIĀNXIÁ: sheeyan-sheeah
QÌ: chee

General Consonants & Vowels

X: similar to English sh (**sh**eep)
Q: similar to English ch (**ch**arm)
C: similar to English ts (pan**ts**)
IU: yoh
UO: wuh
ZHI: jrr
CHI: chrr
SHI: shrr
RI: rrr
ZI: zzz
CI: tsz
SI: ssz
U: When u follows a y, j, q, or x, the sound is actually ü, pronounced like eee with your lips rounded like ooo. This applies for yu, yuan, jun, etc.

Grandmaster of Demonic Cultivation
MO DAO ZU SHI
Glossary

Glossary

While not required reading, this glossary is intended to offer further context to the many concepts and terms utilized throughout this novel and provide a starting point for learning more about the rich Chinese culture from which these stories were written.

China is home to dozens of cultures and its history spans thousands of years. The provided definitions are not strictly universal across all these cultural groups, and this simplified overview is meant for new readers unfamiliar with the concepts. This glossary should not be considered a definitive source, especially for more complex ideas.

GENRES

Danmei

Danmei (耽美 / "indulgence in beauty") is a Chinese fiction genre focused on romanticized tales of love and attraction between men. It is analogous to the BL (boys' love) genre in Japanese media. The majority of well-known danmei writers are women writing for women, although all genders produce and enjoy the genre.

Wuxia

Wuxia (武侠 / "martial heroes") is one of the oldest Chinese literary genres and consists of tales of noble heroes fighting evil and injustice. It often follows martial artists, monks, or rogues, who live apart from the ruling government, which is often seen as useless or corrupt. These societal outcasts—both voluntary and not—settle disputes among themselves, and adhere to their own moral codes over the governing law.

Characters in wuxia focus primarily on human concerns, such as political strife between factions and advancing their own personal sense of justice. True wuxia is low on magical or supernatural elements. To Western moviegoers, a well-known example is *Crouching Tiger, Hidden Dragon*.

Xianxia

Xianxia (仙侠 / "immortal heroes") is a genre related to wuxia that places more emphasis on the supernatural. Its characters often strive to become stronger, with the end goal of extending their life span or achieving immortality.

Xianxia heavily features Daoist themes, while cultivation and the pursuit of immortality are both genre requirements. If these are not the story's central focus, it is not xianxia. *The Scum Villain's Self-Saving System*, *Grandmaster of Demonic Cultivation*, and *Heaven Official's Blessing* are all considered part of both the danmei and xianxia genres.

Webnovels

Webnovels are novels serialized by chapter online, and the websites that host them are considered spaces for indie and amateur writers. Many novels, dramas, comics, and animated shows produced in China are based on popular webnovels.

Grandmaster of Demonic Cultivation was first serialized on the website *JJWXC*.

TERMINOLOGY

ARRAY: Area-of-effect magic circles. Anyone within the array falls under the effect of the array's associated spell(s).

ASCENSION: A Daoist concept, ascension refers to the process of a person gaining enlightenment through cultivation, whereupon they shed their mortal form and are removed from the corporeal world. In most xianxia, gods are distinct from immortals in that gods are conceived naturally and born divine, while immortals cannot attain godhood but can achieve great longevity.

BOWING: As is seen in other Asian cultures, standing bows are a traditional greeting and are also used when giving an apology. A deeper bow shows greater respect.

BUDDHISM: The central belief of Buddhism is that life is a cycle of suffering and rebirth, only to be escaped by reaching enlightenment (nirvana). Buddhists believe in karma, that a person's actions will influence their fortune in this life and future lives. The teachings of the Buddha are known as The Middle Way and emphasize a practice that is neither extreme asceticism nor extreme indulgence.

CHARITABLE MORTUARY: *Yizhuang* (义庄) also called "coffin homes," are a type of morgue where the recently deceased are stored while awaiting burial. They also provide relevant charitable services for those who are too poor to afford a proper funeral, or who have no relatives to claim their body. Charitable mortuaries were generally funded by wealthy families in a given community to demonstrate their generosity.

CLANS: Cultivation clans are large blood-related families that share a surname. Clans are led by family elders, and while only family members can be leaders, disciples can join regardless of blood relation. They may eventually take on the family name, depending on whether the family chooses to offer it. This could be accomplished via adoption or marriage. Clans tend to have a signature cultivation or martial art that is passed down through generations along with ancestral magical artifacts and weapons.

Colors

WHITE: Death, mourning, purity. Used in funerals for both the deceased and mourners.

BLACK: Represents the Heavens and the Dao.

RED: Happiness, good luck. Used for weddings.

YELLOW/GOLD: Wealth and prosperity, and often reserved for the emperor.

BLUE/GREEN (CYAN): Health, prosperity, and harmony.

PURPLE: Divinity and immortality, often associated with nobility.

CONFUCIANISM: Confucianism is a philosophy based on the teachings of Confucius. Its influence on all aspects of Chinese culture is incalculable. Confucius placed heavy importance on respect for one's elders and family, a concept broadly known as *xiao* (孝 / "filial piety"). The family structure is used in other contexts to urge similar behaviors, such as respect of a student towards a teacher, or people of a country towards their ruler.

CORES/GOLDEN CORES: The formation of a jindan (金丹 / "golden core") is a key step in any cultivator's journey to immortality. The Golden Core forms within the lower *dantian*, becoming an internal source of power for the cultivator. Golden Core formation is only accomplished after a great deal of intense training and qi cultivation.

Cultivators can detonate their Golden Core as a last-ditch move to take out a dangerous opponent, but this almost always kills the cultivator. A core's destruction or removal is permanent. In almost all instances, it cannot be re-cultivated. Its destruction also prevents the individual from ever being able to process or cultivate qi normally again.

COURTESY NAMES: A courtesy name is given to an individual when they come of age. (See Name Guide.)

CULTIVATORS/CULTIVATION: Cultivators are practitioners of spirituality and martial artists who seek to gain understanding of the will of the universe while also attaining personal strength and expanding their life span.

Cultivation is a long process marked by "stages." There are traditionally nine stages, but this is often simplified in fiction. Some common stages are noted below, though exact definitions of each stage may depend on the setting.

- ◇ Qi Condensation/Qi Refining (凝气/练气)
- ◇ Foundation Establishment (筑基)
- ◇ Core Formation/Golden Core (结丹/金丹)
- ◇ Nascent Soul (元婴)
- ◇ Deity Transformation (化神)
- ◇ Great Ascension (大乘)
- ◇ Heavenly Tribulation (渡劫)

CULTIVATION MANUAL: Cultivation manuals and sutras are common plot devices in xianxia/wuxia novels. They provide detailed instructions on a secret/advanced training technique, and are sought out by those who wish to advance their cultivation levels.

CURRENCY: The currency system during most dynasties was based on the exchange of silver and gold coinage. Weight was also used to measure denominations of money. An example is something being marked with a price of "one *liang* of silver."

CUT-SLEEVE: A term for a gay man. Comes from a tale about an emperor's love for, and relationship with, a male politician. The emperor was called to the morning assembly, but his lover was asleep on his sleeve. Rather than wake him, the emperor cut off his sleeve.

DANTIAN: *Dantian* (丹田 / "cinnabar field") refers to three regions in the body where qi is concentrated and refined. The Lower is located three finger widths below and two finger widths behind the navel. This is where a cultivator's golden core would be formed and is where the qi metabolism process begins and progresses upward. The Middle is located at the center of the chest, at level with the heart, while the Upper is located on the forehead, between the eyebrows.

DAOISM: Daoism is the philosophy of the *Dao* (道 / "the way") Following the Dao involves coming into harmony with the natural order of the universe, which makes someone a "true human," safe from external harm and able to affect the world without intentional action. Cultivation is a concept based on Daoist beliefs.

DEMONS: A race of immensely powerful and innately supernatural beings. They are almost always aligned with evil. Evil-aligned cultivators who seek power are said to follow the demonic cultivation path.

DISCIPLES: Clan and sect members are known as disciples. Disciples live on sect grounds and have a strict hierarchy based on skill and seniority. They are divided into Core, Inner, and Outer rankings, with Core being the highest. Higher-ranked disciples get better lodging and other resources.

For non-clan members, when formally joining a sect as a disciple, the sect/clan becomes like the disciple's new family: teachers are parents and peers are siblings. Because of this, a betrayal or abandonment of one's sect/clan is considered a deep transgression of Confucian values of filial piety. This is also the origin of many of the honorifics and titles used for martial arts.

DIZI: A flute held horizontally. They are considered an instrument for commoners, as they are easy to craft from bamboo or wood.

ERHU: A two-stringed fiddle, played with a bow.

FACE: *Mianzi* (面子), generally translated as "face," is an important concept in Chinese society. It is a metaphor for a person's reputation and can be extended to further descriptive metaphors. For example, "having face" refers to having a good reputation, and "losing face" refers to having one's reputation hurt. Meanwhile, "giving face" means deferring to someone else to help improve their reputation, while "not wanting face" implies that a person is acting so poorly/ shamelessly that they clearly don't care about their reputation at all.

"Thin face" refers to someone easily embarrassed or prone to offense at perceived slights. Conversely, "thick face" refers to someone not easily embarrassed and immune to insults.

FAIRY/XIANZI: A term commonly used in novels to describe a woman possessing ethereal, heavenly beauty. *Xianzi* is the female counterpart to *xianren* ("immortal"), and is also used to describe celestials that have descended from heaven.

FENG SHUI: *Feng shui* (風水 / "wind-water") is a Daoist practice centered around the philosophy of achieving spiritual accord between people, objects, and the universe at large. Practitioners usually focus on positioning and orientation, believing this can optimize the flow of qi in their environment. Having good feng shui means being in harmony with the natural order.

THE FIVE ELEMENTS: Also known as the *wuxing* (五行 / "Five Phases"). Rather than Western concepts of elemental magic, Chinese phases are more commonly used to describe the interactions and relationships between things. The phases can both beget and overcome each other.

Wood (木 / mu)
Fire (火 / huo)
Earth (土 / tu)
Metal (金 / jin)
Water (水 / shui)

Flower Symbolism

LOTUS: Associated with Buddhism. It rises untainted from the muddy waters it grows in, and thus symbolizes ultimate purity of the heart and mind.

PEONY: Symbolizes wealth and power. Was considered the "emperor" of flowers. Sparks Amidst Snow, the signature flower of the Jin Clan of Lanling in Grandmaster of Demonic Cultivation, is based on the real-life Paeonia suffruticosa cultivar (金星雪浪).

PINE (TREE): A symbol of evergreen sentiment / everlasting affection.

FUNERALS: Daoist or Buddhist funerals generally last for forty-nine days. During the funeral ceremony, mourners can present the deceased with offerings of food, incense, and joss paper. If deceased ancestors have no patrilineal descendants to give them offerings, they may starve in the afterlife and become hungry ghosts. Wiping out a whole family is punishment for more than just the living.

After the funeral, the coffin is nailed shut and sealed with paper talismans to protect the body from evil spirits. The deceased is transported in a procession to their final resting place, often accompanied by loud music to scare off evil spirits. Cemeteries are often on hillsides; the higher a grave is located, the better the feng shui. The traditional mourning color is white.

GHOST: Ghosts (鬼) are the restless spirits of deceased sentient creatures. Ghosts produce yin energy and crave yang energy. They come in a variety of types: they can be malevolent or helpful, can retain their former personalities or be fully mindless, and can actively try to interact with the living world to achieve a goal or be little more than a remnant shadow of their former lives.

GOLDEN BOY, JADE MAIDEN: Celestial servants that are favorites of the Jade Emperor, and who are known to attend to Daoist immortals.

GUQIN: A seven-stringed zither, played by plucking with the fingers. Sometimes called a qin. It is fairly large and is meant to be laid flat on a surface or on one's lap while playing.

HAND GESTURES: The *baoquan* (抱拳 / "hold fist") is a martial arts salute where one places their closed right fist against their open left palm. The *gongshou* (拱手 / "arch hand") is a more generic salute not specific to martial artists, where one drapes their open left palm over their closed right fist. The orientation of both of these salutes is reversed for women. During funerals, the closed hand in both salutes switches, where men will use their left fist and women their right.

HAND SEALS: Refers to various hand and finger gestures used by cultivators to cast spells, or used while meditating. A cultivator may be able to control their sword remotely with a hand seal.

IMMORTAL-BINDING ROPES OR CABLES: Ropes, nets, and other restraints enchanted to withstand the power of an immortal or god. They can only be cut by high-powered spiritual items or weapons and often limit the abilities of those trapped by them.

INCENSE TIME: A common way to tell time in ancient China, referring to how long it takes for a single incense stick to burn. Standardized incense sticks were manufactured and calibrated for specific time measurements: a half hour, an hour, a day, etc. These were available to people of all social classes. When referenced in *Grandmaster of Demonic Cultivation*, a single incense time is usually about thirty minutes.

INEDIA: A common ability that allows an immortal to survive without mortal food or sleep by sustaining themselves on purer forms of energy based on Daoist fasting. Depending on the setting, immortals who have achieved inedia may be unable to tolerate mortal food, or they may be able to choose to eat when desired.

JADE: Jade is a culturally and spiritually important mineral in China. Its durability, beauty, and the ease with which it can be utilized for crafting both decorative and functional pieces alike has made it widely beloved since ancient times. The word might cause Westerners to think of green jade (the mineral jadeite), but Chinese texts are often referring to white jade (the mineral nephrite). This is the color referenced when a person's skin is described as "the color of jade."

JIANGSHI: The *jiangshi* (僵尸), literally meaning "stiff corpse," are the reanimated corpses of dead humans. Their limbs are locked in place due to rigor mortis, meaning they can only move directly forward, hopping with their arms outstretched in front of them. They have some overlap with Western zombies due to their status as a reanimated corpse, general low intelligence and lack of sentience, as well as Western vampires due to their nocturnal nature and desire to hunt living humans and feed off their life force.

JOSS PAPER: Also referred to as ghost paper, joss paper is a form of paper crafting used to make offerings to the deceased. The paper can be folded into various shapes and is burned as an offering, allowing the deceased person to utilize the gift the paper represents in the realm of the dead. Common gifts include paper money, houses, clothing, toiletries, and dolls to act as the deceased's servants.

JUDGES: Broadly refers to the Judges that oversee the ten courts of the realm of the dead, *Diyu.* Diyu is an afterlife in Chinese mythology where sinners are taken for punishment, similar to the western concept of hell.

NIGHT WATCHER: Night watchers announced the overnight hours in villages and cities by way of clappers or gongs. They made their announcements once every two hours (see the entry for Shichen), from 7:00 p.m. to 3:00 a.m.

Numbers

TWO: Two (二 / "er") is considered a good number and is referenced in the common idiom "good things come in pairs." It is common practice to repeat characters in pairs for added effect.

THREE: Three (三 / "san") sounds like *sheng* (生 / "living") and also like san (散 / "separation").

FOUR: Four (四 / "si") sounds like *si* (死 / "death"). A very unlucky number.

SEVEN: Seven (七 / "qi") sounds like *qi* (齊 / "together"), making it a good number for love-related things. However, it also sounds like *qi* (欺 / "deception").

EIGHT: Eight (八 / "ba") sounds like *fa* (發 / "prosperity"), causing it to be considered a very lucky number.

NINE: Nine (九 / "jiu") is associated with matters surrounding the Emperor and Heaven, and is as such considered an auspicious number.

MXTX's work has subtle numerical theming around its love interests. In *Grandmaster of Demonic Cultivation*, her second book, Lan Wangji is frequently called Lan-er-gege ("second brother Lan") as a nickname by Wei Wuxian. In her third book, *Heaven Official's Blessing*, Hua Cheng is the third son of his family and gives the name San Lang ("third youth") when Xie Lian asks what to call him.

PAPER EFFIGIES: *Zhizha* (纸扎) is a form of Daoist paper craft. Zhizha effigies can be used in place of living sacrifices to one's ancestors in the afterlife, or to gods. Joss paper can be considered a form of zhizha specifically for the deceased, though unlike zhizha, it is not specifically Daoist in nature.

PILLS AND ELIXIRS: Magic medicines that can heal wounds, improve cultivation, extend life, etc. In Chinese culture, these things are usually delivered in pill form. These pills are created in special kilns.

PRIMORDIAL SPIRIT: The essence of one's existence beyond the physical. The body perishes, the soul enters the karmic wheel, but the spirit that makes one unique is eternal.

QI: *Qi* (气) is the energy in all living things. There is both righteous qi and evil or poisonous qi.

Cultivators strive to cultivate qi by absorbing it from the natural world and refining it within themselves to improve their cultivation base. A cultivation base refers to the amount of qi a cultivator possesses or is able to possess. In xianxia, natural locations such as caves, mountains, or other secluded places with beautiful scenery are often rich in qi, and practicing there can allow a cultivator to make rapid progress in their cultivation.

Cultivators and other qi manipulators can utilize their life force in a variety of ways, including imbuing objects with it to transform them into lethal weapons or sending out blasts of energy to do powerful damage. Cultivators also refine their senses beyond normal human levels. For instance, they may cast out their spiritual sense to gain total awareness of everything in a region around them or to feel for potential danger.

QI CIRCULATION: The metabolic cycle of qi in the body, where it flows from the dantian to the meridians and back. This cycle purifies and refines qi, and good circulation is essential to cultivation. In xianxia, qi can be transferred from one person to another through physical contact and can heal someone who is wounded if the donor is trained in the art.

QI DEVIATION: A qi deviation (走火入魔 / "to catch fire and enter demonhood") occurs when one's cultivation base becomes unstable. Common causes include an unstable emotional state, practicing cultivation methods incorrectly, reckless use of forbidden or high-level arts, or succumbing to the influence of demons and devils.

Symptoms of qi deviation in fiction include panic, paranoia, sensory hallucinations, and death, whether by the qi deviation itself causing irreparable damage to the body or as a result of its symptoms such as leaping to one's death to escape a hallucination. Common treatments of qi deviation in fiction include relaxation (voluntary or forced by an external party), massage, meditation, or qi transfer from another individual.

QIANKUN: (乾坤 / "universe") Common tools used in fantasy novels. The primary function of these magical items is to provide unlimited storage space. Examples include pouches, the sleeve of a robe, magical jewelry, a weapon, and more.

SECT: A cultivation sect is an organization of individuals united by their dedication to the practice of a particular method of cultivation or martial arts. A sect may have a signature style. Sects are led by a single leader, who is supported by senior sect members. They are not necessarily related by blood.

SEVEN APERTURES/QIQIAO: (七窍) The seven facial apertures: the two eyes, nose, mouth, tongue, and two ears. The essential qi of vital organs are said to connect to the seven apertures, and illness in the vital organs may cause symptoms there. People who are ill or seriously injured may be "bleeding from the seven apertures."

SHICHEN: Days were split into twelve intervals of two hours apiece called *shichen* (时辰 / "time"). Each of these shichen has an associated term. Pre-Han dynasty used semi-descriptive terms, but in Post-Han dynasty, the shichen were renamed to correspond to the twelve zodiac animals.

ZI, MIDNIGHT: 11pm - 1am
CHOU: 1am - 3am
YIN: 3am - 5am
MAO, SUNRISE: 5am - 7am
CHEN: 7am - 9am
SI: 9am - 11am
WU, NOON: 11am - 1pm
WEI: 1pm - 3pm

SHEN: 3pm - 5pm
YOU, SUNSET: 5pm - 7pm
XU, DUSK: 7pm - 9pm
HAI: 9pm - 11pm

SHIDI, SHIXIONG, SHIZUN, ETC.: Chinese titles and terms used to indicate a person's role or rank in relation to the speaker. Because of the robust nature of this naming system, and a lack of nuance in translating many to English, the original titles have been maintained. (See Name Guide for more information.)

THE SIX ARTS: Six disciplines that any well-bred gentleman in Ancient China was expected to be learned in. The Six Arts were: Rites, Music, Archery, Chariotry or Equestrianism, Calligraphy, and Mathematics.

SPIRIT-ATTRACTION FLAG: A banner or flag intended to guide spirits. Can be hung from a building or tree to mark a location or carried around on a staff.

SWORDS: A cultivator's sword is an important part of their cultivation practice. In many instances, swords are spiritually bound to their owner and may have been bestowed to them by their master, a family member, or obtained through a ritual. Cultivators in fiction are able to use their swords as transportation by standing atop the flat of the blade and riding it as it flies through the air. Skilled cultivators can summon their swords to fly into their hand, command the sword to fight on its own, or release energy attacks from the edge of the blade.

SWORD GLARE: *Jianguang* (剑光 / "sword light"), an energy attack released from a sword's edge.

SWORN BROTHERS/SISTERS/FAMILIES: In China, sworn brotherhood describes a binding social pact made by two or more unrelated individuals. Such a pact can be entered into for social, political, and/or personal reasons. It was most common among men, but was not unheard of among women or between people of different genders.

The participants treat members of each other's families as their own and assist them in the ways an extended family would: providing mutual support and aid, support in political alliances, etc. Sworn siblings will refer to themselves as brother or sister, but this is not to be confused with familial relations like blood siblings or adoption. It is sometimes used in Chinese media, particularly danmei, to imply romantic relationships that could otherwise be prone to censorship.

TALISMANS: Strips of paper with incantations written on them, often done so with cinnabar ink or blood. They can serve as seals or be used as one-time spells.

TIGER TALLY: A *hufu* (虎符 / "tiger tally"), was used by Ancient Chinese emperors to signal their approval to dispatch troops in battle. A hufu was in two parts: one in the possession of the emperor, and the other in the possession of a general in the field. To signal approval, the emperor would send his half of the hufu to the general. If the two sides matched, troops would advance.

WHISK: A whisk held by a cultivator is not a baking tool, but a Daoist symbol and martial arts weapon. Usually made of horsehair bound to a wooden stick, the whisk is based off a tool used to brush away flies without killing them, and is symbolically meant for wandering Daoist monks to brush away thoughts that would lure them back to secular life. Wudang Daoist Monks created a fighting style based on wielding it as a weapon.

YAO: Animals, plants, or objects that have gained spiritual consciousness due to prolonged absorption of qi. Especially high-level or long-lived *yao* are able to take on a human form. This concept is comparable to Japanese *yokai*, which is a loanword from the Chinese yao. Yao are not evil by nature, but often come into conflict with humans for various reasons, one being that the cores they develop can be harvested by human cultivators to increase their own abilities.

YIN ENERGY AND YANG ENERGY: Yin and yang is a concept in Chinese philosophy that describes the complementary interdependence of opposite/contrary forces. It can be applied to all forms of change and differences. Yang represents the sun, masculinity, and the living, while yin represents the shadows, femininity, and the dead, including spirits and ghosts. In fiction, imbalances between yin and yang energy can do serious harm to the body or act as the driving force for malevolent spirits seeking to replenish themselves of whichever they lack.

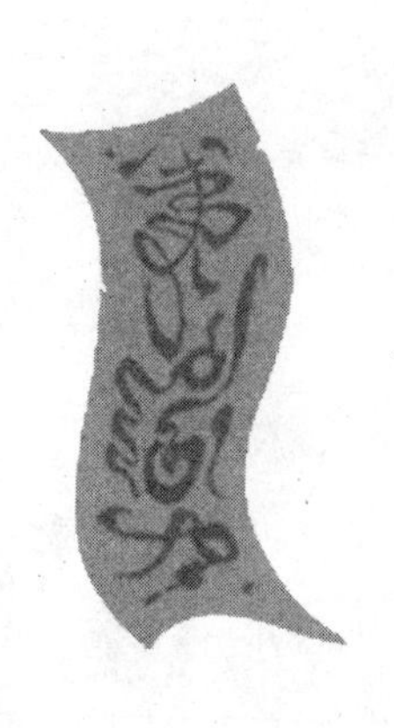